Art Appreciation

Finally, the announcement. Alex crossed her fingers. She intently observed the expectant faces in the crowd, watching their every movement, anticipating the usual lift of an eyebrow here and there, the open-eyed wonder, mouths dropping to *ahhh* their pleasure. Usually her statues garnered pleased smiles, sighs of contentment.

What she saw was startling, to say the least. Eyes wide, mouths agape, hands poised in midair to clap, but frozen in time. The women were gasping, chatting with one another animatedly. A few even shrieked.

And then she saw him.

The man standing on stage—no, not standing, but *stretching*, like a contented cat just risen from a nap—bore a striking resemblance to her statue of Darius. Tall, well over six feet. Extremely well muscled without going overboard, like a real athlete and not a guy who bulked up in the gym. But most of all, just in case someone missed the resemblance, he went for life imitating art.

"What the hell?" she whispered.

He was buck naked.

A Greek God
AT THE
Ladies' Club
JENNA McKNIGHT

AVON BOOKS

An Imprint of HarperCollins*Publishers*

This is a work of fiction. Names, characters, places, and incidents are products of the author's imagination or are used fictitiously and are not to be construed as real. Any resemblance to actual events, locales, organizations, or persons, living or dead, is entirely coincidental.

HarperCollins*Publishers*
77-85 Fulham Palace Road
Hammersmith
London W6 8JB

Copyright © 2003 by Ginny Schweiss

ISBN: 0 00 774041 7
www.avonromance.com

This edition published 2005
First Avon Books paperback printing: December 2003

Avon Trademark Reg. U.S. Pat. Off. and in Other Countries, Marca Registrada, Hecho en U.S.A.
HarperCollins® is a registered trademark of HarperCollins Publishers Inc.

Printed and bound in Great Britain by Clays Ltd, St Ives plc

My heartfelt appreciation to Gina Koziatek,
Assistant Registrar of the St. Louis Art Museum,
for not only answering my questions,
but volunteering information that made the picture whole;
Kathie DeNosky,
for figuratively kicking me when I needed it;
Sue Runde,
for her time and feedback on the final draft;
and Evan Fogelman,
for his enthusiasm, because he understood
A Greek God at the Ladies' Club *early on*
and knew exactly what to do with it
when it was complete.

Prologue

Three thousand years ago

"She loves me . . ."

Darius, a muscular six-foot-four specimen who normally oozed testosterone, lounged against a sun-warmed boulder on Olympus and casually lobbed a pomegranate-sized diamond over his left shoulder. And he sighed.

"She loves me not."

A walnut-sized emerald arced over his shoulder and ricocheted off the boulder. Rolling downhill past his sandals, it finally came to rest next to a she-loves-me-not ruby.

Hermes, in winged sandals, hovered above the hillside, watching his younger brother make a fool of himself. There wasn't an ounce of flab on Darius beneath his tunic. He was wealthy beyond anyone's dreams. Every man wanted to be him. Every woman wanted to lie with him.

And he was reduced to . . . to *this*. Sitting in lush green grass like a lovesick fool, stirring his fingers through the pouch at his belt, tossing gem after gem aside as if they were of no more value than mere daisy petals.

Hermes hung his head. If not for his job, he would fly away and not witness this. He would leave Queen Aara's words undelivered. Messages like hers were bound to be Darius's end someday. But Hermes was messenger to the gods of Olympus, and this had to be done. With a flutter of wings, he landed beside his brother. His friend.

"She loves me . . ."

The hillside was littered with a fortnight of discarded gems, twinkling and glittering in the sunlight.

"She loves me not."

"True," Hermes finally interrupted, "but the king has ridden away. The queen says you may come tonight."

A few hours later, Darius stole through the dark corridors of King Edward's castle, eagerly making his way to Queen Aara's chambers. She was young and beautiful, exotic, talented in the art of making love. Being forced to wait for her favors had been a trial, but one that would be well rewarded, he knew.

Her room danced with candlelight. The scent of lilacs—Aara's favorite—was heavy in the air.

"Darius," she greeted him softly from the center of the room, "you came." Her long braid, draped over one creamy shoulder, rivaled the purest gold. Her eyes danced with the blue of the autumn sky. Generous curves, teased by a diaphanous gown, tempted him with promise of pleasures soon to be his.

In turn, Aara's gaze roamed his body. Slowly. Boldly. He sensed no fear in her at his approach, no hesitation, even though he towered over her, could crush her with his bare hands if he so desired. But she knew well what else those hands could do. The tip of her tongue darted out, moistening her lips ever so slightly, enticing him closer.

With her gown cut to her navel, her breasts delightfully close to escaping at any moment, and moonlight outlining long legs beneath the sheer fabric, Darius couldn't decide where to begin his repast. He would savor the hours ahead.

Her steady gaze perused the jewel-encrusted belt circling his waist. Slowly she reached out and traced the glittering rubies and emeralds with a long, sensual stroke of her fingertip. "Did you bribe the guards with one of these? If so, I'm sure never to see them again."

Darius, wishing her finger traced something more intimate, barely found enough breath to speak. "I gave them something better." Two buxom serving wenches had delivered drugged wine to the eager men.

"Darius, haven't you learned?" Aara sidled up to his chest, laying her soft hand over his heart. "There is nothing better than jewels."

He slipped his arms around her yielding curves and held her to him, struggling to go slowly while his body screamed for haste.

She leaned back, gazing up at him through long eyelashes, and asked, "What have you brought me tonight?"

"What?" He feigned insult. "You want more than me?"

She pouted prettily—his favorite expression on her—and he forgave her coquetry. She would do anything for the gift he'd hidden beneath his tunic. But first he wanted to strip her of every stitch and make love to her until the king came home.

"Psst!" hissed from the night sky beyond the window. "Darius!"

The chamber was high in the castle, set on the edge of a sheer cliff, its window inaccessible to most. Darius had better things to do than to answer his winged brother's call.

Aara leaned in to him again, crushing her breasts against his chest, driving him nearly to the breaking point. He wanted to make this tryst last all night. He wanted to love her so thoroughly that she'd beg him to come back again, with or without his gifts.

"Psst!" With a flutter, Hermes lighted on the window ledge.

"Aara, my sweet," Darius whispered softly in her ear, casually waving his arm behind her back to shoo Hermes away.

He slid the silken fabric off her shoulder, exposing pale skin that never was allowed to be touched by the sun, never to be seen by anyone save her husband and her ladies-in-waiting. If *that* maneuver didn't tell Hermes he didn't want to be disturbed, he didn't know what would.

"Dare!" Hermes whispered, cautious lest Aara hear him.

Darius cupped Aara's ears tenderly with his large hands, hoping she wouldn't notice his distraction, wouldn't hear him speaking to someone else. Just in case that didn't do the trick, he dipped his head and traced her bottom lip with the lightest touch of his tongue until she melted against him.

Hermes persisted. "The king has turned back."

Darius bit back a curse, hoping there would be enough time for at least one romp in the big bed. Pressing his lips to the soft spot beneath Aara's ear, he asked Hermes, "How long do we have?"

Aara sighed lustily. "All night. Tomorrow night, too, if your gift pleases me."

Darius's knees weakened at her words, even as he hardened at the thought of being inside her once again.

"Not *we*, little brother. I'm outta here."

"When . . . ?"

"Soon." Hermes fluttered out the window.

"Soon," Aara whispered, dipping her hands inside Darius's tunic. "What's this?" She sprang away from him, her eyes twinkling gaily, her hands pulling at the box she'd discovered.

Darius caught her loosely by her braid, tugging her against his chest. He wondered how long his brother's "soon" was. "Leave it until later. First, let's enjoy each other."

She smiled coyly. "Darius, let me see. I'll be ever so grateful."

Upon freeing the elegantly carved box, she tilted it to catch the candlelight. "Oh, Darius," she murmured reverently. "I've never seen anything so beautiful." Her fingers, tracing each perfect emerald and every large ruby, ran over the fine, dark wood with long fingernails that Darius preferred to feel upon his back.

"Psst!" came from far off in the night. "He's got his whole army with him."

Aara, having heard nothing out of the ordinary, loosened the tiny bow near her bosom. Her gown slid down bare skin, exposing high, firm breasts, then the curve of her waist and hips, a triangle of tempting curls, and long, long legs. The fabric fell silently, forming a cloud of white at her dainty feet.

She was everything he'd remembered, and more. Perfectly shaped, with breasts full enough to please him and hips wide enough to cradle him.

Darius swallowed hard and found his mouth gone dry. In the distance—he hoped the far, far distance—he thought he heard hoofbeats. Or were they footsteps? He cocked his head to hear better.

"What is it?" Aara asked, though she didn't seem too interested in a reply.

"I thought I heard someone."

"No one would dare come here." She smiled slyly up at him. "No one but you."

The king would undoubtedly take great displeasure with his bride if he discovered her to be unfaithful. "Is it possible—"

"That I want you more than any man?" she asked breathily. She set the box aside and closed the distance between them, crushing her naked breasts against his chest. "That I've never wanted anyone as much as I want you? That I want you all night long? Yes, Darius, it's true."

He was powerless to reason. Cool night air brushed across his heated skin as she disrobed him with quick, skillful fingers. He was hard and throbbing and ready for her.

She led him to her bed, a wide, fluffy mattress nearly as good as any on Olympus. She draped herself across it in the moonlight, a noble, wanton hussy who could have anyone in her bed, and she had chosen him.

"Come, Darius." She patted the mattress. "Lie beside me."

He couldn't draw his gaze from her. Her hands reached for him, and he cocked one knee on the bed beside her hip. Her fingers circled him intimately.

Footsteps echoed through stone passageways. Men's voices raised to the rafters; soldiers' voices. In Aara's need, she seemed not to recognize the danger.

"Oh, Darius, I need you now."

"I must go, Aara."

"No!" She grasped him tightly.

Wincing at the bite of her fingernails, he gently pried her fingers free, one by one. In the distance, he heard Hermes laughing as they battled over Darius's most prized possession.

"It's better for you if I go," he said, concerned for her safety. "But I promise I'll return."

"But why?"

"Listen."

She sat up then and held very still. Her eyes widened in surprise. Her gaze dashed furtively around the room, seeking shelter. She yanked a silken robe off the mattress and cinched it tightly at her waist. "What is it?" she demanded, outraged at the disturbance.

"The king?" he suggested, tongue in cheek. From across the room, he threw the bolt on the door.

"But he rode to the border! He could not be back so soon."

The noise of a hundred men in the passageway said otherwise. "Open that door!" boomed through the wooden barrier.

"It's Edward!" Aara confirmed as she jumped off the bed and hovered at Darius's side. "The passageway is blocked. You'll have to go out the window."

Out the window? It had to be three hundred feet straight down. "You must have me confused with my brother," he said dryly.

She shoved him away from the bed, across the stone floor, toward the window. "Can't you do something? Like disappear?"

"No." He could conjure up musicians, or serving wenches with food and drink. He could move objects using his mind alone. Short of bringing the entire castle down on their heads or pelting the soldiers with food, he couldn't imagine how either ability would help right now.

"Darius!" She stamped her foot and whined.

Bodies rammed repeatedly against the door, threatening to break the hinges free. It was only a matter of time before the king discovered the truth of his queen's crime. The thought of Aara being drawn and quartered was unbearable. He feared not for himself—for he was immortal—but he must protect her.

"As a child, I used to be able to turn myself into a statue," he said tentatively.

"Do it!"

· "But it's been ages." *Literally.* He wasn't excited about the prospect. "My mother warned me if I kept making myself into a statue, I'd get stuck someday."

"Forget your mother! Think of me."

Even frightened, her gaze darting between him and the voices thundering beyond the rattling door, she was still beautiful. He couldn't let anything happen to her, not as a result of loving him. "When can we be together again?" he asked.

Grabbing him by the arm, she backed him into the corner by the window, posing him with one hand on his hip, the other up in the air. Probably to better show off his physique, he surmised. In a bold gesture, she stroked him intimately, smiling as his need for her renewed itself.

"We'll discuss it later, after he goes to sleep," she said wickedly. "Now do your thing."

Wondering if his mother knew something he didn't— Hera was a very smart goddess—he hesitated.

The door cracked beneath the onslaught.

Aara pressed herself against him. "For me, Darius." Her voice was like a purr, mesmerizing, reassuring. Uplifting. "Do it for me."

He took a deep breath, and just as soldiers burst through the splintered door, he turned himself into the finest marble ever to leave Olympus. He was the most perfect sculpture ever created of a young stud god; he was himself.

A half-dozen soldiers tumbled into the room with the remnants of the door, followed by a dozen more with their swords drawn.

Darius extinguished the candles—better the king didn't see Aara's libidinous statue tonight—but he couldn't cover the moon. As the third son of Zeus, he could not command the clouds.

"Out of my way!" King Edward bellowed. Old enough to be Aara's father, he strutted into the chamber as his men deferentially parted ranks.

"Edward," the queen murmured in feigned surprise. "Are we under attack?"

He strolled around the silent room. "I was told you were entertaining a visitor."

"A visitor?" She glanced around the chamber. "There is no one here but me."

"Bring a torch," Edward commanded his soldiers.

Darius cursed the impulse that had led him to immobilize himself without throwing on his tunic first. He didn't take kindly to a torch showing off his enviable attributes to a bunch of angry mortals with swords and hatchets.

"Well," Edward demanded, "what's taking so long?"

"It blew out, Your Majesty."

"You fool! This is some kind of trick." He perused the room, letting his eyes adjust to the dimness. "Never mind, moonlight is good for hunting rats."

Aara inched toward her gown, still pooled on the floor with Darius's tunic. As Edward circled the chamber, she kicked both into a pile and stood squarely on top of them, billowing her robe to cover the incriminating garments.

"Aha!" Edward held Darius's jeweled gift box in his hands. "I wondered which god you'd been trysting with."

"But, Edward—"

"And that large statue by the window, pray tell how it comes to be there."

"It was a gift."

"From whom?"

"My . . . my mother."

The king squared off in front of Darius. He had to look up, but he did so with a glint in his eye. Too late, Darius realized King Edward was not the coward Aara had led him to believe.

"Your mother?" Edward repeated scornfully.

Darius didn't like the king's tone. The man should be honored that a god such as he found his wife appealing. If Edward would turn aside, the arrangement could be advantageous to them all. There was the matter of border wars to the north; Edward could benefit from Darius's assistance in the matter.

Just as Darius decided it might be wise to shed his marble exterior and tell him so, Edward raised his sword.

"It appears your statue desires you, my dear."

Edward's arm dropped. In one clean swoop, the blade severed that part of Darius which no male would be without. It hit the floor with a clunk and rolled across the stone.

In disbelief and rage, Darius's gaze followed its path until it came to rest at Aara's bare toes.

She gasped. "Edward! Look what you've done to him . . . I mean . . . it."

"Mm, yes, I see. I wonder if it hurts." His grin was devilish. "I guess we'll never know." He turned to his troops. "Quickly, lift him up."

Ten men jumped to do his bidding. They tilted the statue and hefted Darius onto their shoulders, bowed beneath the weight.

"Throw him out the window."

"Edward!"

"Silence! Or you'll be joining him on the cliffs below, my dear."

Darius was finished with his quiet suffering. Obviously the king knew of the queen's infidelity; Darius could do her no more harm now by returning to the living, breathing god he was.

It had been so easy as a child—one minute marble, another his heart was beating. But no matter how hard he willed himself to change back now, he couldn't. It seemed his mother had been right—he'd finally gotten stuck.

The soldiers, lined up closely, chest-to-back, carried him progressively closer to the window. Their feet shuffled beneath the weight; they groaned under the effort. Turned and jostled, Darius lost sight of his severed appendage.

"Edward, darling, it was just a silly old statue," were the last words Darius heard as he was hurtled toward the cliffs below.

He couldn't move, couldn't flail his arms or yell for Hermes to come save him. But he could do one thing. He used the very last of his power to whisk his possessions out the window behind him. If he couldn't have them, no one could. Not until he figured out how to put all the pieces back together again. The jewel-encrusted box and belt flew out behind him.

To his chagrin, the last piece—and in his mind, the most important—remained behind.

1

Present day

"**P**sst! Darius, where are you?"

Hermes fluttered around the sky in his winged sandals, searching for his elusive little brother. He couldn't be too loud or too obvious; Zeus frowned on any contact with his shunned son, even after three thousand years. But they were brothers, and Hermes felt someone had to look out for Darius.

Trouble was, he was hard to find. Zeus had been so angered by the tryst with Queen Aara, he'd taken away Darius's rulership of gems. His telekinetic powers were gone, too. He'd been allowed out of the broken, deformed statue, but he no longer had any "body" to call his own. No form, no shape, nothing. Sometimes, when he heard Hermes searching for him, Darius would get inside a star or a tree so Hermes had something on which to focus while they were

talking. Not often though, as he was always afraid of getting
stuck again.

"Psst! I've got good news."

Dust particles around a satellite shifted and took on a new
form.

"That you, Dare?"

"It's me," filtered through what sounded like a yawn.

"What are you doing by the satellite?"

"Listening." Darius didn't sound as morose as the last
time they'd spoken—a mere one hundred fifty years ago.

"Really?" Hermes winged downward, landing gently and
sinking up to his knees in the dust.

"Hey, watch it."

"Oh, sorry." Hermes surveyed his surroundings for a comfortable place to sit, then moved toward the edge. "Okay
over here?"

"Yeah, I guess."

He wiggled into the cloud of dust the way one burrows
into a beanbag chair. "What are you listening to?"

"*Jeopardy!* The history category is a cinch. You ever listen
to The Learning Channel?"

"Uh, no. How you been, buddy?"

"Well, if I let myself get distracted with all the information the mortals have amassed, I don't notice how miserable
I am."

"That bad, huh?"

"Worse." Darius's sorrowful sigh tore at Hermes' heart.
"Do you have any idea how hard it is to get a woman when
they can't see, hear, or touch you?"

He thought Darius would've forgotten about women by
now, but, no—he still had a one-track mind after all this
time.

"Can you imagine how frustrating it is to want a woman when I can't touch one even if I got one? And that's not all—"

"Precisely why I'm here." He thought it better to cut Darius off before he hit rock bottom. "I think I found the answer to your problem. Maybe."

"Zeus is ready to forgive and forget?" Darius asked sarcastically.

"Zeus forgive?" Hermes laughed mirthlessly. "Not hardly. But he said you couldn't have your body back until someone pieced it together again, right?"

" 'Until it's perfect again' were his exact words."

"Right, that's it. So, do you know about Dr. Mickael's team?"

"Yeah, I watched them uncover what was left of me . . . it." Darius yawned.

He couldn't see Darius yawn, of course, but he heard it. A big, openmouthed, I'm-bored kind of yawn. It made Hermes sleepy, so he hopped up out of his comfy seat and paced the edge of the dust cloud before he nodded off.

"They never found all of me, so it was a, shall we say, less than perfect job."

"Right, but get this . . ."

"Can you stand still? You're walking all over the family jewels."

"Oh, sorry." He didn't add salt to the wound and point out that as long as there was no body, there were no family jewels. That seemed too cruel. Instead, he crouched near what he thought was Darius's head, the better to get his full attention.

"Not that I get to use them or anything."

Dare's increasing despondency worried Hermes, which

made the timing of his visit perfect. "There's a sculptor in the United States I think you might be interested in. She's working on a marble statue."

Darius yawned again. "Uh-huh."

"Guess who her model is?"

The dust shifted slightly. "Who?"

"You. Your statue, I mean. The one they found and pieced back together."

"But it's locked up in a museum basement."

"She's got pictures, Dare. Pictures of it . . . of you."

"Pictures?" The dust cloud sat up.

If not for his lightfootedness, Hermes would've toppled overboard. "Yeah, you know what those are, don't you?" He wasn't sure just how well Darius had kept up with the times. Listening to sound waves wasn't the same as seeing the real thing on television or in books.

"Of course, I've been on Earth. I just told you I know where the statue is."

He was pleased to see Dare's lethargy replaced with a crumb of interest.

"Good, then you know where St. Louis is, too?"

"Unless they moved it."

"And you know how things work down there now?" He didn't want to throw him to the wolves if he wasn't ready. If he hadn't seen microwaves and TV and video games yet, he'd think the whole planet was possessed.

"Well, it's been a while, but the satellites keep me up to date. Is the sculptor any good?"

"Oh, very good. Her work is outstanding."

"Maybe perfect?" Darius showed more interest than he had in centuries, and Hermes knew he was doing the right thing in bringing him this news.

"Perfection is her middle name."

"How far along is she? How big is it? Is it—"

"Stop!" Hermes laughed and held up his hands to forestall the questions. Better to let Darius get involved from the ground up. "Go see for yourself. Look for Alexandra de Marco, in the—"

The dust cloud flattened abruptly. "I can't."

So close, Hermes thought. He'd almost had him. *This close* to getting his brother back. "Why not?"

"If it's a statue"—the cloud shuddered—"I'd have to get back into it again."

Hermes kicked at a wisp, scattering dust in all directions. "And this is better?"

"I feel trapped in marble."

"Ah." Hermes nodded to himself. "Claustrophobia."

"Call it what you like, I don't like it. I don't want to do it again."

Hermes sighed theatrically, knowing this attitude called for sterner stuff. He turned his back. "Okay, little brother. I'll see you again in, oh, a century or so."

"Rub it in a little, why don't you?"

"Whatever it takes, bro. I miss you. I hope you'll check it out."

As hard as it was, Hermes winged away. Slowly, so as to give Darius a chance to change his mind. He wanted to take good news back to Aphrodite and the others. Darius was their last hope. Their only hope, actually, if they were ever going to put that young upstart Cytus in his place.

"Hey, Hermes . . ."

"Yes?"

"Where in St. Louis?"

Knowing success was at hand, he grinned, but he made

sure Darius couldn't see him. "Central West End. In a carriage house behind the Ladies' Club."

"I'll go look, but I'm not making any promises."

One benefit to having no body was that Darius didn't need a disguise. He found the sculptor's studio right off and was able to let himself in. He didn't have to make up a story about why he was on the premises, who he was, or what he was doing there.

He'd been this route before. Twice. Both times ended disastrously. Besides worrying about a mortal hacking off part of him again, he suspected one of the gods had it in for him.

In 68, he'd found an artist in Pompeii with an eye for detail and a respect for the gods. He'd waited a whole year for the man to put finishing touches on his statue. But just before he finished, the earth opened up, swallowed it, and crushed it. It was fortunate he hadn't moved into it yet, for Hera, having released him from the statue broken by the king's men, had sworn by the river Styx that she wouldn't be so maternal a second time.

There had been another statue in 79, nearly finished. He'd itched with the need to get into it, to take it, to make it his body. His nickname wasn't Dare for nothing. But then, as luck would have it, Mount Vesuvius erupted. Wet ashes and cinders rained down on the city, suffusing it, molding it into an uninhabitable place. That statue also had been broken and buried.

It was hard to believe his own father would go to such lengths to prevent him from returning to life, but no one else was mad at him. If Darius ever had children, he'd never let anger separate them.

After three thousand years, he hoped Zeus was too old to

care anymore. Or out of touch. Perhaps he didn't know of Alexandra de Marco and her statue.

Upon finding the carriage house, Darius didn't hesitate to enter her studio. If this statue was perfect, he was taking it. *Now.* He'd not lose this chance, too.

Again, he found a statue nearly finished. But unlike before, it wasn't almost perfect, almost life-sized, and slightly flattering.

It was much more. So much so, it brought him up short. Took his breath away. It was too good, too perfect, too wonderful to slip through his hands, so to speak.

"Hermes," he whispered reverently, hoping his brother was nearby. It was a trial to keep his voice calm, but he didn't want to alert Zeus. No more earthquakes and volcanoes erupting for him. Not until he had his powers back and was invincible.

"Yes?" Hermes answered, careful to stay out of sight. "Wow, Dare, it's even better than I'd hoped."

"Does anyone else know about this?"

"I don't think so. There are so many mortals now, it's impossible to keep tabs on everyone. Were you that tall?"

"Yes." He moved right in, settled himself within the marble skin, and waited.

Nothing. No warmth, no slight return of his telekinetic powers, as he'd felt inside the last statue. There must be something about it that wasn't perfect. Something he'd missed.

"But you didn't have muscles like that, did you?"

"I did," he growled. Frustrated and feeling claustrophobic, he nearly moved right back out. But he waited. It might take just one more minute.

"Well, if you say so," Hermes said. "It's been so long, I can't say I remember accurately. Oops, gotta go. Zeus is calling me. Before I go, though, there is one thing I know is wrong."

"What's that?" Darius asked in a tone that should have warned Hermes to leave while the leaving was good. Nothing was going to spoil this for him. Nothing.

"I'm sure—well, I'm pretty sure, anyway—that you didn't have everything that statue has. You'll have to find a way to make her get rid of it."

The claustrophobia was almost overpowering. But it was the right height, right build, right hair. He could almost feel it ready to move with him, to transform into flesh and blood. But Hermes was so sure . . .

"What's wrong with it?"

Hermes rolled his eyes and shook his head.

"The fig leaf, you idiot."

2

"I mean it, Alexandra, let me in!"

"Go away." Alex de Marco gave her sister, Claudia, credit for one thing: she was *the* most persistent woman in St. Louis. She'd been knocking on the studio door for fifteen minutes straight. A lesser woman would've quit long ago.

"You listen to me, Alexandra!"

She preferred Alex, a testament to the tomboy inside, the one who liked to wear old jeans and get her hands dirty. Alexandra sounded so . . . pretentious. Snooty. Rich. None of which described her in the least. She tossed her ponytail back over her shoulder and continued polishing the statue's right quad.

On a nearby easel sat an archaeology magazine, always open to an exhibit of statue parts unearthed from the base of a cliff in Europe. The ancient fragments had been pieced together enough to give her a good idea of what to model her own god after. Only a few parts were missing. Nothing crucial; a few fingers and the penis. Nothing she couldn't work around.

"I've just spent hours with the caterer and the gardener and the suppliers, and I'm *not* in the mood to stand out here and yell at you through this door."

Claudia had begun with a nice request to come in. When Alex wouldn't give in and unlock the door, Claudia had run the gamut through begging, cajoling, whining, and wheedling. Now, apparently, she thought she'd try reasoning with her. Many orphan siblings were separated, but they'd been lucky enough to grow up together, so Alex knew all of Claudia's tricks.

"I mean it, Alexandra." The knob rattled again. "If you don't unlock this door this instant, I'll . . . I'll call the fire marshal and tell him you've had a stroke or something, and he'll take an *ax* to this door to get me in."

Well, that was a new twist. If she'd had time to spare, Alex would've run upstairs and peeked out one of the dormer windows of the old carriage house–turned–studio just to watch her older sister throw a temper tantrum. Imagine, Claudia de Marco Ross Kline—married to a major St. Louis industrialist—having a tizzy just because little sister Alex wouldn't let her watch her work.

Time was short. The weekend would be here all too soon, and with it the sneak preview of her statue at a special Ladies' Club luncheon. Their Forty-seventh Annual Charity Auction was in two weeks, and proceeds from the sale of the statue would benefit their pet project, the Children's Home. One of St. Louis's largest businesses had agreed to make a matching donation, which pretty well secured a new roof and furnace, and would enable the home to remain open.

The event would make or break her reputation as an artist, but it was important for another reason. She and Claudia had a pact. Claudia, the one who'd married money, was researching their roots, working with private investigators, trying to find their father. They hoped that search wouldn't end as the first had, when they'd found their mother's grave and learned her death had preceded their admission to the Children's Home by a matter of days. Alex, the talented one, was using her natural abilities to "give something back" to the home where they'd grown up. If she was a success, she'd be in a better position to keep helping. Everything she did, ultimately, was for the children.

She'd practically locked herself up in her studio behind the Ladies' Club mansion for the past year. Most of the turn-of-the-century carriage house had been remodeled a generation ago into living quarters with high ceilings and few walls, which she'd painted white for maximum lighting. The area over the kitchen and bedroom was enclosed storage, but in the studio itself, everything had been removed up to the peak. Rarely did Alex allow anyone inside, and then only when her work was draped and out of view.

Except the children, of course; her regular visitors. They had permission to walk the two blocks from TCH—the insiders' name for the home—for art classes throughout the week, some individually, some in small groups. She loved the time they spent with her, and she hadn't given up one hour of that for this statue. They were her life, her world; the statue was for them—all of them.

Occasionally Claudia stopped by to chat, as sisters do, and when Alex left the room, she'd peek beneath the drape. Alex knew, but pretended she didn't, and Claudia pretended she hadn't, so nothing was said. No line had been crossed. Claudia hadn't pushed, until now.

"I want to see that statue"—more pounding—"and I want to see it now!"

"Careful," Alex muttered to no one in particular. A tiny grin of amusement broke across her face, even as she continued the painstaking work to eliminate fine little flaws on the statue's muscular thigh. "You'll break a nail."

Not that something so frivolous would matter to Alex. Her clothes were durable; jeans and chambray shirts, their color softened by the fine marble dust coating everything. The only reason her blond hair was long was that she was too uninterested to get it styled; she pulled it back just to keep it out of her eyes when she worked. She knew nothing about pantyhose, thought mascara and makeup were synonymous, and broke her fingernails so often that she'd just taken to filing them with a rasp as she worked.

"Alexandra, I mean it! The preview's Saturday, and I *have* to know it'll be ready."

"Trust me," she said loud enough for her voice to carry across the large, airy room and through the door. "Go away and let me work in peace."

Claudia resorted to whining again. "Come on, give me a break."

In spite of the deadline, Alex was enjoying this new side of Ms. Perfect Woman. Relief from the whining came in the form of the old console television blaring on all by itself—again—which had been happening frequently in the last week and a half. Eventually the volume lowered itself, but it was always a shock the way it blasted on without warning. Not to mention the channel surfing.

She'd complained to the caretaker, who'd called a TV repairman, who'd found nothing wrong and blamed the old wiring in the building. The electrician who'd checked that out said it was ancient, all right, but fine. No shorts or anything. He suggested maybe a ghost had taken up residence—and looked dead serious as he'd said it, too. At that point, she figured Billy, the resident computer guru at TCH, had been experimenting again, this time with her TV. She'd given up and pulled the plug.

Made it damned hard to tune out, knowing it was *still* unplugged. Billy was so computer savvy, he'd get a full scholarship to college for sure. Right now she was just grateful for the noise masking Claudia's intrusion.

With an eye for detail, she perused the marble god from every possible angle. She'd stuck close to the original model, working hers into the atypical, blustery catch-me-if-you-can pose the archaeology team had reassembled, right down to the beautiful, macho smirk on his face.

It stood six feet, four inches tall, not including the base, which raised it up to an impressive seven feet. She'd chiseled it out of the most magnificent hunk of marble she could buy, and since the Ladies' Club—the wealthiest group of women in St. Louis to assemble under one roof—had financed its purchase, it was a pretty magnificent piece. They'd even allowed her to live in the studio rent-free while she worked on it.

Two walls of her studio were papered with a collage— photographs of magnificent, mouthwatering male models and body builders, line drawings of the human anatomy, and a myriad of sketches she'd done on her own. She suspected some of Claudia's visits were manufactured just so she could come in and drool over the walls.

A third wall was filled with artwork the children had done.

They could use more art supplies, she thought, and clothes, games, spending money . . . everything kids need. She knew building repairs had to come first—without them, the city would close the home down—but surely the statue and matching funds would be enough.

And so she chiseled away at the god, because that's what she knew how to do.

After smoothing one last rough spot on its right knee with diamond paste and a felt pad, she stood back and admired what she'd accomplished. Not bad for a year's work. "Mm, mm, mm. You are a handsome guy, if I do say so myself."

"Don't break your arm—"

Damn, she got in. Alex turned, and sure enough, there was Claudia, gazing critically at the statue.

"—patting yourself on the back or anything," Claudia finished with a smug smile.

Alex hated sharing a work in progress. As sensitive as any artist, she was subject to the highs and lows of praise and criticism, and right now she just didn't have the time or energy for either one—or for the distraction that was her sister.

As always, Claudia was elegantly dressed. Today she wore a pink suit and matching pink pumps, and somehow managed to carry that off without looking like cotton candy. Every piece of expensive pearl and diamond jewelry— earrings, choker, lapel pin, the works—was a perfect match. Her way of overcompensating for her spartan childhood.

Out of habit, Claudia stepped around a year's worth of mail heaped on the wide plank floorboards. It wasn't nice, highly polished hardwood flooring, but scarred, dull, and very suitable for a working studio. Why any mail came there at all was beyond Alex. Mostly addressed to "Occupant," it was dropped through the slot several times a week and never touched by human hands again. She had better things to do.

Desperate to cover her work before Claudia started critiquing it, Alex glanced around for the drape, two mismatched, flowery sheets she'd picked up at a garage sale and glued together, light enough to toss over the god's head. Now . . . where was it?

She didn't spot the crumpled heap on the floor until Claudia said, "Oh no you don't," and raced for it. Alex got her hand on it first, but Claudia, even in high heels, was quick enough to jump on it and render it unmovable. Alex tugged for a second, then gave up.

"How'd you get in here?"

Claudia held up a key and smiled proudly, as if she'd single-handedly deciphered an encoded map and discovered a lost treasure.

"Found this." She had to raise her voice to be heard over the TV.

Exaggerating every movement so Alex would know her privacy was gone forever, Claudia held out her pink handbag, opened it, dropped the key in, and snapped it shut again. Back it went beneath her arm, tucked against her ribs and safer than Fort Knox.

The end of Alex's well-guarded privacy. It was a good thing she was done with the statue, or she'd have to have a new lock installed, and she couldn't afford that.

"It took me half an hour rummaging through every drawer in the club to find the extra key, but my goodness, Alexandra!" She lifted her gaze to the statue's broad chest and, hand to her generously rounded chest, sighed lustily. "It was worth it."

Grudgingly, Alex had to admit she appreciated the praise. Claudia had a keen eye for art. Rather than admit it and lose the upper hand, though, Alex busied herself brushing dust off her jeans and shirt. She pretended that nothing her sister said mattered, when in truth it mattered a great deal; her own leftover baggage from childhood.

"Fine," Alex said, punching the off button on the TV with more force than necessary. Blessed silence. "You can go report back to the club that there really is a statue in here, and it really is ready for the preview."

"Now, don't get all huffy, dear," Claudia said soothingly. "You know how important this is to everyone."

"Including me. If I didn't have him ready in time, you and the other ladies might be embarrassed, but it's my career that'd be in the toilet."

With good grace, Claudia—still circling, still perusing the statue from head to toe—nodded in acknowledgment.

Alex retrieved her favorite chisel from the floor. When she tossed it onto the worktable, it landed with a hollow thud and raised a cloud of dust. For the first time in months, she noticed.

"Guess I'd better start cleaning. Have you seen the broom?"

Claudia sighed. "I'm sure it's under something somewhere. Honestly, Alexandra, if you were better organized . . . There it is. Under the sofa."

Alex pulled it out by the handle, then used it to drag the dustpan out, too. Marble dust and tiny chips lingered everywhere. She brushed off her jeans again when she stood up, and tossed the dratted ponytail out of the way. Maybe she should cut it off.

Claudia said, "I thought you didn't clean until you were done."

"Right."

"You always said it was unlucky for you."

"Uh-huh." No sense clearing up that little white lie.

"So wait." Claudia grabbed Alex's arm, stopping her. "Why are you sweeping?"

"Well, gee, maybe because I'm done?"

"Done?" Claudia studied the statue again, from head to toe and then halfway back up. "Oh no no, my dear. You can't be done."

"Trust me, it's finished. It's perfect." Alex bent down with the dustpan to sweep up a load and drop it into the trash can, which she finally found beneath the worktable.

"But, it's not . . . it's not . . ."

Alex followed her sister's horrified gaze, and she smiled. The god wasn't exactly anatomically correct, and she was waiting for her prudish sister to say the words. She feigned innocence.

"What, Claudia?"

"I was afraid of this."

"Yes?" she prodded. This was the first recreation she'd had in months, and she wasn't about to let her sister's embarrassment pass unnoticed.

Claudia sighed. Her cheeks pinkened, and she stammered out, "It doesn't have a, uh . . . It's missing, um . . . Oh, damn it, Alexandra, it has a fig leaf."

Pleased to have the upper hand for a change, Alex grinned. "Yes, I know. Don't look so shocked. I saw you peek last week."

Claudia shook her head, but not in denial of what she'd done last week. More like she didn't know what she was going to do with a little sister who'd obviously committed some grievous error.

"I was afraid you were going to leave it like that."

Alex thought she couldn't possibly have heard correctly. She'd made the fig leaf because that's what she'd thought they'd all want. The majority of the Ladies' Club was, well, matronly.

"The original didn't have a fig leaf," Claudia pointed out, as if that said it all.

Out of curiosity, Alex asked, "And how would you know that?"

Claudia walked right over to the easel and rested one long, Perfectly Pink fingernail on the hacked-off stub.

"No fig leaf."

Alex snickered. "Yeah, no nothing."

"You have to give it a . . . a . . . You have to make it . . . Well, you *know* what I mean."

Alex's eyebrows lifted, along with her sense of humor. She'd been working too hard, too long. "Anatomically correct?"

"Yes." Claudia looked relieved that she didn't have to spell it out. "Now, I understand this might be hard for you, to give it a, you know . . ."

She laughed outright. "After years of sketching male models? Piece of cake."

"Well, sketching is so . . . removed, don't you think? Not hands-on at all. So I brought you something. Wait right here." Claudia rushed out the door, calling over her shoulder, "Don't clean anything until I get back."

"Don't clean anything?" Claudia was always after her to sweep, dust, pitch things out, and sort her mail. Alex took a step closer to the door and called out, "Who *are* you?"

"Ha ha." Claudia returned in a flash, tugging a young man behind her. Six-foot-four, with a chiseled, strong face and a body to die for, encased in a gray Webster University Athletic Department T-shirt, faded jeans with ripped knees, and sandals. Probably not a day over twenty-one. A baby.

Claudia gazed up at him. "I got him as close to scale as I could."

"Wow, and it's not even my birthday."

With a nod from Claudia, he stripped his T-shirt over his

head in one smooth motion, sending ripples through well-toned muscles everywhere, including a nice six-pack.

"I interviewed several, mind you," Claudia said, her back to Alex, as she stared at his broad, sun-bronzed chest. "He was the best I could find."

Alex should've been appalled that the man was stripping when she didn't need a model, but she was more interested in what Claudia had just said.

"You *interviewed* men for me?"

"Of course." She shot a smile over her shoulder at Alex. "I couldn't bring you one that was lacking in the, uh, right department." She turned her attention back to the baby. "Now the jeans."

Quickly, in one smooth motion, he kicked off his sandals and unsnapped his jeans at the waistband. He reached for the zipper.

Alex said, "Hey, wait a minute."

He pulled it down anyway, stuck his thumbs into the waistband, and started shucking the denim down his hips. Red elastic topped red cotton briefs. Bikinis.

"Stop right there," Alex ordered.

Claudia waggled her hand to indicate he should proceed, which he did by obediently kicking his jeans off his bare feet.

Had the man no modesty? Certainly no professionalism. She'd never had a model strip right in front of her. Her cheeks were probably as red as his underwear.

The bikinis followed the jeans south.

"There!" Claudia said triumphantly when he was totally naked. "I thought you might need to see the real thing." She ogled him for a moment, then turned and faced Alex. Her hands were clasped at the button by her waist, probably to restrain them from temptation. "I take it by your open-mouthed stare that you're impressed?"

"I'm staring at *you*."

Claudia jabbed her thumb over her shoulder. "With that right there?"

"I can ignore that. You, on the other hand, are in need of some serious therapy." She looked the real thing in the eyes. No lower. "Get dressed."

He didn't move.

"I'm paying him," Claudia offered as an explanation. "He stays undressed."

"Fine." Alex grabbed the sheet from the floor. "Better close your eyes so you don't get any chips in them," she said to him, then threw it over his head, effectively covering him from head to toe.

Claudia yanked it off again, raking his thick dark hair the wrong direction, giving it a tousled, slept-in look. When Alex tried to grab the sheet back, Claudia threw it onto the floor and stood on it again.

"We want the fig leaf removed."

"We?" Alex asked.

"We voted on it."

Claudia, president of the Ladies' Club, had actually sat at the head of the board room table and made a motion to have the god's fig leaf rechiseled into the real thing? How Alex would've liked to have been a fly on that wall!

"It was unanimous."

She walked a slow circle around Claudia's gift—no sense letting it all go to waste—and smiled slyly.

"And did you all *interview*"—she gave her sister a sly wink—"the demos?"

"No, they left that to me."

She chuckled. "You always did like to head the committees."

"Yes, well, you know the old saying. It's a tough job, but somebody's got to do it." Claudia sounded as if she believed it, which meant she'd missed her calling on the stage.

This is what came of not barring the damned door. She walked over to her perfect, no-longer-finished statue and brushed a spot of dust off his pecs. "Sure, I'll give him a—"

Claudia cleared her throat loudly and pinkened to match her suit. How she could blush at the words but stare unabashedly at a naked man, Alex would never understand.

"I'll make him anatomically correct," she said in deference to Claudia's wishes.

"Good." Claudia beamed triumphantly. She picked up the chisel and ran her finger over it. "Mm, nice. Sharp."

The TV blared to life again.

Over a full blast of *Jeopardy!* music, Claudia hollered, "His name is Matthew and you can keep him as long as you need him. Now, I know how you hate an audience, so I'll leave you two alone."

She came at him with a hammer and chisel aimed at his most vital, most sensitive region.

If Darius had been telepathic, he'd have sent a simple mental message to Alexandra to stop and think this over before she just started banging away at him. He was, after all, a god, a stud with a reputation to uphold. Only the best would do. Matthew, the chosen example, was well endowed for a mortal, but not well enough for Darius.

He had to find a way to show her the difference.

He'd spent most of his time outside the statue while Alex worked on it, perfecting his new body. He liked watching her work, the glide of her hands over the smooth surface, the sway of her hips as she moved around it with a rhythm all her own. It had been many years since he'd walked the earth, figuratively speaking, but he'd seen wheat fields blowing in the wind. Her hair was like that when she left it loose, full-bodied and golden, begging for his touch. Far beyond his present abilities.

Her eyes matched the finest of his aquamarines. He'd give her a necklace to match, as reward for making such a fine body for him.

Her figure—well, suffice it to say, he was eagerly anticipating getting his life back. Especially his hands. But first, he had to be sure he got everything else he needed.

Weak as his powers were at this point, they only worked while he was inside the statue. He needed practice controlling them, strengthening them if possible. So as much as he hated confined spaces, in it he was.

Pure energy radiated outward from him. He turned on a bright floor lamp, successfully aiming the beam directly onto her wall of drawings. His telekinetic skills had grown stronger each day, keeping pace with the final stages of the statue; the more perfect it became, the closer he was to being his old self. It didn't take him long to highlight the sketch he liked best. It was well endowed and would go well with his self-assured grin—the one that drove women crazy.

He wondered how she could have captured his body so well in marble when she'd never seen it in the flesh? All she had were magazine images of a stained, cracked statue. It had been pieced together as well as the team had been able to manage, but it was still a sad, sad image of what he once had been.

Ah, he couldn't wait to be whole and perfect again. How he longed for the women! To smell their perfumed oils, touch their petal-soft skin, hold their soft, female curves against him. To make love again.

For days now, he'd been trying the statue, always hoping that when he returned to life, the fig leaf would drop off and reveal what was supposed to be behind it. What *better* be there. If not, he could vacate it quickly enough, supposing there was no sudden earthquake along the New Madrid fault.

Filling the marble, taking it over with his presence, had good and bad points. He enjoyed knowing that when Alexandra got it perfect, he'd have the means to lift the curse. To do that, he had to be inside it, but he didn't like the helpless, vulnerable feeling of imprisonment. He was a god; he wasn't supposed to know of these things.

The hardest part, though, had begun the day he could feel her hands on him. Often, her fingers roamed over him from head to toe, only it wasn't the head and toes that bothered him. It was everything in between. The lady wasn't shy. She skimmed. She smoothed. She patted and filed and rubbed again. Over and over until he couldn't stand it anymore.

Nor could he stand to be without it.

He'd taken to spending more and more time in the statue as the week progressed. And each day was more sweet torture. He couldn't breathe, couldn't react in a natural way. If only he could move!

And then, quite by accident, he'd found an outlet for his pent-up energy. It had begun with the television. The first few times, he hadn't understood it was he who turned it on. And always so damned loud. After that, he'd experimented with other electrical items in the studio. He'd gotten pretty good with the lights. He'd even learned to make a bell ring, but he'd quit that when it took her out of the room. He didn't want her to leave him; he wanted to be finished.

Except for now. Now he wanted her over at that wall, studying up on what she was about to do. Like a surgeon, she should be prepared. She should be delicate, yet precise. Make no mistakes.

He couldn't imagine what had possessed her to give him a fig leaf in the first place.

"You'd look better without it," she'd said once, standing back in admiration. It was her habit to talk softly as she worked, almost as if she were speaking directly and solely to him, sharing confidences with him in a way no other woman ever had. "To me, anyway. But you in the altogether in front of all those old ladies? I don't think so."

If he'd been telepathic, he'd have let her know immediately upon his arrival that the leaf would never do. But he'd had to bide his time and hope she'd come to her senses. And now she had, thanks to her sister.

Unfortunately, now he could feel her every stroke, and having the leaf forcefully removed wasn't going to be pleasant. Even if he left the statue, it would be torture to watch over her shoulder, knowing he was so close. Knowing one wrong crack would crush his dreams again. But leaving the statue would mean he couldn't feel her hands on him, couldn't come alive at the precise moment when all was perfect. For once he was alive again, there'd be no statue to break. He'd be free for all eternity.

He'd reward her well. Gems. Passion. Whatever pleased her.

And he'd warn her about the stranger who came to her studio each night, shrouded in a hooded sweatshirt. If the door was locked, he jiggled the knob and peeked in windows. If not, he came in and stared at the statue. Once, he'd stood in the bedroom doorway and watched Alexandra sleep. As yet, Darius hadn't been able to figure out who it was or why he came.

Protective instincts welled up inside him, having little to do with needing the statue finished. He'd never spent so much time in the company of one woman. Yes, he couldn't wait to live again and resume his playboy ways—it was, after all, a talent he'd learned at his father's knee—but he'd come to appreciate the great force that drove her to perfection, her love for the children. What did it matter to him the gentle way she guided the children through art lessons, through life? The laughter she shared with them over small jokes. The tears she shed when they cried. By Zeus, this was most confusing.

To protect her, he needed more power. He needed life.

Her palm landed on his chest, pulling him away from his rambling thoughts, back to her silken touch. Lightly, she skimmed her hand downward, as if taking his measure. He could feel it all, every blessed inch, until she reached the fig leaf. It itched, but other than that, he couldn't feel her hand on it other than a certain weightiness.

She tested the balance of the chisel in her hand, turned it to the attack position, and aimed it.

He blinked the light shining on the sketch. On and off. On and off.

"Hey, something's up with the lights," Matthew said.

She jumped, as if she'd forgotten he was there. Darius cringed. Jumping with a hammer and chisel in her hands, so close to him, wasn't good. Not good at all.

"What?" She looked at Matthew, then glanced over at the light. "Oh, it does that sometimes."

"Want me to unplug it?"

"Doesn't matter. If it wants to blink, it'll blink. If the TV wants to come on or if the oven timer wants to ring, they do. I've gotten used to it all." She shrugged it off and came at him again, even though she was still carrying on a conversation with Matthew. "You can get dressed and go."

She placed the chisel at the edge of the fig leaf. From inside the statue, he couldn't see it, but he could feel the sharp point right where he ended and the leaf began.

She raised the hammer.

"Nah, I can't leave," Matthew said.

"Why not?"

Pay attention! He didn't mind her talking to him—he suspected it helped her concentration—but not to someone *else*.

He could leave the statue, go back to being nothing more than air, but he'd waited so long to be whole again, he couldn't bear the idea of a second away from the promise of it. He wanted to be alive again, the very moment she finished. The very *nanosecond* his new body was perfect.

"Mrs. Kline said I had to stay."

Darius kept the light blinking like crazy until Alexandra took time out and turned her attention to Matthew.

"Did she say you had to stay naked?"

"As a matter of fact . . ." He grinned. Not a bad grin, Darius admitted. He probably got his share of women with it, but it was nothing compared to what Darius would be able to do. Soon.

"Well," Alexandra said, stepping back and holding the chisel out of striking range, "did she say you had to do everything I told you?"

Matthew combed his fingers through his hair, straightening it, getting down to business. He studied the statue for a moment, then posed in a similar stance.

"That's what I'm here for."

"Fine." Alexandra put down her tools—*yes!*—and picked up the sheet again. With a flick of her wrist and a warning to close his eyes, she covered Matthew from head to toe.

"Hey!"

"Hey yourself." She picked up her chisel again.

Darius blinked the light faster. Was the woman blind? Any other mortal would have noticed by now, would have walked over to the wall to see if she could stop the irritating flickering.

"Stay under there until you're dressed."

"But—"

"And keep quiet. I don't like distractions. Better yet, go sit in the kitchen."

Under the sheet, with one arm stretched out in front to protect himself from unseen walls, Matthew scooped up his clothes and shuffled out of the room.

Darius tried a pattern with the light, something different to catch her attention now that she was used to it blinking. One short, two long. One short, two long.

This time she noticed. "Honestly, the stuff I have to put up with."

He left it on. He turned off the spots shining on him— something he probably should have done originally, but he hadn't wanted to chance her taking a whack at him in less than perfect light. But now . . . now he had her attention where he needed it.

She glanced up at the dead spotlights and groaned.

He winked the other light in a new pattern, two short, one long. She picked up her hammer and crossed the room in a few quick steps.

"Damn it!" She struck the lamp, denting the shade and shattering the bulb all over the floor.

She was the most frustrating woman! If he could've

moved his arms, he would've paid a premium just to have the ability to pull his hair out.

Darius wasn't giving up though; too much was at stake. Now that he had her where he wanted her, he made the drawing flutter in the breezeless studio.

She glanced at the closed windows, then the door, and frowned. Smoothing the sketch flat, holding it down, she yanked another push pin from the wall and viciously poked it through the bottom edge.

Then, just as he had hoped, her hand lingered. Her gaze wandered to other drawings and photographs around the one he'd selected, hesitating over a close runner-up.

"Hm, what do you think, big guy? Which suits you better?" she said absently, including him even though she didn't know it. "A? Or B?"

Could she *be* more obtuse? He shot the push pin out of the wall and fluttered his choice again.

She stared at the pin lying on the floor. Picking it up, she inspected it, then let her gaze wander the room.

"I think I've been working too hard," she said.

"What?" Matthew asked from the other room, then showed himself at the doorway as he pulled his T-shirt over his head and down his washboard abs. "Did you say something?"

"Can you make tea?"

"Coffee."

She sighed. "Can you boil water?"

"Sure."

She plucked Darius's choice off the wall.

Yes!

"Fine. Call me when it's boiling." She pushed her sleeves up. "I've got some serious chiseling to do."

3

The fig leaf disappeared readily enough, but shaping what was left into *the* perfect male form presented a dilemma.

Alex worked through the week, nearly nonstop. Every muscle in her body protested the extra hours of cramped, fine detail work needed to get the statue ready for Saturday's unveiling and brunch in the Ladies' Club mansion, just across the yard.

Leonard Kline, prominent New York art critic and Claudia's nephew by her second marriage, would be there. The thought of his flying to St. Louis just to view her work made Alex nervous. With a good review, out-of-state buyers might fly in, which would raise the bidding and bring in more money for the children. She couldn't stop to worry about the consequences if he hated it. She had to press on.

If the high bidders were women, she supposed size didn't matter. If they were men, it did. Too large, and the male buyers would be intimidated, wouldn't want the statue anywhere around. Too small, and they'd think the work insignificant.

Leonard Kline might think she couldn't handle the subject matter. She toyed with the balance all week, working slowly, gradually downsizing, approaching what she thought would be the perfect balance.

Until her favorite chisel disappeared.

"Billy!" she hollered toward the kitchen.

The twelve-year-old towheaded computer and science genius from TCH had been there less than an hour. He'd kept quietly to himself, supposedly studying for a test on Monday. Alex understood him well. Like her, he was a perfectionist driven by feelings of inadequacy; if they were perfect, they could win love.

Billy popped into the doorway. "Yeah?"

She waggled her finger at him. "Enough fun for now. I need that chisel back."

"What's a chisel?"

She held up her hammer in one hand, nothing in the other.

"Oh, that. You probably set it down again." A high-energy kid, he wasted no time joining her at the base of the statue for a look-see.

Tapping her toe on the dusty, marble chip–strewn floor, she waited for him to come clean.

"I don't see it," he said. "Did you carry it into the bathroom or something?"

"You know very well I didn't. Look, I don't mind you programming the lights and the TV to do weird stuff . . ." He looked dumbfounded, and she grinned. "Thought I didn't know about that, didn't you? Well, I do."

"But—"

"But taking my chisel's crossing the line. Although I might forgive you if you let me in on how you did it without me seeing you."

"Honest, I didn't. I've been studying. And I didn't program your lights—" His frown changed to a look of scientific curiosity. "What kind of weird stuff?"

"Fine." She got down on her knees and poked through a box of older tools she kept under the worktable. Hoping to make him feel guilty and come clean, she said, "Here's a nice, *dull* one I can use."

The overhead spotlights on the statue flickered out. Hands on her hips, she appraised Billy in a don't-look-so-innocent-kid kind of way.

He dragged a chair underneath one of the bulbs and climbed up. "Probably just the wiring," he said, and Alex was glad he wasn't tall enough to start poking around in the electrical fixtures. No telling what kind of trouble he could get into.

"I had it checked. C'mon, Billy, 'fess up."

"Wasn't me, Alex," he said, as he got off the chair. "Swear. I'll go check the breaker box."

"I've got fuses."

"Fuses?"

He'd played tricks on her before—she was a pretty easy target when her mind was on her work—but he'd never lied about it.

"Never mind. You stay out of my fuse box." She took him by the shoulders, suddenly realizing he'd grown six inches in the past year and she hadn't even noticed. He didn't look like he was lying, though; he had no trouble meeting her eyes and he wasn't trying to sidetrack her. Stumped, she turned him toward the kitchen and gave him a light push. "Maybe I did carry it into another room."

"Better let me help you then. I know you have to have him done in another hour, and with the way you keep house, it could be anywhere." He blushed as soon as he realized what he'd said. She laughed, and he said, "Well, it's true."

She gazed around the studio. "Yeah, well, I'll start with this old chisel—"

The TV blared on, full volume.

"—you go ahead and look around."

He trotted over to the TV and turned it off, but it came right back on. He reached around behind it, pulled on the wire, and came up with an unplugged plug. "Whoa! This kind of weird stuff, Alex?"

She grinned, thinking, *Boys will be boys*, wishing she could have some of her own. "And you know nothing about it?"

"Sure, I know something about it." He turned the wire over in his hand. "I know it's not possible."

"Anything's possible." Especially with the amount of energy she'd felt in the studio lately.

"Nuh-uh."

"Yeah? Watch this." She aimed the chisel at the statue's groin, raised the hammer, and said, "I need light!"

And the light clicked on.

"Whoa!" Ricocheting expressions mapped Billy's thoughts: natural curiosity at war with knowing that whatever was going on, it wasn't right, and maybe he should be afraid. "This place is haunted."

She waved off his worry. "Get outta here. It's all in the vibrations or something. Now, are you going to find that chisel or not?"

His face paled and his eyes grew rounder as he whispered, "It's right behind you."

And there it was, peeking out from beneath the flowered sheet. "Now how'd we miss that?"

He ran into the kitchen, reappearing almost immediately with his books, papers, and backpack cradled haphazardly in his arms. Stooped over so he'd drop nothing, he bolted for the door. "Later, Alex."

"Wimp," she called to his retreating back. She retrieved her chisel, tossing the older one aside, missing the toolbox completely. She'd worry about the possessed TV after the auction, if someone didn't 'fess up first.

.She flexed her wrist muscles, stretched her neck from side to side, and tossed her loose hair over her shoulder. That was another thing! Both her scrunchies had suddenly, inexplicably, disappeared. She didn't have time to hunt for them now. Back to work she went, for half an hour before she took another break, when she noticed something quite peculiar.

She'd thought it had been her imagination this past week, but the marble seemed to be getting warmer, taking on what seemed like body heat. It had increased each day. At first she'd chalked it up to her fevered pitch to get it done, but it was so warm now, she knew that had nothing to do with it. Billy was smart enough to have rigged up some thermodynamic thing, but he'd never touch her artwork. Besides, he stuck mainly to electronics, and there wasn't an electronic component anywhere in her statue.

So she was left with an inexplicable warmth in her statue, which wouldn't hurt the selling price, but that one minor flaw on his hand might. And he was to be sneak previewed in . . . She hunted for a clock, any clock. When she found one under a thick layer of dust on the bookshelf, she used her shirttail to wipe the crystal. It didn't come perfectly clean, but enough so she could read it.

"Half an hour! Where the heck are the movers?" she said, then realized she was talking to the statue again. She'd caught herself time and again, whispering thoughts better kept to herself. Not like Pygmalion—for who could fall in love with a statue?—but private thoughts that every woman has about sisters and children and friends.

She picked up the phone and dialed the Ladies' Club. The studio was going to seem lonely after her captive audience was taken away to his new home.

"Is it ready?" were Claudia's first words.

"Of course!"

She couldn't believe Claudia wasn't standing over her shoulder, but apparently she'd gotten the message last night. She had come bearing a pizza as a peace offering in exchange for a peek at the statue. For being interrupted, Alex had shoved her out the door and thrown the pizza at her, with the lid wide open.

And then all night she'd lain awake, wondering if she'd made a mistake by removing the fig leaf after all. Was the decision really unanimous? Did the rest of the ladies realize this was a life-sized male god, in the nude, not some little two-foot statue that would sit quietly unnoticed on a corner table? Did they realize what a stir it might cause at a private brunch instead of an impersonal museum?

Too late now.

"So where the hell are the movers?"

"Right outside your door, sweetie."

Her reputation was on the line, and she didn't want to get labeled "Temperamental" and "Delivers late." She nearly ripped the door off its hinges as she threw it open to reveal two men and a dolly. Big men, for sure, but only two?

"You're it?" she asked, afraid to hear their answer.

"We're it, lady." The logo above his breast pocket read Tom, and he sounded overly confident, as if he'd never met his match with a stationary object and never expected to in his lifetime. "We was told to wait out here till you opened the door, no matter what. I guess it's time, huh?" He spit in the flower garden. "Where's it at?"

She stepped aside. Tom trod over Occupant's mail. The

second guy, Jim, kicked it aside with his heavy shoe, which was the only article of clothing on his body that didn't have a tear in it.

"Holy shit," Tom said, halfway into the room, gazing up at the marble statue. He reached under his cap and scratched the back of his head, which made the bill bob up and down over his nose. "We ain't movin' that, lady."

"Yeah, you ever heard of a hernia?" Jim added.

"You ever heard of a stacker?" she snapped back, ticked off that they'd come unprepared. The two of them standing in the studio only made her Greek god look worlds better, not that it needed any help.

"A hernia? Try double hernia," Tom said.

"Triple hernia," Jim added.

She didn't dare scream at them; among other influential people across the yard, the art critic might overhear. So she grinned, but she was sure it wasn't a pleasant sight, as both men quickly backed toward the door.

"I suggest you get a lot more men in here *pronto*," she said.

Tom glanced at his watch. "Before the preview? You crazy? Where we gonna—"

"I don't care where you get them," she yelled, her voice escalating beyond all attempts to keep it professional and ladylike. "Get them out of the crowd for all I care, just get a whole damned bunch of them!"

Okay, so "Temperamental" was a label she could live with.

Darius felt it happening. As soon as Alexandra finished buffing his fingernail, he felt warmer, stronger. He couldn't move yet, though. Couldn't tell the ten men tipping him precariously toward the floor to wait just a few more minutes and he'd move himself. On foot.

Not onto any stage, though. A few more minutes, that's all he needed. Then he'd be off to Olympus to show Zeus that he'd found his perfect body again, that he was back on the playing field. After that, he could survey the female population on Earth and do some serious choosing.

Though . . . Alexandra de Marco had some interesting qualities, the best of which was that she'd provided him with the perfect body. For that alone, he owed her. He'd been in and around her studio for two weeks, and in that time, no man had visited, much less made love to her. She hadn't even mentioned one. Her telephone barely rang, let alone with a man on the other end.

It wasn't that she wasn't desirable. He'd seen her every which way but naked, and sometimes darned close, and he knew for a fact that her body was just fine. Sometimes, when she got hot working under the lights, she'd strip down to a tiny little stretch top that hugged her breasts.

Once she'd even gone to take a bath, then run back out in two bits of cream-colored fabric to make a quick adjustment on a sketch. No matter how much satellite he'd listened to, none of what he'd heard had prepared him for the little scraps of material that clung to her curves as she stood there with no self-consciousness, scratching her pencil across a page.

As a matter of fact, she was better than just fine, and it had nothing to do with his being out of commission for centuries. Maybe—

The room spun before his eyes. His stomach churned as the statue started to drop on one side.

"Hey, watch it!" Tom hollered.

Yeah, watch it.

With much grunting and groaning, the men prevented the marble from crashing to the floor. Barely. At least four of them carried their own excess weight around the middle and had no business hefting him around. The fifth was pasty-faced; he couldn't be healthy. And the sixth volunteer, well, maybe that limp was due to uneven leg length and not weakness. That left a lot of dead weight for the two who were young and strong, probably in better shape than the movers, but only two.

An accident now could ruin his perfect body beyond repair, could send him back to limbo. To nothingness. Alexandra might not have time to fix him, or the damage might be irreparable. As the men lugged him across the studio and out the door, one slow step after another, he figuratively held his breath. And waited for the change to happen.

He experimented with his telekinetic abilities and found them limited to things outside the statue. He could open the door and hold it from banging against the marble, but he was powerless to just pick up the statue and move it himself.

Perhaps if he extricated himself? Left the statue before he came fully back to his normal godself? The thought was anathema to him, but perhaps better than being broken again. He'd just made up his mind to pry himself away when he felt a thud against his shoulder.

"What's up?" Tom asked.

"Damn lamppost's too close to the door," Jim replied.

"No it's not. Just watch where you're going and let's take it slow. Did we hurt anything?"

"Nah, it's cast iron; can't hurt it."

"I meant the statue, dumb ass."

Darius felt Jim's fingers probe him, right there on the shoulder where he'd felt the thud. He didn't need Jim to answer, though. Already he felt cooler. He tried to extricate himself, and couldn't.

Don't panic. Think.

"Just a scratch," Jim whispered, so the impromptu helpers wouldn't know.

"Well, don't tell the lady. She's crazy enough already."

Unless she could see that he needed fixing, his chance to regain a body, and hence a life, was gone, not to mention maybe being stuck for eternity in this damn thing. Where was she when he needed her?

"What's the hold-up?" she asked. From the sound of her voice, he could tell she was approaching his feet.

"Nothing," the two movers answered in unison.

He cursed them, their stupidity, their incompetence, their mortalness. They carried him into a ballroom, under cover of a temporary, curtained stage. There they stood him up again, threw a new drape over his head, and beat a hasty retreat.

Moments later, he heard Alexandra's footsteps, coming to check him over one more time, he hoped. He did a quick check to see how much power he still had. Close enough to perfect to still have some, he quickly let the drape "slip" to a lopsided position, exposing his damaged shoulder to her sight.

"Really, Claudia should have called the museum for a referral for movers," Alexandra said absently, as she did a quick visual inspection. He had to agree.

Claudia appeared then, a virtual moving garden in a long, flowing floral dress and emeralds. "Great, Alexandra, a whole minute to spare."

"Sarcasm doesn't become you. Just let me fix the drape, then you can open the curtains."

Alexandra tugged on it, straightened it, played with the folds until they met her satisfaction, and all the while, he wanted to scream at her, "My shoulder! Fix my shoulder!"

Clipping her words, Claudia said, "It's fine, go get dressed. And for heaven's sake, how do you ever expect to catch another man looking like that? Do something with your hair!"

"It's long, it's straight, it doesn't *do* anything."

Darius had heard this argument before. While Alexandra sought perfection through art, Claudia strove for it through appearance. Personally, he thought Alexandra in anything was a vision.

"You could at least brush the dust out of it."

"It's not dust, it's marble chips."

"Oh, so that makes it all right, I suppose. Honestly, Alexandra, I've spent the last week making sure everything's perfect to debut your statue. You have no idea how much . . . The Greek columns had to be delivered and set up just so, and they were the wrong color when they arrived. They clashed with the centerpieces, if you can imagine that." She rattled on, distracting Alexandra so much that Darius wanted to throttle her. "Well, I suppose you could, you *do* have an eye for color. But honestly, there's so much more to . . . Those paintings didn't just walk over here from the art museum, you know. And that ten-foot rain lamp! Do you know how much oil one of those things takes? It took forever to find a store that carried it. And then there was—"

Darius slid the cloth down the far side so it would rise again on his damaged shoulder.

"That's odd," Alexandra said. As she raised up on tiptoe to grab it, her hand rested on his arm. Out of habit, thank Zeus, her fingers wandered over his skin. "Oh, darn."

"What?" Claudia asked.

"I've got to fix a spot."

"Fix a spot?" It would've been a shriek if Claudia hadn't been whispering. "There's no time to 'fix a spot.' Everyone's at the tables, waiting. Get off the stage now so we can unveil it."

"It'll just take me a minute."

Yeah, leave us alone. If Alexandra got him out of this, he swore he'd make it up to her. Diamonds, rubies, anything she wanted, as much as she wanted.

"I've got some felt in my back pocket."

"Jeans," Claudia said on a moan. "We're about to unveil a masterpiece, and you're in dusty old jeans. Honestly, I don't know how you can do such perfect work and not give a damn about your clothes or your hair . . . or your mail . . . or your . . ." Her mantra faded as she walked away.

As Alexandra smoothed the damage, Darius warmed again, felt hope again, darned near fell in love, if he were capable. But why limit the field? He had a lot of down time to make up for.

"Mm, mm, mm," she said. Seemed to be her way of admiring him. She finished with the felt, ran her fingers over him one last time—by Zeus, he could feel work-roughened calluses on her hands now!—and then stood back to admire him.

A young woman, about Alexandra's age, stopped to gawk. Fanning herself with her clipboard, she said. "Oh, Alex, too bad he's not real. Every woman in America'd want *him*."

Alexandra grinned saucily. "Jan, if he were real, every woman in America would die waiting, 'cause I'd rip my own clothes off and never let *him* leave the bedroom."

By Zeus, hold that thought!

Jan laughed and said, "Okay, we're ready," into her lapel. A drum roll sounded.

"Drums," Alexandra muttered. "For a Greek god. Sorry, big guy."

"Ladies and gentlemen . . ." came over the loudspeaker. "The St. Louis Ladies' Club is proud to have this opportunity to preview its Forty-seventh Annual Charity Auction with a life-sized marble statue of the Greek god Darius."

Alexandra patted his arm, said the oddest thing, "Knock

'em dead, Darius," then drew the cover over him and slipped away. Already he missed the warmth of her body resting against his arm, her womanly softness pressing against him.

"Darius, first god of gems, was a real favorite with the ladies."

First god?

Suddenly he was able to draw breath into his lungs, to feel his chest expand. He exhaled, then inhaled again, just to be sure it wasn't a fluke.

It wasn't! He could move!

"Darius was sculpted by St. Louis's own talented, award-winning sculptor Alexandra de Marco, whose work has drawn New York art critics to our fair city today."

He could wiggle his fingers, his toes. Shift his weight from one foot to the other. Blink his eyes. With one hand, he did a quick count of the pièce de résistance. One, two, everything was there, and in the right size.

"Please join me as we now welcome . . . *Darius!*"

The drape was snapped off his head, leaving him on the stage alone, alive, and impressed with the view of hundreds of women seated before him. Openmouthed women, to be sure, as they gazed at his beautiful, perfect body. Old ones, young ones; fat, skinny, short, and tall; each one was beautiful in her own way. He was a bit out of practice, but he used to be very good·at finding each woman's beauty. All he had to worry about was where to start, and how to keep the peace until he could get around to all of them. He grinned in anticipation.

By Zeus, that felt good!

Several women shrieked. One swooned. Most smiled and sighed lustily.

Men jumped up from their seats, approaching him, yelling

orders at him to cover himself, at one another to throw the
drape around him and throw him out. *Peasants*. There was no
need to cover his beautiful, perfect body.

"Psst! Congratulations," Hermes said from his hiding
place behind the stage curtain.

"Glad you could make it."

"I knew it would work!"

Darius beamed with pleasure and pride. "It seems the
ladies missed me."

Seeing no one about, the audience simply assumed he
spoke to them, perhaps playing a part in keeping with the
theme, and they swooned, as women always did for him.
They weren't so different from the women he used to bed,
who'd thought winning a god's attention increased their
stature in life. Golden blonds, deep brunettes, shiny silvers—
they dotted the room, with a few shades of red thrown in for
good measure. All his favorites, except he kept looking for
one in particular. One the color of ripe wheat.

"Where's Alexandra?" It seemed only fair she be his first;
he owed her. And if what she'd told Jan was true, he was going to be busy for quite some time.

In the distance, outside the window, lightning flashed, followed by a thunderbolt that rocked the building.

"Uh-oh," Hermes whispered.

"What?" Darius asked. He really hadn't been paying attention, but the second thunderbolt was unmistakable.

"Zeus is on to you now," Hermes said.

Preposterous! "He said when I found a perfect body—"

"You've heard the expression 'When Hades freezes
over'?" Hermes said, tongue-in-cheek. "Same thing. I'm
outta here. And you'd better find a place to hide."

4

Alex hadn't been watching the unveiling. It was more important to her to observe the predominantly female, totally wealthy and influential luncheon crowd get their first glimpse of her latest work. Claudia had practically shoved her out the back door to go change into more respectable attire than marble dust–coated jeans, but Alex needed to be *here*. Now. So she'd slipped right back in without changing and positioned herself along the side wall, at the midway point where she wouldn't be too obvious, yet could see as many faces as possible. How better to gauge the public's response to Darius? He looked almost perfect to her.

The key word was "almost." Every project, by the time she was done with it, was "almost" perfect. Given unlimited time, she supposed she'd never be truly finished with anything because there was always a way to make it better.

But as he'd neared completion, Darius had approached perfection, had made the gradual, logical transformation, in Alex's opinion, from "the statue" or "it" to "him." And if several people noticed something wrong with him—a rough spot, a slightly askew proportion, an intrusive line—she could tackle that in the coming week.

While she waited for the unveiling, she studied the crowd actively anticipating the same, in surroundings carefully orchestrated by the Ladies' Club to lend extra excitement. The auction committee had transformed the mansion's first-floor ballroom into nothing short of a Greek marvel. Fat Corinthian columns, faux finished to look magnificently old and cracked, decked out with twisting, climbing grape vines, created inner and outer colonnades of dining tables. To remain inconspicuous, Alex practically pasted herself to one of the giant pillars.

Paintings on loan from the St. Louis Art Museum and private collectors followed the Greek theme, ranging from fact, the Parthenon and the Acropolis, to myth, the mighty Zeus hurling his thunderbolt. Each server for the fifty-some-odd tables of eight was decked out in a white, floor-length chiton, edged with golden embroidery. In a ceremonious line, they paraded into the ballroom, carrying golden trays laden with crystal flutes bubbling to the rim with champagne. Centerpieces on the circular tables echoed the columns and twisting vines, each one sheltering an artistic cluster of round, grape-colored candles.

And this was just the preview!

One thing she could say about these ladies: they had a lot of faith in her. Not only all this hoopla, but they'd generously supported her with room and board for the past year, waiting for just this moment.

Finally, the announcement, and Alex crossed her fingers. She intently observed expectant faces in the crowd, watching their every movement, anticipating the usual lift of an eyebrow here and there, open-eyed wonder on almost everyone, mouths dropping open to *ahhh* their pleasure.

What she saw was startling, to say the least. Usually her statues garnered pleased smiles, sighs of contentment . . . even *laughter* wasn't out of the ordinary, as some of her pieces were quite whimsical.

But this! Eyes wide, mouths agape, hands poised in midair to clap, but frozen in time. The only clap she heard was from thunder outside. Twice. Only . . . it was sunny out.

The women were gasping, chatting with one another animatedly. A few even shrieked. Mrs. Osstrander leaned over, grabbed a knob on her portable oxygen tank, and without taking her eyes off the stage, increased the flow to her nasal cannula.

Men, too, exhibited bizarre behavior. She'd expected some mixed reaction there, but a few had stripped off their coats and were now sprinting toward the stage. What on *earth*?

And then she saw him.

She eased out from behind her column. It's wasn't as if her presence would distract anyone and temper his reaction—not at this point.

The man standing on stage—no, not standing, but *stretching*, like a contented cat just risen from a nap—bore a striking resemblance to Darius. Tall, well over six feet. Extremely well muscled without going overboard, like a real athlete and not a guy who bulked up in the gym. But most of all, just in case someone missed the resemblance, he went for life imitating art.

He was buck naked.

My oh my, how he could stand there in the altogether without blushing was beyond her, though—wow—a man built like that certainly had nothing to blush about. As an artist, she'd been studying the human form for years, and his was the best she'd ever seen.

But wait, what was she thinking?

A perusal of the stage behind him, toward where her statue should have been, told Alex that this . . . this *impostor* had somehow hidden Darius, who weighed upward of seven hundred pounds, before executing this practical joke.

Who *was* he?

Not Matthew, that's for sure. She hadn't seen him since the day Claudia dropped him by. He'd boiled her some water for tea—which, come to think of it, she'd forgotten to drink—spent the day napping on her sofa, fully clothed, and left when his time was up.

Had someone put the impostor up to this, or did he think it up himself? Was it supposed to be a joke on her, or on the whole club?

Only one thing wrong with the whole image. Well, maybe not *wrong*, exactly. While shaping the statue, Alex had always pictured the real Darius—the mythical one—with raven black hair. This guy was blond. Not pale and washed out, but sun-bronzed to a deep golden tan. And manly. Oh yeah, no doubt about that.

Without even consciously thinking about it, Alex approached the stage, threading her way unerringly around the fat columns, between tables, and through clumps of guests who'd stood up for a better look, crowding the floor with a traffic jam of disarranged chairs.

A petite, white-haired woman of aristocratic bearing grabbed Alex's arm before she got twenty paces. Her grip was surprisingly strong and steady. "Absolutely marvelous, my dear! I had no idea there was going to be entertainment. These things are usually so boring." She held a pair of glasses up in front of her eyes but didn't put them on, taking another gawk at the impostor. "Simply *mahvelous*."

Alex smiled and laughed nervously, as if she agreed. One thing she'd learned about living behind the Ladies' Club for the past year and conversing with the women as they came and went—how to be gracious. A smile and a calm tone went a long way toward smoothing ruffled feathers, and from the furious, appalled looks on many of the club members' faces, there were quite a few old birds going bald this afternoon.

"Excuse me," Alex said with deceptive graciousness, gently twisting her arm until she could get free without throwing the elderly woman to the floor.

She didn't get far, maybe another twenty feet, when a heavyset matron snagged her aluminum cane out, landed a direct hook over the crook of Alex's elbow, and reeled her in for an upbraiding. "Haven't you people ever heard of the health code?" She had a cell phone up to her ear, probably to report the violation.

A feminine arm draped gracefully over Alex's shoulders. "Oh, don't mind her," the owner purred, squeezing gently, probably trying to be reassuring. Whoever she was, she looked great in a size one silk dress and diamonds. Her orthodontically perfect smile alone must have cost more than the statue would fetch. "Mom's just jealous—bad hips, she can't stand up and get a better look herself." She released Alex and snatched the cell phone out of her mother's grasp. "Aren't you, Mother?"

Alex escaped toward the stage, dodging more attempts to intercept her, knowing there was going to be one hell of a spat when Claudia got ahold of her. Claudia wasn't responsible for this . . . this . . . *joke*—she'd never risk her position at the Ladies' Club—but she would of course blame Alex.

As would the rest of the ladies, who had impeccable reputations to uphold in the community, as if Alex didn't, but no one would consider that. If she didn't do something fast, her career would be in the proverbial toilet, never to be retrieved. When that happened, she'd no longer be in a position to help the children.

She needed to do some serious damage control. She needed to get to *him* before Claudia got to her.

Darius's first step felt about as graceful as a newborn fawn. Hermes had warned him to hide; Darius could barely coordinate his legs to walk without wobbling, much less dashing off for cover. Not that he would hide even if he could.

All he could think about right now was *feeling*.

For the first time in three thousand years, he had skin. His sense of touch was alive again. The first sensation that registered, after breathing air into his lungs and expanding his chest a few blessed times, came from the bottoms of his feet. It wasn't exactly pleasant. The stage looked as if it were covered with rich, green grass, but the texture was too stiff to be real. Obviously man-made, and therefore too inferior for him, third son of Zeus, to walk on. Listening to the satellite waves these past few years, he'd learned that mortals loved "synthetic." It wasn't all it was cracked up to be.

As he perfected his first few wavering steps, spreading his arms to maintain his balance until he got the hang of it again, one sense overrode all others. The stretch and bend of long unused muscles and joints—toes, ankles, knees, hips—was nearly overwhelming. The swing of the family jewels—ah, yes, he'd forgotten how wonderful being alive could be. How wonderful to have women gazing at him in adoration, vying for his favors. At the edge of the raised platform, he contended with one large step down to the main floor—a beautiful inlaid wood surface that felt hard and cool against the soles of his feet. Now that he thought about it, the room was unseasonably cool—not that it bothered him, he just noticed it—with a draft that set the candles flickering on every table. Why would mortals burn candles in the middle of the day when the room was as bright indoors as out?

Looking around, he decided he'd much prefer a warmer room, one where the ladies would have to part with some of their cleavage-concealing clothing in order to be comfortable. Although many of them were fanning themselves now as they stared at him, their faces flushed with a very becoming, rosy hue.

"Hermes, look, a standing ovation," Darius said, hoping his brother was still nearby to see how well he was being received on Earth again after his forced absence. Amazing that mortals remembered him after so long, but here was proof that his reputation had been enduring. Mothers must have passed on stories of his prowess to their daughters, and they in turn to their daughters, and so on. How else could this warm reception be explained? Greek gods had fallen from favor over the centuries, replaced by more modern Higher Powers, and yet here was incontestable proof that he was still revered.

He tested his arms, at first stretching them to their full length, then splaying his hands on his hips as he surveyed the crowd gathered before him. The lovely Alexandra was nowhere in sight. Need he wait for her when all these other women were so pleased, so eager to see him?

Perhaps Alexandra was testing him?

Well, Queen Aara be damned! He wasn't going to let another female get the upper hand again. Ever. That resolved, his mood brightened again. He had much to look forward to.

"By Zeus, where do I begin?"

Several hands shot up in the air, the women competing for his attention. Pure delight rippled through him, escaping in a laugh, which only made him giddier. A score more hands waved in the air. But then sparkles—millions of them—caught his attention.

My, what a lot of diamonds. The room fairly danced with their glitter. Bracelets, rings, pins—

His diamonds, though he didn't know how so many came to be *here*. He'd generously bestowed many upon his former conquests, of course, but that didn't account for all of these. This was certainly something he'd look into. Later, after he had time to sate more immediate desires.

He strolled past five men shoving garments at him, as if he'd be impressed with a gift of their coats. Scratchy damned things. But then mortal men never had appreciated him as much as the women had. Quite the opposite, as a matter of fact. He understood, though. They were jealous, of course. Who could blame them?

"Hermes?" Darius looked around for his brother. His gaze landed on the one thing in the room he really didn't want to see right now: a painting of his father throwing his thunderbolt. Didn't look much like him, really—mortals and their imaginations!—but the thunderbolt was unmistakable. He grunted. "Do you see that painting?"

"Yeah, I see it," Hermes replied softly, blending in with the costumed servers. He liked to play tricks now and again, but declined to be the center of attention. "You see how mad he is in it?" True, Zeus's likeness exhibited quite a scowl. "Picture him ten times angrier than that. No, a hundred. No, a thousand. A thousand thousand."

"But why is he angry?"

"Maybe he never figured you could beat the curse. I don't know, but I'm telling you, Dare, you'd better get up to Olympus and talk to him."

"All in good time."

First things first. Darius brushed past the men and paused by the first cluster of women, who smiled and tittered and stroked his arms and chest as if he were a prize stallion. He even felt a pinch of his buttocks, but when he turned to see who was so bold—to reward her, after all—the ladies circling him just laughed and smiled, oh so innocently through their blushes.

"Come now, ladies, don't push," he said, holding out his arms so as many as possible could touch and share him. Nothing worse than a pack of jealous women. They tended to go for the hair every time; not his—each other's. Their wrestling on the ground wouldn't bother him, but the *shrieking*. He'd never get used to that. "Everyone will get a turn."

Apparently the art of batting eyelashes and gazing up beneath coquettishly slanted lids hadn't gone out of style, though these modern women were a bit bolder about the whole flirtation game. He decided he liked that. He liked it a lot.

A loud, prolonged crash of dishes drew his attention toward the back of the pack. Looking over a sea of stylishly coiffured heads, he finally caught a welcome glimpse of Alexandra. It wasn't difficult, with her popping up on a chair seat, catching his eye, then jumping down and popping up on a closer chair a moment later. Several other women noticed her tactic and climbed up on chairs, too, but they generally held their places, swaying from one foot to the other, striving for the best possible view.

Suddenly the cluster of women nearest Darius parted like

rushes at the edge of a lake. Not voluntarily, but because Alexandra was shoving and elbowing them aside.

"Coming through. Make way. Coming through." She lunged at him, falling against his chest, throwing her arms around his waist.

By Zeus, that feels good! His arms, all limbered up now, easily slipped around her, pressing her to him, relishing every millimeter of contact with his skin.

No, by Zeus, *she* felt good. Warm, soft in all the right places, though her spine was rather rigid. Given a few minutes, though, he'd melt that right out of her.

"Alexandra, I was searching for you." He inhaled deeply of her hair, which was loose the way he liked it and scented with something he'd never encountered before. Floral? He inhaled deeply again. No, spicy. "Mm."

"Cut that out!" She planted her hands on his chest and shoved until there was space between them.

Ah, she wanted to play before they went off and made mad, passionate love. It had been a long time for him; he didn't know how much temptation he could take. Just thinking about stripping her garments off her, beholding her naked in front of him, her skin pinkening from the intensity of his gaze—

Alexandra's arms slipped around his waist again, and he swelled with desire and considered taking her right there on a table, but knew she'd never go for it. Few women did.

"Is there someplace we can go?" he asked.

"Oh, you bet," she snapped, wrapping something around him with a yank so hard that it jerked his body and threatened his infantile balance.

Looking down, he saw a snowy white cloth draped around his hips. "What's this?" he asked.

"Oh, I don't know," she said, rolling her eyes. "Common courtesy maybe?" Her gaze lifted to his, eyes blazing, flashing a rare, blue-green aquamarine fire. Irresistible. If she pleased him—

Well *hell*, as the men nowadays would say, she'd please him all right. All she had to do the first time was *be* there.

But no, he owed her. Not that a god could owe a mortal much, but these were extenuating circumstances. Forget the necklace he'd thought to give her. Earrings would suit her better. Long, dangling ones that would sway with her every movement. On the surface, Alexandra seemed quiet, but like a stream that can never be stilled, in reality she was always in motion. Even when she was deep in thought, her fingers would idly trace an object, feeling its texture, or she'd shift from one foot to another to view something from different angles.

Now those fingers were struggling to knot the bulky cloth at the side of his waist.

"Who the hell put you up to this?" she demanded, glancing around the crowd as if she wanted him to name someone she could behead.

The instant Alexandra was done tying, Darius tested his telekinetic powers to see if they were back to normal. Sure enough, the knot melted away; the rough cloth slid to the floor. Alexandra bent down to retrieve it, but surprise, surprise, several feminine feet were already firmly planted on it.

She yanked on it. She tugged. She yelled, "Get off!" But no one did. "Okay." She shoved her sleeves up her arms, baring wrists that seemed too delicate to work with stone. "All right. Be that way," she snapped.

The ladies were only too happy to part ranks and let her leave.

"Wait," Darius said.

"Let her go," Hermes urged.

"But I owe—"

"Damned right you do," Alexandra muttered, spinning

back, planting herself beneath his nose, glaring up at him. Even pointing her finger. "You owe me an explanation, mister. Where's my statue? What'd you do with it? You owe these people an apology for . . . for . . ." Her hand fluttered about in the air, drifting downward, indicating his magnificent natural state. A camera flashed. "Oh yeah, and you owe the reporters a quote admitting that I had nothing to do with this . . . this . . . *prank*. Ooh," she groaned, covering her eyes with her hands, her fingers clawed with frustration. "I can't talk to you like this. Stay right there."

She ducked through the bevy of women again. With his height advantage, Darius had no trouble watching Alexandra stop at the nearest table, grab hold of its tablecloth, and yank. Hard. Dishes, glasses, and lighted candles flew every which way, as did women quickly darting out of range.

She returned to his side then, arms encircling him again, tying another cloth around his hips. Okay, so she hadn't been hugging him before, out of gratitude that he'd returned to life. She yanked the knot tighter this time, then pulled it again for good measure. Hands on her hips, she nodded at her handiwork.

"There, that ought to hold."

"It's no good."

"So go get dressed."

"If it will make you happy."

Jamming her fingers through her hair, she growled, "Yes!"

Darius thought it was a good move on his part, making her ribbons—she called them scrunchies—disappear days ago. He liked her hair all wild and loose about her face, even wilder now that she'd jabbed her fingers through it a number of times, rumpling it, giving him a glimpse of her future as a well-bedded woman. Nothing like a delightfully frustrated female to pique his interest. How fortunate that it was Alexandra.

Too bad she insisted on covering him with cloth far beneath his station. The latest knot melted away, but not before several women had stuffed small pieces of green paper inside, next to his skin. He tossed the fabric over his shoulder. It landed on a table behind a tightly knit group of women, pretty much out of Alexandra's reach. When she disappeared again, he had no doubt she'd gone to clear another table, though she really should be more careful tossing lighted candles around.

A woman peered up at him through thick eyeglasses. He didn't notice what she wore, other than ruby earrings and a matching choker. Fluttering yet another piece of green paper beneath his chin, she pouted. "Now there's no place to put this."

"You may keep your paper, madam." He had other interests. So many new smells, most of which were delightful, tickled his nose. But not the one that suddenly had become strongest in the room. "What *is* that awful scent?" He leaned closer to the women around him, sniffing each one in turn. "Ooh, I like that one. What is it?"

She batted her eyes and gushed, "White Diamonds."

"Madam, my diamonds don't have a scent."

"Your—?" Her hand guarded her necklace, and then, with an embarrassed smile and a nervous laugh, she shook her finger at him. "Oh, you naughty boy!"

"Smoke!" a man behind Darius yelled.

Yes, that was it, the smell he'd been trying to place. Turning, he looked over the heads of the women behind him. Sure enough, smoke was rising from a nearby table. A second later it caught hold, throwing up flames.

"It's that damned tablecloth he threw. Idiot!" a man growled. "Where the hell's the fire extinguisher?"

Alexandra was by Darius's side, then. This time, to reward her for returning, he let her tie another cloth around his waist. If it made her happy, if it meant he could get her out of there, alone, sooner . . .

"Oh my God!" she whispered breathlessly.

Please at her reverent tone, Darius grinned and said, "So, finally you see me for who I am."

"What I see is a fire," she snapped. "Nine one one!" she shrieked. "Nine one one!"

At her words, everyone in the room jumped into motion, men and women, guests and serving wenches alike. Somewhere overhead, loud horns began to blare intermittently.

What a powerful woman!

Alex's career was already in the toilet; what was a little fire? The lid on the coffin? The stake through her heart? The extra bullet to make sure she was truly, deeply dead, never to surface again?

Probably. But for the children's sake, she couldn't go down without a fight. She had to find some leverage and force the impostor to reveal where her statue was so the guests could go ahead with the preview, so momentum would continue for the auction as scheduled. The children needed clothes and computers, and a plethora of odds and ends that just allowed kids to be kids.

The statue was heavy marble; it couldn't be far. Unless a truck had been standing by to whisk it away, these people should still get to see Darius before they left.

"Ladies! Ladies!" In her own inimitable, very ladylike fashion, Claudia raised her voice over the commotion. Somehow she could do that, without appearing to yell. Baffled the heck out of Alex. But Claudia was in her element, in control, ready to organize everyone, drawing their attention effortlessly. "And gentlemen," she added with a prolonged, radiant smile, as if she had all day before the fire raced off to another table, and then another. "If you would all pick up your glasses of water and throw them on the fire, I'm sure we could have it out in no time."

Alex could have said it a lot faster: Throw water on the damned fire!

High heels clicked on the hardwood floor as the race was on to grab a glass of water, any glass off any table, kind of like musical chairs. Everyone got into the swing of things, running around, laughing. No one wanted to be empty-handed, not now that it seemed like a game, even though the blazing fabric was shooting hot embers onto the upholstered chairs. Maybe they weren't going to hate her after all.

The first few drinks they tossed turned out to be hard liquor. Hot flames shot toward the ceiling. The automatic sprinkler system responded with heavy showers.

Okay, so they were going to hate her, no doubt about it. Especially the art critic who'd been imported just for this event. Alex glimpsed his back as he charged out a set of French doors, rescuing two of the museum's paintings, one under each arm, barking orders at other men to grab the remaining pieces. No, hate was too mild. He'd label her destructive. No one would ever invite her to show her work anywhere again. At least not indoors.

Following him out the door was a drove of rich, influential, half-drowned women, carrying upturned plates over their heads like china umbrellas, trying to protect what was left of their hairdos. Which wasn't much. It was a big room. The exits were far away. The sprinkler system was very efficient. They weren't laughing anymore.

Finally the ballroom was deserted, except for a lot of sodden tablecloths and chairs, and Alex and the impostor. *He* was laughing with unbridled glee, his face tipped up to the ceiling, his arms spread wide as he circled round and round, like a small child playing in a gentle rain shower. Water dripped off his jaw and his hair, mingling with the drops streaming down his bare chest and back. His tablecloth was drenched, clinging to him, outlining him as though he wore nothing at all.

"Rain!" he crowed, as he twirled round and round in a puddle. "Indoor rain! How do you do it?"

If only she could flush him down the sewer with her career.

As the sprinklers finally tapered off, the impostor did a good imitation of a toddler. He gazed up. Then down. He held out his arms for more. When nothing happened, he looked crushed.

Bemused by his childish dejection—there *was* a bright side to everything—Alex folded her arms across her chest. "You're not going to cry, are you?"

The ladies of the club began trickling back into the ballroom, complaining about getting their leather shoes wet, tiptoeing to minimize the splattering, looking like refugees from a flood. Many of their guests, however, had a completely different outlook. The damp ones seemed mildly amused, with hesitant smiles as they doffed their pumps, dodged media photographers, and eased in to retrieve purses and whatnot. The drier ones were gabbing among themselves, giggling like schoolgirls, corralling the same photographers to capture them as they swallowed Darius into their midst and posed with "the entertainment," as they called him. They couldn't keep their hands off him.

Caught in the pictures with them—they refused to let Alex go, as if she'd orchestrated this wonderful party—she had no choice but to paste a smile on her face. It became a real smile when she imagined what she was going to do to this man when she got him in a room without witnesses. In the meantime, she smiled pleasantly, while muttering under her breath.

"You . . . you one-dimensional pin-up." Name calling among the children was always discouraged, so Alex's repertoire was a bit limited. She felt bad about that. "Just wait'll I get you alone."

He clapped his arm around her shoulders, hugging her tightly to his side with an intimate gesture that would look to all the world as if they were in cahoots together.

"That's what I've been waiting for," he said enthusiastically.

"*What?*" she said through gritted teeth.

"Being alone with you. Oh Alexandra, my love, you have no idea," he said, turning to face her and her alone, grasping her shoulders gently in his strong, well-proportioned hands.

He ignored the women around them, who still reached out and touched him as if he really *were* her statue, and the photographers, who seemed glad to use up their film on anything that might smack of blackmail later. If he'd been her boyfriend, such undivided attention would have gotten him an immediate yes to a proposal. Any proposal. Since he was a total stranger, his directness was rather unnerving. What was that "my love" crap anyway? She gritted her teeth and remembered what he'd done.

"What I have 'no idea' of is what you've done with my statue."

"I will explain everything afterward."

"*Now.*"

He gazed at her with longing . . . No, that couldn't be right. He didn't even know her. What an actor!

"Stop that," she hissed, making an unsuccessful attempt to dislodge his grip. "This has gone on long enough."

"Yes, you're right, I've waited too long already."

"Good." Finally they were getting somewhere. He'd tell her where her statue was, she'd lead everyone there . . . "Hey!"

She hadn't expected the ol' caveman carry, but sure enough, she found herself upside down over his shoulder.

"Put me down!" she shrieked, blinded by a volley of camera flashes from all sides.

He patted her rear—the jerk!—and she exploded with a bombardment of back pounding that was only ineffective because she didn't have a hammer.

"Alexandra!" Claudia gasped. "Get down from there immediately."

As the impostor carried her through the crowd, Alex focused on her sister's red face. "Me? Don't tell me, tell him!"

He grabbed a glass of wine and downed it. "Mm, better than I remember," he said appreciatively, quickly following it with a second and then a third, working his way from table to table while Alex ineffectively grabbed at chairs, dragging them in his wake in an unsuccessful attempt to trip him up and halt his progress.

Along the route, she got an eyeful of dozens of feminine hands patting his cheeks right beneath her nose. Yeah, it was a nice butt, but come on, their age spots obviously outnumbered their IQs. She only hoped they didn't tear off his tablecloth. She was embarrassed enough.

"I seem to have gotten turned around," he said. "Which way is your studio?"

"Put me down!"

To Alex's dismay, most if not all of the ladies pointed toward the nearest exit. Like she *wanted* to leave with him?

5

"That sneaky little . . . So *that's* who she got to model for her," Claudia murmured to no one in particular as she and most of the ladies of the club trailed after Alexandra and her poor taste in men.

Not that there was a darned thing wrong with his body; it was fine. It was better than fine; no wonder she hadn't been interested in Matthew modeling for her. After having her husband desert her as he had, and a long period of celibacy, she'd probably met this guy, fallen down on her knees and thanked her lucky stars, then thrown caution to the wind and locked him in the bedroom. It wasn't as if she could afford to let another one get away.

But even if he were the best lay in the land, his manners could use some work. Hiding the statue—what was he going to do, ransom it? Leaving his clothes behind, like this was the gymnasium in some private men's club! Dragging her sister off like that, over his shoulder, like . . . like a caveman, for God's sake. This was the twenty-first century—

A tall young man sidled up to Claudia's shoulder, interrupting her thoughts as he poised there, pencil and notepad in hand. "*Post-Dispatch*, Mrs. Kline. Can you tell me who was in charge of the entertainment today?"

He thought it was *entertainment*?

Touching her emerald necklace, running her Hydrangea Pink nails over the brilliant green stones in an effort to distract him, to buy herself some time while she sorted things out, Claudia glanced at the other ladies, wondering if they'd heard.

Should she report the statue stolen now, right up front to the media, in the hope that it could be tracked down sooner? Because after all, she'd seen it on the stage one minute, and the next it was gone. Completely gone; she'd checked. But that was ridiculous. It was huge, and heavy, and the moving men had hung around—for refreshments, they'd said, which from the looks of them probably translated into liquor. Alexandra had been right; she should have called the museum for more experienced, more professional movers.

Or should she try to pass this off as a preplanned activity and hope to save the day? Maybe Alexandra was part of this. Maybe the statue was back in the studio already, and if that were the case, she'd come off stupid claiming it was stolen, wouldn't she? No thank you very much.

Most of the ladies were gabbing among themselves about the caveman's impressive body, his dark chocolate eyes, his aristocratic bearing—which was really impressive when you thought about his carrying this off, first in the buff, and then in a drenched tablecloth. They were laughing with delight and intrigue, following him and Alexandra toward the old carriage house. Irene—good ol' vice president Irene—was right there by her side, though, and she caught on just as quickly.

"Why, it was a joint effort," Irene informed the reporter in her slow, smooth-as-whiskey Southern accent, catching Claudia's eye. "Wasn't it, dear?"

"Uh, yes, yes it was." Claudia gave the young reporter a gracious smile, hiding her concern that her sister had just been hauled into her studio. And if she wasn't mistaken . . . but no, it couldn't be . . . but it looked as if the door just opened for them, before they even got there. It closed just as quickly behind them, and Claudia could swear she caught a glimpse of something—someone?—flutter through the opening just before it was shut. "A joint effort. I think most of the guests took it in the manner in which it was intended, don't you?"

He scribbled on his notepad. "Looks like it got out of hand to me," he said, expressing Claudia's true view, only milder. On a scale of one to ten, it was his minus one to her ten plus. "Important New York art critic, everybody in the Who's Who of St. Louis in the room—" He shook his head. "I don't know. I'm not buying it. We gonna see the statue soon?"

Claudia pasted on her most confident smile. "I'm, oh, sure we are. Excuse me," she said, escaping toward the carriage house herself. If she had to trip that exhibitionist and stomp him and her sister with her heels, she *damned* well was going to get to the bottom of this.

When she reached the studio door, she found Griff, the club's gardener, already hunkered down on the cobblestones, picking at the lock.

"Move aside. I have a key," she snapped. Lucky she'd stuck it in today's purse. She'd been afraid she'd have to force her way in with the moving men earlier.

"So do I," he grumbled. "Won't work." Mark Griffin stood up and pummeled the door with the flat of his fist, rattling it on its hinges.

Claudia looked at the normally mild-mannered gardener as if he'd lost his mind. He'd been around forever, first working odd jobs at TCH, and now, for the last ten years or so, head gardener at the Ladies' Club. Not that he was "head" of anyone else, but the ladies liked to hand out titles. They claimed it was to make people feel important, but the majority just preferred to give a laborer a prestigious title instead of funding his 401(K).

He hauled off and kicked the bottom of the door with his work boot. Claudia had never known him to raise his voice, much less strike anything.

"Gonna get me a hammer," he said, running his work-roughened fingers across the glass top half of the door. "Something hard."

"You will *not*." Claudia shouldered him aside before he plucked a brick off the garden wall and broke the irreplaceable leaded glass. "Those panes are over a hundred years old. Not to mention the fact that he's got about six inches and twenty years on you."

Griff growled his frustration, turning away after getting one last kick in at the door. "A crowbar. Yeah, that'll work. A crowbar."

He'd watched a lot of orphans grow up, but he'd always had extra time for Alexandra, who liked to dig in the dirt with him. If he felt protective toward any one of them, Claudia guessed it made sense it was her sister.

Which was a good thing for Alexandra, because Claudia was going to wring her neck when she got hold of her. How she must have been laughing behind her back when Claudia had shown up with Matthew and actually confessed to having "interviewed" him for the job.

"Oh little sister, you are going to *pay*."

* * *

Hermes barely managed to flutter through the door to Alexandra's studio before it slammed and locked. It was good to see Darius back to his old self, with his old joie de vivre firmly in place, as well as all his telekinetic powers. Good, good, he'd need them and all his strength later, when it came time to put Cytus in his place. Before that, though, there was a bet on Olympus as to which long-denied pleasures Darius would indulge first.

Flying up to an overhead beam, Hermes perched on the edge of it, rubbing his hands together in anticipation, in a position to miss nothing as Darius set a furious Alexandra on her feet. By Zeus, but that woman could punch! A mortal man would have been knocked off balance from the sheer force of the blows she dealt him. But Darius laughed and grinned at her, as if he thought they were love taps. Not the direction Hermes wanted him to go.

Come on, Dare, get on with it. Food, you idiot. Food!

He couldn't say it out loud, of course. Wouldn't be fair. The bets had been made among the few siblings who knew of Darius's plan to regain his life, and Hermes was there solely to report on actual occurrences and the order in which they happened.

Aphrodite had bet that Darius's first priority would be to make mad, passionate love to Alexandra, until he slaked the thirst that surely had built up over three millennia. If that started to happen, Hermes was outta there.

Apollo bet that Darius would forgo that until he'd summoned him and requested a song on the lyre, in order to first woo Alexandra properly. *Fat chance*, thought Hermes, noticing the flush of Alexandra's cheeks and her long, rumpled hair. No way Darius was staring at her, touching her, and thinking about music.

Personally, he thought Darius might *want* to go for

Alexandra first, but Hermes had hung around the studio a bit
lately, too, observing her at work. She was a focused woman,
not easily distracted, never indulging herself. A good match
for Darius, who'd end up frustrated and at his wits' end. Then
he'd have to occupy himself while he figured out how to bed
her, and so Hermes had made his bet: food from Olympus.

It wasn't a bet to see who won. It was a bet to see who
lost, akin to drawing the short straw. The loser had to break
the bad news to Darius about Cytus. Hermes shuddered, not
even wanting to think about what that would mean. Had he
picked common wine, he'd already be off the hook, as Darius had sampled several glasses on his way out of the ballroom. But noooo, he'd picked food fit for a god. *Fool.*

It was only a matter of time now, if Darius would get on
with it before Zeus tore himself away and came down to
Earth to see just what the Hades was going on.

"I don't believe this!" the impostor thundered, dumping
Alex onto her feet in the middle of her studio.

"You? Oh God," she said, her hands reflexively snapping
up to grasp her woozy head. It had been spinning before
he'd set her vertical. Now she felt as if she had a top on her
shoulders, gyrating for balance. Eventually she thought to
bend over until her circulation stabilized, and then she came
up slowly.

In the meantime, he was still carrying on about something, though she couldn't imagine what *he* was upset about.

"Have they no respect?" he demanded in a barely controlled roar, which only served to fire Alex's blood.

Good thing Claudia hadn't brought this guy in to model
for her, instead of Matthew. *This* guy was way too distracting, in every good sense of the word. Too much of a hunk to

keep her mind on what she was chiseling, to keep her gaze from drifting back to the most magnificent pecs she'd ever seen. Too *male* for her to even stand there in the same room with him without noting how the backs of her thighs still burned from where he'd held on to her with way too much familiarity during their trip across the yard.

"What is the matter with those mortals?"

Mortals? She blinked, suddenly distracted by his strange choice of word. Thinking it would all make sense in a minute.

"Excuse me." She held up one hand like a school crossing guard, repeating herself until he finally quit his ranting and glanced in her direction. He didn't meet her eyes; he was too busy pacing for that. "Excuse me, but I've just had a major transfusion to my brain, could you stand still? Please. For a minute. Thank you. And why are they *banging* on the door like that?"

Meeting her eyes now, he stood his ground and grinned broadly. "Because they want me."

No self-esteem problems there. Had she not been furious with him, she supposed his grin could be considered devastatingly handsome, one that would've melted her into a puddle except for the fact that she *was* furious, far beyond furious, so she'd never know.

Lightning quick, his face evolved into a furious frown. "Although some of them think I need . . . help."

"Yeah, well"—Alex snickered—"if you want to talk to someone who doesn't think that, you grabbed the wrong woman, buddy."

Just as fast, his grin was back. Beguiling, this time. "You think I'm perfect," he said with the most self-assurance she'd ever heard from anyone. Almost convinced her, and she was a pretty tough case right now.

"Yeah, a perfect lunatic maybe." Now that her equilibrium was back, she found herself pacing. Must've caught the jitters from him. Moving around took her mind off missing his shoulder in her gut. She was curious, too. "How did you think you were going to get away with this?"

"With what?"

"Well, gee, where do I begin?" she asked facetiously, holding her ground now, almost ready to advance on him, but he was so . . . big . . . and perfect . . . and masculine. And naked beneath a clinging tablecloth, which was white except for where it was plastered to his skin, leaving little to her imagination. *Focus, Alex.* "How about with taking my statue, for starters."

"I need it."

She waited for more of an explanation, but he didn't elaborate. "That's it? You need it?"

"Yes, that's right."

"So, what, when you need something, you just take it?"

"I needed a perfect body and you made one."

"Uh-huh." She didn't get it, not really. And wasn't likely to as long as the annoying crowd outside continued clamoring to be let in. Couldn't blame them, though. They'd been promised a work of art and lunch, and it was a sure bet they weren't going to get lunch in the soggy ballroom.

"Alexandra . . ."

She bit her tongue in time to stop her habitual retort: *Call me Alex.* Only her sister and a few of the older club members insisted on using her given name. The younger members, her friends, the children, everyone at TCH, all knew her as familiar, approachable Alex, not snooty old Alexandra. Although it didn't sound quite so snooty the way he said it. With a soft X, more like Alesandra. Made her knees go soft, too. Made her remember the feel of his fingers, hot through the denim, surely burning an imprint on her thighs. The absolute ease with which he'd hoisted her up. The way he'd said, "Duck," when he'd dipped through the studio door, not because he risked hitting his head, but so she wouldn't raise up and hit hers.

"Is everything all right?"

"Hm? Oh," she said, surprised to find he'd moved into her space without her noticing. Caught off guard, uncomfortable, she reeled backward. And then tried to cover up the fact that she'd done so by walking around him, wanting to put as much space between them as possible, as soon as possible. She didn't mind the children getting so close. Or her sister; they'd shared a bed on more than one occasion, abandoned children comforting each other. But not him.

Not wanting him to know he flustered her, she moved closer to the door, pretending interest in the commotion outside. She glanced over her shoulder and found him watching her intently. It made her self-conscious, when she'd rather be getting down to business.

"Is everything all right?" he asked.

"Other than you taking my statue, you mean?"

"Yes."

"Oh yeah, everything else is just peachy."

"Peachy? That's good?"

"Mm, yeah." She noticed the crowd outside was quieter now, though someone was still picking at the lock. "The lock," she murmured. He'd had one hand on her thighs and a wineglass in the other; none free to turn the bolt on the door after they'd entered, and he'd been nowhere near it since. Her earlier discomfort rapidly faded. "How did you do that?" She turned and looked him right in the eye. "How did you lock the door?"

He winked at her.

She rolled her eyes, frustrated to know she wouldn't be getting any straight answers out of him. She'd have more luck with a two-year-old. No, she'd have more luck with an *infant*.

"Okay, you've got thirty seconds to tell me where my statue is or I'm calling the cops."

She marched over to the bookcase that housed the phone—let it sink into his tiny little brain that she was really serious—but before she got there, it rang. Her answering machine, a garbled but happy chorus on the greeting message, picked up. The children had given it to her for her birthday, and though the greeting they'd recorded was far from professional, it was priceless. These kids didn't have parents to go to for handouts; they'd worked and saved and bought it with their own hard-won money.

"Hi, this is Alex's phone—" Billy began.

"She's really cute. Ask her for a date." Sounded like Keiko.

"Shut up, dork!"

"Happy birthday, Alex! From Billy and Maria and T.J. and Keiko and Kesia and Julian and—"

The chatter went on, getting more garbled by the minute. She considered them her younger siblings, friends every one of them, and there was no way she'd change that message.

"Leave a message at the tone."

"Ask her for a date!"

And then the tone.

"Alexandra? Alexandra, I know you're in there. Pick up," Claudia said. "Okay, don't pick up, but I know you're in there and I know you can hear me and I want you to march right over to this door *right* now and open it and let me in. Right now. I'm standing *right* here. *Right* now, Alexandra."

She was tempted to do just that, to open the door and let

Claudia at the impostor, but was afraid she'd come after her instead, like any of this was her fault.

As soon as Claudia gave up and hung up—thank God people couldn't slam down cell phones the way they could the good old standard models—Alex said, "Okay, I'm calling the cops now. I'm picking up the phone. I'm dial . . ."

When the receiver didn't immediately lift off the base, she wiggled it. Then she tugged, and the whole unit lifted off the bookcase, in one piece. Taking it into her arms and trying to forcefully wrench the two pieces apart didn't work either, so she gave up and slammed it back onto the top shelf. Still, the parts magically stuck together, as if glued.

"Darn kids." What could she do to make him tell her what he'd done with her statue?

Open the door and use Claudia's cell phone!

Alex whirled around, thrilled to have a solution, but was brought up short the next second by the sight before her.

"Where's your tablecloth?"

"May I ask you something?"

" 'Oh, Alex, do you mind if I get naked now?' " she said for him. "Well yes, as a matter of fact, I do."

He didn't take the hint and cover up.

This was a great situation to learn to make and keep eye contact. She didn't dare let her gaze drop lower than his chin. Here she was, alone in her studio with a beautiful naked man who wasn't modeling for her, a pack of judgmental women about to burst through the door, probably with a photographer or two in tow. It seemed so much more . . . *tawdry* than in the middle of a crowded ballroom. Certainly more scandalous to her reputation. And what affected her reputation affected the children's welfare. Speaking of whom, any number of impressionable little minds could pop in at any moment; *they* knew about the back door.

"I wish you wouldn't do that," she said.

"What?"

She waggled her hand in the direction of his birthday suit. "I don't even know you, for God's sake. And even if I did, it'd be rude to just drop your clothes whenever you feel like it, now wouldn't it?" She snickered at her own foolishness. "Ah, geez, look who I'm asking. The little kids have more sense than you do."

"I know times have changed, and maybe, well . . . May I ask you something?"

"Only if you get dressed."

"Why do those women think I need . . . help?" He wasn't roaring anymore. He was clearly baffled, and seemed shy about asking.

Confused by the change in his manner and the question, Alex asked, "What kind of help?"

"They kept tucking paper in. I don't need stuffing," he said, affronted.

Alex followed his gaze to the floor where he'd dropped the tablecloth, making sure she hastily skimmed over the good parts on the way. For a minute she thought, *Now where have I seen . . . ?* But that was too preposterous. She laughed at herself and waved the thought right out of her head.

Validating his complaint, the dark plank floor was littered with stuffing, all right. The green kind. Jackson, Jackson, Jackson. Who was on that fifty? She crouched and saw that it was Grant. And there—over there was a . . . a *Franklin!* And another! She scooped those two up first, before he quit playing his part and decided he wanted to take the money and run.

"Do they think I'm not gifted enough?"

"Oh, I'm sure that's not what they're thinking." A laugh

bubbled up out of her throat, just a tiny one, though she tried hard to suppress it. This really wasn't funny. Not at all. She picked up more greenbacks, stacking them in her fist. And the more she picked up, the more she found. Sprinkled in with them were a dozen monogrammed calling cards with personal phone numbers hastily scratched across the backs. Those, she ignored.

"Geez Louise," she whispered, barely able to believe it as the number climbed. "Seven hundred. Seven twenty."

"I don't understand."

"Suuuurrrre you don't. Nine hundred. Nine fifty." She'd slaved over the statue for almost a year, never seeing more than twenty dollars at a time, worried whether the home was going to be able to make ends meet for the kids this year, and these women just *threw* this much cash away. She closed her fingers tightly around the cash, taking possession of it.

Well, he *owed* her, for God's sake. He'd stolen her thunder today, along with her statue. He'd done irreparable harm to her reputation and her career, while his was virtually assured if he was planning on making it as a magician. He'd embarrassed her in front of hundreds of influential people, the media, the art world. He was doing nothing to make amends, no public apology. He could start paying up right now with this, his gratuity.

"Please, Alexandra." He spread his arms wide, in supplication. His voice was gentle, yet urgent. "You must look at me!"

"Oh no, no way."

"You must tell me what is wrong with this body."

She snatched up the soaked tablecloth as she rose to her feet. He'd worked his way into her space again, but she didn't back off this time. It was easier keeping her gaze pinned to his face, and no lower, when they were close enough to bump elbows.

"Not a darn thing."

"Truly?"

"Yep." She nodded, not having to double check. "And that's my professional opinion, too." She smiled brightly. She could afford to be sunny and cheerful. She had twelve hundred dollars to pay an attorney to keep this guy's ass in jail until he 'fessed up.

"But then why did they stuff my cloth?"

"With this?" She held the money up between them, gaining a little satisfaction about rubbing his face in the fact that she'd picked it up first and possession was nine-tenths of the law, or so she'd heard.

"Don't they know a god when they see one?" he said, reverting to his imperious highness tone.

Oh brother, he deserved whatever she could dish out. For emphasis, she fan spread the cash right in front of his chest, then waved it under his nose, hoping to torture him. Though he didn't look too tortured. Weren't actors underpaid? He should've been salivating.

The studio door swung inward just then. A photographer burst to the head of the pack, getting a lovely picture of Alex offering cash to a naked man with one hand while dangling his garment with the other. The only question was: would they think she was accepting money from him, or propositioning him?

6

In the two weeks that Alexandra had been completing what would become his perfect body, Darius had never seen her feisty side. Sure, she was pretty, feminine, curved in all the right places; a worthy conquest. Patient with the children who visited for art lessons or just to chat. Polite to the gardener, the electrician, the television repairman, and the pizza delivery girl.

Well, okay, there was that one time she threw the pizza at her sister. And now that he thought about it, she *did* scream at the moving men earlier today. But other than that, she'd seemed a kind, gentle creature.

But now! Her aquamarine eyes had darkened, and were they ever flashing! Hoo-boy—he'd picked up that expression from a sitcom, and it certainly fit his mood right now— he was mentally rubbing his hands together in anticipation of bedding such a passionate woman. First, though, he had to get rid of everyone crowding in through the studio door- way, especially the man who kept flashing the bright little light at them. Alexandra would like that. She'd be grateful.

As agonizing as it was to turn away from her, he did so, rounding on the crowd and roaring, "Out!"

By Zeus, that felt good! Picked his mood right up again.

He heard a squeak from Alexandra behind him. A protest? Seconds later, a cloud of sheets flapped over his head, the same glued-together ones she used to throw over the statue when she wasn't working on it. They were mismatched, dusty, and made him sneeze as they settled on him, covering him from head to toe. He battled his way back to the light, and then since he was going for points, instead of discarding the scratchy, inferior fabric out of hand, he wound it around himself until most of him was covered, tossing the excess over one shoulder. Neither a fine himation nor a chiton, but more like a Roman toga; it would do. Though as a god, he shouldn't have to put himself out just to win a mortal woman's favors. He owed her, of course, but only so much. He had his limits.

"Get . . . out!" he roared, hastily advancing on the startled ladies.

The photographer was quick to recognize the danger and flee, though he had trouble retreating through the blockade of women at the door. He snapped a few more pictures, then turned, and hunching over at the waist to protect his camera, torpedoed through the maze of skirts.

"The rest of you, be gone!" As soon as the words passed his lips, Darius realized it was an outdated expression, but he couldn't be concerned with that right now. He stretched to his full height and adopted his sternest expression, scowling for all he was worth, but it was difficult in the face of such a lovely group of admirers. But Alexandra would be grateful. Some women didn't like to share.

He had to physically encourage them to leave, a hand here, an arm there, a general shove in the direction of the door. A whispered promise to get back to them later, when he was done here. After all, he had a lot of pent-up energy to dissipate, and Alexandra was only one woman.

While he was ushering the bejeweled bunch out, it seemed as good a time as any to repossess what was rightfully his, and so he began. And when they were all gone, none the wiser for his lightening their load, he bolted the door, using nothing more than a simple thought.

"There," he said triumphantly, pleased to have gotten rid of everyone so quickly, turning back to Alexandra. Beautiful, feisty, sure-to-be-grateful Alexandra. He crossed the room with quick strides of anticipation to stand proudly before her. "They're gone."

She said nothing, just stood her ground, clutching the slips of paper to her breast, staring up at him as if she didn't know what to think of him. But it didn't look good. A lesser god would have been put off.

"Alexandra, my sweet," he crooned softly. "We are alone now."

Now why did those words bring a sense of déjà vu?

Never mind, he scolded himself. *Ignore it. Keep focused.* He wished he were close enough to whisper sweet flattery in her ear, but the murderous gleam in her eyes made him think twice. She was going to be a tough one, this woman. A real challenge, he thought with glee.

Her eyes never leaving his, she folded the green papers in half and stuffed them into her jeans pocket. "You're not getting this money back," she said, with a sexy little jut to her chin.

Oh yes, this would be worth the wait. Not the three-thousand-year wait, of course, but the extra fifteen minutes it was going to take to get her clothes off.

"I have no use for it," he said.

"Must be nice." She leaned backward as his gaze roamed her flawless complexion, but stood her ground otherwise. "What?"

He could learn to like that—her feistiness. From what he'd seen on television, women stood up for themselves a whole lot more nowadays. He'd hoped it was pure fiction, until confronted with it in such a tempting package.

"Why are you staring at me like . . . like that?" she asked.

As he leaned over her, homing in toward lips that he knew would be sweeter for the waiting, she slyly outmaneuvered him, moving away until the worktable stood between them. He followed. She circled the table, keeping a few strides ahead of him.

"They all know you're in here, you know," she said with bravado. "They've called the police by now, so if you want to avoid trouble, you'll just tell me where the statue is, and we can get on with the preview."

The statue? That brought him up short. "Alexandra, don't you recognize me?"

"Oh yeah. Yeah, I recognize you. You're the actor somebody hired to take the place of my statue on stage. Or the magician somebody hired to make it disappear."

By Zeus, but she was obtuse!

"Although," she said, as if contemplating the whole issue, "I can't figure out why. I mean, if the club wanted more publicity, this"—she laughed without mirth, holding her arms wide, indicating nothing specific, but her day in general— "this'll sure do it. Missing statue . . ." She picked up a rasp and tossed it into a box beneath the worktable. "Naked man . . ." Another tool followed, and she cleaned her way around her whole work area as if he were no longer there. "Sprinklers and fire alarms."

It took several more tools thunking into storage before

Darius realized that Alexandra was crying. She did a good job covering it up, with all that cleaning and sorting and tossing and muttering, but he caught the telltale swipe of her fingers across her cheeks more than once. Puzzled, he stopped following in her wake. Most women *wanted* him to know when they were crying; they used tears to get what they wanted from him. Had women changed so much after all these years? Or was Alexandra just different?

She slammed a hammer down sideways onto the wood table and glared at him across the surface. "Damn it, why won't you just tell me where my statue is?"

She had no clue? She could stare right at him, as she had been for months, and she had no idea?

"Hm," he said. "I see this will take longer than I thought. How about something to eat?"

"How about I apply this hammer to the back of your head and when rigor mortis sets in, we'll auction *you* off?"

"Lamb, perhaps?" he asked lightly, ignoring her challenge. "Or veal? Never mind, let's see what the servers have." He rubbed his hands together at the prospect, not unaware that the mere thought of food had his mouth watering. He savored the sensation, etching it into memory.

Buxom serving wenches flowed gracefully into the studio through Alexandra's kitchen door, bearing golden platters brimming with a colorful selection of aromatic foods. He sniffed hungrily, savoring every scent. It had been so long! Mortals had a term for old favorites: comfort food. If he couldn't have the comfort of Alexandra's body in the next ten minutes, he'd take the food.

One after another they came, the fifth and last wench carrying diamond-encrusted goblets of what Darius knew to be the finest wine on Olympus. He took one for himself and held out the second to Alexandra.

She stood there mute, her jaw hanging open. Such a tempting sight, his lips ached to touch hers, but he'd give her a few more minutes to adjust. Maybe the wenches had brought too much, too soon; she was clearly overwhelmed with so many choices.

"Drink," he encouraged, gently waving the goblet in front of her face until she grasped it. Even then, he kept his hand on it, helping her raise it to her lips. "Sip it slowly, savor the body—"

She pushed his hand away and chugged the wine down like water. Then she held out her arm. "Pinch me."

"Alexandra—"

"Go on, pinch me."

No sense arguing with her. He reached around and pinched her behind.

She squawked, jumping away from him. "Hey!"

"Not what you wanted?"

"Who *are* you?" He started to explain, but she cut him off. "Who are all these women?"

"Alexandra, my sweet—"

She rolled her eyes.

"I am Darius, third son of Zeus."

"Oh, puh-leeze."

"These women serve me whenever I desire food or drink."

"Really?" she asked, eyebrows raised toward the wenches, all of whom were pleasant, smiling, and nearly bursting out of their colorful, silky garments.

"Alexandra—"

" 'Darius' my ass." She rounded on him again. "If this is *Candid Camera*, I'd better see some normal people out here, pronto." She tapped her foot impatiently, then turned and headed for the door. "I thought not; more like *Twilight Zone*. Well, doesn't matter. I'm sure Claudia's phone will work."

"You don't believe me," he guessed.

She stopped short of the door. A wench refilled her goblet. Alexandra looked at it, said, "What the hell?" and chugged that one, too.

"That's it." He laughed, relieved that she didn't dislike him, she was just confused about everything, her feelings included. He'd be able to clear this up in no time and then get on with seducing her. "You don't believe me. But you know of the statue Dr. Mickael found, you know the story behind my downfall."

"*Your* downfall?"

"Yes, Alexandra, *my* downfall. *I* am Darius. *I* moved into the statue." He paused in his explanation, letting that sink in as he closed the distance between them. Then, daring to stroke her silky hair, the same tresses he'd wanted to touch these torturous two weeks while he'd been locked in immobile marble, he said softly, "I swear by the Styx this is true. Do you need further proof?"

She gazed into his eyes for a moment. And then she laughed. "Oh, that's good."

Maybe his wine was too potent for her. Normally that was a good thing.

"You're good," she said. "I've gotta hand it to you, you get right into your part and stick with it." She emphasized her words by digging her fist into the air in front of her belly. "I should be madder'n heck at you, but you're just soooo goooood. Wait, no, I *am* madder'n heck at you." She held out her goblet for a refill. "Fortify me for meeting my sister."

"Yes," he said to himself as much as to her. "I think further proof is in order. Though I must tell you, I'm not happy having to prove myself—this is a first—but I realize I've been out of circulation a long time. So I will make an exception this once."

He flipped on the overhead spotlight telekinetically and held up his hand, letting the beam shine on the gems dangling from his fingers.

Alexandra stepped closer. "That's . . . that's Mrs. Wilson's necklace!"

"No, it's *my* necklace. I am the god of gems. They're all mine until I give them away, and I never gave these away. Nor these." He set his goblet down and showed her a circle of opals, set in gold. Technically, he didn't rule metals, but it wasn't his fault the women had set his stolen gems in precious gold.

"Oh my God."

That's it! She was beginning to worship him already.

"You like these? You may have them, or I have others from which you may chose. I'm thinking aquamarine, to highlight your eyes." He laid half a dozen pieces of jewelry on the worktable. Alexandra practically ran to his side.

Good girl! Though he would have liked it better if she'd wanted him without his gems, if she weren't like every other mortal woman. He'd have his fun with her nonetheless and then move on.

She dropped her goblet on the table and grabbed his arm. "Come on."

His mouth went dry. He grabbed up his wine and drained it.

"Now you're talking." He laughed with delight, thrilled that now he was getting somewhere. Turning her toward him, he engulfed her in the circle of his arms.

Just as quickly, she ducked free.

"Ah, foreplay," he said, laughing. "I've heard of this."

"See if you've heard of this," she said, drawing him by the hand across the room.

"But, Alexandra, the bedroom . . . isn't it that way?"

"Trust me," she said.

And he did, allowing her to draw him to the door leading outside. Perhaps she had somewhere else she'd rather make love? A field of daisies, perhaps? A shaded glen with a babbling brook?

She yanked on the knob, brought up short by the lock. Never touching it, he turned the bolt for her.

"Refill my glass, ladies," she said over his shoulder. "I'm gonna need it. Right this way, Darius."

He'd explain later that they were wenches, not ladies, right after—

Halfway out the door, she shoved him. Taken by surprise, Darius found himself on the other side of a closed and bolted door. Not that a lock could stop him, but he was taken aback. Confused. Was this part of foreplay? He faced the door.

"What do you call this?" he asked.

"Retribution!"

Alex was on a roll. She'd just thrown out any connection to the crime that she had, but *really!* who could get any information out of that man? Other than what he wanted her to believe, of course. A Greek god!

Give me a break.

He was even pretending to be interested in her; after all she'd been through, that was just plain mean.

She wheeled away from the door, prepared to deal with the servers who'd been hired to work at the luncheon, but who'd obviously been better paid to take part in someone's prank. For the life of her, she still couldn't imagine who would go to such lengths. Such expense. It was a shame, really, when all that money could have gone straight to the children. Tax deductible, too.

To her amazement, the room was empty. The servers—and all the food—were as gone as . . . as the impostor. No way she was thinking of him as Darius. What a desecration that would be.

No problem, she'd just return the stolen jewelry—as soon as she figured out what she was going to say to the ladies. It was important they know she had no part in this. She'd think Claudia would believe her, except that when Claudia had told her to get down off the impostor's shoulder—as if she'd had a *choice*—she certainly hadn't been on Alex's side. She'd assumed the worst.

Had they all?

Realistically, she could understand why. Only an insider could pull off a stunt of such magnitude. And such timing! Someone with connections. Someone with something to gain. In her case, publicity. Media attention, a mystery—these would build attention, intrigue, entice a larger crowd to the auction. Most likely raise the winning bid. She wasn't the ultimate recipient, though. The children were.

As if on cue, Billy and five of the girls came in the back way, popping through the kitchen door, laughing and giggling, bubbling through the entrance like champagne after a cork.

"Oh!" Billy said, stopping dead in his tracks, his hands—and what was in them—flying behind his back. "Uh, hey everybody, it's Alex." He said this loud enough for most of Missouri to hear.

The girls, a kaleidoscope of age and race, also stopped dead, as if playing the red-light, green-light game, frozen in various ridiculous poses before they, like Billy, straightened up and shot their hands behind their backs.

"Uh, hi, Alex."

"Yeah, hi, Alex."

Billy, looking uncomfortable, glanced toward the front door. "Aren't they going to let you have lunch with them?"

Formulated plan or no, Alex thought she'd better return the jewelry before it got mixed up with the kids' art projects.

"Just a minute, guys," she said, rushing over to the work-table.

Six kids backed away from her, like little magnets turned to opposite polarity.

She didn't have time to think about that, though absently she asked, "What're you guys up to?"

"Nothing," six voices chanted. The closer she got, the more they scooted backward.

"All right." She faced them, arms akimbo. "What've you got there?"

"Where?"

"There, behind your backs."

Emily sniffled. At six, she was the youngest one allowed to walk to the studio under supervision of one of the other kids.

"Hush, Em," Billy whispered.

Alex didn't want to make anyone cry. Heaven knew they'd had enough hardship in their short lives. Softly she said, "Okay, Billy, looks like you're the ringleader. Confession time."

"Aw gee, Alex, we wanted to surprise you." Hands behind his back, he danced from one foot to the other and back again, clearly torn between what she wanted and what he wanted for her.

Could they be part of this prank? This *fiasco* of a day?

Just as quickly, she knew, *No.*

"Believe me, I've had enough surprises for one day. What am I saying? For a year—no, a decade! C'mon. Tell me."

He glanced at the girls, he and Maria nodded between them, then to the others, and all the hands came forward.

"What's this?" Alex asked.

"Napkins."

"Matching plates."

"Candy."

"Popcorn."

A rainbow-colored, computer-generated banner that said CONGRATULATIONS ALEX! A matching card signed by all the children and staff at the home. Pretzels and raisins. In short, a party in the making.

"Since you got the statue done in time, we wanted to give you a preview party," Kesia whispered, barely loud enough to hear.

"Oh, guys," Alex said, sighing, touched deep in her heart at their thoughtfulness.

People were knocking on the studio door again, and it just as fast progressed to banging.

"Didn't they like it?" Billy asked, with a nervous glance toward the racket. "The statue?"

Alex shrugged. "Don't know. It disappeared."

"You . . . you mean . . . the *G-H-O-S-T* got it?"

"What ghost?" Emily shrieked.

"There is no ghost," Alex said firmly, to all of them. "Now, I'm going to return the ladies' jewelry and then—"

Kesia opened the door, letting a crowd of anxious-looking women inside. Bare-necked and bare-eared and bare-wristed women, except for Claudia. She still had her emeralds. The rest of them milled about, searching the floor, stooping down and checking under and through the mail, tossing it every which way while they searched frantically.

"Some of the ladies think they may have dropped their

jewelry while they were in here," Claudia said, with her usual genteel display of tact.

"I have it," Alex said. She sounded dejected, even to herself. The kids were here to throw her a party, and she just wasn't in the mood. "It's on the table. I'll let you sort out whose is whose."

Unhappy that she hadn't worked out quite how to state her innocence in everything that had happened—or *not* happened—today, she set her own problems aside for the minute and turned to her first priority, the children.

"You wouldn't happen to have any chocolate in there, would you?" she asked them.

Keşia's hand shot out. "I've got chocolate bubble gum."

"Ooh. May I?"

Alex was rewarded with Kesia's wide grin, which always lit up the room.

"Alexandra?"

"Hm?" Unwrapping the gum, Alex turned to see what Claudia wanted now.

"So where is it? Their jewelry?"

"Right—" She pointed to the worktable. "Uh-oh."

The empty worktable. After her cleaning spree, there weren't even any tools to look under. Like the statue, the jewelry had disappeared.

Could this day *get* any worse?

Dejected, Alex sunk to the floor. She drew her knees up, dropped her head onto them, and in a muffled voice said, "Call the police. I need to file a report."

"They're already on the way," Mrs. Wilson said huffily.

"Oh, Agnes," Claudia said unhappily.

"Well, you don't think we're going to just stand by and watch your sister steal everything, do you?" Her gaze darted to Claudia's emerald earrings, then quickly took in all her matching pieces. And then she got really huffy, drawing herself up two inches taller and looking down her nose.

"What's the matter, Alexandra? No black market on emeralds?"

7

By sunset, Darius was ready to admit something was wrong—really wrong—with his new life. And it had begun with such promise!

Alexandra had thrown him out. *So what?* Now there was a nice new expression he'd learned. Fit the bill perfectly. Here he was, in a new city that sprawled over boundless square miles, promising a large population, which, to his way of thinking, also promised a boundless number of women. Many of whom would be young, beautiful, and—since his life-altering run-in with Queen Aara's husband, he looked forward to this most of all—*single*. With a jaunty step, and thankful that the contingent of women had suddenly swooped into the studio, he turned his back on Alexandra's door and strolled off the well-maintained grounds of the Ladies' Club, eager as could be to go exploring.

Immediately as he left the umbrella of towering oak trees, golden rays of sunshine showered over him, suffusing him with warmth, toasting his skin, producing a glorious, heady feeling, again validating that he was, indeed, alive. Life didn't get better than this.

Well, maybe a little better. There was that boundless-number-of-single-women thing he was looking forward to.

He strode briskly along the gritty, blistering hot sidewalk, almost giddy with delirium as he put his muscles and bones further to the test. Legs pumping, arms swinging, heart beating. Ah, it was good to be alive! And to be away from all those screaming females. *Ay-yi-yi-yi-yi*—he'd picked that up from watching . . . what was his name? Ah yes, Ricky Ricardo. (All these new expressions; he could hardly wait to try them all. He was eager to tower over a bad man and say, "Make my day.") Anyway, from their hysterics, you'd think those ladies owned the gems they'd been wearing. It was a sure bet they weren't going to calm down and tell him how or why or from which god they'd received them, not anytime soon.

He stretched his legs in a long, ground-eating stride, constantly aware of the poor-quality sheets brushing against his skin. The fabric wasn't nearly fine enough for a god, but he supposed it would have to do. He could conjure up wenches bearing food and drink, musicians who played notes so sweet as to make the heart soar and eyes weep, but he had no power to whisk up new garments. For that, he'd have to wait until something better came along, if mortals were capable of something better, or return to Olympus.

Not an option. Not yet. He'd waited so long to enjoy life again that he didn't want to lose even a minute en route to Olympus. His goals were simple: he'd spend the day looking around the city, seeking adventure and romance.

Now why didn't that sound good? Isn't that what he'd been waiting for? Over the centuries, he'd had ample opportunity to "reflect," to "examine his feelings"—chick words, he knew, and not activities he enjoyed. But then he'd gotten pretty bored, and for the last several years, there'd been *alllll* those talk shows. It was a wonder mortals weren't talked to death by the time they were six.

So why *didn't* that sound like a good plan? For the past two weeks, every day while Alexandra worked on him—

Oh yeah, now he remembered. Her hands, skimming over his every surface. The top of her head, always in his view as she completed him. The undeniably feminine way she jumped when he startled her by unexpectedly blasting the TV on. He'd gotten a kick out of that, no matter whether she jumped, laughed nervously, or angrily threw a rasp at it. Made it worthwhile every time. Any which way he saw her, she was ultimately enticing. Slowly but surely, he'd started thinking she should be his first conquest. The idea had grown on him. It seemed just; after all, she was the one giving him his life back.

He'd been ogling her for two weeks, impatient to get *his* hands on *her* body. Run his fingers through her spun-gold hair and see if it was as soft as silk. Stroke *her* body for a change, and see if she was as tormented as he.

But after that display back at the studio, it was obvious she needed time to cool off. A gift always eased the way with a woman. He'd find a local artisan, have him set some gems in a unique gift, something just for her. Maybe embedded along the handle of a rasp? The way she tossed tools around, though, he'd better select durable ones. Diamonds.

That decided, he shifted his focus to his surroundings. Late summer in St. Louis demanded to be noticed. The trees were green, but limp. Grass was as brown as straw. Flowers wilted and faded on their stems. No breeze ruffled through the sagging trees, either too small to shade the walk or set too far back on the grounds.

Traffic was much as he'd seen it on television, only larger. And faster. And what were those fumes attacking his pristine lungs? He, a god, actually *coughed*. No wonder mortals rode by with their windows rolled up. He didn't want to breathe this crap, either, except that it beat not breathing at all.

"Hey, whoa there, buddy." The lone mortal who'd followed him actually *touched* his arm—it was one thing for women to make contact with him, but quite another for a man—urging him back onto the curb. "Better wait for the light."

With a pen and small notebook in hand, he'd mentioned he was with the local newspaper and persistently dogged Darius's heels right from the studio door. Darius didn't have enough recent experience to guess the man's age, but his dark hair was mixed with gray at the temples and his belly looked soft above his belt. His round face appeared soft, too, totally at odds with the look of determination etched in his eyes.

"I kinda thought you'd head over to the park," the reporter said casually. "There, the light turned."

Darius stepped off the curb, absorbing his surroundings the same way a man dying of thirst takes in water. Had the sky been that shade of blue before? Or the clouds so white?

"Whoa!" The reporter grabbed Darius's arm again, yanking him back as a low-slung red vehicle whizzed by in front of him, its driver showing off his middle finger. "Not from around here, are ya? Gotta watch those right turns, buddy. Okay, you can go now. St. Louis ain't exactly pedestrian friendly, if you know what I mean." His stride was a good deal shorter than Darius's, but he kept up nonetheless, blotting perspiration from his face with his sleeve. "You know the park's the other way, don't you?"

Darius had no clue where he was going. A couple of minutes ago, it hadn't mattered. He hadn't cared; he just wanted to get out, move about, see people, *feel* things. But if he expected to find adventure and romance in a hurry, he could use a guide.

"You know your way around this city?" he asked, bending at the waist to smell a bush covered with tiny yellow flowers.

Ahh. He closed his eyes, relishing the moment. Concerned that the anticipation might have been better than the experience, he was relieved to discover that touching and feeling were ever so much better for having anticipated them in the first place.

"Well, yeah, I better," the reporter answered with a chuckle. "They don't pay me to get lost and make the stories up, you know."

"Hm." As long as the man was going to tag along, he might as well be useful. "The park?"

"Yeah, Forest Park. Isn't that where you Greeks are having the picnic this year?"

"A picnic! Really?" Picnics meant people; lots of people—*women*—in a jovial mood. Perfect! "How delightful."

The reporter flipped through pages in his notebook. "Yeah, right here." He stabbed an entry with a blunt finger. "Officially started half an hour ago. I was gonna go after lunch—those ladies put out a real fine spread every year—but," he said with a rueful laugh, "guess that's down the drain. Course, an exclusive from you would go a long way toward making it up to me."

"A picnic sounds good."

The reporter, seeming to think they'd struck a bargain, stuck out his hand. "Patrick Pulsar. And you are?"

Darius hadn't been studying movies and television for

two weeks for nothing. Without hesitation, he slid his palm across Pulsar's and said what he was supposed to say.

"Hey, bro, 'sup man?"

Pulsar looked dumbfounded. Probably couldn't believe a god could be so with it.

"The park?" Darius prodded.

"Uh, sure, this way. Follow me."

Washington University's Annual Greek Week Picnic was in full swing on a hill in Forest Park. Darius could hear them half a mile away, and he headed straight for them, barely listening to Pulsar's commentary on points of interest along the way, like the outdoor theater and zoo and art museum.

"Some of these date from the World's Fair in . . . uh . . ." Patrick stumbled over the date.

"What was 1904?" Darius said automatically. Until he'd actually seen *Jeopardy!* he'd been very impressed, wondering how one man—Alex Trebek—could know all those answers himself. Talk about disillusionment.

"Oh, yeah, that's right, 1904. No good with dates, never have been. Gotta write 'em down all the time."

Forest Park was a haven in a city wilting under ninety-eight percent humidity. A Shangri-la of trees and shade, an occasional trumpet from an elephant in the zoo, and laughter drifting on the air. Darius looked both ways and crossed the street to a smoother walk.

"This is a bike path," Pulsar said.

Darius didn't think that was of much interest. Behind them, Hermes fluttered down—all the way down to the pavement.

"You're walking?" Darius asked, too surprised to greet him otherwise.

"Don't want to attract attention," Hermes said.

Pulsar glanced over his shoulder and did a double take at the winged sandals. "Nah, won't attract any attention that way. Lessee, if I remember my mythology, you'd be Mercury, right?"

"I prefer Hermes."

"Oh Greek, yeah, I get it." He scribbled in his notebook. "You guys look kinda old for Greek Week. You professors or something?"

Several men and women on Rollerblades streaked past them on the asphalt path, wearing short, tight pants that left little to Darius's imagination. The two bringing up the rear sported golden wings painted on their leather boots.

"Look," Darius said, laughing, "Hermes wannabes."

"Hm, yes, I see that." He didn't sound flattered.

A young man with a shaved head roared by, rudely brushing against Hermes and intentionally crowding Darius. "Move off the path, bozo."

"Hey, Dare—" Hermes began.

"Got it under control, brother. Under control."

A perfectly healthy overhead branch fell to the ground, unexpectedly landing in front of the skater's wheels too late for evasive action. Instead, he took a nasty spill, head and hands blazing a new trail across the thin grass and into the dry weeds at the edge of the woods.

"Why, thank you, Dare."

"Hey, what're brothers for?"

Pulsar frowned, but kept his thoughts to himself.

Sheltered from the midday rays on a hillside dotted with mature oak trees, four dozen young men and women were swathed in a rainbow of solid, striped, and floral sheets, the likes of which no ancient Greek would have been caught dead in. They were on their feet, for the most part, milling about, laughing, loud; in short, slightly sloshed.

"Hey, here come some more!" someone shouted as Darius and the others approached.

"Come on up!" a woman invited, urging them up the hillside with a wave of her arm.

"They have *food*," Hermes said, with special emphasis. "We should have food. I'm *starving*, aren't you, Dare?"

"Already taken care of."

Behind Hermes were five beautiful serving wenches, wearing embroidered chitons, carrying large woven baskets brimming with food and drink.

Pulsar said, "Where the hell did they—" but forgot the rest of his question when one of the wenches fluttered long, sooty lashes at him.

Darius whispered, "Try to keep up with me, Pulsar," and with the tips of his fingers, pushed the man's slack jaw shut.

Darius led his band up the hill.

"Hey look, more food!" someone in the college crowd announced.

"All right!"

Pulsar followed, sniffing the air as he fell in behind the basket-bearing servants. "Is that lamb I smell? *Grilled* lamb?" There wasn't a fire in sight.

Darius and his contingent were welcomed into the bosom of merrymakers, half of which were female and, from the way they pushed and shoved for the privilege of latching onto his arms, very interested.

Now this was more like it!

Hermes pretended to be absorbed by the banquet of food spread out on four picnic tables lined up in a row, while the young "Greeks" gorged themselves on Darius's lamb and seafood and dates, and discussed Socrates and Plato as if they were still alive.

"Take a bite," Hermes muttered under his breath.

Technically, the bet among his siblings and him was still open. True, Darius had summoned food back at the studio, but he still hadn't tasted any. He was a lot closer to doing that than he was to having Apollo play a tune, or to making mad, passionate love to Alexandra, but Hermes felt he couldn't really relax and enjoy himself until he knew *he* wouldn't have to be the one to give Darius the bad news. That kill-the-messenger saying was all too true at times, which is why he often hovered while delivering messages.

A silly maid tilted her face up to Darius, laughing at something he'd said, teasing him with a small bunch of red grapes. "Open up," she said, dangling the fruit-laden stem above his lips, draping herself across his arm so he couldn't get a finger free to help himself.

Could the woman be more obvious?

Well, what did he care? He just wanted Darius to eat. Unfortunately, that bunch of grapes wasn't from Olympus and wouldn't fulfill the terms of the bet. But it was a start.

Darius partied all afternoon with the students. Their food wasn't the best, but the young women were so lovely and so insistent on sharing with him that he hadn't the heart to refuse a nibble.

For entertainment, they had a lyre, at which none of them was adept. Darius hadn't known it could make such horrible sounds in untutored hands. And yet Apollo—the *real* one— just stood by, flirting shamelessly with the women and tossing food to a small flock of crows, letting the partiers murder the music until Darius begged him to please take pity on his ears and play something.

They'd generously offered him wine, but his made theirs taste like stale river water. And his was endless. His poor brother was intoxicated early on.

Hermes must have really missed him over the centuries because, no sooner than Darius had attacked his first leg of lamb, Hermes started dancing about, laughing and carrying on, giggling something only half intelligible. Darius, who had more important things on his mind—half a dozen women whose togas were getting looser by the hour and slipping off their shoulders—deciphered some of it as "Welcome back, Dare," and a childish chant, "Aphrie lost, Aphrie lost. Ha ha ha ha ha ha." He'd lost track of him for a while then, and shortly thereafter, his older brother was wearing a mortal's striped toga, still giggling, and when asked about his new garment, said, "Even trade," and quoted, "When in Rome . . ."

By early evening, Darius's new friends were drunk enough to stop pretending they were back in ancient Greece. The picnic was winding down, though he knew everyone would go somewhere else and party long into the night. Personally, he had other plans. He'd spent all afternoon relishing the feel of grass beneath his feet (he could have done without the acorns), the roughness of the wooden picnic tables, the scratchiness of tree bark; in short, touching anything and everything he'd missed and quite a few things he'd seen only on TV, until today.

Now . . . now it was time to move on. He'd wanted Alexandra to be his first, but she'd thrown him out, and he had other anticipations to experience. He'd selected two lucky young women to bed. Later he'd join the others and check out the city's nightlife at a place they called the Landing.

As the sun dipped low in the western sky and rain clouds

moved in, he noticed an increasing number of visits to the small stone building at the bottom of the hill. Men through one door; women the other.

"What's that?" he asked Ted, who sported several very un-Greek-like tattoos on his biceps.

"Wha's wha'?" Ted slurred, bleary-eyed.

"That building."

"Bath"— Ted belched, then used both hands to steady his head and focus on Darius—"room."

Bath house! thought Darius, sure that's what Ted meant, as bathrooms were found inside mortals' personal residences and didn't attract so much foot traffic. Coed bathing, now that sounded great. It seemed a mighty small building, though. Must be an entrance to underground springs. Maybe hot springs.

"You ladies want to join me?" he asked the chosen two.

They giggled. And wiggled. "Sure, I better," one said, and was quickly followed by the other with a "Me, too." A blond and a brunette in a coed bath house on his first day here. What a great city!

"I'm ba-ack," he whispered with glee.

Not wanting to buck tradition, he followed the unspoken rule. While the women headed for the far side, Darius admired the last rosy rays of sunset playing over the stone wall, then entered the door with the stick figure without the tunic painted on it. Inside, the room offered little. More disconcerting, though, was the heavy feeling coming over him. Working its way through his bones. Making it difficult to lift his feet.

He stumbled over to the nearer stall and sat down, hoping it was just bad wine making him feel this way.

"What the—"

He looked at his hand, studied it from all angles, and with

great effort, flexed his stiff fingers. They were slow to re-spond. Too slow. Damn it to Hades, he couldn't make love to two women with reflexes like this!

"By Zeus, what's happening to me?"

Suddenly, when he could no longer move a muscle, could not so much as lower his hand, he found himself regretfully missing not the blond and brunette, but the lovely, exasper-ating Alexandra.

Wondering if he'd ever see her again, ever feel the touch of her hand running over his skin again. Ever be able to tell her how grateful he was for the hours of life she'd given him.

Under cover of darkness, Cytus steered his matched team of heavily jeweled, obsidian-black horses to a secluded spot behind a thick grove of oak trees. Leaving them and his equally bejeweled chariot where they wouldn't be noticed, he pressed forward, lurking in the rain-drenched forest, spy-ing on his handiwork.

Half god, half mortal, able to pass as either, he'd badgered Zeus for centuries for the privilege of taking over Darius's rulership of gems, since the legendary philanderer of Olym-pus was permanently exiled and not likely to find his way back into Zeus's good graces. Hera had lobbied in Cytus's fa-vor also, because she was partial to him, which might also have been the reason it took Zeus so long to come around. But finally he had. Taking great pride in his exalted position, Cy-tus wasn't about to relinquish his rulership now. He was there to send Darius back to whatever or wherever he'd been for the last three thousand years. Any way he could. He'd lined up lo-cal gang members to do whatever had to be done—didn't want Zeus blaming him, just in case he still had some paternal feelings toward Darius—paid them a few paltry rubies, and pointed them toward their living, breathing target.

They'd returned almost immediately, explaining their quarry had disappeared and the only thing out of place in the building was a statue. Poof! Just like that, Darius was gone. Inexplicably, he'd left the statue. He'd waited three millennia to come back to life, and then vacated? Didn't make sense.

Had Zeus had a hand in this, angered by Darius's solution to the curse, determined to keep him in a state of nonexistence? Or had Darius simply caught on to Cytus's plan and decided he was safer elsewhere?

Too bad. Cytus would deal with whoever'd warned him later. Right now he simply modified the plan. In case Darius came back, he'd find his perfect statue had become—oh the shame of it!—most undesirable.

Cytus watched with childish delight as local gang members again surged into the stone bathroom, relished their hyenalike laughter as they did his bidding and damaged the marble statue positioned on the toilet. He pictured skin gouged with metal tools, fingers broken off and flung into dark corners. Wouldn't it be ironic if Darius's penis was lost *again*. Oh joy! Not only would it be the coup de grâce, but it'd certainly make Darius think twice about trying another statue. Ever. With that thought in mind, Cytus waited until the punks retreated to wreak mayhem elsewhere, then strode into the small building, careful where he stepped.

But there were no small pieces of marble lying about to trip him. Even though a mortal could have missed seeing some in the dim light, he had excellent vision and could see there was none. Not one. He peered over the top of the stall.

Paint?

They'd sprayed it with paint? What were those morons thinking? Why, if he had the power, he'd turn them all into cobras and let them spend the rest of their days slithering about, spraying venom to get their next meal.

But wait; all wasn't lost. He'd always heard that Darius took great pride in being so magnificent, so perfect, so desirable to women. A true legend. Turning him into a graffiti target was bound to be demeaning, bound to teach him some sort of lesson and put him in his place.

If it didn't, if Darius had already fulfilled the terms of the curse and earned the privilege of coming and going anytime he pleased . . . well surely he'd never want to get back into such an ugly hunk of marble now.

But if he did, Cytus would be ready for him. Next time, though, he'd hire professionals. And he'd pay them *after* the job was done.

8

Alex's studio was quiet at two A.M., save for the various rumblings visiting children make in their sleep as they roll over and bump one another in their makeshift beds on the floor, or stretch out a foot and send an empty popcorn bowl scooting across the wood. It was good to have them nearby, especially after the afternoon she'd had with members of the Ladies' Club, discussing unavoidable topics like lawyers and lawsuits, fraud, insurance claims, theft; in short, anything they could hurl at her.

"Look at Julian," Maria said with a soft laugh, amused by the ten-year-old boy's openmouthed sprawl. She was seventeen; in her mind too adult to go to sleep for at least another hour, though she was fighting heavy eyelids with every yawn.

Alex was thirty and wished she could have gone to bed right after dinner. It would've been a nice, quiet place to hide out and lick her wounds, but the children would have none of that.

Six-year-old Emily had propped a sassy hand on her hip and said, "You always tell us to look forward, not back."

Brat. Alex promised never to say something so trite again. Instead she set a whole new example—how to drown your sorrows in pepperoni pizza and chocolate sauce. Together. The kids' shrieks of disbelief and laughter had cheered her up for a short while, and all of them had eagerly dived right in and started what would probably become a new tradition at late-night TCH pizza parties.

She was tired of putting on a brave face, always trying to teach by example. Maybe kids needed to know that adults could be just as lost coping with adult-sized problems as children were with theirs. She'd had too much chocolate pizza and Kool-Aid, her stomach hurt, and she couldn't concentrate on this newest revelation or what Maria was saying at the moment. Now she just wanted to go to sleep and not wake up until this nightmare with the statue was over.

"Cute, ain't he?" Griff agreed with Maria. The children viewed the gardener (and sometimes TCH handyman) as a surrogate grandfather, and since there was no way he'd been invited to the exclusive preview, either, he'd been included in this party.

Julian slept on without a clue.

"Wish I had a camera," Maria said.

They spoke softly, even though an earthquake probably wouldn't wake Julian or the others.

"I've got one," T.J.—Maria's twin brother preferred the short version of Tomás José—volunteered, jumping up to get it.

Poor Julian—doomed to blackmail sometime in the near future.

Griff pushed himself up off the blanket-strewn floor, first

to his knees, then to his feet. "Damn arthritis. I'm getting too old to be sitting on the floor."

"You're not old," Alex said automatically.

Though he was starting to show gray at the temples. And she'd noticed lately that after he'd been weeding the flower beds for awhile, he had to stand up and stretch before he moved on. When had that happened? He didn't seem older than the first day she could remember him sweeping up at the home, but after a few mental calculations, she realized he must be fifty-five, maybe sixty. And life hadn't been kind.

Would her father look old? Had life been kind to him? Probably not, forced to give up two children, from all indications shortly after their mother had died. What kind of circumstances those must have been.

"Guess I best get going," Griff said once he was vertical, stretching and yawning simultaneously. "Bosses want me here at seven sharp."

"Seven?" Alex asked, surprised. Though Griff often started groundswork earlier in the hot summer months, it was solely by choice. "Why seven?"

He grimaced. She knew immediately it had something to do with cleaning up after the "big day," and that he regretted mentioning it in front of her at all.

"Sorry," he said, patting her shoulder in a fatherly manner. "Didn't mean to bring it up." He glanced around at the sleeping children. "You did good, lettin' 'em have this party for you. Couldn'ta been easy."

She bit her lower lip to stop it from trembling—she wasn't ready to let her tears loose just yet—and patted his lingering hand in return.

"I'm just five minutes away," he said. "You know you can

call me if you need me. 'Night, Maria, T.J. You all lock up behind me now, you hear?"

"Take some pizza with you," Alex said.

"Think I'll pass." He rubbed his stomach. "Too much cheese already."

After bolting the door behind Griff—he tested it just to be sure—Maria returned to her cross-legged position on the floor beside Alex.

"How come he doesn't have kids?"

Alex shrugged. "Single, I guess."

It wasn't true; Griff once had confided that he'd had two daughters, sent to live with relatives in California after his wife had died. But it wasn't her secret to share. And it only raised more questions, to which she hadn't any answers because Griff had changed the subject and never gone there again.

"How come he never adopted anybody?"

"It's hard enough for single men to adopt now. Used to be impossible."

"I bet he wanted to adopt you."

She was in the mood to lick her wounds, not add salt. Eager to end the direction this conversation was headed, she rose to her feet abruptly, grabbing an empty pretzel bag on her way only because she could crush it noisily, drowning out any more of Maria's comments.

T.J. shoved his sister in the arm, saying, "Good one," sarcastically. She punched him back.

Alex stumbled toward her bedroom. "Don't kill each other on the premises. I can't handle the publicity."

"Where're you going?"

"To bed?" she suggested, turning and staring at T.J. as if he had two heads.

He grinned mischievously. How he had any energy left was beyond her. "Good luck. There's five kids in there."

Five? she mouthed.

"Yeah, remember you sent Daniel in for a time-out and he fell asleep?"

She couldn't remember why the others had joined him. She couldn't hold her eyes open long enough to shuffle one around, much less all of them. "Okay, so I'm going to sleep."

"Where?"

"Who the hell cares?"

Smart kids, they didn't point out the error of her ways. Not tonight.

She didn't go far. She shuffled back across the room to the worktable, dropping the snack bag on the first horizontal surface she found, though if anyone had asked her where that was, she wouldn't have been able to tell them.

"If the kids get up before I do, keep them away from Sabrina and her kittens." Sabrina, a muddled mixture of grays and browns, was the feral cat who'd turned a hidey-hole in the club garage into her personal nursery. Through a yawn, she said, "I won't be able to face cat bites and claw marks."

"Alex?" Maria asked after the last light was out.

"Hm?"

"If you thought any one of the ladies was your mother, which one would you think it is?"

It wasn't as startling a question as it could have been; she and Claudia had played similar games as children. *If any one of the women in the grocery store is our mother, which one is it?* Then of course, they'd check them all out; hair color, eye color, height, whether any of them smiled at little girls. *If*

any one of the men in church is our father, which one is it?
Were any of them studying little girls, searching for a familiar face?

"Don't know." Alex sighed, too tired and too old to play.

Maria and T.J. bantered over who it would be. Then T.J. said, "If we're guessing father, Alex's could be Chef Ramon."

"What?"

"Well, look how he's always giving her 'leftovers.' I've looked in some of those to-go boxes. That's pretty fancy leftovers."

"He cooks fancy lunches," Alex said, yawning. "Now shut up and go to sleep."

Then, rolling over onto her right side, she fell asleep without even looking for a towel to pillow her head. What did it matter if she was comfortable? Tomorrow the ladies would come to a consensus and have her arrested or something.

Then, because she'd never make bail, she'd be sleeping on a moldy old mattress in a tiny cell. To make matters worse, she'd probably dream about *him*. The impostor. Everything that had gone wrong, after all, was his fault. Him and his big ego, his infuriating insistence that he was Zeus's son. His dreamy dark chocolate eyes, firm pecs, and oh, she dared not go on.

When the phone rang, Alex groaned and rolled over, not too happy to have her dream interrupted, certain she'd been in bed no more than ten seconds. According to the clock, she wasn't far off. It was two-thirty. A power nap, to some people. Personally, she needed more sleep than that.

She rolled over and slid off the mattress, falling farther than she expected. Sprawled on the cold, hard floor, she glanced around. Even in the dark, she could tell she wasn't in her bedroom. She'd fallen off the worktable. What the heck was she doing sleeping on the table?

The long, hellish day and evening came back in an unwelcome rush while the answering machine picked up, did its thing, and then a male voice boomed across the room.

"This is Officer Dietrich, with the St. Louis Police Department."

Oh God, *now* who'd gotten arrested? She tried to remember which children were there, sleeping. Had to be one of the other ones, afraid to have the police call TCH or notify a caseworker. Any one of them was capable of substituting Alex's name as their "responsible adult" and looking quite innocent as they did so.

"I'm sorry to call so late, but we've got a situation and need to speak with Miss, uh"—Alex could hear papers rustling in the background—"Alexandra de Marco. Uh, are you missing a work of art?"

She bolted upright, her feet tangling in a blanket on the floor as she stumbled through the darkness toward the phone. "Don't hang up, don't hang up!"

"A statue of a man? Because—"

Was that a snicker?

"Hello!" The machine whistled annoyingly as she picked up. "Hold on, I'm here. I'm here," she said, punching buttons to shut off the damned recorder.

"Are you Alexandra de Marco?"

"You found my statue?" *Oh God, please say yes.*

"I guess that's a yes."

"How? Where?" She *knew* that impostor couldn't have been her statue. What had she been thinking?

"Forest Park, ma'am. Uh, I'm supposed to ask if you can come down here and identify it."

"It's mine."

"We need you to identify it in person, ma'am."

"Really?" she asked, taken aback by his insistence—not that anything could keep her away—and feeling just a little bit sassy now that the world was turning right again. "Just how many full-size nude statues of Greek gods went missing yesterday?"

"For God's sake, Alex, slow down!" Griff yelled over the rush of wind through the club's old, un-air-conditioned maintenance van.

The windows were rolled all the way down; good thing—gave him a good grip on the frame as Alex propelled the van through the streets, the headlights cutting a narrow tunnel through the black night as she streaked a beeline for the statue in the restroom in Forest Park. Alex sneezed and rubbed her itchy eyes; didn't take long outdoors for her allergies to kick in. The temperature outside had dropped to eighty-five; the humidity hadn't. Moisture dripped off the trees, landing momentarily on the van, then blowing off on its journey downward to slake the earth's thirst. Alex stuck her hand out the window until it was wet. Then, raking her fingers through her loose hair, she pushed it off her face.

"Relax," she told Griff, though she was far from it herself.

He'd had a beer at his place, and once she found that out, she wouldn't let him drive. Nor would he let her venture into Forest Park alone in the middle of the night. What if it was a crank call? Considering the only cop he trusted was Jimmy, who'd been raised at the home, coming with her was quite a concession on his part. He had a record and wasn't particularly comfortable around cops.

"Done some time," he'd told her one afternoon.

Digging in the garden together made for long hours of shared confidences, on both sides, as Alex grew up. He'd waited until she was twenty for that particular conversation. The revelation hadn't made a bit of difference; the years had already proven him a good man. Just like him to tag along now.

The roads through Forest Park were hilly, winding, and unlined on the best of nights. Tonight the slow drizzle had slickened them. She'd pay more attention to her driving, but there was so much to think about. Getting her statue back. Meeting up with the impostor some time in the future on a more level playing field; she hoped he turned out to be as sane as he was sexy. She wouldn't mind getting to know him a little better.

"I didn't teach you to drive like this!" Griff pointed off to the side up ahead. "Is that a wolf? See, you gotta look out for stuff like—Yeah, that's a—Look out!"

She slammed the palm of her hand against the steering wheel, blowing the horn, venting some of her pent up energy. The animal didn't run off, but it didn't step in her way, either, and she sped by without having to slow down and waste precious seconds. As if the statue were going anywhere.

"Wow, a wolf in Forest Park!" Griff craned his neck out the window as they zoomed past, trying to keep it in sight as long as he could. "Wait'll I tell the kids."

"Well, if you're telling the kids, you might mention it was a raccoon."

"Was not!"

"Most definitely *was*. When's the last time you had your eyes checked?"

"Don't need my eyes checked, girl." He settled back in his seat, shrugging further into his jacket, for once not mentioning how the damp night air made his arthritis ache. "'Sides, I passed my vision test when I renewed my license."

"Uh-huh." As Alex approached a fork in the road, she finally slowed. Choices, choices. "Darn, I always get lost in here."

"Where we going?"

"Some restroom outbuilding over by the zoo."

"If you promise to drive like a rational human being, I'll tell—"

"Never mind, I think I see flashing lights." She spun the wheel right and zipped off again, the rear end fishtailing until it caught hold. "Yeah, I do! See, it wasn't a crank call." In her excitement, she reached across the seat and grabbed Griff's arm.

"Both hands on the wheel!"

"Oh God, I can't wait to get Darius home."

Griff nervously rubbed his whisker-stubbled jaws and muttered, "Never thought I'd be glad to see cops again."

She parked the van by the patrol cars. Well, actually, she hit the brakes and it slid to a crooked stop next to enough cruisers to put the rest of the city at risk. As Alex slid out the driver's door and asked the nearest officer where the statue was, Griff yanked the key out of the ignition and pocketed it.

"This way," a female officer said, falling in step beside Alex and leading the way to the restroom. It was a small, stone building with a narrow doorway.

"Oh no. Not in there."

"Is that a problem?"

"Shoot, yeah." She'd made a frantic call to a professional mover she'd used in the past, promising him triple time to get out of bed and meet her in Forest Park. Anything to get that statue back to the studio ASAP.

A dozen officers parted rank and let her through. She thought more than a few of them were wearing smirks, but she ignored them. She had to get in there and evaluate the situation before the heavy equipment arrived. Unless she found enough police volunteers to carry Darius out to where the mover could maneuver his equipment, the statue was doomed to stay until normal working hours.

"Maybe I should warn you before you go in . . ."

Alex glanced at the officer's name tag. O'Leary.

"There's been some damage." Alex figured she must look grief stricken, because O'Leary hastened to explain. "Nothing's broken that I can see, or anything. It's graffiti."

"Graffiti?" On her perfect statue?

O'Leary nodded. "Gang symbols, I'm afraid."

Alex wondered if it could be restored for the auction. She must have wondered it aloud, because she heard a male officer snicker and say, "She thinks someone'll buy that? Christ, I guess it takes all kinds."

Inside, she found more officers standing around. Fortunately not making use of the facilities.

The room was no larger than ten by fifteen. Urinals, two stalls, one rust-stained sink with a drippy faucet, and a metal trash can. No statue. Maybe she was still asleep on her worktable, having a nightmare. Maybe she didn't really have these achy bruises down her right side where she'd fallen off and hit the wood-plank floor, which appeared to be softer than a modern-day hardwood floor due to marble dust blurring the grain, but that was only an illusion.

"So? Where is it?"

All officers present pointed toward the stalls, neither of which had a door. Warily, due to the way they parted rank for her, she eased herself on over there and glanced inside.

Her first impulse at seeing anyone sitting on a toilet was to shield her eyes and look away. But this wasn't a man; it was definitely marble.

"Oh . . . my . . . God." How embarrassing to stare at it, though, with a pack of men staring at her, whispering comments among themselves. Or was that just her perception?

"That your work?" one of them asked. Oh yeah, she definitely heard a smirk in that question. Faced with this, though, it was best to ignore it, because she certainly couldn't explain this away.

She stared down at her once-beautiful hunk of marble, sitting on the toilet in a near perfect *Thinker* position, except for staring at one, upraised, supinated hand, his fingers curled loosely. Someone had set a half-empty roll of toilet paper on end in his palm, the tail of it wrapped around his head like a crown.

She knelt in front of it, beneath the unshaded, overhead light bulb. Lifting the sheet, ignoring the suggestive comments all around, she inspected every inch. It was, unmistakably, her work—except for the multitude of gang symbols tattooed on its forehead, chest, almost all exposed areas. It was, unmistakably, her Darius.

If she'd thought it impossible that her statue could turn into a man earlier—hell, who thought about things like that?—she had no words to describe what she was thinking now. How her statue, without a break or a crack in it, could have changed position. Not just a finger or a toe, but every friggin' joint. Disbelief warred with unbridled hope. Definitely a nightmare. Desperate for that to be the logical explanation, she pinched herself when no one was looking. Hard.

"Ow."

"Ma'am, is this your statue?"

She broke out in a cold sweat. No one could have duplicated his hair, his bone structure, his corded muscles. No one could have made marble flexible . . .

She was as open-minded as anyone, thanks to where she

grew up. The orphanage was housed in a creaky, old building, built around a log cabin dating back to the time of Lewis and Clark. A boarded-up tunnel in a forgotten part of the basement was rumored to be part of the Civil War's Underground Railroad movement. Add to that several decades of orphaned children from a variety of backgrounds and beliefs, and you got stories, fresh stories and those passed down over the years, one generation of parentless children to another. Ghost stories to explain creaks in the middle of the night. Ouija boards pulled out of dark cupboards for conversations with the beyond. Midnight seances.

But this was pushing open-mindedness to the limit.

"Ma'am, is this your—"

No one would believe she was sane if she claimed this was her statue.

My God, the myth was true!

"Yeah, it's mine," she heard herself whisper, as if from far away. Hoping they wouldn't label her unstable and hide the children from her.

A man cleared his throat. "The report you filed yesterday says your statue stands, and I quote, 'approximately seven feet tall.'"

Oh, he would notice *that.*

"Miss de Marco? You want to explain that?"

It did last time I saw it?

It shrunk?

It got tired?

"Well, it, uh, would. If it were, you know, upright."

He muttered something about flaky artists and walked out of the restroom, shaking his head in disgust.

"Lord God Almighty," Griff gasped from behind her. "How the hell'd that happen?"

"I don't know." She shook her head slowly, afraid to even

admit out loud that something so unreal could be possible. "I don't know. Griff, what'm I going to do?"

"How're you planning on moving it?" O'Leary asked.

Alex looked around the inside of the stone building. A mini fortress. No way the movers could get the equipment through the doorway. No room to maneuver it inside.

"Maybe some of you officers wouldn't mind—"

"Oh no, honey. No no no." Faster than Alex could smile and say please, O'Leary and every other uniform disappeared out the door, like rats deserting a sinking ship.

"Then I guess it'll have to stay," she said.

Griff moved closer to her and softly said, "Alex, honey, I didn't want to say nothing while they was in here, but that can't be your statue."

"I know, I know," she said, shaking her head. "I can't explain it. But it is. It's Darius."

"But, Alex—"

She turned to face him. "Look, Griff, you know I'm not crazy."

"Desperate, maybe."

"Right, and there just happens to be a stray statue in a john in Forest Park that I'm *desperate* enough to claim? Oh come on, Griff, I know this doesn't make any sense. Believe me, I know it doesn't." She stared at the statue, absorbing every muscle, every joint, every surface inch she'd created. "But I know my own work, and this is it."

If this was it, and the impostor hadn't really been an impostor at all, then maybe he hadn't been pretending. Her heart skipped a beat at what that meant. Maybe he, as a man, really had wanted her.

It was a notion so unexpected, so contrary to everything she believed, that the moment she'd dared think it, she felt a heavy *whump* of a heartbeat thud inside her chest. Like a warning to remember that if she let herself care, no matter how he felt about her now, later he'd leave.

It was safer to think he was really hard up. No pun intended.

Back to business—safer territory—she stepped farther into the stall, her hands skimming over the entire statue, searching for the worst, but thankfully finding no irreparable fractures or unsightly gouges.

"Except for the paint"—she rubbed a smear between her fingertips and noted that it hadn't completely dried yet because it was old, cheap, or both—"it seems to be okay." Giddy with excitement, she turned to Griff. "If I can clean it up in time, the kids'll still get winter clothes and everything else they need, and the home won't have to close." All she had to do was clean off the paint. Surely that could be done.

After a moment—a long moment in which Griff stared at her so hard, Alex thought he might call O'Leary back in and tell her to cart her away to the mental ward—he said, "Well, look at the bright side."

"What's that?"

"It's not using the urinal."

She got a mental picture of trying to auction *that* off, and agreed wholeheartedly.

"We sure can't leave it here," he said.

Knowing he'd accepted this statue as her statue because she had, relief flooded through Alex, escaping in a long exhale that allowed her to breathe again. But no sooner had she started to relax than an unbidden little fear crept in, a doom-and-gloom voice that said maybe, since it had come alive once, it could happen again.

Quickly she shoved that thought away, far back into the recesses of her mind. All that mattered was that the statue was here now. It had to stay that way. It just had to. She had to keep her mind on the business at hand.

"You think they'd let me tear down the wall?" She traced the beautiful, thick stones with her palms. "It's probably historic. Didn't they have the World's Fair here once?"

"I doubt it's that old."

"Hm." More rubbing.

"But I'm sure they won't let you tear it down, neither."

"Well, maybe the mover can get a bunch of men over here first thing. What time do you think they go to work?"

"Better post a guard here tonight if you don't want more paint on it."

"I'm not leaving," she said, meaning there was no need for a guard. "I'll be here cleaning it." She rubbed her itchy eyes again, making a mental note to tend to her allergies when she went back for supplies. Wouldn't it be nice to live where there was no crime and no allergies?

Car doors slammed outside, signaling departing police. Departing manpower.

Alex sighed. "Maybe the gang'll come back now, and I can pay *them* to move it outside."

"Over my dead body!"

A car engine revved. More than one man shouted.

"Just kidding." Not really. "What's going on out there?"

Alex and Griff both listened intently.

"Did someone yell, 'Get out of the john'?" Alex asked.

"Sounded like it."

Curious, they both headed for the door. Just as they reached it, the whole building shook. The wall opposite the stalls began to crumble.

"Get out!" Griff grabbed Alex and pushed her out ahead of him.

They were blinded by the number of spotlights shining on

the restroom, but they could make out the lone patrol car with its grill buried in the stone wall, its back tires spinning at top speed on the damp grass, quickly making ruts. Officers ran everywhere, trying to get near the car, but being very cautious. And Alex could see why. The driver's seat was empty.

The nearest officer yanked open the door, jumped in, and threw it into park with a horrendous grinding of gears.

"Turn it off!" someone shouted, as the wheels continued to spin, digging deeper into the earth with every rotation.

The officer jumped back out.

"Why didn't you turn it off?"

"There's no goddamn key in it, that's why!"

"Well, we gotta do something."

"It's hung up. We'll need a tow to pull it out so we can get into the engine and disable it."

"That won't work. Check the gas gauge."

"You check the gas gauge!"

"Park a car behind it in case it decides to go backward."

"Ohhhh shit!" someone shouted as another engine revved.

"What the hell—?"

"I ain't never seen nothing like this," Griff whispered, standing behind Alex with his hands closed protectively over her shoulders.

"I have," she said. "Remember the television?"

"Those tricks're done with cameras, Alex."

"Ha ha. I mean mine, how it comes on by itself."

"It doesn't *move*."

"Tools did." Was she crazy to be thinking this way? "Jewelry did." It sounded crazy, even to her. "I swear it, Griff, it's happened in my studio."

Two patrol cars later, the wall had fallen and the roof listed at a precarious angle overhead. Lots of angry testosterone in blue was milling about, looking for a scapegoat because patrol cars weren't possessed, so someone must have done something. Alex didn't care. As soon as those cars were out of her way, there'd be room to send the heavy equipment in after the statue. She'd have to find something to sit Darius on other than a toilet, maybe a marble tree stump, but once the graffiti was removed, there *would* be an auction.

Beneath a heavily cloaked moon, Cytus paced agitatedly under a wide span of oaks, watching intently as the statue was hoisted from the wreckage. Mumbling unintelligibly for the most part, except for the occasional outpouring of rage he was prone to.

"Is she really claiming that ugly thing?" he demanded.

Hermes perched overhead on a thick branch—a power position over Cytus, a bully who used his limited powers to maximum effect in his efforts to prove he belonged among the gods. If not for the family bloodline, he'd have been barred from Olympus long ago, back when he'd been a spoiled brat, before he'd become mean and vindictive.

"The horses are restless," Hermes noted, afraid they'd draw attention. They used to be such a well-behaved team, back when—

"What is she thinking?" Cytus ranted. "She's taking it back to her studio, to do what with it? Surely she can't make it presentable again!"

"No, no, I'm sure she can't. You got what you came here for, didn't you?"

Cytus's wicked laugh revealed just how pleased he was with himself. "Almost."

"Then you might as well go and leave poor, defeated Darius to his misery." Hermes wasn't known as the Trickster for nothing. "Poor, poor Darius. He'll never try this again."

"He should have come to me, you know," Cytus said grimly. "Immediately upon taking his first breath, he should have come. He owes me an apology. On his knees. Groveling!"

Like *that* would ever happen!

"Mm, yes, I'm sure he realizes that now." Hermes sighed dramatically. "Too late, though, don't you think?"

Cytus grinned. "Too bad." Then frowned, suspicious. "Why are you here, anyway? Have you been talking to him against Zeus's orders?"

"Oh no, no I wouldn't dare. Wouldn't go against Zeus's orders. I just, uh, came to see you."

Cytus frowned. "Well, what is it then?"

"What?"

"The message. You did bring me a message, didn't you? I can't imagine you followed me otherwise."

"Oh yeah, the message. Hades wants to see you."

"Hades? But he never leaves the underworld. That means I'll have to go there."

"Yes, I know."

"But it'll take too much time!"

"I can tell him you said so." He fluttered up off the branch, as if to depart immediately.

"No!" Cytus visibly shuddered. "Don't do that."

They both glanced across the way as the heavy equipment deposited its ungainly prize crookedly on the grass, its sheet covering its head but little else as it tottered over. Hermes liked to think of it as Darius mooning Cytus.

Apparently of like mind, Cytus growled, "I'll go."

Ignoring the horses' nervous dancing in place, not even

pausing for a moment to calm them—he'd never deserved that team!—Cytus stepped into his chariot, then turned and glared toward Darius, his eyes as stark and cold as winter.

"But I'll be back."

9

It was the most humiliating dawn of Darius's existence, dumped out in the open, on wet grass, on his forehead and knees with his bare ass sticking up in the air.

Only a few hours ago, when Alexandra had seen him upright and proud and perfect, she'd told her friend how much she wanted him. That she'd tear off her clothes and keep him from all other women. Then, his heart had soared with anticipation.

But now . . . Now that she'd seen him this way—by the Styx, he swore he'd find out why this had happened to him!—did she still desire him? How could it be possible?

As bad as it had been to turn back into marble a few hours ago—he'd repeated an endless cycle of panic, curses, and promises made—he only fully realized the gravity of his situation when hoodlums entered the building. He recognized the type: young men full of testosterone with nothing better to do than show off how macho they were, each one feeding off the others until they were in a frenzy, out of control, unstoppable.

And there he was, sitting on a toilet, immobile and vulnerable to attack. It took but a few moments to gauge his diminished powers and figure out how to clog the spray cans—an invention he wasn't familiar with—and thankfully after he did so, they ran off instead of trying other forms of mayhem.

Only when Alexandra arrived on the scene did he feel safe again. She touched him, checking him out, running her hands over his skin, reminding him of the days of sweet torture before he'd come to life. His panic fled, his curses changed to murmurs of pure rapture, and he'd stopped making promises he'd never remember. The one bright spot in this dark night was that he might get to endure that again, with the same end result.

His sense of touch was no longer as heightened as that moment when he'd been perfect on stage, when he'd felt every callus on her hands, calluses made by the hard physical work she did to hone her craft. To make him perfect.

Now that she was here, she wouldn't let anyone else harm him. All she had to do was take him back to her studio. But even though he hadn't been long on this earth, Darius realized she needed help. And it didn't look like she was going to get it from the mortals in uniform.

Having seen cars move earlier in the day, Darius needed only a few minutes to figure out how to propel a couple into the stone building. Zeus must have a crumb of compassion, after all, to have left him with some abilities, but as before, he couldn't do a thing to move himself.

How frustrating it had been to watch Alexandra pick through the heavy stones to reach him, and then the heavy equipment roaring closer and closer, finally scooping him up off balance—it was all too much. He was at the mercy of the machine and its driver, who was now, in between fits of yawns, complaining about the hour. And then finally he was outside, wrong side up, making all sorts of desperate promises that if he could just come alive again this instant, he'd do whatever Zeus asked.

He complained bitterly, but of course no mortals could hear him in his condition.

Hermes fluttered around overhead, whispering for Darius to leave the statue before it got broken.

"Can't," Darius replied.

"Fool! The man can hardly keep his eyes open. He'll drop you again for sure."

"No, I mean I *can't*."

"You mean . . ."

"Yeah, it's too late." He'd hang his head in shame and dejection, but of course, he damned well *couldn't*. Sounding morose was as close as he could come to showing how depressed he truly felt. He had a gift for Alexandra enclosed in his fist; it was doubtful he'd ever be able to give it to her now. "I'm stuck. Trapped in here."

"But . . . the cars . . ."

"I know, I know. I can still do some things. Like when Alexandra had me almost finished and my powers started to return." But a fat lot of good that was doing him. "You have to get me out of here, Hermes. It's so tight in here, I can hardly breathe. It's closing in on me, the pressure, like being caught in a cave in. I don't know if I—"

"Calm down, calm down! What can I do?"

" 'Calm down'? I'm encased in a stone coffin and that's the best you can do!"

It drizzled off and on for hours. By dawn Darius was finally mounted upright on a flatbed truck and driven out into the streets, his soaked sheet flapping in the breeze, snapping like a wet flag. In case his bare ass wasn't noticeable enough on its own, he had a police escort complete with strobing lightbars to draw everyone's attention. Early morning traffic came to a virtual standstill, and he was lined up with them, mooning everyone behind him.

This all resulted in a lot of horn tooting for the long, slow, crowded mile back to Alexandra's studio. It was a damned parade—at his expense. Men jumped out of vans with cameras on their shoulders—big ones—so he'd make the evening news. How was he going to get women after this?

"No no no!" Alexandra shouted as the mover dropped him outside her door, balancing his bare butt on the cold brick garden wall, leaving him tilted at a ridiculous slant. "I need you to take him in through the big door. Around the other side."

"Sorry, lady. No can do."

"But you have to. I can't get him ready out here."

The man at the controls laughed. "Face it, you can't get him ready, period."

"I have to!"

Yes, she has to! Darius didn't know if he'd get a second chance to come back to life if she fixed the statue, but it was an option he wasn't willing to forgo. His new pose was embarrassing, but once Alexandra fixed him as good as new, maybe he'd come alive again, and the position would be moot.

He hoped.

It started to rain again, a hard summer shower, chilling him thoroughly. If he weren't solid marble, he'd shiver. He longed for Alexandra's warm touch.

"I gotta get home so my wife can get to work, or my ass is grass."

"I'll pay for her to take a cab."

He shook his head, reversing away from Darius. Alexandra followed on foot, wiping rain out of her eyes.

"It's not the car," he shouted over the receding rumble of the motor. "It's the kids. I'm late already."

She followed him down the driveway, splashing through puddles, arguing all the way out of earshot. Darius hoped she'd be able to change his mind, but it looked doubtful. His whole future looked doubtful. He'd taken a risk, moving into the statue. It might all end here. He'd probably be shuttled off to some museum basement, never to see the sky again. And this time, he wouldn't even get to hear the broadcasts off the satellites. No more "History for one hundred." No more "Lucy, you got some 'splaining to do." Bored to death.

Only he couldn't die.

But worst of all—and this was a surprise—was that he'd miss Alexandra. He'd never again see her first thing in the morning and last thing at night. She used to kiss him. Well, not exactly a *kiss*, he admitted, but every night she'd press her fingers to her lips and then she'd tag his cheek or his shoulder or his thigh, usually whatever she'd been working on last.

He'd miss her laugh; it was all light and air and genuine merriment as she enjoyed her hours with the children, with seemingly more fulfillment than most mothers he'd ever witnessed. Didn't matter if they were doing art projects, watching TV—his choice of shows most of the time—or sharing a snack.

He'd miss how she cradled the little ones and kissed their scrapes and, when asked, advised the older ones who sometimes had problems too big for bandages.

Oh, how could this have all gone wrong?

"Hermes, you still here?"

His brother landed on the roof of the carriage house. "Right here."

"What happened? I was *perfect*."

Hermes fluttered closer, inspecting the statue from head to toe now that there were no strangers around. "Nothing's broken, Dare. Except for your colorful new look, you still are."

"You think she can get it all off?"

"Maybe. Looks like it might be running a little bit in the rain." Dabbing at the graffiti with a corner of the sheet, he grunted doubtfully. "But even if she could, then what? You were perfect and you still turned back into marble." Hermes shook his head. "I don't know, Dare. Looks bad to me."

"You think it was Zeus?"

"Maybe."

"Nah, he'd want me to know if it was him," Darius said. "He'd throw a thunderbolt so I'd know for sure."

"I'll check around." Hermes rose in the air.

"Not now! Get this crap off me first."

"Hey. One, I don't know the first thing about paint. Two, I don't have the patience, and three, it's raining out here."

"Like I don't know that?" Darius couldn't believe Hermes was deserting him. "Whatever happened to 'He ain't heavy, he's my brother'?"

Hermes' laugh filtered back from the sky. "Don't look now, Dare, but you *are* heavy. And I'm only your half brother."

Bastard!

"Wait. Go to Zeus, will you? Tell him I fulfilled the terms of the curse. Tell him you saw me come alive again. Tell him—"

"Maybe he's the one who turned you back."

"Then talk him out of it."

"Zeus?" Hermes laughed.

Obviously he needed a little incentive. "I'll give you half my gems if you're successful."

"Half of *all* of them?" Shocked, he sank to the ground like a rock.

Only because he was desperate. "Yes, yes. Now go!"

"You're my brother, Dare," he said, perturbed. "You don't have to bribe me."

"One would think that were true."

"But what the heck?" Hermes said with glee, rising again. "I accept."

Left in the pouring rain to drown his sorrows by himself, Darius had nothing to do but think and regret and worry and plot and promise. What had gone wrong?

Had he turned back to marble because his time ran out? Perhaps he should have visited Olympus first, when he'd had the chance. Was there a way to do so now? Sending Hermes to intercede with Zeus seemed a good start.

Had he wandered too far from Alexandra before repaying her? Could that be it? Now he regretted leaving her side before rewarding her with gems, as he'd planned. He'd do that, if he got the chance. He promised. In the meantime, he'd use what limited powers he had to get her whatever gems he could. Surely some of those wealthy ladies would come by to see him.

Did Alexandra have the ear of one of the gods? Perhaps he'd angered her by leaving, and this was his punishment. He could fix that, too. He'd be agreeable. If he could come back to life, he'd spoil her with wine and food fit for the gods, obsequious servers, and music so sweet, it would bring tears to her eyes. He'd make love to her ten times a day.

If only he got the chance again.

Later that same morning, little-girl giggles rippled through the studio, floating on air like notes from a harp. Little-boy laughs echoed a beat behind. Children sang the A-B-C song, broken down in increments and echoed by a deeper, male voice that didn't get all the letters right, bringing on another fit of giggles. Mixed beneath them all were sounds of children eating breakfast, the clatter of dishes and glasses and utensils.

Alex curled up on her side, surprised to find herself on

something soft. It smelled like the thirdhand sofa she'd been given when Mrs. Ketterman's mother had gone into a nursing home last year. She could've sworn she'd seen a pair of children snuggled on it earlier, when she'd run in for cleaning supplies, then back out again to work on the statue in the rain. Could've sworn she'd collapsed on the worktable hours later from exhaustion, after the marble was cleaned up and polished to perfection. Sure she had; she'd even picked up one of the kids' discarded T-shirts and used it to pillow her head.

She'd often thought waking up to the sounds of small children every morning would be heaven on earth. They were giggling and guffawing the way little girls and boys do. Years ago she'd had reason to believe the children she heard would be her own. She'd moved out of TCH after high school graduation, struggled with a little help from her sister, worked her way through college, earned her degree, and married. Bam, bam, bam, right in order.

If not for the accident, she'd have kids by now. If she were whole and perfect, her husband wouldn't have left her. If she were successful—which might happen now that she had the statue back—someone might love her again.

Well, the kids loved her, of course. They didn't care about emergency surgery or scars, perfection or success. But if she weren't both of the latter, the auction would be a bust; without a new roof and furnace, the orphanage would close and they'd all be shuffled off to other facilities. Wait until she announced the statue had been found!

"I want another one," Julian said.

"There's plenty to go around," the deep male voice soothed. "Selena, over here. Tell Selena what flavor you'd like." He started the alphabet song this time, cracking the kids up when he stumbled through L-M-N-O-P.

That wasn't Griff. She didn't know a Selena. And she'd only once smelled food that heavenly, but she'd had too little sleep to remember when.

"Mm, what is that?" she asked, uncurling, squinting until she grew accustomed to the bright light streaming in through the windows. Even on the overly soft sofa, she felt every bruise down her right side, sharply bringing the night before into focus. She rolled to her feet, stretched the kinks out of her neck, remembered with great joy that the statue was back and undamaged.

The phone rang twice and forwarded to the answering machine.

"Hello, Alexandra? This is Marcie Wilcox at Webster University."

Alex was scheduled to kick off a series of guest lectures at Webster's College of Fine Arts the week after the charity auction.

"Uh, look, in light of the circumstances, we've rethought our policy on—"

"No no, wait! Don't hang up!" Alex made a dash for the phone, got her feet tangled up in a wet sheet crumpled on the floor, and stumbled past a young woman playing a harp that hadn't been there yesterday. She missed most of what Marcie said next, but knew exactly why she was calling.

"I'll, uh, call you back if we decide to reschedule—"

"Hello, I'm here! Don't hang up," Alex said, pushing buttons until the machine stopped recording and whistling, thinking, *Don't fire me before I even get started.*

"Marcie? Hi, sorry I'm so slow getting to the phone. I was up to my elbows in—" She noticed the children were all ears—good Lord, where *did* they get all that heavenly smelling food?—so she turned her back to them and lowered her voice in an attempt to cover her little white lie and segue into the good news. "I was busy cleaning up the statue. Did you hear that the police found it last night? Isn't that great? The thieves didn't get too far with it."

Sounding upbeat, she babbled on about finding it in Forest Park, while mentally she reviewed who knew that *her* statue had been upright, and who would require a creative explanation about the new one.

"Well, as I was saying," Marcie said when she finally got a word in, "this was just a courtesy call really, to let you know there might be a problem, but my secretary, uh, just popped in to say everything's been worked out. I'm so sorry to have bothered you on the weekend, and we look forward to seeing you after the auction." She hung up.

"Disaster averted!" Alex announced to the room in general, laughing with relief. Until she turned and faced the children. "Oh my God!"

They were seated around her worktable, a banquet of food spread out on golden trays in a veritable rainbow of colors and garnishes in front of them. The extra chairs—she didn't own more than four—were from the club; good, upholstered ones that would be ruined by crumbs and shoes. Worse, though, were the people circling the children: five women, just like the day before, dressed in gold-thread embroidered chitons; one man, Darius.

He moved about the children, patting a head here, a shoulder there, unhampered by the red satin sheet toga wrapped around him, a delicate lace edge tossed over one magnificent shoulder. Mrs. Ketterman's elderly mother had given the set away, complaining that the sheets were so silky, her blankets kept sliding off the bed, and she feared some night, in her sleep, she'd do the same. Alexandra thought they were sexy, and even though she had no need for them, she'd saved them in a drawer, hoping someday she'd have a man to share them with.

Try as she did not to admit it, they were pretty darned sexy now, draping over his big, masculine body.

"Oh . . . my . . . God."

Darius turned then, beaming a smile in her direction that warmed her way beyond a slight blush. Way down to regions that hadn't been warmed since her husband had left.

"No!" she said, panicking as she realized what his presence here meant. "It has to be there."

She'd heard the cliched expression "My heart stopped." She was sure hers really did, as she could feel it cramp up in her chest, rendering her incapable of motion, rooting her to the floor for what seemed like minutes until it started beating again. Then she tore across the room, flung open the door and checked the low garden wall that, a few short hours before, had supported the sitting statue. It wasn't there. She ran outside, barefoot, searching all around the perimeter of the studio, praying the mover had taken pity on her, come back, and was, even now, circling around to the big door.

No such luck.

Darius followed a few steps behind. "Looking for me?"

Feeling hopelessly outmaneuvered, she sank onto the garden wall where she'd left her future only a short while ago.

"Can you do that at will?" she asked, and felt stupid for doing so.

"You mean come and go?"

She nodded. He sat beside her, invading her space again, *sniffing* at her hair!, and she scooted away as unobtrusively as possible. But then she felt cold and wanted to scoot back, longing to feel his bare arm brush against hers again.

"I've always had the ability to turn into a statue and back, even as a child. My mother used to say, 'Darius, you keep doing that and one of these times—' "

"Wait a minute! You can go back." Alex brightened, seeing a solution to all her problems. She perched on the very edge of the wall now. "Can you choose how you do it? You know, go back to the same position I sculpted?"

Darius leaped to his feet. "No!"

She followed in his wake, gripping his arm with excitement—oh Lordy, he felt as good as he looked!—circling the biceps she'd shaped with both her hands. "You can. You said so. That's great! You can do it before the auction. Hallelujah, I have a guardian angel after all!"

"No way."

He crossed his arms over his chest, trapping her fingers against his steadily beating heart until she wrestled them free. She resisted the urge to step away and shore up her space again.

"Oh please. It's not for me. It's for the children. You have to do it."

"I don't have to do anything. I am a god."

"Look, I might be willing to buy into you being able to turn into a statue and back—What am I saying? I've seen it and I still have trouble believing it. But it's not going to be so easy to convince me of the god thing."

He shrugged and offered up an apologetic little grin, but the irrepressible, irresistible twinkle in his eyes said he was incapable of being sorry for anything. And somewhere, deep in her heart, was the realization that if he truly was a god, this was as it should be. But of course he wasn't.

"Prove it," she challenged him. Her hands fluttered in the space between them, defining it as the area she wanted him to fill with marble. "Do it in front of me. You know, turn into my statue. Do it. Do it now." She backed away to give him plenty of room.

"Psst! Don't do it, Dare."

"Jesus!" Alex said, ducking and looking overhead at the same time, certain she'd heard something out of place. "What the hell was that?"

"My brother. Hermes, come meet Alexandra."

A man appeared at the edge of the carriage house roof, wearing a low-crowned hat, a simple short tunic, and winged sandals. Involuntarily, Alex gasped as he stepped off into thin air, then watched spellbound as he gracefully sank beside them.

She blinked. She stepped up onto the garden wall and waved her hand over his head, checking for invisible safety lines, even though she could tell there weren't any, but she *had* to check, just in case.

"Okay, so maybe *he's* a god."

Yesterday that would have been ludicrous. Today it made more sense than a statue turning into a man and back again, which was where she needed to focus right now.

"But I still want proof from you." What she really wanted—no, *needed*—was her statue back, right now, and for his mother's prediction to come true. What she *wanted* was another matter, solely due to the fire in his eyes, as if he wanted her right here, right now, and no one else would do. While it was the stuff dreams were made of, she was afraid it was more than she could handle. More than she was prepared to give.

Darius closed the gap between them, sending her reeling backward through the door and into the studio, shadowing her every step of the way.

"Never. I will *never* turn myself back into a statue again." He shuddered at the thought.

Sensing his weakness, glad to be on more even ground, she grinned. "You're chicken."

He frowned, obviously perplexed.

"That's it, you're chicken. You're scared to turn back into the statue."

"I'm scared of nothing," he said, his chin raised imperiously.

"No, uh-uh, I'm not buying it, mister. Afraid of getting stuck?" He winced, and she could see that she was right. "That's it, isn't it!" She sidestepped around him, circling, perusing him from head to toe, thinking as she moved. "So, how can I convince you?"

"Impossible."

"But you have to. That disaster I averted on the phone with Marcie was only temporary. They think I never produced a statue in the first place. They think I'm a cheat *and* a liar."

He turned away, as if that in itself were the last word.

"Come eat. We're having what the children call brunch. Selena can provide you with any kind of juice you name. She also has an assortment of pastries. Or some cheese or lamb if you prefer."

She followed in his wake, saying, "You can't change the subject with food." She sniffed the heavenly aromas again, saw the children were eating the food so it must be real, and then spotted a tray in the center of the table with her downfall: a golden brown pastry with dark red cherries oozing out the seam.

He noticed the tug of war between her priorities and grinned; she scowled, knowing instinctively that he'd use any advantage to change the subject.

He picked up the cherry turnover, took a small bite, then held it to her lips and said, "Careful, it's hot."

She pressed her lips together.

"Alexandra."

There was that soft, sexy X again, the one that melted her insides. Saying it that way should be outlawed.

"Anybody ever tell you you don't play fair?"

"Many mortals." When she didn't acquiesce, he took another bite and chewed slowly, overtly savoring the taste until he'd swallowed the last crumb. "But what fun is playing fair?" Then quite unexpectedly, before she could even bolt out of his reach, he pressed his sugary, cherry-scented lips against hers.

Part of her wanted to reel backward, gain her space again, get some perspective, win this argument. And part of her realized she'd never, in her whole life, not even at one of her sister's two ritzy reception dinners, tasted anything so sweet, so wonderful, so *decadent*.

Was it the food, or his lips?

He was watching her expectantly, waiting as she warred with the sizzle of sexual tension within, the look in his eyes letting her know he knew what she was fighting. No way was she letting him think *he* might have had some tongue-tying effect on her. His ego was big enough.

"Once I get some food in me, I'll be able to think clearly," she told him, struggling to focus anywhere besides his lips. "And then I'll think of something." Some way to get him to turn back into marble, and hopefully get stuck that way. At the very least, to stay inert through the auction. Let the buyer deal with it . . . him . . . *whatever* afterward.

Resolutely, she stepped around him to get her own pastry, one that wouldn't have the memory of his lips on its edge.

"I've got it!" Alexandra declared some fifteen minutes later.

Darius had been waiting for this. He'd watched her for many days in her studio, studying her for hours on end. He knew how she worked. When faced with a problem, a perplexing spot or bump or whatever on his statue, she'd step away. She might pace slowly around the studio, or go into the kitchen and fix a meal, or call the children to tell them it was okay to visit. Then while she worked or played with them, she'd glance at him every so often, thinking.

It was no different now. She ate. She talked to Selena, some nonsense about workers' rights and sexual harassment. Apparently her mind was elsewhere, as she didn't even laugh along with the children when he stumbled through their alphabet song. He finally got it right, and they pulled out paper and pencil and showed him what the letters looked like and how to form simple words like "cat" and "dog." It became much more interesting when they showed him what "Darius" looked like.

Billy snuck up behind him and poked him in the arm.

"Told ya!" chorused around the table.

"What?" Darius asked.

"Nothing," Billy said.

"Billy thinks you're a G-H-O-S-T," Emily said. She took pity on his blank look and said, "Ghost."

"No I don't," Billy said, then muttered, "not anymore."

"Good, because I'm not a ghost, I'm a god."

"Yeah, right. Bet if I cut your arm open, I'd find wires."

Darius continued to bide time with the children, and Alexandra continued to glance at him every so often, still thinking, puzzling it out until she had the answer.

Or so she thought.

"You need a perfect statue, right?" she said.

"Exactly." He drew a line with the pencil, noting how the feel of the table transferred itself up the shaft to his hand.

"Well, I have others." Her triumphant smile was radiant. "You may choose."

She should sculpt herself for posterity, Darius thought. If she did so, then he could carry it back to Olympus with him and have it always to remind him of the lovely woman who'd given him his life back.

He glanced around the open studio and saw none other.

"Where?"

"There's a beautiful one beside my bed."

It must be very fine indeed if she kept it so close. Six-year-old Rashida volunteered to fetch it and was back in a blink with a life-sized turtle, a small variety.

"You're proposing I spend the rest of my days eating insects and lumbering about with my home on my back?"

Rashida crawled onto his lap, giggling when the slippery satin sheet nearly dumped her on the floor, snuggling contentedly into his protective grasp. He couldn't recall ever holding a child before; he had none of his own and there weren't many on Olympus. She was soft, warm, and totally reliant on him not to let her tumble off. He'd never had someone rely on him before.

It was . . . nice.

"Darius? Did you hear me?" Alexandra said. He struggled to look attentive. "I said, after the auction, couldn't you leave the turtle and then take over this statue again?" She gestured at his body. "You know, the one you've got now."

"I *could*." He shuddered at the thought of turning into any statue again, ever. Voluntarily or otherwise. For what she was proposing, he'd have to do it two, no, three times. "But I won't."

"Maybe he doesn't like turtles," Rashida said.

"There's that clay statue," Billy said, turning to Darius. "It's not a turtle. How'd you like one of Aphrodite?"

"How'd you like to change into a girl?" Darius shot back.

"Y-you can't do that, can you?" Horrified, Billy stumbled through the words fearfully.

"No."

"Is the Minotaur male?" Maria asked, a bite in her voice. Unlike the other children, this one didn't like him, didn't approve of him, though he didn't know why. " 'Cause she's got a Minotaur. Horns and all."

Oh yeah, half bull, half man; he'd get lots of women that way. Which reminded him, he'd been here a full day now and hadn't thanked Alexandra properly. Awfully slow for him, considering how long he'd been out of action. He hoped he hadn't lost his touch.

Quite unintentionally, his gaze was drawn to Alexandra, immersed in a brainstorming session with the children trying to find him the perfect alternate statue. Just looking at her heated his blood. Puzzling, though, that that didn't happen yesterday in the park with the Greekettes. Not that he'd been immune to them, but they hadn't ignited this steady heat he was feeling inside him now. Alexandra had.

How odd.

"Sure, go get that one," she said to one of the kids, still planning his future.

"Enough!" He stood up, settling the small girl safely on his chair. "I don't want to change into anything. I don't want to be small. I don't want to be female. I don't want to be an animal. If these other statues are so perfect, auction them off."

"I promised them a life-sized god. It has to be you."

"Well, *I* want to be me." He spread both hands on his chest. "I'm very grateful to be me. Which reminds me. Alexandra, I picked this up yesterday with you in mind. A small token of my appreciation. I know it doesn't make up for the trouble I've caused you."

He proffered the diamond tennis bracelet he'd liberated

from one of the Greekettes at the park, dangling it in front of Alexandra's face.

She blinked.

"Wow," Maria said with feminine admiration.

"Holy cow," Billy said. "You know what kind of computer that would buy?"

Why wasn't she taking it from his hand? Wasn't it good enough for her? Big enough? *Women!*

"Is that real?" she asked.

"Of course it's real. I have no use for glass." Still, she didn't reach for it. "There will be more, I promise."

She stood up and started stacking dishes and trays, clearing tables again, which he recognized as a sign of agitation. He nodded at Selena, who directed her crew to clean up and go away, which they did instantaneously. Alexandra suddenly had empty hands.

Stunned, she landed on the seat of her chair, hard. She massaged her temples, talking to herself more than to him.

"Obviously I'm outgunned here. You want the statue, you've got the statue, there's nothing I can do about it. Okay, I accept that." She looked up at him then, with a steely gaze that spoke of her determination. "But I will not accept stolen jewelry." She surged to her feet. "And I will not have these children exposed to a thief! Now—"

"I am . . . not . . . a . . . thief," he enunciated clearly. He held up the bracelet. "These are mine. I own all gems above and below the ground—"

"Hey, unless your name's on the title to a diamond mine—"

"—until I give them away and, by the Styx, I assure you I never gave these to that girl in the park, nor any of those the women were wearing yesterday."

"I'll take 'em," Billy said, reaching for it.

Alexandra, her true colors surfacing, he thought smugly, snatched it out of Darius's grasp. Nothing like a little competitive edge to make a woman want something.

"Kids, make some found signs to put up in the park. Don't say it's diamonds, just a bracelet. Put my phone number on them. Maybe we can find the *owner*." She glared at Darius as she pocketed the bracelet.

"What are you gonna do?" Keiko asked.

"Me? Get on the phone and see if I can find another piece of marble. Oh, I know! Billy, can you get on the Internet and see what you can find? And while you're at it, see if there's a free lost and found board on the St. Louis site. Darius, can I see you in the other room?"

She headed for her bedroom.

Finally, Darius thought, feeling his blood heat in anticipation. Of course! She wanted to thank him for the diamonds in private.

He'd had his food. He'd had his wine. Now it was time to have Alexandra. Did she want it slow? He hoped she wanted it fast, because he'd waited a long time for this and didn't know if he could go slow. She knew the children were there, would be in the very next room. She must want it fast.

With a bounce in his step and a silent admonition to remember last night's vow to make love to her ten times a day, he followed.

10

A diamond tennis bracelet! Who did he think she was!
   Alex would've thrown the stolen goods back in Darius's face, but she wanted the owner to have *some* chance of getting it back. Darius seemed overly fond of collecting other people's expensive jewelry.

She should throw him, *the thief*, out on his ass. But now that she knew he and the statue were one and the same (she'd deny it to any rational adult), there was no way she was going to encourage him to leave, in spite of his attitude and the way he flaunted his shortcomings. Pacing the bedroom, waiting for him to join her, she reviewed what she knew to be true, as preposterous as that knowledge seemed to be, but there was no denying what she'd seen, what had happened.

Somehow Darius had reverted to marble last night. Definitely trapped, otherwise he'd never have endured the paint and forklift. Must have been pure hell for a guy with an ego the size of Texas.

If it happened once—if she could suspend disbelief that far, what was one more step?—it could happen again. Therein lay her chance, though she hadn't a clue how to use it. She'd work on that, but first she had to protect the children's immediate welfare.

Behind her, Darius's bare footsteps across the plank floor were barely audible, but discernible nonetheless. The man exuded a presence like none other. At least no one she'd met. Was that what charisma was? An inaudible, indefinable magnitude, quiet, but as effective as a round of trumpets announcing he'd entered the room?

The door closed and locked, and she knew without looking that he hadn't used his hands to do it. She spun around to give him a piece of her mind, a lecture about how important it was to set a good example in front of the children, and came face-to-face with Darius in the altogether, the red satin sheet pooled on the floor behind him, his erection standing as proud as the smirk on his face as it led him across the room toward her.

Her hand shot out in the universal stop sign. Her gaze was a little slower rising to the level of his face. Why, she hadn't seen a man that aroused since her ex-husband left . . . No, that wasn't right. Not since before her accident.

True to form, Darius ignored her stop sign, shot past her hand, scooped her up in his arms, his exuberant laugh all pride and primitive, dominant male. Lord, what a sight! For a split second, her carefully guarded feelings betrayed her as her heart soared and swelled with triumph, knowing that a man wanted her again.

Of course, he hadn't seen all of her yet.

No, not *yet*. Never *yet*. Even if she were attracted to him—she swore she wasn't!—he was going about this all wrong. He was strong, hands roaming everywhere, lips scorching a trail right behind.

"Hey, whoa, wait a minute," she said, not even aware at first that, as she spoke, the heel of her hand landed a quick pop on his nose. At his startled yelp, she rolled out of his grasp and landed on her feet. She needed to catch her breath, to put some space between them so this sizzle would dissipate, so she could think through whatever this was between them, this *heat* that made it difficult for her to think. With nothing better at hand, she put a chair between them, a simple wooden one piled high with clean laundry that never seemed to make it into nice little folded piles in dresser drawers.

It was that fast that a possible solution started to form in her mind. He had to have a *perfect* statue, right? She feinted left and right in turn, as needed, both of them circling the chair, spilling washcloths and underwear to lie in pastel pools on the darkened floorboards. If possible, he looked even more thrilled by the chase.

What if he—it?—became *im*perfect, say like a broken nose? Would he have to relinquish the statue? Not his nose, though. She didn't want to decrease the statue's value with a crooked nose staring a buyer in the face.

Caught off guard with this new supposition, this marvelous insight into another world for which she was totally unprepared, she darted to the left when she should have dodged to the right, losing traction on a pair of underpants. Darius caught her effortlessly, swallowing her up in the circle of his arms with a triumphant laugh, aligning the lengths of their bodies, crushing her breasts against his hard chest. Not much of a challenge, considering her whole mind was no longer against it.

Could she reach up and rip his perfect ear? Again, no, it would decrease the statue's value. A knee to the groin certainly wouldn't work, not the way she wanted. Hard to pull off, too, when her feet weren't even touching the floor.

His lips covered hers then. Oh God, gentler than she'd thought he'd be, considering how his mind seemed to be working on one track. Soothing.

Uh-oh, that was dangerous.

Think!

As he bent forward and her feet touched down again, his hands took on a life of their own, wandering from the back of her neck down to the swell of her hips, always pressing, always moving. Lord, but he played her like a concert pianist caressed ivory keys, and she feared she might start humming along, picking up his tune.

Concentrate!

Inching around to the sides now. Could she break his fingers? Wait for him to go for her breast, then grab a pinky, twist it back, throw her whole body into it? Or would she have to catch him unawares? What else could she break? Maybe stomp on his toes, smashing a couple of them. Where were her boots?

"Alexandra."

Oh no, no, don't say it like that. She'd be lost for sure if he did.

"Alexandra!" he whispered urgently against her lips.

There was a dreamy "mm?" in response.

Was that me?

"How does this come undone?" He was tugging at her jeans, the top button open, the fly still zipped.

She tried to push his hands away, but he'd have none of it. The zipper suddenly edged downward beneath his touch and—shit, she'd worn bikinis today—before she could stop it from exposing the horrible scar on her abdomen, Darius had lifted her shirt halfway over her head, trapping her hands. She froze, waiting for the inevitable gasp, the abrupt cessation of motion that would tell her he'd seen it.

"Ohhh," he said quietly as his hands stilled.

Alex's heart plummeted. No, she hadn't wanted him, but she could live without the rejection, thank you very much. Slowly, she worked her way back into her shirt and began pulling it down, her face burning with the heat of shame, the torment of having lived this moment before. Her eyes welled with tears she refused to shed in front of him.

"No. Wait."

He grasped the hem in one hand, gently traced the scar below her navel with the fingers of his other, until it disappeared beneath the top elastic of her plain underpants. It made no sense to wear bikinis, but as luck would have it, she'd grabbed them in the dark. His gaze flew up to hers, locking, all the playfulness gone from it now. Tucked away somewhere, never to be seen again. Not that she wanted to.

She wasn't as adept at lying to herself as she'd like to be.

"Who did this to you?"

The fierceness of his query startled her into muteness, into awareness that something very different was going on here. Something she thought she wanted but wasn't ready to face.

"Alexandra, who harmed you like this?" He dropped to his knees in front of her and pressed his lips to the puckered skin.

Oh good Lord, she couldn't breathe, could only feel his hands and lips, even the brush of his eyelashes, across her belly. There were no words to describe what his gentle attention was doing to her, to years of being too afraid to long and hope and pray.

Then, lifting his tender gaze to hers, he said, "Tell me, and I will torture him before I kill him."

The dam of emotion broke. Shorn up by years of practice, tears burst free, streaming down her cheeks, sobs catching in her throat. Oh, she'd cried over this before, many times. But never for this reason. Never because her scar brought out the tenderness in a man.

"Tell me," he repeated, and she did. Told him all about the auto accident, the damage, the surgery. The husband who rejected her, who said she was so ugly now, no man would want her. She sobbed into his shoulder, wearing herself out, knowing he'd come to his senses and set her aside and leave her as soon as he could escape her clinging embrace, but not caring, because right now, this just felt so *right*.

She knew men like this existed, of course. Fictional ones. She'd read about them in books, seen them in movies. But when it came to actually finding the real McCoy, she hadn't been so lucky.

Until now. Until he forgot about sex and just held her, whispering tender words about what he'd do to her ex if he ever met him, some of which were quite creative, if not archaic.

"I could turn him into an ass," he offered.

"He's already an ass."

"A real one that eats grass and carries heavy burdens and brays. I'd sell him to a cruel master who'd beat him every day."

"Could you neuter him, too?"

"That goes unsaid."

His brisk reply made her chuckle, made her realize that he wasn't just a playboy with a huge ego, but a god with a heart of gold.

And the damned thing was, she couldn't keep him.

* * *

Darius wandered through the wide, ornate halls of the Ladies' Club, smiling benignly at each woman he came across. He spoke not, preferring to dwell on what he'd felt while kneeling before Alexandra. In the past, he'd been aware that he'd angered mortal men over their wives, and he'd had concern over said women's welfare from time to time. But never like this. Never had he felt such anger, such *hatred* for whoever had done that to Alexandra, such intense longing to put someone to the sword. Slowly.

When the club members began skittering out of his way, he realized he needed to replace his scowl with something more attractive. He needed to concentrate on something else, like what he was here for. The ladies had something he wanted.

At first, their guard was down and they'd start to preen. They laughed delightfully, probably at the red satin sheet, but he had nothing better. Then they went through various reactions. Some got huffy. Some expressed confusion, asking him if he was promoting the auction, and if so, did that mean the statue had been recovered? Others sidled up to him, close, bathing him in the heavenly scents of their perfumes, and asked if he was available. He smiled, answered noncommittally, and continued his stroll, leaving each lady several carats lighter without her knowledge.

Was he available? The mere fact that he hadn't jumped into the nearest closet with several of the younger ones left him puzzling that very question. Now, the thought of Alexandra and him in a closet—

"Psst! Dare."

"Yes?" Darius continued walking, mentally cursing his brother's timing.

"Aphrodite wants to talk to you in the ballroom. You know, the same room where you came alive."

The ballroom had been dried out and put back together. Everything was still there, waiting: the snowy linen-draped tables; the grapevine-wrapped columns; the paintings, including Zeus and his thunderbolt, which reminded Darius he should probably go visit his father, but he was afraid to stray too far from Alexandra. Just in case.

Aphrodite appeared on the stage in a flowing white gown and a delicate circlet of violets crowning her head, looking only slightly older than when he'd last seen her. Maturity became her. When he offered her his hand to step down, she flung herself into his arms.

"Oh, Dare, I thought I'd never see you again."

He'd never hugged his sister before. He found he liked it. With joy, he laughed and twirled her around, making her shriek girlishly before setting her on her feet. "What are you doing here?"

"Why, I'm fine, thank you." She'd always been after him to learn the social graces. "You're looking well."

"All right," he said, laughing as he gave in to her subtle demand. He held her at arm's length. "Why, you're even more beautiful than I remember. Now tell me, what are you doing here?"

She sighed in frustration, though her smile ruined the effect. "I guess that'll have to do for now. But don't think I'm giving up on you. Which do you want first? The advice or the bad news."

"News is Hermes' job."

"Yes, well, he and Apollo won that stupid bet, so that means I have to tell you."

"So, times have changed on Olympus also."

"Oh, you have no idea. But that can wait. Come, sit beside me. Let me tell you about Cytus first—promise you won't yell at me—and then I'll tell you how some things are still the same."

He joined her on the edge of the low stage, where they were hidden by tables and not likely to draw attention should someone peek into the room. Aphrodite laid out the background of how Cytus came to take over Darius's ruler-ship of gems while he was in exile. How he'd abused the privilege, giving away far too many gems to mortals, deflat-ing their value and, in part, contributing to the gods losing superiority in mortals' eyes.

She obviously didn't want to dwell on any of this, but ended with an uncharacteristic "Believe me, Cytus is one mean son of a bitch. He's caused the rest of us nothing but trouble—do you know he resorts to *blackmail*?—but Zeus won't do anything about it because then he'd have to find an-other god to take over the rulership, and heaven forbid, he's far too busy playing with his computers to take the time. So it's up to you."

"Me? I'm having enough trouble here with one mortal woman, and you and my brothers want me to deal with some young pup who needs his ears boxed? Gang up on him. That's what you used to do to me."

"But you were never dangerous. We need you, Dare, please, you're the only one who can help. Put Cytus in his place. Now. Once and for all. Dethrone the brat. Take back your rulership—before it's too late." She brushed her hands together, as if dusting them off. "There, I've explained it to you. Hermes can get off my back. Now, about you and Alexandra."

Cytus had to be pretty high up in the family to gain such

an important rulership, yet he couldn't be too dangerous if Aphrie switched gears so quickly, so Darius followed her lead and dismissed him.

"This sounds like the advice part."

"Well, don't take this the wrong way, Dare, but it looks like you need my help if you're going to get her."

He almost stuck his nose up in the air and said, *Hmmpf! I never needed your help before.* But he quelled that reaction because, of course, he needed it now. Desperately. Slumping forward under the weight of his failure, he rested his elbows on his knees.

"I don't understand her at all," he admitted. "I offered sex. Women always want to have sex with me. She didn't. Then I offered to avenge her. Women like that, don't they?"

"Sometimes."

"Apparently not Alexandra," he said wryly. His anger was twofold. If she'd died from her wounds, he wouldn't exist. But more than that, how could someone hurt such a caring woman? She was beautiful, talented, open-minded, good with children—

Hm, he'd never cared about that last one before. Why now? Why all these unsettling changes? Life used to be so simple.

"What you haven't realized yet, little brother, is that you want Alexandra for a very different reason."

"I want to repay her."

Aphrodite smiled with warm compassion and patted his knee tenderly.

"I know you think you do, Dare, but face it. If all you wanted to do was repay her, you would've left her a pile of gems and gone your merry way already."

"I tried that. She won't take them." She'd never wear the bracelet; she'd comb the park trying to return it. "I never met a woman who wouldn't take gems. They usually demand more."

Aphrodite saw the need for a different approach. "Why do you care? You could just leave them in a drawer and head back to Olympus, you know."

"But then she—" He paused to gather his thoughts, but it didn't help. "But she needs—" He sprang to his feet and started pacing between the tables and the stage, but that didn't help him sort things out either. He turned abruptly. "I need fresh air."

Aphrodite followed him out to the garden, where they walked among the roses, their scent strong, almost overpowering in the heavy air. With a crooked, knowing smile, she asked, "Is it helping?"

"What?"

"The fresh air. Is it clearing your poor, muddled, male brain?"

"Okay, if you're so smart, you explain it."

"I'm not the goddess of love for nothing, you know."

"Love has nothing to do with this."

She let that slide for the moment. "Your feelings for Alexandra are different than for any other woman in your past, am I right? Oh, don't answer that, I know I am. I won't use the L-word because I know that would lead to the C-word and totally freak you out, and I want you to hear me out."

"Aphrie!" When had she learned to talk like this?

She pressed her fingers against his lips, hushing him so she could continue. "Even a playboy like you has to admit that your feelings for her are different. Right?"

She pinned him with a stern gaze until he nodded, then she removed her hand, but held up her index finger to forestall any comments.

They strolled past the gardener, who watched them curiously at first, and then presented Aphrodite with a white rose. It was at that perfect stage, not quite open, with beads of moisture shimmering along its delicate edges, begging to be touched.

Now why did that remind him of Alexandra?

"What a nice man," Aphrie said, and Darius was grateful for the interruption. "A few relationship problems . . . remind me to help him later. Where was I? Oh yes. You want to repay her, but you want it to be meaningful. So you have to understand the woman within. Listen closely, because this is where things are still the same, and you never got it before. You have to discover Alexandra's true needs, Dare. Only when you know those can you meet them. Only then can you truly repay her."

"Her needs? She says she needs the statue. If I give her that, then I haven't repaid her at all, because I'd have nothing to repay her *for*."

"Her *true* needs, Darius. A statue's just a hunk of marble. No one needs a hunk of marble to be happy."

"Worked for me."

Her eyebrows arched gracefully. "Did it?"

Her *true* needs, Darius mused as Aphrodite left him alone to figure out what he should do next.

"She's right, you know," the gardener said.

He placed a hand on one knee and levered himself to his feet. Something about the way he moved bothered Darius, but he was hard pressed to say what exactly.

"I've known Alex all her life. Well, 'cept for a coupla the early years." He shook his head slowly, keeping some thoughts to himself. "She thinks she has to be perfect. She thinks everything she does has to be perfect."

More perfect than she was?

"I guess I'm partly to blame, so I don't mind speaking up now. Your friend's right. Ain't no way a hunka marble's gonna give that girl the happiness she deserves. But I have to wonder why you're here, why now?" He shook his trowel beneath Darius's nose. "I know it damn well better to make her happy."

Darius glared down at him, but the old man didn't scare so easily.

"You think I'm worried you'll turn me into fertilizer?" Darius asked, exasperated.

Something had turned him back into a statue last night. Possibly some*one*, like Zeus. If Cytus were truly pissed off over the rulership deal, he'd bear watching out for.

"Nope, ain't saying that. I may be older'n you, and smaller and weaker. But just remember, I know how things work here."

Her *true* needs, Darius mused late that afternoon. He'd spent most of the day within a few blocks of the club, observing women, trying to assess what made them happy as they went about their errands. They drove all different kinds of cars, wore all different kinds of clothing. They traveled singly and in packs. He wasn't sure any of them knew what made them happy, as he'd stopped a few and asked, but hadn't gotten a direct answer. Unlike the ladies at the club or at the picnic yesterday, most eyed his red toga with suspicion and gave him a wide berth.

Everywhere he looked, it was just as he'd seen on television. Words. Literally millions of them. Printed on shop windows, doors, and sides of buildings. On cars, trucks, and buses. On banners flying from tall poles flanking the main street, and metal signs on shorter poles doing the same. Tiny words in neat columns on papers folded and stacked in metal boxes located at street corners. Even after two weeks of television, he couldn't decipher them.

Never before had he been faced with puzzles he couldn't solve quickly, and now, in this new life for which he'd waited so long, he was faced with two of them. Words, and Alexandra's true needs. If he solved one, would the other fall into place?

Eventually he was stopped by a solid man in dark blue, one of the police officers who'd been in the park last night. He asked polite but firm questions. What's your name? Do you know where you are? What's your business here?

"I'm trying to find out what women need."

"Get in line."

Darius looked around, but there was no line. "But—"

"He's with us, Officer."

Darius recognized T.J. and Maria. Both seventeen, blond, still in team sweatpants from cross country practice, with matching tops tied around their waists. They were the home's two oldest residents, and from the strained look on Alexandra's face each time they left her studio, they were the two she worried over the most, though he didn't know why. They were quiet children, never sassed her, always helped with the youngsters. Maybe if he knew what trouble awaited them, he'd have a clue how to make Alexandra happy.

He wished Aphrodite would put in an appearance and at least let him know if he was on the right track.

"Yes, I'm with them," he said eagerly.

"Not me, you're not," Maria said, still looking upon him as no better than horse droppings.

The officer was about to pursue that when T.J. again spoke up for him.

"Better move along, then," the officer said. "The store owners are complaining about you chasing their customers away."

"But—"

Two more women got out of a car, gave the driver some money, and entered a shop. They reminded him of the women who'd stuffed his cloth with money and small cards, the latter of which had words printed on one side and scrawled across the other. What had they said?

Darius looked after these two women longingly, as if they might hold a clue, but he no longer knew what to ask.

"But I haven't found out what women truly need."

The officer scratched the back of his head. "Good luck with that. But do it someplace else. And tell your fraternity buddies that I don't mind a little Greek Week fun, but don't hassle the shoppers."

"Yeah, come on, Darius, back to the studio," T.J. said, bouncing the back of his hand off Darius's arm, the way mortal men communicated with each other, touching but not touching.

On the short walk back to the Club grounds, T.J. and Maria didn't let him stop any more women.

"You can't just do that, man. Not dressed like that," T.J. said. "You'll scare 'em."

"I didn't scare the ladies at the club."

"That's different, they had a Greek theme going. They thought you were part of it."

As at the picnic, Darius realized.

"Oh let him," Maria said. "Maybe one of them'll run him over."

"I just wanted to find out . . ." No, he couldn't tell children what he was doing. Though T.J. was friendly and almost grown. "You seem to be very close to Alexandra," he said instead.

"She's like our big sister," T.J. said.

"Then you know what she—"

"Yeah, if it weren't for her, the home'd have to close next month. It's an old building. Things keep breaking. Administrators think foster homes are better."

"We thought that was all taken care of, until *you* came along," Maria said, "and took the statue."

"Ah, that's why you don't like me."

"No, that's why I *hate* you." She sniffed and ran ahead.

"She was counting on Alex's support to help her through med school," T.J. explained. "She wants to be a doctor, maybe a pediatrician or an orthopedist. Family Services doesn't provide any help after we're twenty-one."

"That's what the statue was for?"

"Nah, it was to keep the home open. Alex was counting on her reputation for Maria's tuition. Mine too."

"Oh," Darius said, wondering why there was a little pull at his heart, and what it might mean. He hadn't any experience with children. Why did he suddenly care about the twins' higher education?

Because they were important to Alexandra?

They arrived at the studio just behind Claudia, who was dressed all in white. Alexandra would have an alliterative pet name for that, like Winsome White. Only hers would be better. He almost missed standing in front of her, privy to all her quiet mutterings. At least then he knew what she was thinking.

"Psst! Dare, wait a minute."

Darius stopped outside to see what his brother wanted.

"Got an urgent message for you from Aphrie."

"Ha! You know what she's got me trying to do? She's got

me trying to find out what women want. By Zeus, if I knew what women wanted—"

"Wrong," Hermes intoned, and the single word caught Darius's attention more effectively than trying to bellow over him.

"Wrong? I'll tell you what's wrong. Me, a god, having to solve an age-old riddle—"

"Would you shut up?" Hermes waited until Darius vented a little steam. "Aphrie says to tell you—"

"She's here? 'Cause I've got some questions for her."

Hermes sighed impatiently. "If she were here, would I be doing this? She outlined for me what you'd probably do— and I must say, she came extraordinarily close this time— and then told me what to tell you. Are you going to listen or not?"

"Proceed."

"She says to tell you it's not what *women* want, you dolt—her words, not mine—it's what *Alexandra* wants that counts. What *she* needs. Concentrate! Oh, and one more thing. Times've changed—"

"So I'm learning."

"You might reconsider the toga. You've heard the saying, 'When in Rome . . . '?"

"Yes, recently, I believe."

"Well, Dare, when in 2004 . . ." Hermes fluttered upward. "We love you, brother."

"Yeah, sure you do," Darius muttered. Cytus was probably blackmailing the both of them. So let them suffer awhile; Darius had problems of his own he considered more important than what he was or wasn't wearing. Major problems.

He stepped into the studio to meet his. Unexpectedly, he was just in time to see Claudia, decked out in a matching set of fake rubies from earlobes to fingers, surreptitiously slip

Alexandra's brand new diamond tennis bracelet into the side pocket of her white jacket. Alexandra didn't see this, as her back was turned while she and half a dozen of the smallest children put their art supplies away, tucking them into low cabinets beneath the telephone.

"I'd love to help you," Claudia was saying, "but, dear, you know Geoffrey believes the only way to help others is to—"

" 'Let them help themselves.' I know, I know."

"I'd give you some money, but honestly, I have to account for every dollar. Paying this agency to find our father is straining my creative money management, believe me," she said with a wicked smile.

Darius noted that she patted her pocket nervously, as if to reassure herself that she had what she'd come for and no one was the wiser.

"They're good, but very expensive," Claudia said. "I'm supposed to meet one of them in an hour with another payment. But I'm sure it'll be worth it. I just know we'll know any day now," she continued, bubbling over with excitement, backing toward the door, bumping into Darius. "Oops. Oh. Well, gotta go, won't keep you any longer. Just think, in a couple of days, we could actually be talking to our father!"

He was impressed with how quickly she got out the door on those high heels.

Finished with her task, Alexandra stood up and brushed her hair out of her eyes. Not that it needed it, but on seeing Darius, a pretty blush stole across her face, and she was probably trying to distract him from noticing.

How to find out what she wanted?

No, that wasn't right, he remembered. Aphrie said to find out what Alexandra *truly needed*. Sounded the same to him, but his sister was the relationship expert. He could follow all that talk show advice and try to talk it out, but modern men were having enough trouble learning that technique and he didn't have a modern bone in his body. Undoubtedly, he'd stumble through it. He might even anger her, and then how would he ever find out what she wanted?

"I can't believe Claudia didn't snap your head off," she said. "She's really very mad at you."

He carefully laid the diamond bracelet on her worktable, spotlighting it, displaying it to best advantage, drawing her attention against her will.

"Better keep a closer eye on that."

"How'd you get—hey!" Her blush forgotten, she glared at him suspiciously as she grabbed it up. "I told you I'm returning that to its rightful owner. You keep your hands off." Her blush deepened at her double entendre.

"Yes, well, better tell that to your sister."

"Claudia?" She glanced toward the door. "Don't be silly. She's got more diamonds and emeralds and—didn't you see the rubies she was just wearing? What would she want with a little ol' diamond tennis bracelet?" She barely paused for a breath. "Nothing, that's what."

He was just about to tell her the truth about her sister's supposed gems, when instinct told him that wasn't the way to accomplish the task Aphrie had set out for him. Instead he picked up the little girl shyly tugging on his toga and settled her on his hip.

Alexandra's icy aquamarine gaze softened to liquid warmth.

By Zeus, I believe I just scored points!

"Mind if I hang around awhile?" he said. "It's about time for . . ." The television blared on, surfed through channels, and landed on *Jeopardy!* He beamed with satisfaction and said, "Yes, I thought so," as he headed for the couch. If Alexandra thought his holding Rashida was so sweet, wait'll she saw how attentive he was as the little girl taught him some of the printed words.

Alex rolled her eyes, not wanting Darius to know how happy she was to have him back. Embarrassed, sure, over this morning's fiasco in the bedroom. Crying on his shoulder like that—what was she thinking?

Well, she hadn't been. She'd been reacting. Here was a man—okay, not a man, but as close as she was going to get—who wanted her, who didn't mind touching her, who actually seemed emotionally *moved* by her scar, toward her, not away, and what was her plan? To injure the son of a bitch and see if that'd turn him back to stone.

It was that or face the fact that, outside of the nicely boxed meals Chef Ramon gave her nearly every day, her refrigerator was as empty as her wallet. She'd tucked Darius's tip away in the bottom of a drawer; it was for the children or dire emergencies, whichever came first. Without a statue to auction off, she'd need to get a job to pay the bills, which meant she couldn't devote all her time to more sculpting, which meant the home, and the children, and oh, it was just too depressing. Better to wallop him in the back of the head with a hammer before she remembered how comfortable she'd felt in his arms. No, not comfortable . . . *cherished*.

If it worked, great, she'd have her statue, but not a man. No change there. If not, he'd think she was mentally unbalanced, run the other way, and she still wouldn't have a man. No change there, either.

Besides, he wasn't a man, he was a goddamn statue, and how perverted was that? She wasn't interested in humping the marble, of course, but she'd always, always, for the rest of her life, wonder what it would've been like to make love with the living, breathing, oh-so-tender stand-in who hadn't backed away in revulsion.

So, here he was, back in her studio—*thank you, God*—presenting her with this golden opportunity. His full attention would be on the TV. All she had to do was get rid of the witnesses. And get this done before she changed her mind. Because, God Almighty, she wanted to change her mind.

"Okay, kids, time to head home."

11

Alex received a rousing chorus of "nu-uhs" as Kesia, Daniel, and three small children vaulted with great theatrics onto the couch, landing beside and on top of Darius. At first he looked quite uncomfortable, almost horrified, Alex thought, but as six-year-old Rashida burrowed under his bare arm and snuggled into his side, he seemed to soften beneath her trust and morph into a couch-daddy. A pretty strange-looking one in a toga, but the kids didn't seem to mind, so why should she?

Besides, if she was successful, he wouldn't be here much longer. She hoped that wouldn't mean getting caught up in his embrace again, because that played havoc with still-tender emotions, not to mention tempting her out-of-practice hormones way too much.

There was so much at stake. She'd have to catch him off guard.

Rashida extended her tiny index finger and delicately traced the diamond brooch pinned on the toga to hold the single shoulder in place. Alex didn't even have to ask if it was real. She should demand he turn it over right now, so she could ask around the club and find the owner, but Rashida was so mesmerized by it, outlining it over and over, and Alex didn't want to deny the little girl such a simple pleasure. She'd get it from him later.

Selena appeared for a short while, passing out healthy snacks to the children, startling Alex, giving her pause. When she and his other little handmaidens were out of sight, were they watching, always waiting, always prepared to appear instantly? Would they know it was she who injured their, what, their boss? Their god? Would they intervene? Or take revenge?

Hm, so many variables; so little time.

Were there other risks? Probably. She wasn't experienced at plotting against people, much less a god who probably had powers she hadn't seen yet.

"Who was Alexander the Great?" Darius chorused to one of the answers with Daniel, a pudgy, pale, round-faced nine-year-old with a smirky smile and a Harry Potter haircut.

Whatever the risks, Daniel and Kesia and Billy and dozens of others' futures were definitely more important. Not just the children living at the Children's Home now, but many to come, too.

Okay, so she had to get everyone out of here, sneak up on him, and do the deed.

"Why don't you move the couch closer to the TV?" she suggested, trying not to sound as devious as she felt. "It's so far away back there by the wall. You can move it out here into the center of the room." *The better for me to get behind you after they're all gone, my dear.*

"What is the Nile?" Darius answered.

"How'd you know that?" Kesia groaned.

"He paid attention in school?" Daniel suggested, while everyone else shushed him for the next selection.

They weren't shushed for long, however, because Darius took Alex's suggestion and telekinetically slid the couch out to the center of the room and lined it up in front of the television, much to the children's delight. Irrepressible Rashida bounced up and down and begged him to make it go again, until he promised her he would, later, at which point she contentedly settled onto his lap. Wasn't that sweet, the way he cuddled her?

Don't go there. It'd do her no good to note his better points.

"Who is Mickey Mouse?" the kids chorused.

"Who was Steamboat Willy?" Darius countered, garnering looks of amazement from the kids when they found out they were wrong, and he, a stranger to this time and place, was correct.

Alex was pretty amazed herself, but refused to weaken her resolve. There was nothing she could do for a while but watch him, study him, debate and discard various plans of attack.

More questions, and a high five between Darius and Daniel.

A high five? "For a guy who bit the dust—literally, I might add—three thousand years ago, you sure know a lot of current stuff," Alex remarked.

He tossed her a playful wink and sent the TV surfing through channels (the children all yelled, "Hey!"), reminding her of just how much culture exposure he'd had while she'd finished the statue.

Oh yeah, she really had to do him in.

* * *

Darius wasn't born yesterday. He knew Alexandra was up to something, he just didn't know what. Mind reading wasn't his specialty; if it had been, he'd have been able to answer Aphrie's riddle by now.

What did Alexandra truly need?

Well, she obviously loved the children and did all she could to help them. That's what the statue had been intended for—their benefit. But there were other ways to help. For instance, after Darius had questioned ten answers in a row, Daniel shook his head and said, "Boy, I bet you're good at homework, too."

So when *Jeopardy!* ended and Alex was ushering them toward the door, Darius said, "Daniel, did you need help with your homework?"

"Yeah!" He slipped free of his backpack and retrieved his geography book from inside it before Alex could stop him, and try to stop him she did. He zipped across the room, eluding her, and Darius settled on the edge of the couch with the youngster, side by side, mentally whipping the coffee table over as a desk.

"He has to go home now. With the group," Alexandra said pointedly.

"This'll just take a few minutes," Darius said, keeping his head down so she wouldn't see the conspiratorial wink he shared with Daniel.

"Then I wanna see the kittens," Rashida said. The rest of the group concurred excitedly.

"But—"

"You promised," Kesia whined. "If we wait any longer, we won't be able to catch them."

Sabrina, the feral cat with fur the color of marbled mud, and her mixed brood of five kittens had captivated the children's attention for weeks. Rescue and adoption to loving homes was their goal, as if transferring their own need for parents to the kittens.

Alex hadn't had any psychology beyond one requisite course she'd taken, but even she knew the kids needed to do this to feel, in even the smallest measure, somewhat in control of their lives. But from an early age, the kittens weren't cuddly and friendly, more likely to hide and hiss. Billy printed information off the Internet about taming wild-born kittens, and now everyone knew they had to wait until weaning, take them home where they could be monitored, and wait a few days for the kittens, who are naturally curious, to approach them.

Alexandra sighed. "Okay, let's go see how they're doing. But then you have to go home."

They all agreed. She went with them through the kitchen and into the attached garage, which wasn't what Darius wanted because, if he was going to impress her with taking an interest in the children, she had to be there to see it.

"You want to go see the kittens, too?" he asked Daniel.

"Nah, that's girl stuff. I don't understand this page about France and England." He pressed the tip of his finger against the black letters on the page.

"Um, read it to me," Darius said. "Slowly. Use your finger to follow the words."

"But I'm not supposed to—"

"It's for me. I . . . I can't, uh . . ."

Daniel blinked. "You need glasses?" he asked with disbelief.

"What of it?" No need to let a mortal, even a small one, know he could do something a god couldn't.

Ten minutes later, Daniel understood more about France and England than he thought possible, Darius was no closer to understanding the printed language, and everyone else returned with an open box of snarling, hissing kittens. In spite of his earlier disdain, Daniel was instantly off the couch, begging to hold one.

"Watch out for her claws," Kesia said, handing him a tiny tortoiseshell furball with the attitude of a cornered lion.

Alexandra hovered about, and Darius studied her, trying to figure out both what she was up to and what he could do to give her whatever it was she needed. Life was getting more complicated by the minute. Perhaps he should have spent more time on Earth over the past hundred years. He might have learned something valuable. If he hadn't imploded first from frustration.

"Where does Selena go?" Alexandra asked. "When she's not waiting on you, I mean."

"Wherever she wants."

"So she's not . . . *around*?"

"Learning more mortal female tricks from you, you mean? No."

"Oh." She smiled slyly. "Come on, kids, time to go. You don't want to be late and make the others wait."

The children all groaned, "Oh all right," the way only children can.

While Kesia took a kitten in turn from each one and placed it back into the box with its mewling, hissing siblings, Daniel handed his to Alex. "Watch her claws," he said.

"Yes, I know—oh, Darius didn't get a turn, did you?" She smiled at him so sweetly, totally at odds with the maternal cooing and wicked gleam in her eye. She dropped the kitten onto his stomach, a move guaranteed to bring out every tiny, sharp claw.

His thin, silky toga was no match for the kitten as it alternately hissed and tried to climb its way to the highest possible perch—his head. Darius jumped to his feet. The children scrambled after the kitten, on the run.

"What in Hades did you . . . do . . . ?"

His face felt heavy. His speech slowed. And why was Alexandra staring at his chest?

Slowly, and with great effort, bending his head forward, he could see his toga was awry, his broad chest nearly bare. Except for the drops of blood seeping through tiny punctures.

"Oh my my," Alexandra said airily. "Whatever happened?"

Quick as a wink, she was all over him, moving his left arm here, his right arm there, turning his wrist, crooking a finger. As he grew heavier and heavier, she worked faster, molding him back into the position in which she'd first sculpted the once-perfect statue.

Oh, Alexandra. His heart felt heaviest of all; a massive, immovable stone lodged deep within his chest.

When she could no longer budge any part of him, she folded her hands in front of her and whispered, "Oh please please please don't be . . ." Much to his mortification, now that he could do nothing about it, she lifted the edge of his toga and checked him out. "Thank you, God."

How could you do this to me?

She stood back and studied his face, frowning and *tsk*ing quietly to herself. "Well, it'll have to do."

What? What's wrong with it? If he were going to be stuck in it for the rest of eternity, he preferred it not be ugly. Being upstairs in some museum would be a heck of a lot better than being shunted off to some dark basement. Not much, but better.

"See you later, big guy."

She rested her hand softly on his arm. Almost longingly, or did he imagine that? No no, he was sure it was a tender touch. Wasn't it? Oh, damn it to Hades, he could barely feel it.

"Okay, kids, I'll walk back with you," she called jubilantly.

No sooner was she out the door—tossing one last smirky smile of defeat over her shoulder—with kids and kittens alike, than Darius was telekinetically sorting through the tools of her trade, tossing them off shelves and out of boxes and cabinets, searching, searching.

"Aha!" he said, when at last he found the diamond paste and a soft pad. Just what he needed to fix himself.

It was only a matter of moments, though, before he realized he couldn't see what he was doing. Stuck in the statue, with his head tilted to its original, sculpted, proud position, he found that the puncture wounds on his chest were no more visible to him than his feet. He needed help if he was to win over the one person on whom his life depended—Alexandra. And he needed it now.

"Hermes!" he roared.

Cytus wasn't alone in his bid to keep his rulership over gems. He had spies, one of whom had relayed a conversation between Hermes and Zeus, in which Hermes had tried to convince Zeus that Darius had beaten the curse by fair means and should no longer be hampered by turning back into a statue. Zeus was old and wise, changed the subject, and soon had Hermes admitting that Darius had bribed him with half his fortune, even though Hermes maintained every word was true and he didn't need bribing.

With this information in hand, Cytus reassessed the situation. If Darius was so willing to give up half his wealth to stay alive, perhaps he'd be willing to give it all up to forestall a fight.

Not that Cytus was afraid of a fight, but why not take the easy route, right? With this in mind, and now that Darius was immobile and had to listen to him, Cytus dropped in for a little visit.

"Mm," he said grimly, circling Darius slowly, taking his time for effect.

"What?" Darius growled. "Where's Hermes?"

"Oh, there was an urgent message from Aphrodite to Hera." Or so Cytus had led him to believe. "But first, I've come to make you an offer."

"Who are you to offer me anything?" he demanded, sounding dubious and hopeful at the same time.

"Cytus, ruler of gems." He bowed mockingly. Over Darius's sharp expletive, Cytus grinned wickedly, adding, "Your replacement. Ready to hear my offer now?"

"You have nothing I want."

"I believe there's a small matter of"—he paused for effect—"your old rulership?"

"It's still mine, you insolent young twit. It'll always be mine."

Cytus laughed. "Not in the shape you're in."

"Won't be this way for long." Not so haughty now.

"Last chance, Darius. Your *supposed* claim to the gems in exchange for your life. What'll it be?"

"You'd better get out of here before Alexandra gets back."

Cytus chuckled at the mere thought that he might somehow be concerned about Alexandra seeing him. He poked around on the worktable, sorting through her tools.

"Must be annoying, a god one minute, a statue the next.

Back and forth, back and forth. Tell me, have you found out yet what causes it?" Not that he gave a flying fig. "Cat got your tongue, huh?"

It was damned difficult carrying on a conversation with a statue that had no facial expressions, no body language, and muttered something that sounded like, "You don't know the half of it."

"Well, no matter. I know getting broken got you into this mess. Surely the same state will keep you out of my hair." He glanced around, then grinned tauntingly. "Too bad there's no cliff to toss you over. Remember that, Darius? Remember how it felt to find out you were stuck in the marble and couldn't save yourself?"

"What would you know? You weren't even born yet."

"Ah, but I can imagine. You plummeting toward the rocks . . . Tell me, do statues fall headfirst, or kind of end over end?" No reply. "Hm, I could find out. There's a window upstairs, one over the drive." He paused again, wishing there would be some look of fear on Darius's face, but of course that was like hoping to see a rock cry. "Nah, too much trouble."

From the table, he selected a hammer.

"This will do nicely instead, I think." He tested its weight in his grasp. "Yes, I'm sure of it. A few missing appendages and, whoops," he said, laughing coldly, approaching the statue slowly so as to cause the most trepidation, "no more Darius."

He could feel the tug at the hammer; Darius's feeble telekinetic attempt to rid him of it.

"You'll have to do better than that." He stopped in front of the statue. "Oh, can't?" He *tsk*ed. "Too bad."

He touched Darius's upraised hand with one of his own,

noting the genetic similarities, measuring the distance. He'd never used a hammer before, but it couldn't be too difficult.

"Should've accepted my offer, Darius," he said, swinging the hammer in a downward arc.

12

Man? Or marble?

Alex lagged a few paces behind the children as they walked back to the home, mulling over how to handle her dilemma. She barely heard them arguing over the best way to carry the box of kittens, the best way to handle them once they got there, the best way to handle the change from mother's milk and dead mice to kitten food.

If only her problem was as simple to solve as theirs. Yes, the statue was back. But would it stay that way? It had changed too often now for her to hold her breath on that outcome.

And yes, as of now, it was in good form overall. She'd made all the necessary postural corrections she could before he'd frozen up, and basically, given the alternative, she was pleased with them. Thank heavens he wasn't the kind of man who passed out at the sight of his own blood, because she had no idea how she'd ever market a life-sized, supine nude with its eyes rolled back in its head. She'd be the laughingstock of the art world, and she wasn't sure that was any better than being thought a crooked sculptor who took charity money and didn't produce a work of art, at the expense of innocent orphans.

God, it sounded worse when she analyzed it!

At the last minute, she'd even managed to tilt his head up into the proud, chin-upraised position she'd originally sculpted. But there was that little matter of the sad look on his face, the unspeakable grief in his eyes. The end result would be breathtaking—if he were a king looking over a bloody battlefield, proud of winning the war, but disheartened by all the men he'd lost. With all the publicity on her statue of Darius—long-lost son of Zeus, god of gems, playboy—it was a little too late in the game to claim she'd sculpted a despondent king instead.

Overall, she had what she wanted. Why then did Darius's anguish—which was so obviously painful—plague her? Hang heavy on her mind? He wasn't happy as a statue; he'd do anything to reverse the situation.

She shouldn't care, she told herself. He was meant to be auctioned off for the children. He was created *solely* for their benefit.

But he's not just a hunk of marble anymore, she grudgingly admitted to herself. Sure, he had feelings when he was alive. Remember how he was cuddling Rashida on the couch? How happy he and Daniel had been as they played along with *Jeopardy?* How tender he'd been when he'd kissed her scar?

And when he'd tempted her with the cherry pastry, those certainly hadn't been marble lips he'd pressed against hers. Warm, soft, his touch so gentle, it almost tickled.

Don't go there, an inner voice warned.

It'd be easier to think he didn't have any of those same

feelings when he was marble, but she knew he did. Why else would he keep coming back? Oh, not for her, of course; never for her.

Then there was the conversation she'd had earlier with Claudia. Alex suddenly realized how precarious her own position was. She needed to build a nest egg, and fast. Working part-time would limit the hours she could put into her art, but that couldn't be helped. She only had to make sure it wouldn't cut in on the time she spent with the children.

It was dinnertime when they arrived at TCH; everyone was in the dining room.

"Alex, honey, I heard all about it," Mrs. Wallis said. She'd been in charge of the Children's Home since Alex had arrived as a four-year-old, and had aged gracefully into a diminutive, white-haired, no-nonsense woman who was still sharp as a tack. She left her place at the table now, putting her arms around Alex. It felt just as comforting as when she'd been half Mrs. Wallis's size, not the other way around. "How are you?"

"Oh, okay."

"Like you look okay," she scoffed, and dragged Alex by the hand into the kitchen. "Haven't I taught you that sharing your troubles cuts them in half?"

"Not this time."

"Let's try it again. How are you? Really."

Maybe it would help somewhat, help her work through her tumultuous thoughts. Couldn't hurt, she supposed.

"Not good," she admitted, as they settled on stools at a scarred wooden table set against the white-tiled wall. Already it felt better just to admit that much out loud to someone who cared. "I have the statue back, but it's not quite the same."

Her gaze roamed over the stove—one burner didn't work;

the wide-open windows—the air-conditioning was kaput; and the bag of garbage—it should have gone down the disposal, but they didn't have the funds to fix that either.

"I don't think it'll go for as much money, Mrs. Wallis. I'm so sorry. I—I don't know what to say."

"Hush now, it's not your fault if the police can't keep up with the thieves."

No one ever lied to Mrs. Wallis; Alex didn't dare tell her the whole truth.

"Don't give it another thought, dear. I know you've done your best. I don't care what the Board of Directors says, my Alex is *not* in cahoots with a pack of no-good—"

"What? Wait a minute, what'd you say?"

"I said, a pack of—"

"No, before that. The board's been talking about me? Why?"

With some of the club's members on the board, it shouldn't have come as a surprise.

"Oh, now don't you go worrying about them." Mrs. Wallis patted Alex's hand in a comforting gesture, but it didn't do the job. "You leave them to me!" With that, she was on her feet, changing the subject. "Have you had dinner?"

She let it go for now, thinking she'd catch Mrs. Wallis in a more talkative mood soon; mealtime was always hectic, as only kids can be, no matter how many adults were on hand at the time.

"I had a snack. Sorry, so did the kids, but it was healthy. You'd better get back to yours before it gets cold."

"Not much chance of that in this heat, but I will, all the same. Stop by tomorrow and check on the kittens, okay?"

Alex grinned, knowing Mrs. Wallis just wanted to get a look at her tomorrow and gauge how she was holding up. "Sure. See you later."

Alex took an alternate, longer route back to the studio, by way of three blocks of small shops, boutiques, and cafes. After she reviewed her situation—a less valuable statue, no support, no shining example for the children to model—her path seemed clear. She'd apply for a job right away.

Why was the Board of Directors of the Children's Home discussing her?

Well, why not? Undoubtedly the rest of St. Louis was, as well. When she passed a newspaper box on the corner and saw Patrick Pulsar's byline under "Greek God: de Marco's Comedy, Children's Tragedy," she made a point to watch traffic instead. No sense rubbing salt into the wound. With any luck, Darius was stuck for good and the tide would turn.

This area of town was used to an eclectic crowd, ranging from hippies with dreadlocks and studded eyebrows to yuppies in Banana Republic and hundred-dollar haircuts. No one even blinked an eye when she entered the first boutique in shorts and a T-shirt and inquired about a job.

Just in case.

The heat of the day waned gradually as the sun coasted lower in the sky, casting longer shadows on the sidewalk, barely diminishing some of the heat that reflected upward.

Any other evening, Alex could've enjoyed the walk home. She was accustomed to rejection. Abandoned by her parents, then continually rejected as a possible daughter for some lucky couple. For a whole year, she'd thought her husband loved her, but he'd ended up rejecting her, too. At the beginning of her career, she'd had to develop a thicker skin to survive rejection by juried art shows and galleries.

But even with her experience, twenty-five *Sorry, don't need any help right now*s in a row didn't set too well. Life hadn't prepared her for that. She was feeling pretty glum at the moment. She'd thought that when college kids went back to school, clerk positions opened up; turned out that, weeks ago, they went back to school all right, right *here*, and filled the few positions there were. Without a car, she'd have to continue her job search soon via busline. Or maybe borrow a bike somewhere?

She stopped and visited a few minutes with Griff, patiently watering the roses with a hose, and ended up telling him her problems, because he knew the truth about the statue and wouldn't think she was crazy. By the time she finished unburdening herself, ending with her latest rejection woes, he, too, looked rather pensive.

"Oh, now I've gone and done it," she said glumly.

"What?"

"You're thinking about your girls, aren't you?"

He scrutinized her face, started to say something, then nodded sadly and looked away.

Was that moisture in his eyes? "Sorry, Griff."

He cleared his throat. "Mm, no matter."

"Guess I'd better go inside before I make anyone else miserable."

He patted her arm, but he didn't look at her again.

She longed for the days when life was simpler, when they used to garden together, digging through the dirt, sorting through her childhood problems. Back when she didn't know what it was like to share space with a hunk she alternately wanted to maim and to seduce.

She was tempted to pull a few stray weeds outside her studio door, but as she approached the threshold, sounds of a heated argument emanated through the leaded glass panes.

"Usually you do your dirty work without witnesses, Cytus."

Cytus? *Damn.* Sounded Greek to her, and right now, Greek meant anything but good.

She rushed inside, prepared for the worst because that was the kind of evening she was having, and laughed with relief when she found the statue still standing, rock-solid, in the middle of her studio.

Then swallowed that same laughter when Hermes patted the statue's chest, said, "There, I think that's got it, buddy," stepped back and tossed the diamond paste and rag onto the worktable.

"Oh no! No no no." Surely he hadn't been able to—of course not, but . . .

She ran over to the statue, hoping to see scratches still marring the surface, but they were gone. She closed her eyes and ran her fingertips over the area, concentrating, hoping to feel something, *anything*, out of place.

But Hermes had touched it up perfectly, and beneath her fingers, Darius started to stretch and smile. Gone was the sad king.

"Noooo," she wailed, throwing a justifiable tantrum and flinging herself supine onto the couch, her arm covering her eyes, mindless of the three men in the room as she castigated herself.

Why, oh why, had she left him alone?

What was she thinking? She was probably nothing more than a mere inconvenience to a god; Hermes would have just brushed her aside to fix his brother. No, next time, she'd have to do a job that even a god couldn't fix.

And there *would* be a next time. Darius had to sleep some time. Didn't he? Sure he did. Once that was decided, their argument caught and held her attention.

"I don't need to worry about witnesses," Cytus said.

She guessed he was Cytus; no one was making introductions. He was golden-haired, brown-eyed, almost as tall as Darius, with the same muscular build shown off by his embroidered tunic. Not as good looking, though, because while Darius had a boyish grin and a playful twinkle in his eye, Cytus had a stony face and cold gaze.

"After all, I'm Zeus's favorite—"

"Why you insolent—"

Maybe they'd start flinging lightning bolts at each other. Maybe Darius would get hit. Yes! She sat up straight, watching eagerly, fingers crossed. Just don't break anything. Leave something for me to work with.

"There's no place for you anymore on Olympus," Cytus said. "You've lost favor."

". . . arrogant . . . impudent . . ."

Impressive vocabulary.

Cytus picked up a rasp and threw it at Darius, who stopped it in midair without so much as twitching a muscle.

". . . ill-mannered . . ." he roared.

Wait! Cytus was on *her* side? Well, how had she missed that? Sensing a turning tide, she rose to her feet, inadvertently drawing his attention.

"You, uh, don't want him alive either?"

In reply, Cytus picked up tool after tool, growling, flinging them toward Darius as quickly as he could, but none came within three feet of doing any damage.

"Now might be a good time to remind you, Cytus, that Darius is Zeus's son." Hermes fluttered overhead, out of the path of flying rasps, hammers, ice picks, cans, books, telephone. "He won't take kindly to your attack."

"Nonsense. It was Zeus who put a curse on him."

"All the same . . ."

"He's lost favor on Olympus."

"On the contrary, he still has many allies on Olympus, and you'd be wise not to run afoul of them."

"Like who?" Cytus growled. He picked up an cordless drill and seemed quite startled when his grasp hit the button just right and powered it on. "Ooh." He glanced at Darius and grinned wickedly. "This is interesting."

"Do me a favor," Alex began, then hesitated when she saw the hungry gleam in Cytus's eyes. "I . . . I know you don't know me, or owe me anything, but could you, when you, uh, use that drill on him, could you make it somewhere inconspicuous? You know, so when he turns back, I can still sell the statue?"

"Alexandra!"

Cytus roared with laughter, and Alex got the feeling she'd just received her worst rejection of the day.

"Well, come on, it won't hurt you any," she continued to argue why he should help her this way. "You'll have what you want, I'll have what I want."

"I want him to suffer."

"Oh." She chewed the inside of her lip nervously as he walked slowly toward Darius, who stood his ground, while Cytus aimed the cordless drill at Hermes anytime he winged close enough to be a hindrance. "Well, he will," she said. "Suffer, that is. I mean, it can't feel too good to have a drill run through your toe. Maybe the little toe? Or better yet, between his toes?"

"Ha! How 'bout right in his—"

"Cytus!" Hermes yelled over the drill. "Our brothers won't like this," he warned, darting a glare in Alex's direction, warning her to keep out of it.

If he'd come down here, like a man, she might be able to tackle him and keep him off Cytus.

"Ares, in particular," Darius said calmly.

Cytus hesitated. Suddenly he turned off the drill, resting it at his side. Clearly he didn't want to bring Ares, god of war, into this personal fight.

"No, I have a better idea." Cytus studied Alex, giving her a cold shiver up her spine, then smiled maliciously at Darius. "She won't love you anymore, you know—not when I'm through with you. And I can do it all without angering Zeus or Ares. I know just how to do it." He was laughing as he tossed the drill down with a clatter and then hurried out the back door.

It was Hermes' turn to slump on the couch, wiping his brow. "Whoo, that was *too* close, brother! And you"—he pointed his finger at Alex—"you ought not mess in affairs you don't understand."

She picked up the drill, turning it on. This time, Darius moved away, circling around to the other side of the worktable.

"You weren't afraid of him, but *I* scare you?" she asked incredulously.

"That was a fair fight. I don't want to hurt you."

Hermes snuck up behind her, snatched the drill out of her hand, and whispered in her ear, "He loves you, you see."

"Do not!" Darius roared.

"Do so. Aphrie told me."

"Well . . . well . . . she's wrong."

"Aphrie's never wrong."

He loves me? In spite of his firm denial, perhaps because of its intensity and Darius's subsequent sputtering, she was tempted to believe. Just a little bit. Could it be possible?

"Aphrie?" Alex asked.

"Aphrodite."

"Oh. Right." She took that with a grain of salt. "She's been, uh, here then, I guess?"

Hermes winked. "Taken quite a shine to the gardener, too. But no, don't ask, please, I can't say any more than that. Confidential, you understand."

She looked from one god to the other. "Oh, sure, why not? Hey, every girl has gods dueling under her roof. Excuse me, I need to go outside now and find a nice, rusty tool to slit my wrists."

"Darius!" Hermes said as Alexandra slammed the door behind her. "You're not going to let her—"

"Don't worry, little brother. She was just kidding. She'd never hurt herself."

"But how can you be sure?"

"I've seen her scar."

"Then she's hurt herself before?"

"No, someone did it to her."

He wanted to see it again, kiss it gently, swear to her he'd kill anyone who ever harmed her. He wondered if he ever dared expose himself to her in such a manner again. A vulnerable position like that could get him bashed over the head with the nearest lamp. And yet he wanted to stay around.

Was Aphrie right? Was this love?

"I hope you're right," Hermes said.

"She'll be back soon, and I'll wager she has one hell of a plan to do me in." His mind was only half on what he was saying, as he was still mulling over the love question.

"What do you think about what Cytus said?"

"Hm?"

"You know, that threat about her not loving you anymore when he's through with you?" Hermes snickered. "Who's he kidding? All women love you."

"No," he said, far more introspective than he used to be. "All women love my gems."

"Well, whatever he meant, I don't like the sound of it. Darius, are you listening to me?"

"Do you think she does?"

"Does *what*?"

"Love me?"

"She's a woman; who knows?"

"Because she won't take my gems. Not any."

"If she truly loved you, Dare, she'd let you have the statue."

Was she as torn as he? Wanting two opposite things? As quickly as he thought it, he knew it was no longer true. He *used* to want other women *and* Alexandra. Now he wanted only her.

Darius strolled through the remnants of Alexandra's studio, her floor littered with nearly every hard object formerly residing on shelves and in boxes, shaking his head over the mess and, feeling somewhat responsible, wondering what to do about it. Cytus had good aim, a strong arm, and hurled objects as fast as Zeus's lightning bolts. But not fast enough to defeat Darius's telekinetic powers; he had only to see the objects coming to deflect them. And he'd deflected them all over the place, he noticed, grinning triumphantly as he stepped over a broken lamp, careful not to cut his foot.

Wouldn't that be ironic? Win the battle, and lose the war over a piece of broken glass.

Maybe, he feared, he'd been here too long. Never before had he concerned himself with the state of a woman's abode. Never before had it occurred to him that she might be distraught to have her place trashed. Oh, there'd been a time or two when he'd been troubled that a jealous husband might have his wife drawn and quartered, but that had never come to pass; amazing what ruffled feathers could be soothed by a few rubies.

But this was different. It was only a messy floor, and yet he was far more than troubled. Almost contrite, ashamed—but that was impossible; he was a god, by Zeus! Above those feelings.

Or he should be. Used to be.

Love? Or simply responsibility? He didn't know.

Summoning Selena, he was joined immediately by her and her oddly dressed staff. If he wasn't mistaken, those were some sort of military jackets covering the women to the tops of their bare legs, with coordinating brimmed hats perched jauntily on their heads. No doubt Alexandra had something to do with this.

"Interesting," he said. Not them, but the vision of another pair of legs he'd rather see.

"You like?" Selena asked.

His visions not to be shared. "Actually, I was thinking that I need to replace this toga with something more appropriate."

"Yes, when in Rome . . ." Selena said with a knowing smile. "I'm certain Alexandra would appreciate it."

Well then, he would do it!

"So, what can we serve you today?"

"Actually, I'm not hungry. I was hoping you'd tidy up."

After a stunned moment, all five women burst out laughing, but with a steadily piercing gaze from him, they quickly quelled that into giggling behind their hands.

Selena picked up a piece of the broken lamp. "Did she come close?"

"She didn't do this."

"Don't tell me you threw this at her!"

He tried to put her in her place with an imperious glare,

but it didn't work. Centuries of training, and Alexandra had corrupted her in a day.

"No, Cytus threw it all at me." He was a god; she was a servant; he really shouldn't have to explain anything.

"*Cytus*. Oh, Darius. Come on, ladies, let's get this picked up before she gets back. She *is* coming back?"

"Oh, I'm sure she is."

"Good," Selena said triumphantly, as if she knew something he didn't.

They started picking up, then all at once Selena stopped, drew herself up straight, propped her hands on her hips, and stared at him. "You'll never be right for her if you don't learn to get your hands dirty," she said.

Could that be true? With a deep, heartfelt sigh, knowing he'd do this for no one but Alexandra, Darius sat on the couch, extended his hand for a drink, and began to pick up the room.

With a flourish, Selena served a full goblet of Olympus's best. He barely had it finished before Cynthia glanced out the window and whispered, "Quick, she's coming! No, wait, it's okay, she's watching the sunset."

"We're almost done."

"Look how pretty orange the wall's turned."

"Oh, she's changed her mind. Here she comes!"

"How does she look?" Darius asked, holding out his goblet for more.

"Mad. No, determined. Yeah, determined."

"Quick, ladies, let's leave them alone."

"A refill first!" he shouted, and Selena complied before they vanished.

He flew the base of a broken statue back onto the shelf, wondering where the top of it was. Probably under something, like the couch, and he wasn't about to get down on his hands and knees in front of Alexandra and search for it.

Humming softly to herself, she walked past him as if he weren't there, and he wasn't sure if the color in her cheeks was a blush or a reflection of the setting sun.

"Hello," he said to break the ice. No reply, not even a sideways glance. "Uh, I'm still here."

"So I see," she said with a bright smile, though it was far too innocent-looking for his peace of mind.

Picking up a pile of mail from her worktable, she proceeded to sort through it, though Darius had never seen her so much as blink at it before; she had in fact always kicked it aside where it fell through the mail slot. So he suspected she was trying too hard to ignore him, and wondered why.

"I picked up while you were gone."

She grinned knowingly. "Right." She walked over to him, helped herself to a sip of his drink, and licked her lips slowly, temptingly, savoring every drop.

Darius's mouth went dry.

"Pretty expensive goblet for Selena to leave behind."

He'd give anything to watch her lick her lips again.

"Ha—" He cleared his tight throat. "Have another sip."

She did, with the same theatrics, though she looked perfectly oblivious to his state of mind.

He'd give anything to have her lick his lips; he feared she'd bite him instead. If she'd give him a five-minute head start, he'd have her so mindless with passion, she wouldn't be able to resist him.

"Go ahead and finish it. We can watch the sunset together if you like."

The light was fading fast, the wall barely a pastel pink. "Too late."

As the color drained from the wall, so, too, did Darius's energy wane. It was at that moment that he realized exactly when he'd frozen up in the park—at sunset. Two nights in a row now. Only he felt it sooner this time; recognized exactly what was happening. If he didn't do something fast, he'd be at Alexandra's mercy, as helpless as he'd been in the public restroom, as helpless as he'd been with Queen Aara's husband. Knowing how much Alexandra needed the statue, well, he'd already had enough statue experience with a treacherous mortal female to last an eternity, thank you very much.

"Hermes!"

No reply. No time to waste.

"Hey," Alexandra said, as he circled her wrist in an unbreakable grasp and made sure they were out of reach of any hard objects. "Hey!"

This was no good. He'd turn into the statue and be fine until morning, but he couldn't keep her standing here in the middle of the room all night. She needed her sleep. She needed to be safe if her nightly visitor developed a mean streak.

"Where are you taking me?" she shrieked as he dragged her to the bedroom.

"To bed." No time to explain.

"I'm not going in there—" She was dragging her feet and grasping the door frame, and generally doing anything a woman could do to slow down a man hell-bent for the bedroom. "Well, I'm not going to bed with—"

He was stiffening up, and not in a romantic way. No time to lose. He had to see to her comfort as well as protect both of them. Directing his rapidly diminishing telekinesis in different directions, he ticked off all he had to do, before it was too late: close and lock the bedroom door, slide the dresser over in front of it, clear the nightstand of all potential head bashers, push her onto the mattress, and at the last moment, fling himself horizontal.

Turning into marble in midair, he hit the bed like the nearly three-quarter ton of solid mass he was.

Alexandra squealed as the bed cracked with an ear-splitting pop, splintering beneath his weight, which dragged the mattress through the supports and down to the floor on his side. Her side listed toward him, rolling her onto his chest.

By Zeus, she felt heavenly against him! He could feel every push as she tried to shove herself off him, as she tried to scoot up and maintain a hold on her side of the bed. But gravity was against her. She'd get little sleep, he knew, lying on a cold, hard hunk of marble.

He'd get even less, feeling her warm thigh wrapped intimately over his, rubbing against him every time she moved, and her small, strong hand upon his chest, right over where his heart should by rights be beating. How could he get any rest, knowing he had the only woman he wanted in his grasp. So close.

And damn it to Hades, he'd finally gotten her into bed and he couldn't even put his arms around her!

13

The only thing good about going to bed with a hunk of marble—and Alex was being generous here—was that it was cool to the touch. Other than that, it was hard, the evening was barely dark, there was nothing to read or listen to, nothing to sketch with, and no hope of the children coming back to hand her a tool, any tool.

In short, she was the most miserable she ever remembered, outside of her accident-imposed hospital stay. Those days hadn't been fun, lasting nearly a week before she could go home, and then she was on restricted activity. Watching her husband leave hadn't been entertaining, either, but at least she hadn't been bored to death.

She suspected, if she didn't figure out some way to get free of Darius's grasp beforehand, that she'd be here only until morning, and she viewed that with mixed emotions because now she had her statue, and then she wouldn't. She wasn't certain, of course, but his last non-injury-inflicted turn into marble had lasted only overnight.

Over the next few hours, she became quite adept at maneuvering pillows and comforter into various positions to pad her against the unforgiving marble. Since none was comfortable more than five minutes, she got lots of practice. She was also aware that Darius, though weakened, was using what power he had to further break her bed. Every once in a while, usually when she'd just settled into a new, and therefore relatively comfortable position, one of the two remaining legs would creak and shift. Around midnight, just about the time she drifted off from fatigue, her side of the bed came crashing down, giving her a somewhat level mattress. At least she no longer felt as if she were sideways inside a sleeper sofa.

He'd have no reason to do this, that she could think of, other than her comfort. And that just wasn't fair. She was doing her best to do him in, and then he went and did something totally selfless. She preferred to think of him as the thief he was.

Idly, her fingers grazed the marble out of habit. Still so perfect. Smooth chest. Broad shoulders. Muscular arms. Toga-wrapped in a silky sheet, he'd made a pretty magnificent hunk, too. Then, with his dark chocolate eyes dancing, always following her, twinkling when he teased her, sparking when she'd pushed his buttons . . .

Keep this up and I'll never get to sleep! Better concentrate on the statue, girl. Not the man.

If he never turned back, the only way out of his hold was to break his hand. Brutish, but true. The Venus de Milo might be art-worthy without appendages, but Alex had no illusions of what her statue would be worth without its hand. It wasn't, after all, a rescued antiquity. No, it was worth far more in perfect condition, and if he continually outmaneuvered her, the only way she could see she was going to get that was to convince him to give it up.

As long as she had a captive audience . . .

Darius remembered the last time he'd been in bed with a woman, three thousand years ago, and how different the scene—outside of the fact that he'd been an active participant then, alive and erect.

Lilacs had perfumed the air in the young queen's bedchamber, high in a castle perched on a cliff. Flickering candlelight had teased over Aara's skin, masking imperfections—

Whoa! as mortals said nowadays. When had he ever thought she'd had imperfections? When had he ever noticed?

Never.

The vision of Aara dimmed with Alexandra snuggled up next to him, and—if he weren't a statue right now this would scare him to death—it had nothing to do with proximity. What a daydream—to woo Alexandra and bed her, finally! To touch her petal-soft skin, caress her scar, kiss away her tears of joy, wind her limbs around him, feel her fingers skimming over his body while hers writhed beneath him—

Now there was an exercise in frustration—one of godly proportions. If he'd felt confined by the marble before, he was getting downright claustrophobic now, with no room to expand the way he felt he must. By Zeus, he had to think of something else!

After an hour, she was still talking. Softly, quietly, weaving vivid stories of the orphaned children for him to see.

Billy, the scientific one, whose brain worked as fast as the computers he loved. Her wish for him was a recent-model computer with software to challenge him. At the same time, she knew his knowledge would benefit the other children.

T.J., with an uncanny knack for understanding the little ones. Without help, he'd miss out on the college degree he needed to go into social work.

Maria—even though she was a resident of the home, not staff, it was her touch that soothed a fevered child during the night. Without financial help for years to come, the road to becoming a doctor might be too heavy a load; maybe a pediatric orthopedist.

Kesia, who loved animals intensely, cried when a baby bird fell out of its nest.

Stories of Daniel and Rashida and Emily, how they'd come to be at TCH, their troubles and talents and aspirations.

All these children had hopes and dreams. He didn't want to know that. He didn't want to understand that mortals had worthy goals, worth meeting at any price. Not one of them seemed focused on an art career, yet Alexandra would help them, mentor them, provide for them in any way she could. Her art, as he listened to her, seemed more a means to an end than an undying devotion to creating something out of a rock, perfection her most important tool. It was all for the children; always the children.

She talked more through the night than all the days it had taken her to finish the statue. He had a long day ahead of him tomorrow; he could use a little sleep. And still she kept talking, almost a whisper really, a low soothing murmur, occasionally chuckling over a favorite memory that tickled her emotions.

Resisting mightily—as if she were an enchanting Siren luring him toward his own destruction—he nevertheless felt a steadily growing warmth in his heart toward the children. Why was he coming to care for them?

Because Alexandra cared. And because, with her words,

she painted an irresistible picture of why they deserved to have him care.

Briefly, he toyed with the idea of putting one of the pillows over her mouth to muffle her words, though his powers were so weak, she'd likely win that struggle.

When she finally drifted off to sleep, leaving him to think in peace, it hadn't been peace he'd found. He knew he had to leave her. He must travel to Olympus, make up with Zeus and soothe old hurts that were best forgotten. Then Zeus could free him from this hellish half-god, half-statue curse that was ruining his life. He'd be free to return to Alexandra, woo her, make love to her, blind her with passion until she was so happy to have him in her life that the thought of doing away with him would never enter her mind. He'd give her babes of her own, as many as she wanted, as often as she wanted. He hoped they would please her more than his gems.

"Hm, interesting dilemma," Hermes said when he finally answered Darius's bellows. Unlike Darius, whose voice was mute to Alexandra as long as he wasn't alive, Hermes spoke softly, so as not to wake her. "Tell me, can you feel her?"

"No," he lied.

"So what'd you want? And please don't say you want me to intercede with Zeus again. He's so wrapped up in his new software, he darned near bit my head off last time."

"My chariot—"

Hermes grinned. "Hephaestus thought you might be needing it. Soon as he heard you were back, he dragged it out of storage and started checking it over. Needed a new axle or something—don't ask, he's the blacksmith, not me—but it should be travel-worthy by now."

Oh, to see Olympus again: Hera, his mother—he'd no longer mind her damned peacocks. His siblings—he missed them one and all, and probably had a few nieces and nephews he'd never met. Fruitful, aromatic gardens where nothing wilted or died. The dozen tile-roofed, whitewashed residences of the gods, where he'd known many happy centuries. Open meadows of lush green grass, beckoning him for a warm nap beneath the afternoon sun while his horses grazed nearby.

"And my horses, have Onyx and Obsidian grown fat and lazy?"

"Uh, no."

"Someone's seen to their exercise? Splendid! Who?"

"Well, *someone* has."

"Who—no, not Cytus! By Zeus, my gems *and* my horses! If I'd been married, would he be sleeping with my wife, too?"

Hermes wisely kept his tongue about that, as their family wasn't known for its impeccable morals. "So, uh, when do you think you'll be, uh, you know, *alive* again?"

"Sunrise."

"Really?"

"I think so. Say, how'd you get in here anyway?"

"Uh, the door?"

"I blocked it."

Hermes glanced toward the door, then back at him. "Guess that's why the dresser's halfway across the room, huh? Nice try, though. I won't ask why you're trying to shackle her to you and barricade the door, too. No, no, don't want to know."

Crestfallen, Darius realized his powers had been too weak. He'd tried to do everything he could to protect Alexandra, and he'd failed. Maybe the stranger wouldn't come tonight. He could have his team there for an early departure, or he could ask Hermes to stay and scare the stranger away.

"Stay awhile."

"Thought you wanted your team and chariot here right away?"

"I do, but . . ."

Hermes grinned. "Can't sleep like that, huh? Lying next to her, I mean."

"You think I can do anything else?" Darius growled, giving himself away.

Hermes laughed. "Want me to throw a bucket of cold water on you?"

"Want me to drop the ceiling on your head?"

Hermes whispered, "Think I'd better stay a few minutes."

"Why? You haven't tormented me enough already? Witnessed my humiliation?"

"Well, yes, that's been rather enjoyable, but I'm more concerned with the two mortals sneaking around in the studio right now. Flashlights mean they're up to no good, right?"

"Two?"

The stranger always came alone and never used a flashlight. Darius struggled in vain against the marble, needing to lift his head off the mattress, feeling more frustrated than ever.

"Yeah, and that's on top of the first one I kind of scared off when I got here. At least he was outside, not like these guys."

Being helpless to save himself was one thing. Being totally helpless to protect Alexandra from danger, he found that the mere thought of her suffering so much as the tiniest bruise at their hands frightened him more than he'd ever been in his whole life. He didn't scare easily, and he'd had a long life.

"Don't worry, I'll hang around until they leave." Hermes picked up one of the broken bed legs, swinging it horizontally through the air, testing it for its effectiveness.

Darius knew his brother loved him, but if their safety was left up to Hermes alone against two others, oh boy. He was light, agile, quick, a great distraction to a mortal enemy with his ability to fly, but not built for hand-to-hand combat. He prayed they scared easily.

Darius levitated a loose edge of the comforter. "Quick, cover her up. Hide her."

"Oh hey, good idea."

Hermes dragged the fluffy comforter—what wasn't crammed between Alexandra and Darius—over her sleeping form, covering her completely. Then suddenly he drew himself up against the wall by the head of the broken bed, assuming the rigid position, though not the form, of a statue, his new weapon behind him.

Darius, unable to lift or turn his head, could only watch the strangers as long as they were within the focal path of his rigid position. The bigger of the two carried a bag, no, a pillowcase, bulging at the seams with its heavy load.

"Find a place yet?" he asked.

"That statue's staring at me."

"So what?"

"I dunno. Gives me the willies, that's all."

"Well, the sooner we find a good spot, the sooner we're outta here. She could be back any time."

He backed away from the foot of the bed, keeping his gaze on Darius. "The other room was better. Let's put it out there and get outta here."

"Fine. But it has to be where nobody finds it till the cops get here."

"Hermes," Darius whispered as the men left.

"I'm on it."

He returned a few minutes later, laughing to himself.

"What?"

"You're never going to believe what they hid out there."

"Really?" Darius sounded deceptively interested in Hermes drawing this out.

Missing the sarcasm, Hermes said, "I'll give you three guesses."

"How about I give you three seconds to tell me before I clunk you over the head with that stick you're holding?"

"Ooh, touchy. Sure you didn't hire them?"

"Hermes!"

"Okay okay, guess not. They had a drawerful of jewelry and watches in that bag, so you can see why I thought maybe you'd hired them. Why would they collect all that and deliver it to you otherwise? Unless . . ."

"They want the police to find them!"

"Who're they trying to frame, you or her?"

"I don't know. Go move them."

"Where should I put them?"

"I don't care, anywhere else! I'll take care of them . . . later, when I can move."

"Okeydoke."

"Okeydoke," Darius muttered to himself after Hermes had left. Some mortal expressions deserved to die.

For the moment, he set aside his anger and frustration over being unable to protect Alexandra—it solved nothing—and shifted his focus toward what was important now. By Zeus, she must be hot beneath that comforter. Struggling for control, he managed to uncover the top half of her. She was still moist, sweating from the heat, dots of perspiration on her brow. He blew gently, trying to create some sort of cooling breeze, but he was unable.

Resting, regrouping his powers, he waited impatiently for Hermes to return. He'd waste no time when the chariot arrived. He'd make up with Zeus. He'd never apologized to his father before, but to be with Alexandra, to be able to help her as he wasn't able to tonight, he'd do it this time.

Then, and only then, he'd be back to himself. He could do all those things he'd been daydreaming of earlier: woo her, make mad, passionate love to her until finally she'd be won over and thoughts of doing away with him would never enter her mind again.

Not that it would do her any good, because once the curse was completely removed, scratching his skin with an innocent kitten or bashing him with a lamp would do nothing. Once she saw that, once she knew he was again immortal, she would look upon him differently.

As a mortal woman looks upon a god.

And then, would she want him for himself? Or like other mortal women, would she want him solely for what he could give her? His gems.

Toward morning, Alex tossed and turned fitfully.

She'd slept—that was a laugh—crammed against the hard marble, not well rested because who goes to bed at sunset in summer and stays there until sunrise? It was like being sick and confined to bed when you really didn't feel sick at all, only after a while, you just feel lousy from doing nothing.

She felt the change at sunrise, instantly aware of Darius growing warmer, the rise and fall of his chest as he began breathing again, the beat of his heart beneath her ear as she cuddled closer and laid her head on his chest.

"Alexandra . . ."

"Just hold me," she whispered. *Let me pretend I don't have to find a way to do you in. Just for a little while.*

Doing him in would be so easy. Get him in the throes of passion, rake her nails across his back, and voilà—instant statue.

Well hell, she'd be crushed. Literally. Maybe even figuratively. Better to be on top when he returned to marble, though as his arms encircled her, enveloping her in a warm cocoon, she sighed and fell back asleep, and dreamed she could keep him—for a little while at least. Until something out of the ordinary woke her, and she found herself alone in bed.

Was Darius there, or was he gone? She caught herself hoping he was in the studio, but that was simply because she wouldn't mind having another go at him. Had nothing at all to do with the fact that, even though he wasn't a man—strictly in the sense of what was human, or mortal, as he called it—he certainly was a hunk and worth looking at.

She swallowed before she drooled on her pillow and made a liar out of herself.

And he certainly had a tender side that begged further exploration—now how attractive was that? Helping Em with juice, snuggling Rashida, studying with Daniel. Leveling her bed last night. Sure, you could say the whole broken-bed thing was his fault in the first place, but he was just protecting himself. Fair enough. Didn't take anything away from this paradox that was Darius: both alive and not, both strong and tender.

Nothing she could do about him now but stretch out for a few minutes to get rid of some of these kinks. Now the ladies of the club could sue her for breaking an antique bed. Lordy, was there any end to the trouble she could get herself into lately?

Well, she wasn't doing this to herself, come to think of it. It was all Darius's fault, really, though he'd be pretty hard to pin down with the blame. If he felt any responsibility at all, and she was sure he was above all that, he'd try to pay them off with a stolen ring or something. Honestly! Shouldn't gods have some morals?

Noises on the other side of the wall—the remainder of the old carriage house, what wasn't her studio, was now used as a garage—ruined any chance to enjoy a few minutes of peace and quiet. Sounded like Sabrina tearing the place apart to find her kittens, though she hadn't put up any fuss when the kids had taken them. She'd hidden beneath the van, watched them carefully, and then casually lain down and licked her paw.

It was probably Griff. Alex peeled off last night's sweaty clothes, changed into her shortest shorts and briefest tank top—maybe a tan would make her look healthier and help her get a job—and headed out the back way to join him in the garden awhile.

Finding two six-foot-plus hunks arguing in her small galley kitchen, she paused on the threshold; Darius and Matthew, the model.

"Look, man, I told you, Mrs. Kline said she dropped it here the other day and asked me to come find it. That's all I know."

"Dropped what?" Alex asked.

Darius turned, the beginning of a smile freezing on his face, his gaze never wavering as he took her in, over and over, from head to toe. Maybe he hadn't realized what was on TV was often in real life, because he certainly was fixated on her bare legs. His eyes darkened, nearly smoldered.

"Good morning," he said, his gentle tone at odds with the proprietary glare he cast toward her.

She should be insulted; she was flattered. She got hot all

over again, and this time she couldn't blame it on sleeping in her clothes.

"Well, hel-lo," Matthew said, his gaze also roaming over her.

"Oh stop it. I'm too old for you, and excuse me, Darius, move over a little bit, would you? I've got to close that window before I start sneezing my head off."

On tiptoe, she reached over the sink and cranked the window shut. The backyard was shady this time of morning, and she would've liked to let a cool breeze inside, but she knew better. She could still feel Darius's gaze on her, felt a feminine sense of satisfaction knowing it was she who'd replaced the customary twinkle in his eyes with something of a more heated nature.

Heated, hell. *Volcanic.*

When she turned around, she discovered he'd moved closer. Was in fact now standing between her and Matthew, blocking the younger man's view by plucking at the sides of his toga and holding them out wide.

"Hey, nothing wrong with me looking," Matthew complained. •

"Go look somewhere else." He glanced over his shoulder at her. "Have you no decency, woman? Get dressed!"

"I am dressed. Remember? TV? Hey, wasn't me who turned on *Baywatch.* Matthew, what're doing here?"

"Like I was telling him, Mrs. Kline asked me to come look for the bracelet she dropped here the day she brought me by. She didn't have time, and she was worried it might get kicked under something and, how'd she put it? Oh, lost under a dust bunny, I think. Anyway, I found it, but this kook took it away from me."

She grabbed the diamond tennis bracelet dangling from Darius's hand. "I told you to leave this alone."

"You know that's not your sister's."

She'd say Matthew was a thief who made up the whole story to cover his ass, but how many jocks used the expression "dust bunny"? He had to have gotten that from Claudia, but why would her sister send him after a bracelet that wasn't hers?

Instinctively covering for her sister, she said, "You got the wrong one, Matthew."

"Oh. Oh! Gosh I'm, uh, I'm sorry. I didn't know there'd be more than one. Geez, you must think I'm—oh no, I'm not a burglar or anything like that."

"Relax," she said, laughing softly because every time she moved, Darius was careful to keep her shielded. And plucking at his toga like that did nice things in the bun region. *Mm, mm, mm.*

"You're not going to call the cops or anything, are you?"

"No."

"Not *if* . . ." Darius left the thought dangling.

"Oh no, not that again."

"What?" Alex asked.

"He wants me to undress."

"*What?*"

"Says he wants my clothes."

"Feeling shy?" Darius asked. "As I recall, you were only too happy to discard every stitch you were wearing a few days ago."

"Yeah, well, you weren't in the—hey, how'd you know about that? Were you spying on me?"

"Oh God, *relax*, you two! He wasn't spying on you."

"Then how'd he—"

Think fast.

"This is the Ladies' Club. You think they don't have security cameras around here?"

"Oh. Guess so. Sorry, man."

"Your clothes . . . or the cops?"

"Geez." Matthew whisked his gray Athletic Department T-shirt over his head.

"Not in front of her!"

Alex was speechless about the whole situation. Darius in a T-shirt, with fleece shorts hugging every, uh, bulge she'd given him? It'd be too much to take in. He'd seem more mortal, more human. It'd seem wrong to maim him. She'd already begun to have second thoughts about that, but honestly, she'd been half asleep and curled up next to his big strong body, and therefore such thoughts weren't to be taken seriously. She could justify bashing a mythological god, but to humanize him? Might be a problem.

Especially if he kept looking at her like that, as if he thought she was desirable and sexy.

Yeah, right.

Damn, but the possibility made her think the same kinds of thoughts about him, and that would never do. Never.

Matthew looked past them, obviously noting that Darius wasn't standing aside to let him pass. "Where then?"

Darius pointed at the connecting door. "In the garage."

"I need something to put on." He looked at Alex hopefully. "You got some boxers around, you know, that you sleep in or something?"

She finally found her voice. "Darius, why do you want his clothes?"

"I'm tired of walking around in a sheet. Get out in the garage. You may have my sheet after I get your clothes."

"That?" Matthew, horrified at the thought, pointed at Darius's red satin sheet with the lace edging. "I can't walk home wearing that! I might as well wear a sign saying I'm perverted, rape me."

Darius raised his arm, probably only to point to the door again, but Matthew scuttled into the garage without waiting to be sure.

He scuttled right back in, slamming the door behind him and leaning against it.

"Out!"

"I can't. There's two monsters out there. No way, man, I'll take my chances with you first."

"It's a cat," Alex said.

Matthew laughed, but not humorously. "Oh no, that's no cat. They're bigger'n me. Lots bigger. They're so black, I couldn't tell what they are, but I'm not going back out there. You want the clothes, they're coming off in here." He threw his T-shirt onto the counter.

"Black?" Darius mused. He brushed past Matthew and opened the garage door. "Onyx! Obsidian! By Zeus, am I glad to see the both of you!"

"I'm outta here," Matthew said, grabbing his shirt and brushing past Alex at top speed. "Tell your sister I couldn't find it."

Alex was watching Matthew run away, and listening to what sounded like horses in the garage. Horses!

She flipped on the light and checked for herself. Sure enough, two massive black heads were buried against Darius's chest, making deep rumbling noises as he stroked their gracefully arched necks.

Black Stallion, eat your heart out. These guys not only had long wavy manes, tails that reached the floor, and coats so silky they shone in the light, they were also decked out in jeweled harnesses that would pay off the national debt of a few countries.

"Yes, yes, 'tis I," he murmured to them. "Did that mean old Cytus mistreat you? Well, never mind, I'm back now.

Yes," he crooned, scratching their favorite spots. "I missed you, too. Oh, such good boys. You're so loyal, aren't you? Yes you are."

She'd heard him speak kindly, gently, to the children, but this was downright erotic, all that murmuring and crooning and petting and scratching. Astounded by the revelation, she realized she wanted this kind of attention from a man. Worse yet, she realized she wanted it from *him*. Dangerous thoughts; very dangerous.

Well, stop watching, dummy.

Better yet, make him stop, before she grabbed him, knocked him down, and had her way with him right there on the garage floor. He wanted her; she knew it. She was willing. Hell, she was darned near desperate. Wouldn't take long. A few hours, at most. They could pick up their battle where they left off, later.

"Dare—"

"Alexandra!" He turned and hugged her fiercely.

Yes.

"Let's go inside," she said.

"Can't waste a minute."

"I know."

"The sooner I leave, the sooner I may return."

"Leave?" She was throwing herself at him, and he wanted to leave? *Now?*

14

Darius's flashy, jeweled horses and chariot raced upward, reaching the clouds in short order, then breaking through them to the peaceful sky above, leveling off once they were far above Earth, far above his feelings of claustrophobia. He set a course for Olympus, regretting leaving Alexandra behind already, yet knowing it was best. No telling what changes had occurred in his long absence; he wouldn't risk her safety. And if Zeus, in an angry fit, turned him back to nothingness, then Alexandra would be stranded far from her loved ones. While he'd thought little of it since finding the statue, now he was eager to get home and straighten out his life.

Home. Funny that he thought of it as home, when he'd been exiled for three thousand years, when his siblings and other gods had been forbidden to speak to him. Yet . . . it was the only home he knew and it held many warm memories, memories that had kept him sane over the centuries.

It was also the only place where everyone didn't *want* something from him.

It was there he'd find Zeus, the only being capable of removing his curse. Only then would he be able to return and make love to Alexandra properly, without concern over turning back into marble at an inappropriate moment. Having that happen when he finally got her into bed, well, it could scar the woman for life.

He urged the horses on faster.

She'd had enough trouble in her life already: orphaned, injured, scarred, saddled with a sister who'd tried—*twice!*—to steal the diamond bracelet he'd given her, and though he didn't want to admit it, losing the statue had made her many enemies among the ladies of the club and damaged her reputation.

Simply holding her that morning had been one of the hardest things he'd ever done. Never had he lain with a woman, just lain with her and held her, without seeking a release. Not only had it never occurred to him to do so, but if anyone had even suggested it as a possibility, he would have laughed at the thought:

"What in Hades?"

Suddenly he noticed he wasn't alone in the sky, though at first he didn't know exactly what was keeping him company. What had a long, streamlined body, wings, and a tail, though none of those appendages flapped? Curious—it would take only a moment to see what it was, he'd still be home before he knew it—he steered his team closer, until he saw it wasn't alive at all, but a . . .

What did the mortals call this invention? A missile? No. An airplane! Close enough now to see the pilot staring back at him with far more curiosity, Darius gave a jaunty wave and turned his team eastward.

                                    •

He laughed without inhibition, purely, joyously; exhilarated to be free, unfettered, and in command of his powerful team again. Crossing paths with Helios as he carried sunlight to the world, Darius tossed him a wave, too, pleased by Helios's unbridled smile at seeing him alive again.

"I'm ba-ack," Darius called across the sky to him, finally able to use another one of those mortal expressions he'd learned. Some of them just stuck; he didn't know why. He was dying to run into Cytus again and use Dirty Harry's line.

Across the Atlantic. Over Spain. Following the Mediterranean to Greece, then turning inland toward Thessaly.

"Ah, home," he said to his team as they, sensing a manger of oats in their near future, picked up even more speed near Olympus.

He could see the gate of clouds now, watched over by the Seasons. Extending his fist overhead in triumph, he stormed through in his own version of a victory lap, shouting "I'm ba-ack," for all to hear. He headed straight toward Zeus's home, the most magnificent of all on Olympus, and on the highest peak, as befitted the most powerful of gods.

On the way, he noticed more residences now, smaller and of lower altitude than the magnificent palaces of old. More crowded than he was used to, and he didn't like it at all. Why, there on the hillside where he'd last sat, tossing gems, musing whether Aara loved him or not, sat not one but three houses. Pity. He gladly left them behind and below, shaking off some of his dissatisfaction and disappointment.

At least the weather hadn't changed. Sunny and mild, it bathed him with the fresh scent of outdoors. No pollution here. No allergens; wouldn't Alexandra like *that*. He took a deep breath, then another, cleansing his lungs gratefully, then turned to the business at hand.

"Ze-us, I'm ho-ome," he sang out, chuckling over how

similar it was to Ricky Ricardo's "Lucy, I'm ho-ome." He didn't think Zeus would get it, though, so he didn't repeat it. No sense acting silly when he was here to prove a point and request—no, demand!—to have his life returned to him 24/7.

By Zeus, but mortals had a way with their expressions! 24/7—couldn't get any clearer than that.

Hermes fluttered to Darius's side as he strode with confidence through the great hall, which, on a smaller scale, reflected the changes he'd seen outdoors. A noticeable difference from thirty centuries ago. Later he'd ask about the trees growing inside, and those two new oil paintings. Later, when he had time to deal with all the changes that left him with a vague sense of unease, as if nothing would be the same ever again.

This unease urged him to hurry, to do what he came for and return to Alexandra before matters there changed also, for the worse.

"Where is he?" Darius asked Hermes.

"In the control room."

"The what?"

"Control room. Go out this door. Wall-to-wall computers, satellite receivers, shelves full of software we've developed to control the weather."

"Really?"

"Yeah, rain, thunder, lightning, lightning-related fires, you name it. We got Uranus's input on wind, Poseidon programmed the flood software . . ."

Darius halted abruptly in the wide, stone passageway, thinking all that traveling must have affected his hearing.

"Zeus and Uranus? Working together?"

Not possible! Zeus had defeated and banished his grandfather, father, and most of the clan from Olympus long before Darius's time, then split up the territory with Poseidon and Hades. Why, Darius had never even met his great grandfather, and now he and Zeus were sharing office space?

"Yeah, well," Hermes continued, "Uranus says he's too old to keep up with all the details, so he's been happy as a lark playing on his own computer and letting Zeus iron out the bugs. Poseidon's keeping control of the oceans, but he's using software to do it, too. Gives 'em all more time to play on the Internet."

Darius opened his mouth to say something, couldn't imagine what would be appropriate, and decided to move on and solve his own problems before trying to sort through the new family dynamics.

"Won't be long, Hades should have volcanoes and earthquakes under wraps. Hope they don't have any glitches, like Zeus did the other day, you know, when you came back to life and there were those stray thunderbolts. This way." At the top of the wide staircase, Hermes pointed down the hall to the left. "Sure you're ready for this?"

"Couldn't be readier." Had no choice really, not if he wanted Alexandra to see him as a stud.

"You may want to see if he's busy first. If he's got his face buried in the monitor, or if he's cussing at the computer, don't say anything, just wait until he finishes whatever he's working on."

"He hasn't seen me in three thousand years—you think the computer'll be more interesting?"

"In there. Good luck."

"You're not coming?" Darius paused outside the door, suddenly wary after all Hermes had told him, or not told him.

"Uh-uh, not until I hear whether he's in a snit or not."

Darius pushed opened the heavy, well-oiled door, entering a large room with several desks and monitors scattered about the lush green foliage, like boulders half hidden in a tropical forest. They didn't seem to go together, but hey, it wasn't his control room, and he really didn't care how Zeus spent his time as long as he removed this damned curse.

"There, take that!" Zeus said, pounding the keys in front of him, then sitting back to watch colorful activity flashing across his screen. "Ha! I knew it!"

"You got it?" a voice Darius didn't recognize responded from the other side of a bushy hanging plant. Whoever it was sounded older than Zeus. Maybe Uranus.

Maybe Darius had better slow down just a little bit, kind of take in the new lay of the land, so to speak.

"Yes! Finally!" Zeus rose from his chair, dancing a little jig, obviously pleased with himself. "That's the last time I'll have to—"

Turning around, he saw Darius and stopped in midsentence.

"Darius!"

"Father," Darius said with a hint of uncertainty. Not that he didn't recognize his father; that wasn't the problem. He wasn't sure what he'd expected, but it wasn't what he got.

Zeus burst out laughing. Not with joy, pleasure, pride, nor happiness to have him back, but a roar that, after a few minutes, brought tears to his eyes. Finally he caught his breath.

"Oh, I'm sorry," he said, wiping his eyes without embarrassment.

Tears? From Zeus?

"Son, what *is* that you're wearing?"

"Oh. Uh . . ."

"It looks like . . . Is that a bedsheet?"

"Well . . ."

"Uh-huh, nearly got caught by another jealous husband,

right? Son, I thought after all this time, you might've learned your lesson."

"Oh I did, I did. That's why I'm here, Father, I—"

"In a sheet? I like the color, though. Looks silky, too." Zeus came forward and fingered the fabric over Darius's shoulder. "Not bad."

He still had a smirk on his face, and Darius realized he'd just have to go along and be the butt of this joke if he was going to get anywhere today.

"Yeah, well, you know how it is, Father. Three thousand years of nothing, and then a whole planet full of women."

Zeus clapped him on the shoulder. "What I wouldn't give to be young again! Sit down, tell me all about it. You hungry?"

"As a matter of fact—"

Zeus snapped his fingers, and his personal serving wenches appeared. They still wore traditional garments, kept their heads bowed as they offered tray upon tray of delicious food and drink, and didn't dare address their master by name. Unlike Selena and her staff.

"Something the matter, son?"

"Huh? Oh no, no, Father, just thinking how great it is to be back. Can't believe how much I missed this place." He rushed to add, "And you and Mother, of course. And the others."

"Relax, Dare. I know I used to be an ogre."

Zeus casually leaned back in his chair, something he never would have done long ago. He seemed more mellow, warmer, approachable.

For perhaps the first time in his life, maybe *because* Zeus was so mellow, Darius remembered Aphrie's admonition about observing the social amenities. He'd rather jump right in and get his life fixed, but maybe she was right. He'd try it. He perused the room slowly.

"Quite a change in here."

Zeus beamed. "Yeah, added some skylights for the plants—did you know they counteract the negative energy from the computers? Huh, neither did I until one of the grandkids told me. Don't dare move any of them, though. Aphrodite has this thing about the flow of sheng chi."

"What is feng shui?" Darius said automatically, then felt foolish for having listened to way too much TV. "Uh, sorry."

Zeus didn't seem to notice. "Went over big with the Chinese. Anyway, did that. Hephaestus designed the desks, built them special. Ergonomic, he called them. Did you ever think we'd have so many new words?" His voice trailed off. "But you're not here to discuss architecture or vocabulary, are you? No, didn't think so. What's on your mind?"

"The curse."

"Why, it's gone, of course! So what do you think of my control room? State of the art! All satellite hookup. All wireless."

"Nice."

This was the trouble with social amenities; they got in the way of what he really wanted to talk about. Like *why* it had taken his father three thousand friggin' years to give him back his life. If he was going to end up forgiving him this easy, without any lectures, by Hades, he could've done it sooner!

But, he must have learned something from all those talk shows, because for the first time, Darius didn't spout off and dig himself in deeper. He wanted to see Alexandra again. Zeus went on talking, and Darius went on pretending to listen, while all the time he was wondering what Alexandra would think of Olympus.

Would she like it here? No allergies—she could throw her antihistamine away. No cooking. No mail to pile up. No dust. She'd like that, wouldn't she? Would his family like her?

Whoa!

"You okay, son? You've gone a little pale."

"I'm, uh, fi—I, uh—*water.*"

Zeus didn't even get to snap his fingers, and Darius had a goblet of fresh water from one of Olympus's wells.

What in Hades was I thinking? Alexandra? Here?

Once he got over the fright of thinking of her in his life in a more permanent manner than what he'd been thinking earlier, he found he sort of liked the idea; it could grow on him. Olympus held all the marble she could ever need. She could spruce up the place with some magnificent statues. One of Zeus and one of Hera would go a long way toward their acceptance of her in the, uh, family.

Oh boy.

He chugged the rest of the water and a refill.

"Got a few extra computers around, of course," Zeus was still talking. "Even on Olympus, this stuff goes obsolete before you know it."

"Extra computers? Really?"

"Oh yeah. Better than anything Gates has come up with."

"Mind if I take one?"

"You?" Zeus studied him closely. Suspiciously. "What would you want with a computer?"

"Billy needs one. Well, Alexandra says Billy needs one, and she would know." He was rambling. He shouldn't have mentioned Alexandra. Not yet.

"Billy's an orphan," Hermes chimed in. He'd dared to enter the control room when he hadn't heard any bellowing.

"An orphan!" Zeus said with admiration. "Now there's a worthy cause. Of course you may take one. Glad to see you're taking an interest in the less fortunate. Good to have you back, son. Couldn't be happier."

He leaned forward and clasped Darius warmly on the shoulder, something Darius didn't recall ever happening before, at least not since he'd reached puberty. Usually they'd been at loggerheads about who got which woman, as their tastes were similar. Like father, like son.

"You know, son, Aphrodite mentioned you met someone . . ."

Uh oh, here it comes. *What's her name? Where does she live?*

"Someone special. Ever since we heard you found a perfect statue to move into, your mother's been talking grandchildren this and grandchildren that, and, never thought I'd say it, but I'd kind of like bouncing a grandbaby on my knee while I surf the Net. And heaven knows, we could use some fresh blood on Olympus. She have family that would object to her living here?"

"Just a sister." If Claudia objected, he'd offer to replace her fake gems with real ones. That should satisfy her.

A beeping sound diverted Zeus's attention.

"Blast!" he roared at the computer, propelling his wheeled chair across the floor until he faced his desk again.

"Lost him," Hermes said. "He'll be like that for hours. At least you caught him at a good time."

Still in shock at this new side of his father, Darius stood, not sure whether to wait around or go. They used to roar at each other until one of them stormed out.

"It's like he's someone else."

"Yeah."

"Since when does he care about orphans?"

Hermes shrugged. "Long time ago."

"Why?"

"Not sure. Hera's waiting for you." He ducked a playful swipe of Darius's arm. "Hey, don't blame me. When Hera says to tell her when you return, I tell her."

"You couldn't say you forgot over how many centuries? Ah, never mind, I'm kidding. I want to see everyone, as long as it doesn't take all day. *After* I change into my own clothes. Then I'm going back for Alexandra. She'll love it here."

Try as he might, Darius couldn't get away before dark. Hera wanted to spend time with him; turned out she had an ulterior motive, as she repeatedly mentioned a sweet young goddess she'd "handpicked" to be his wife. Zeus hadn't been kidding about that grandchild thing.

And he'd thought mortals were bad, wanting a few of his gems.

Darius didn't want to argue with her, so he just avoided the whole topic. She'd know soon enough when he showed up with Alexandra, and when faced with a genuine prospect, she'd be thrilled by Alexandra's grace and beauty. Why, she'd start furnishing a nursery the very next day!

At the family dining table in the royal hall that evening, Aphrodite elbowed Athena aside so she could sit next to Darius. Zeus was at the head, Hera opposite him. There was an empty chair midway.

"Anyone know why Cytus isn't here?" Hera said.

Aphrie quietly muttered that he no longer had any horses, Hermes snickered, and Apollo covered it all with a burst of lyre music.

"Not now," Hera ordered. "We want to be able to talk to Darius. He's been gone so long." She signaled to the harpist to resume her background music.

One thing Darius noticed right off today, as he visited around, was that most of the Olympians were up-to-date in their idiomatic expressions, much more so than he was. He'd had benefit of the satellite transmissions, but they'd been able to practice with mortals.

"Darius, tell everyone what's been happening since you've been back," Hera prompted.

By back, she meant alive. Halfway through his story about indoor rain at the charity auction preview, they explained sprinkler systems to him. Darius laughed along with them, never remembering a more comfortable time with his family. Aphrie had made changes in here, too; maybe there was something to that chi thing.

"I did the walls in soft shades to soothe the mood in here," she explained. "Got rid of those dark corners. Moved the table over to the west. Don't the plants make all the difference?"

His family quickly changed the subject.

He hadn't forgotten Alexandra and his eagerness to return to her ASAP—another wonderful, succinct mortal expression!—but it was better he didn't risk the horses traveling at night, and so he enjoyed this repast.

Until Cytus thundered into the hall, demanding to know who'd stolen his horses.

Darius stood, mellow with drink and good food and familial warmth. Calmly he stated, "They are mine."

"You!" Cytus advanced on him, rage in his eyes. "I should have known!"

"Cytus," Zeus said mildly, "sit down and eat your dinner."

"But—"

"No buts. Darius is correct, the team is his."

"Oh yeah? I suppose next you'll be wanting to give him

back his house and everything else, too, huh? Well, forget it! Hades can freeze over first!" He stormed out of the hall.

"Now there's a hothead," Darius said.

"Remind you of anyone?" Zeus asked, laughing.

"Like father, like son, I always say," Hera said. "With that tramp Aara for a mother, what can you expect?"

So, Darius thought, Zeus had decided to have Aara. Of course there'd been no competition, with Darius broken and useless at the bottom of the cliff.

Still, that was a long time ago, and he let it go.

He turned to Hermes. "You didn't mention he took my house, too."

"Just sitting there empty," he mumbled. "Athena, pass the salt?"

Darius was constantly afraid Hera was going to start back in on the "sweet-tempered, young goddess; very biddable" conversation.

Biddable! After dueling with Alexandra, he couldn't even imagine being interested in such a female. Not only had Alexandra ruined Selena and her staff, she'd done a pretty good number on him, too, he realized. *Twenty-first century, here I come!*

Cytus stormed back into the hall shortly thereafter, took the seat opposite Darius, and grinned evilly.

"So how's your girlfriend? Think she misses you?"

Refusing to be baited, Darius slowly lifted his goblet and sipped, covering how he felt inside. There, not too far from the surface, was a need as strong as any he'd ever known— so strong it almost scared him—to whip that chair right out from under Cytus and bash him over the head with it. He wouldn't even have to rise from the table to do it.

But wait, if Zeus was Cytus's father, then the brat wasn't

as inconsequential as he'd thought, but another half brother. Not that he put much store in pesky relatives, but this new, kinder, gentler Zeus might.

"Better yet, will you miss her?" Cytus prodded. "You know, say, if something should happen to her?"

15

On Tuesday after Darius left, Alex congratulated herself on not falling into bed with him, then moped around for hours. If she stayed in the studio any longer, she'd have to face Claudia coming by to check on the statue, which, obviously, was nowhere in sight, so she pulled herself together, faced the inevitable, and went job hunting.

She couldn't believe how many shopkeepers and store owners were so darned well informed about her life. What gave them the right to look at her with mistrust when she gave them her name? Eyeing their inventory protectively, memorizing every piece, checking it repeatedly until she exited their stores. Locking display cabinets and pocketing keys. Alerting reinforcements. You'd think she was a klepto the way they watched her.

Her luck was no better in the cafes and restaurants; something about the security of their cash registers, they said. The manager of the only day care center within walking distance—and she was up to a two-mile radius here—mentioned that her facility served a very elite group of parents (her nose was up in the air as she said this) who would most definitely object to exposing their innocent young children to a common thief.

"Common?" This was pushing her too far. "Hey, it takes more than a *common* thief to make a full-sized statue vanish in front of four hundred people," she'd said as she stormed out.

When she got home, her problems weren't over. It was early yet, but she'd be spending another night with little sleep, this time wary of the stranger Darius had told her about before he'd flown off, warning her to lock her doors and windows. Apparently someone wearing a hooded sweatshirt had been paying regular nightly visits, and Darius had finally seen fit to pass on that bit of information. What a guy.

She'd take a hammer to bed with her. Her rasp would make a good weapon; its handle had disappeared long ago, leaving the long, narrow, pointed shaft exposed. She'd shove her dresser in front of the door, barricading herself in until morning.

Should she call the cops?

Sure, like they didn't already think *she* was the one who needed watching, not some peeping Tom.

"Who exactly has seen this stranger, Miss de Marco?"

"Darius."

"Last name?"

"Third son of Zeus. He's been staying with me since he moved into my marble statue and came to life."

Uh-huh, sure.

She needed a good night's sleep so she could clear her mind and decide once and for all if it was better to lust after him or plot his untimely end.

At home, she walked into a squabble between Kesia and Daniel over who could have what out of her suddenly fully stocked refrigerator. It didn't take more than a quick glance inside to see that none of the items were store-bought. Damn, just when she thought she could stay mad at Darius until he was completely out of her system, he went and did something nice.

Julian shouted for her to come talk to the cop at the front door. A comforting sense of warmth rushed over her and filled her, to think that Darius, with her welfare in mind, had alerted the police to the peeping Tom. Logic slammed in a split second later; she knew he'd done no such thing. Still, though, the warmth clung to her like a security blanket.

Did other women go through these roller-coaster emotional swings?

"So . . . didja get it back in one piece?" An officer from the park had forgotten to get her signature.

"Mm-hm." She didn't read the form; better to get him out of here as fast as possible.

Julian had let him in, so he didn't have to ask permission to look around. "Where is it?"

"I sent it out for cleaning." She shoved the signed form back at him.

"For—what? Who does—"

"Thank you for coming." She practically pushed him out the door, then warned Julian again about not opening doors to strangers.

"But policemen are our friends."

She muttered, "Not at this address."

T.J. and Billy dragged the broken bed out of her bedroom, with "Way to go, Alex!" from T.J., "What's that mean?" from Billy, and a sniping "You can do better" from Maria. One look at the lopsided box spring, and she had the boys remove it, too, leaving the mattress parked on the floor like a raft adrift at sea. She wouldn't be sleeping tonight anyway;

she'd be sitting up, waiting for a sweatshirt-hooded visitor, thinking about someone else entirely.

Where was Darius sleeping tonight?

Olympus, she guessed, not knowing how long it took gods to flit around the sky. How fast did horses pull chariots, anyway?

Would he turn back into marble there, after sunset? Did the sun set on Olympus?

Would he get injured and turn into marble permanently? A hangnail was all it would take.

Would his father remove the curse and let Darius leave Olympus again? Or was he still so mad that he'd just lop his head off?

Did thinking about him mean she cared?

Well, hell, he'd been a big part of her life lately, of course she'd *think* about him. He probably wouldn't think about her, though, or the children. He'd become part of their lives for a while, but not the other way around. She shouldn't be wasting her time. She should be ordering more marble and starting a new statue to show the club she had her priorities in line, that she'd do everything in her power to replace the "stolen" one. She'd work day and night, except for when she had to go to a job to earn her keep, and then the club could hold a semiannual charity auction, right? Just this once.

Except the home would be closed by then, the children shuttled off to who knew where, making it hard to keep track of them. And keep track of them she would. She would *not* abandon them.

Damn Darius, anyway.

"Oh hell," she said. "Hermes, if you can hear me, I have a message for Zeus. If he—or anybody up there, for that matter—is just going to kill Darius or do something, you know, equally drastic, tell him I could sure use the statue back. In good shape. You know, for the kids."

She didn't dare ask for what *she* wanted, didn't dare hope to wake up in the middle of the night to find Darius, the man, in her bed. Living. Breathing. With all parts working.

Unable to face another day of useless job hunting on Wednesday, unable to order more marble without a legitimate invoice number from the Ladies' Club (and she knew they wouldn't give her one), what was a woman to do? Darius's gratuity wasn't enough. Alex finished off a bowl of the most heavenly fruit salad, then wandered outside to poke in the garden with Griff.

"Thought you'd be coming out here," he said, setting her bucket in front of her.

When she was six, he'd bought it for her very own, a pink one filled with shiny new, green-handled garden tools. You could no longer tell the color of the handles, but after two decades and more than a few teary conversations, he'd kept the tools rust-free.

"I should've come out here yesterday," she said, sitting beside him on the grass, in the sunshine, turning her attention to weeding around the geraniums. Later they'd move into the shade.

"What'd you do?"

"Looked for a job." *Sat up all night.* Well, until she'd fallen asleep. She checked out the young man blowing grass clippings off the driveway, idly wondering if he could be her nocturnal visitor.

"Any luck?"

"Hm? Oh, a job. No, seems my reputation precedes me."

"He's too young for you."

"What?"

"That boy you're staring at's too young for you."

"No kidding. Oh!" She laughed at the thought of her and a twenty-year-old, then sobered again. "Has he been working here long?"

"On and off the past few weeks. Mrs. Wilson's grandson, needs some spending money, you know how it is."

"Nepotism."

"Yeah. But he seems okay. I was worried at first, 'cause he always shows up wearing long sleeves. Thought maybe he's hiding something, you know. But he works in the sun awhile, sheds his sweatshirt, no tracks. So I ask him about it, real casual-like. Says with all the heat training he did this summer for road races, he chills easy." He reached over and helped her with a stubborn root. "You're still staring."

"Only because there's been a man coming into my studio at night, wearing a hooded sweatshirt. Or jacket maybe. I don't know if Darius knows the difference. So I was just wondering, you know, about *him*." After her sleepless night, she'd be wondering about everything on two legs.

"He *saw* someone inside?" He didn't even wait for her nod. "Well, that has to stop right damn now. You go sleep at your sister's tonight."

"Uh, no-o." Alex liked her freedom and space way too much to give it up so easily.

"There you are!" Speak of the devil, Claudia had found her. Dressed all in red linen, she rivaled the geraniums for color. "Where the hell is the statue?"

Pull weed, drop in bucket. Pull weed, drop in bucket.

"Alexandra!"

"Gone."

"Shit."

Alex arched her eyebrows at her socially perfect sister's uncustomary curse, then almost passed out as Claudia plopped down on the other side of Griff and started pulling weeds, too. Her Radiantly Red nail polish wasn't going to hold up to this.

"Claudia?" Alex whispered.

"What?" she groused.

"Just checking to be sure it was you."

"Oh, maybe it's my fault. Griff, can you put your bucket between us? Thanks. Maybe I've been spending too much time searching for our dad instead of keeping an eye on you."

"Keeping an eye on me?" Alex said slowly, her tone edged with warning.

"You know what I mean. Seeing if you needed help. Taking some of the pressure off. You must have been under a lot, and so was I, what with getting the unveiling ready, but really, I guess I could have spent more time with you. But you know, I'm getting so close to finding . . ."

Maybe, Alex realized, she could have spent more time asking Claudia how that was going. Hey, what was a little more blame today? "Sorry. What've you found out?"

"Well, for one, the detective thinks Mrs. Wallis knows something."

This could be great news; she should have asked sooner. Much sooner. She'd been too focused on that statue. Unearthing her roots was just as important, always had been.

Claudia continued. "Did you know she used to be a member here? Yeah, me neither. His question—and I'm in perfect agreement—is why someone with enough money to belong to this club would take a job at an orphanage."

"Maybe that explains why the home has always been a pet project."

"That's something else he's looking into, her relationship with some of the ladies. Like maybe one of the former members placed *two small children* at the home."

Funny, this topic had come up at the pizza/slumber party the other night, though with a different slant then. Had their mother been close to a member of the club? Is that why they'd cut this art deal with Alex? The committee had approached *her*, not the other way around. She'd always thought it was because Claudia was a member, but maybe that wasn't it at all.

"He also has a bit warmer trail on an uncle, on Mom's side, who may or may not still be in St. Louis. If he can find him, then we're one step closer."

Griff cleared his throat. "This search . . . it's really important that you girls find out about your dad?"

"Yes!" they answered in unison.

"One of you's not sick or something? Some mysterious illness you're trying to nail down?" he asked, a faint tremor in his voice betraying his concern.

"Sick of being abandoned," Alex said.

"Curious, too," Claudia said. "There's a big hole in our lives, Griff. You know: Who do we look like? Is our dad still living? Do we have aunts and uncles and cousins? Other sisters and brothers, maybe. Maybe even here, in the city. We could celebrate birthdays together," she said wistfully.

"Holidays," Alex added, in the same tone. They'd lain awake many times in the girls' dormitory, voicing this same dreamy scenario. "With people we're related to. Enough of them that maybe we'd always have someone who'd never leave, no matter what."

Intuitively, Alex reached across Griff and met her sister's outstretched hand.

Griff cleared his throat again and ran the back of his hand

across his cheek. "You know, you two could be openin' a kettle of worms." They said nothing. "Might find out something you don't want to know."

Claudia caught Alex's eye over Griff's back as he stretched way forward to reach behind the geraniums. "Like what, Griff?"

He sat back up, dumped a handful of weeds in his bucket, and surveyed the area. "Lookin' better."

"Griff," Alex said warningly.

"What?" He looked back and forth at the two of them. "Did I miss something?"

"Yeah, you know something we don't?"

"About the parent thing? Nope, not a durned thing. Just heed what I say, though. Plenty so-called orphans've found their folks only to find out they're not wanted."

"And plenty go the other way," Claudia said.

"Yeah," Alex said. "We have to know, Griff. Look at us, our relationships leave a lot to be desired. Claudia's on her second husband. I'm divorced. Psychologists say we have issues that have to be resolved." Wouldn't a psychologist love to hear she'd fallen in love with a—

Wait a minute! Not love, no way. She didn't even want to admit she *liked* Darius. She could list fifty reasons to not like him, a hundred to not lo— No, she couldn't even think the word. Preposterous. He was a *statue*, and meant for the children. She wasn't playing Pygmalion to his Galatea.

Yet she remembered how he'd cuddled Rashida, joyfully played along and sang the alphabet song with the children, fed them—

Stop it.

The sensuous way he looked at her, touched her, kissed the scar that her husband said made her ugly . . .

Stop it right now!

"I ain't no psychologist," Griff said, "but even I know there's different ways of going about that."

"Yeah, well, we choose this way," Claudia said, wiping perspiration from her brow. "Why are we doing this in the sun?"

"That's where the weeds grow," Alex said, determined to drag her focus away from the unthinkable, back to a sane, productive conversation. "Griff, you've been around a long time. Do you remember back when we were left at the home?"

He shook his head. "No, sorry," he said sadly. "You were already there when I got the job."

They pulled weeds in silence until Claudia said, "Well, we better find out something soon. This search is breaking the bank."

Alex thought this was as good a time as any to test Darius's theory. "Does your husband know about your fake jewels?"

"*What?*"

Now no one was pulling weeds, and Griff's head swiveled back and forth between them.

"Your emeralds, for one," she bluffed.

"What are you talking about? I never heard such—"

"And that diamond ring you're wearing. Were any of them ever real?"

"Of course—" Claudia glanced around nervously, checking the yard for eavesdroppers, then whispered, "How did you know?"

"Darius told me." If he was right about that, what else was he right about?

"Oh for goodness' sakes! What would a two-bit pretty face know about precious stones?"

"Darius. You know . . . god of gems?"

Claudia lowered her voice to Griff. "Has she been like this long? Confused about reality, I mean."

"I am not confused about—"

"Oh no, you just think because you made a piece of marble look like a mythological god of gems, that the model you used—never mind, I can't even say this."

"And you tried to steal the diamond tennis bracelet from my studio."

"I never!"

"Twice. The second time, you sent Matthew."

Claudia started to deny it, then snapped her mouth shut. Then just as quickly struck back with her own accusations. "What about the ladies' missing jewelry? You going to return *it* any time soon?"

"I don't have it."

"Oh, right, I forgot. The *god* probably *repossessed* it."

"He's *real*. And that's exactly what he did."

"You hocked your jewelry to finance your search?" Griff asked, his voice husky with disbelief.

"That was our deal," Claudia said, her chin raised defensively. Her husband thought she'd spent too much on this long ago. "Alex'd help the children by way of the auction— she's got the talent to do it—and I'd find our dad."

"But I didn't know you'd sell your jewelry!"

"Well, you never really asked, did you?" Claudia sighed. "Just like I never asked how your end was coming. And now you've cracked under the stress."

"I have *not* cracked."

Claudia rolled her eyes.

"Well, maybe I can help out here," Griff said, then grinned. "Just like old times, huh? Claudia, your sister isn't cracking up. The statue is . . . well, Darius is . . . ah, heck they're one and the same. Now no, don't say nothing. I've seen it for myself, and you know I wouldn't lie to you, and I'm not cracking up, either. I can't explain it, but there it is. Just accept it and deal with it.

"And Alex, you've got to convince your sister to quit this search. When her husband finds out about her jewelry, well, that's not a pretty picture, is it? If all that money hasn't turned up anything yet, then it likely never will. Maybe there's a reason you're not supposed to find out anything. Maybe someone like that uppity Mrs. Johnson's son is your father."

Claudia looked aghast, as Ted Johnson was constantly in and out of legal trouble for one shady deal after another.

"There go the warm, fuzzy holidays," Alex said wryly.

"Make light of it if you want, but sometimes terrible things happen in families, secret things you're probably better off not knowing."

Darius rushed back to the Central West End as fast as the horses could carry him, which was a bit slower since he'd detoured past Pompeii and picked up a little something extra that he knew Alexandra would love—an ironclad solution to their dilemma, and wouldn't that please her?

After Cytus's threat, Darius feared for Alexandra's safety, but while he'd been getting things together, Hermes kept watch on Cytus's whereabouts, promising to notify him immediately if Cytus attempted to leave Olympus.

Halfway back to the studio, Darius was overcome with a sense of urgency as he realized Cytus probably had accomplices. For the first time ever, his horses heard the crack of his whip.

Would Cytus harm Alexandra?

I must protect her!

Because he owed her? No, if he merely owed her, he

wouldn't have put the thought he had into the cargo he was carrying. Even Aphrie had been impressed.

Did he love her? Aphrie said he did, but he didn't believe it. Love meant giving up what he valued, giving up his life, losing power, gaining heartache. He might've been without a body for three thousand years, but that didn't mean he'd had his head in the sand. He saw things. He knew love ruined strong men. Nope, wasn't love.

He wanted to establish Alexandra in his house, be her protector, and make her the mother of his children, but that wasn't love. Was it?

He sure liked her a lot. He probably looked like a fool, one minute grinning from ear to ear in anticipation of seeing her again, the next, frowning over her safety, driving his horses as fast as the wind. Not an hour went by he didn't think of how sweet it would be to finally make mad, passionate love to her. In that respect, and only that respect, he could use the L-word. To strip off her clothing, taste her lips and her body, inch by glorious inch, until she writhed beneath him, begging him for release, screaming out his name—

"Hey, easy there," he soothed the team as they suddenly swerved off course. Totally his fault for letting his mind wander, so he reined it in until he landed safely behind Alexandra's studio. Turning the horses loose to graze, he unloaded his gifts, eager to see the expression on her face. He entered via the back door, peeking around the corner to see if she was there, telekinetically transporting everything behind him.

"Alexandra?" Upon receiving no reply, he jauntily entered her bedroom, hoping to find her waiting for him in bed.

No such luck. But it looked as if he owed her a bed. He stood there awhile, letting time slip by, staring at the mattress on the floor with longing, wondering if her pillow smelled like her spicy shampoo, if the sheets were still warm where she'd slept.

No one was watching. No one would know.

He sank to his knees on the mattress, wishing she were there beneath him. Bending forward at the waist, pressing his nose into the linens, he inhaled deeply and, yes, there it was, that special scent that could only be Alexandra. A spice he didn't know so many centuries ago. He stretched out, resting his head on her pillow, closing his eyes and dreaming again of how he would adore her body.

"You're in over your head," Hermes said.

Darius groaned, annoyed at getting caught. Hundreds of thousands of women in this city alone, and here he was, sniffing an empty bed, pining for the woman who'd slept there. "Go away. I want to enjoy this."

"No, wait, you've lost your mind. I'll tell Aphrie you need help."

Too eager to brag to remain irritated, Darius rolled over and sat cross-legged in the center. "Actually, she saw what I was bringing back and said I did pretty well."

Hermes' eyebrows arched in disbelief. "Really? You think bringing Billy a computer's going to get you into her bed? Which, by the way, looks different."

"I didn't bring the computer to get her into bed." Darius grinned, rising fluidly to his feet, still aware of every movement he made, every muscle and joint, every surface he touched, even now. "I brought something better for that."

"Really? What?"

"I'm not going to show you before I show her."

"Oh come on, I'm your brother."

"Precisely."

"Aphrie thinks it'll work?"

"I didn't tell her my purpose."

Hermes snickered.

Darius scowled. "Don't you have somewhere else to be?"

"Well, I have a message for the gardener, but I'm waiting until he's alone. Alexandra's with him outside."

"Really? Outside?" With a bounce in his step, Darius strode out of the studio like a man with a mission. He found Alexandra on her knees, digging in the dirt, a pile of limp weeds overflowing the bucket beside her. "Alexandra," he said, shocked to see her engaged in menial labor.

She turned slowly, her gaze starting at his sandals, working its way up bare legs to his thigh-length tunic, lingering on his chest, then rising to his eyes. For a moment, just a moment before she caught herself, he thought he saw interest. No, not interest . . . well, yes, that too, but . . . pleasure. She was happy to see him alive again! Yes, no matter how hard she tried to cover that, he'd seen it, recognized it, and it made his heart swell with joy.

"Come inside," he said gently. He held his hand out to her, waiting with bated breath to see if she'd take it, if she'd look upon him as a live male—not a wannabe—and let him help her to her feet.

"Well shoot me now," she said, turning the trowel in her grip, maybe getting ready to plunge it into his foot.

"Alexandra," he said warningly.

With a reluctant sigh, she jabbed it into the pile of weeds. For a moment, she did nothing but think, fighting her own battles, and he let her, because some steps she had to take on her own.

"Wouldn't work anyway," he said.

"I have to—"

"I'll clean this up," Griff offered.

She nodded at him, then turned and looked up at Darius

again. There it was, just the hint of a smile, as if she'd realized that if she couldn't have the statue, she could at least have the god.

Perhaps she'd come to realize it was the better deal. Wait until he told her his plans! Many women would sacrifice their firstborn to receive the honor he was about to bestow upon her—a home, with him, among the gods on Olympus.

Her hand, when she placed it in his, was rough from work, dirty from the garden; nothing had ever felt so good. So right. Rising to her feet, she followed him toward the studio. So did Hermes.

"Get lost," Darius said.

"But I want to see what you brought—"

Darius slammed the door in Hermes's face and locked it, never taking his eyes off Alexandra, nor his hands.

Yet, all too soon, she pulled free. "I have to, uh, go wash up. If the kids get here before I get back, will you give them a snack? They're always hungry after school, and they concentrate better on their artwork if they've got something in their stomachs."

The kids—*again?* His admiration for her dedication was in grave danger of morphing into frustration.

"And can you get those horses out of my backyard before somebody calls the cops?"

He attributed her rambling to nerves, as surely she knew why he'd returned. Surly she'd missed him and recognized her own need to feel his hands on her again.

Well, he'd give the children their presents first, then send them home. Aphrie said he'd chosen well, that Alexandra would be pleased. This was a new concept to him, how giving someone a gift could make someone else happy, but he'd thought about it all the way here, and maybe there was some logic in it. The children were Alexandra's life, and he was making them happy, therefore she'd be happy too. Why hadn't he figured that out before? Was that why he'd chosen the gifts he had? Had it been subconscious? Or was he starting to like children, to see them as people, more so than a nuisance to deal with before bedding the woman he wanted?

Whoa, this was way too deep for an unmodern guy!

"Hey, Alex!" Billy, Kesia, and little Rashida charged into the studio, each of them aglow with excitement. "Alex, Alex, there's horses outside!"

"And a wagon!"

"It's a chariot, silly."

"And a chariot! Oh, hi, Darius. Where's Alex?"

"Is it yours?"

"Of course it's his," Billy said. "Hey, Darius."

"Hey. Alexandra's washing up. She'll be out in a minute."

Rashida pointed at the stack of gifts on the worktable. "Wha's that?"

"I brought some things I thought you might like."

"Okay, all clean," Alexandra said, coming out of her bedroom in clean shorts and a T-shirt. Barefoot. She had pretty feet, nice delicate toes, graceful arches. He could start kissing her there and lick his way up to—

Later.

"Darius brought us presents!"

"Here, Billy," he said, "the computer's for you."

"Wow!"

"You brought him a computer? Oh, Darius," Alexandra said softly.

Now *that* was a tone he liked, tinged with awe and gratitude, he thought. Perhaps Aphrie had been right. Perhaps he *had* chosen well.

"You didn't steal it did you? Because if you did—"

"No, I didn't steal it, my father sends it with his blessings." Then, catching the boy's excitement, he said, "Well, turn it on."

Billy examined all sides. "There's no cord."

"Hm, Hermes didn't mention a cord, but he said to tell you to just turn it on. And when you get it home, put the round thing in a sunny window."

Billy glanced at it, then turned very big eyes toward Darius. "It's totally wireless *and . . . solar* powered? I never saw—" He flipped the switch; the computer beeped. "Holy shit! Omigod!"

Darius grinned at the boy's appropriately reverent tone. "'Twas nothing." By Zeus, it felt good that *some*one around here appreciated him. "Here, Kesia . . ." He reached into his tunic and withdrew a soft, furry, green-eyed kitten. "I brought this little guy for you."

She didn't look overly excited. When the small white bundle mewed at her, she reached for it, her heart in her eyes. "I . . . I guess I can find her a home, too," she said sadly.

"This one's for you to keep."

She cuddled it, then handed it back. "Thanks, Darius, but I can't take it."

He knew she wanted it. Never had he met such stubborn—

"What *is* it with females in this century? Will none of you take *anything* from me?"

"I will," Rashida said, raising her hand.

He reined in his exasperation, remembered this was the twenty-first century and people were supposed to talk to each other. He asked Kesia to kindly explain.

"I only had enough money to buy the food for the kittens I'm giving away."

"She'll catch her own mice." That solved—maybe this talking thing wasn't so bad—he smiled and placed the kitten gently into her arms again.

She cuddled it for a moment before saying, "She'll need to be spayed, and I'll have to get her shots."

Picturing Dirty Harry blowing the poor, defenseless thing away, he snatched it back. "By Zeus, why would you shoot her?"

Startled, she studied him for a moment to see if he was serious. "Shots," she explained. "Vaccinations."

"Oh." That word he understood better, and he returned the kitten to her arms. "She won't need them—"

"She's had them?" Her smile lit up the room.

"—because she is immortal."

Alexandra yelled, *"What?"*

Kesia looked at Billy uncertainly. "What's that?"

"She'll live forever," he scoffed.

"Wow. Thanks, Darius."

"Oh no no. No no no," Alexandra said.

"Do not worry, Alexandra."

Did she seem to melt when he said her name? Come to think of it, he'd noticed that before. So she wasn't as unaffected by his return as she'd have him believe.

Rashida gazed up at him imploringly, hoping she hadn't been forgotten. Remembering how much she'd liked his diamond brooch, Darius draped a string of crystals around her neck and fastened a matching one on her wrist.

"Ooh, look, Alex." She twisted this way and that, watching them glitter in the light.

Finally, a female who didn't mind accepting a gift.

"They're not—" Alexandra began.

"No," he said. "Not diamonds. Not stolen." He winked, just to let her know he knew how her mind worked. "Ready for yours?"

She sounded suspicious when she said, "My what?"

16

She needed time to think! Darius was handing out presents left and right. Questionable presents. She didn't know much about computers, but from Billy's reaction, should he have one light-years ahead of the rest of the planet? How could he explain that to anyone? If he told the truth, he'd be branded a liar. If he lied . . . well, that was just wrong. But he needed a computer.

A kitten that grew into a cat that never died would be simpler to explain. Somehow. Kesia didn't need it, but it was far less obvious than a computer. She couldn't take Kesia's gift away and let Billy keep his.

As for Rashida's beads, Darius said they weren't diamonds.

"But they're not valuable, are they?" Alex asked.

"No," he whispered.

"Magic?"

"I can't do magic."

"Stolen?"

"*Quit asking that.*"

"Given your past—"

"I don't steal. The gems are mine, remember?"

"And this—whatever you brought me—is it yours to give?"

"Technically it's no one's."

She rolled her eyes. "In other words—"

"Now it's yours. Or it will be in a few seconds, if you'd let me get on with it." With a theatrical flourish, he extended his arm, indicating a vertical object covered by her art drape. The flowered sheets had hidden his tall form pretty well, but they drowned this four-foot-tall gift in a pool of cotton.

"I'm not liking that 'technically' part."

"You're going to love it when you see it, and it'll solve all your problems. You won't think twice about the statue of me anymore."

That certainly sounded promising.

"It's a little marked up because of the eruption, but I know—"

"What eruption?"

"Pompeii, 79, a lot of rubble . . ."

He'd brought her something from Pompeii? "No way."

"Yes way," he said, his chest puffing out with pride at his up-to-date response.

Well, a cordless, solar-powered computer . . . maybe he *had* brought her something from Pompeii. If anybody could, it was he.

Seemingly thinking he was on a roll, he telekinetically whipped off the drape.

It stood there in front of them without fanfare; could be any common work of art in any studio. But it wasn't common. He was right, it was a little marked up. Scratched, banged, with hairline cracks, it was a marble statue of an older, smaller god, with horns, cloven hooves, and a curlicue tail. She didn't know whether to ooh and aah, or snicker.

"This is supposed to solve all my problems, how?"

"Clean it up and auction it off."

Tentatively at first, her hands wandered over it from top to bottom, taking its measure. How could someone, using only rudimentary tools, turn out something so perfect? As her hands caressed it, she was honored to be in the presence of a work of art so ancient, so precious, so magnificent. It belonged in one of the finest museums in the world, under controlled conditions. Never in a million years could she have dreamed of this moment, when she'd be the first to see—and touch!—such an exquisite work, crafted so long ago by a true artisan.

It could fetch a nice price at the auction. It, and the matching donation, could put the home back in the black—until the truth was discovered and it got her thrown in jail.

Why was it that so many things Darius did threatened *her* freedom? Now she was sorry she'd given an inch on the computer and kitten; having done so made it harder to justify why they were okay, but this wasn't. Didn't matter, though. She couldn't use it, and she said as much.

"Why not?"

"Gee, maybe because it's a stolen antiquity?"

He shook his head. "Not stolen."

"Darius, anything unearthed from an ancient site and transported here, without permission, is stolen."

"So don't tell anyone it's old."

She laughed at his naiveté. "Yeah, like any expert wouldn't know. And even if they didn't, I do. I could never take credit for someone else's work."

"He's dead," he said dryly.

"Doesn't matter. Take it back." She folded her arms across her chest and glared at him.

He mirrored her pose just as stubbornly. "I thought you wanted to help the children."

"By getting arrested?" And she'd wondered how her reputation could plummet further. "I don't think so."

"You won't take my gems. You won't take a statue no one owns . . ."

"Can't you get it through your head? Those are temporary, stop-gap measures. Without my *widely advertised* statue of Darius, my reputation is shot. I'll never be trusted again. I'll never get another commission to make any more statues to bring in any more money. I won't be able to help the home this year, next year, or the year after that. I won't be able to help Maria and T.J. when their maintenance stops. I'm telling you, take it back."

"I'm not leaving for a while."

Funny how such a casual statement made her all warm inside again. And though his words were simple, the way he gazed at her was hot and complicated, made her think he wanted her, made her remember he wasn't repulsed by her scar, made her want him.

"What about Zeus's curse?" she asked, knowing the myth.

"Gone."

The single word made her smile. "You sure?"

"I watched the sun set last night." His eyes twinkled with merriment. "So you can quit planning your next attack."

Darius worked to get Alexandra alone for the next couple of hours, while she seemed to work to keep the mood light. She wouldn't let Billy give up his art time for the computer, no matter how much he argued that he could trade the time doing computer graphics instead; it was a lighthearted argument at best.

From time to time, while the children created art, she admired the statue he'd brought her. Being Alexandra, she couldn't keep her hands off it. Wasn't long before she was checking it out, every square inch of it (he *would* have to bring her a nude!), and he knew it was crazy, but he suddenly found himself dealing with feelings of jealousy. Over a dirty statue!

It wasn't until after they'd walked the children home— they made him look as if he were carrying the computer when, in fact, he telekinesed it—that he was able to get her alone. At last.

Sunset wasn't far off. It would be the first they'd enjoy together. The first of many, he hoped, visualizing a radiant sky, goblets of heavenly nectar, and three thousand years of testosterone-build-up lovemaking. It would be a perfect night.

Ah, to wake with her in his arms tomorrow. He'd tell her then of his plans to introduce her to his family, to establish her in his home on Olympus. She'd be delighted to leave her allergies behind. Of course she'd never leave without helping the children first, so, without the distraction of her trying to maim him, they'd put their heads together and solve that dilemma; she would have to give in and accept some gems, and together they'd come up with a plausible explanation. Once she was situated on Olympus, the kids could visit from time to time. While he hadn't surfed the Net himself and didn't know how it worked, he was fairly certain Hermes or Zeus could set up a way they could all keep in contact between visits.

Yes, he had it all worked out. Now he was getting the hang of this alive business. He just hadn't had his feet under him before, that's all. Took a while to catch up so many centuries.

"What are you thinking?" she asked, strolling beside him on a sidewalk cracked and canted by tree roots.

He'd tucked her hand into his when they'd left the home, and she hadn't objected, though he thought she was slightly uncomfortable by the contact. Nervous, perhaps. So this was good, a warm-up to let her get used to touching him.

"Oh look, a help wanted sign," she said suddenly, dragging him along in her wake. "I have to go inside for a minute."

She didn't need a job; she was coming home with him, but he'd already decided not to surprise her until tomorrow morning. He released her hand, feeling an odd twinge of abandonment as he was left to browse the boutique.

Again, words everywhere, just like outside. Here they were on signs above the racks of clothes. On small tags. Taped to the walls. If he learned this modern-day script, he'd be able to leave little love notes around the house for Alexandra. She'd like that. Hermes could teach him.

"C'n I help you?" the clerk mumbled, something attached to his tongue.

Darius crouched low, staring at the clerk's mouth, aiming for a better look. "Is that a gem?"

"Darius . . ." Alexandra warned.

With all the unrepossessed gems out there, he supposed he didn't need to pry this guy's mouth open to see what was inside. He could miss one here and there, especially if doing so avoided angering Alexandra before showing her what a stud he was. Besides, the jewelry in his eyebrow was cheap, so probably the other was, too. On the other hand, maybe he wore it in his tongue to keep it safe. Mortals were strange; he definitely couldn't wait to return to Olympus. With Alexandra there, he need never deal with men again.

Knowing he might be here a couple more days, he thumbed through a rack. "I need some clothes." A few minutes later, Alexandra, all smiles, ushered him out the door. "But I—"

"No money, no clothes."

"What about what the ladies stuffed in my cloth?"

"That's for the kids. You didn't take anything from the store, did you?"

He sighed mightily. "I only take—"

"What's mine," they finished together.

"I know that's what you say," she said, smiling ruefully. "I'm just not sure I believe it."

He noticed how her smile turned warm and silky when he grasped her hand again. How she walked closer to his side, bumping arms every other step. He held her hand close, intentionally brushing the backs of her knuckles against his leg.

"Oh, I got the job!"

"So I heard." He squeezed her hand tenderly, raised it to his lips and kissed it. "You want to watch the sunset from the studio, or go to the park?"

"Uh . . ." She stared at her hand. He kissed it again, pleased to see her eyes darken with desire. She licked her lips.

My, if one little kiss had her speechless, well, he didn't dare anticipate how erotic the rest of the night would be. He might not be able to wait until after the sun set.

So *this* was foreplay.

He summoned Selena as soon as they walked in the door. Gold goblets of nectar were in their hands within seconds, and Selena left. Tomorrow he'd order one crafted especially for Alexandra, fit for a goddess, set with aquamarines that he would hand select.

"Let's go outside," he said, slipping his arm around her shoulders, savoring the feel of her slender body tucked against his side, even if she resisted that a bit. He'd noticed long ago that she let only Claudia and the children get in her personal space. With Matthew and the movers and the club members, and even with him, she frequently took a step back.

She'd come around. Indeed, he already felt her softening against his side, her hip brushing his as she allowed him to draw her along. Finally, her resistance melted away through and through, and she slipped her arm around him, her fingers cupping his waist.

She flowed in step with him toward the door, toward the waning sunset, though he could tell by her shaky smile that she was nervous, surely knowing what was to come later. Finally they were meeting on familiar ground: the pursuer and the prize.

By Zeus, if he made it through the sunset without having her right out there on the garden wall, it'd be a miracle. Turning her against his body, he engulfed her within the circle of his arms, hastily sent his goblet off to a table, and with his thumb, gently tipped her face up to meet his lips.

So sweet. So tender. He was about to suggest they skip the sunset when he noticed two things. The pink light was already fading from the wall, and there was a knock at the door. More like a pounding.

"Ignore it," he whispered, his lips brushing against hers as he spoke.

"Yeah," she agreed, just as softly. "Let's just stay in here."

"Alex! Are you in there? Alex!"

"Uh-oh, that's Jimmy. Sounds like it's urgent," she whispered against his lips.

"They got a search warrant for your studio! They're on the way now."

Slowly, reluctantly, she pulled out of his arms, looking up at him for help. Regretfully, he admitted to himself, he hadn't a clue.

Instinctively, he wanted nothing more than to hold on possessively, but it might frighten her, so he allowed her to ease away. He didn't know who Jimmy was, but when Alexandra opened the door, a uniformed officer stepped inside. She let him touch her shoulder, and when she didn't back away, Darius felt his hackles raise.

"Wha—What does that mean? What'm I supposed to do?"

"Calm down, honey," Jimmy said. "There's nothing you can do." Before he went on, he took a minute to tell Darius how he and Alexandra had grown up at the home together. "They're looking for stolen jewelry." He grinned down at her. "You haven't been knocking over any stores, have you?"

Uh-oh. Now where did Hermes put that stuff?

"No, of course not," Alexandra said with a forced laugh. Not because she knew about the loot, but probably because she was worried they'd find the gems he'd repossessed, which could be just as bad, he supposed. He quickly sent them out to the roof. But as for the burgled loot, he hadn't a clue.

"Holy shit!" Jimmy said.

"What?" Alexandra wheeled around. "Darius!"

"Hm? Oh." He'd been so distracted, he hadn't realized he was growing heavy. Changing. Solidifying.

"You *lied* to me?" she accused, as the pink rays dimmed. "I can't believe you *lied* to me!" She threw her goblet at him, making a direct hit smack in the middle of his chest before it fell to the floor with a clatter and rolled away.

It reminded him of other things rolling away, long ago.

No cuts, no blood; she hadn't hit him hard enough.

"Hey, Alex—" Jimmy said. From the shocked look on his face, Darius didn't think Jimmy'd ever seen this side of her before.

"I can't believe I was falling for a *liar*. Where the hell's my hammer?" She stormed across the room to her work area.

Jimmy followed. "Alex, what're you doing?"

Darius could barely draw air into his stiff lungs, let alone explain that he hadn't lied, that he *had* watched a sunset on Olympus, that he'd believed he was alive to stay. He knew what was happening. He knew there was only one way to stop her from injuring him. He had to make himself too ugly to sell, so ugly that she'd pray he came back to life in the morning.

Alex was beyond furious. Way beyond. She couldn't see straight as she shuffled through box after box, searching for a hard, sharp tool, any tool. Where was the drill when she needed it, anyway?

What had she been thinking? He was real? He was sex material? *Get a grip.* He just wanted to get in her pants before he left, that was all.

She settled for a hammer; she'd have to aim carefully. Wouldn't do to break too much. She strode toward him, ready to do some unfixable damage, something Hermes wouldn't be able to smooth over.

He blinked once, giving her pause. She didn't like to think of him as alive; she'd never intentionally attacked someone. Then slowly he raised one hand, holding her gaze captive with his progressively hardening eyes as he did so.

"You got any last words?" she gritted to the condemned god.

Jimmy squared off between them, grabbing her wrist. "Alex, no. You've worked too hard."

"Let go, Jimmy." Over his shoulder, she didn't like the look she saw in Darius's eyes. What was he up to?

"Think about what you're doing." Jimmy glanced over his shoulder. "What the hell—"

"Oh no! You wouldn't!" She couldn't get past Jimmy fast enough, and apparently Darius would.

With the last of his power, he assumed a position he knew she couldn't market. He stuck his finger up his nose.

"Oh shit."

The rest of the evening passed in one long horrific blur. At least the other officers entering her studio didn't take one look at her tussling over a hammer with Jimmy and shoot her on the spot. Though that might have been better all around. Then she wouldn't have had to endure the slow, tedious search, which resulted in a pillowcase of watches, cufflinks, and all sorts of jewelry, none of which looked like anything the club members would wear.

They didn't believe she'd never laid eyes on it before. Who would, given her recent history? Well, maybe Jimmy, but they'd grown up together and he loved her like a brother.

She wouldn't have suffered the ride in the back of a patrol car, the wait while Claudia contacted an attorney, the night in a cell, with a cot she wouldn't be caught dead on.

In addition, they charged her with stabling livestock within the city limits, or some such crock. She loudly pointed out that the property wasn't hers, therefore it wasn't her problem. Unfortunately, the club had big lawyers, and it did turn out to be her problem.

She was castigating herself, seeing how low she could go by replaying in her mind what she'd been about to do with Darius. God, what was *wrong* with her? Was she so sex-deprived that she wanted him then, still wanted him now? Was she so hard up for male affection that she actually *wanted* him to be alive in the morning? Maybe he hadn't lied to her; maybe sunsets on Olympus were different. Maybe the judge would order a psych evaluation, find her insane, and get her some serious help.

Giggles interrupted her maudlin, sniffling, head-in-her-hands reverie as she gave in and perched on the very edge of the cot. She tried to ignore the two women in the next cell, but the giggling got louder. Her head sunk lower.

"Psst!"

Reluctantly, she peeked between her fingers. "Oh, go away."

"Dare sent me to see if you're all right." Hermes slipped between the bars—she didn't see how—but when he crouched beside her, she rose and paced the small cell to avoid him. He was quicker on his feet, though, and he cornered her with a hand on her shoulder. "Should I break you out?"

"No!"

Both neighbors enthusiastically accepted his offer. To his credit, he ignored them.

"You're sure?"

"Break anything you want, I'm not leaving." Though, speaking of breaking, it was three A.M. and, if she was home before sunrise . . .

But no, she'd already admitted to herself she'd gotten past

that. If she were home before sunrise, she'd sit there patiently and wait for him.

"I'm pretty good with locks."

"You'll just get me in more trouble."

He glanced around the cell, his nose wrinkling when assaulted with the multitude of long-accumulated odors. "Is that possible?"

She shot him a cutting look.

"They don't torture prisoners anymore, do they?"

"Go away."

"Strip search maybe?"

"Too late, bozo. There was a ring missing from the jewelry store heist; they thought I might have it *in* me." She was pleased to see him wince. She was less happy about the hug he imposed upon her. Did all the gods practice this touchy-feely crap? Against his shoulder, she asked, "You wouldn't know anything about all that jewelry, would you?"

"Yeah."

She shoved him away, her jaw dropping open. Then she got it together and demanded, "Well, what?"

He explained about the night Darius had shackled her into bed with him and the men who'd left jewelry behind, then offered to explain to her jailers that she'd been framed by Cytus.

She started laughing, punchy from too much stress and too little sleep. "Sure, why not? You go out there and tell them everything you know. And then let me know how it goes, because I think they lock the men up somewhere else."

Without Hermes there to bug her after that, she cocooned herself in what he'd told her. How Darius had protected her by barring the bedroom door. How he'd hidden her from the thieves with the comforter. How he would've gotten rid of the loot if he'd known where it was.

At ten A.M., she was released. She simply signed everything Claudia's lawyer told her to. What more could they do to her?

Claudia drove her to the studio. "I don't know why you want me to bring you here," she said.

"It's where I live."

"You haven't been listening. You've been evicted, girl. Everything's locked up tight. They even took away my key. Probably Griff's, too."

"Just drop me off, okay?"

Claudia sighed heavily and did as she was asked. Griff and Chef Ramon were standing outside, talking. Each of them hugged her, and in her ear, Ramon whispered that he'd been banned from giving her any more meals, but if she could wait until dark, he'd sneak her something.

"Thanks," she said, "but don't get yourself in trouble. Won't do anybody any good if you lose your job."

He hugged her again, looked as if he had more to say, then let her go.

"You can check the doors if you want, but I'm telling you, they're locked," Claudia said. "I'll wait here five minutes, and then I'm going home."

Alex went around to the back door, where she'd be out of sight. She couldn't believe this, but she knocked on her own door, and placing her mouth close to the seam, said, "Darius?"

Hermes fluttered down beside her. "He's gone."

She took a deep breath and, willing herself not to cry, turned and walked away. "I need sleep. Bad."

He fluttered after her. "Where are you going?"

"Mrs. Wallis'll let me sack out for a few hours. When I wake up, I'll think of something. Maybe."

Ludicrous. She'd laugh, but didn't have the energy, knowing she couldn't successfully defend herself without lying, and even if she had practice, no lie was good enough. When she could express herself coherently again, she'd ask Hermes to take Darius a message.

"What about your sister?"

She shook her head. "Her husband'll never let me stay."

"Griff?"

"Maybe. For a while." If she'd been more alert, she would've wondered why Hermes followed her to the home's back door.

"Alex!" Mrs. Wallis said, coming out onto the porch. "Oh, poor thing, you look awful." She wrapped her arms around Alex, comforting her, bringing all the carefully controlled strain to the surface. "Tell me about it, sweetheart."

Alex didn't have to hide her feelings here. "Can't." Tears started, burning a path down her cheeks. "I need sleep first."

"Oh. Well."

Alex tried to step toward the door, but she couldn't carry Mrs. Wallis's weight with her.

"We have a bit of a problem," Mrs. Wallis said quietly. She couldn't meet Alex's eyes at first, but she finally sucked in some courage and made eye contact. "I'm afraid it's the board, Alex. You know some of them are members at the Ladies' Club. You know how angry they are. There's nothing I can do. They're very influential women. They decided— and I don't agree for a minute!—that you're a bad influence on the children, and—"

"What! Everything I've done is for the kids."

"Alex, Alex, I know. Believe me, I know. But they have control, you see. Money is power."

She didn't see, not at all.

"What's happened?" Hermes asked.

Alex heard Mrs. Wallis's words as if from far away. "I'm sorry, Alex. They've barred the children from having any contact with you."

No!

"If I disregard their order, if *any* of us lets you speak to the children, they'll begin moving them immediately."

17

Alex dreamed she was flying. Quite a shocker, considering the last thing she remembered was entering her studio to find it trashed.

Hermes had walked her back, as she wasn't functioning much better than the walking wounded. Not after hearing what Mrs. Wallis had to say, knowing how terrible this was for the children. If the board carried through with its threat, each child could be moved at least once, maybe twice, before the system accommodated everyone. Their routine would be disrupted. Many would end up in new schools with different teachers. Children who'd been together for years would be separated. Boys and girls alike who considered her their big sister and confidante would be scattered from one end of the city to the other. Those who looked up to her would likely hear terrible, untrue things about her and be reprimanded if they defended her.

Maybe she was exaggerating this all out of proportion, but

really, these weren't children coming from a strong family base that would see them through the troubling times ahead.

Then there was the lock on the studio door. "I can't get it," Hermes admitted after a few minutes of fiddling with it.

When he turned to give her the bad news, she sailed an old red brick past his head, sending it crashing through the leaded glass.

"That'll work," he said, and then she was in.

Broken dishes. Broken statues. Scattered tools. Upturned furniture. Sketches ripped off the walls. She sunk amid the crumpled pages, picking up two, curling into a fetal position on the floor, holding them close to her heart as she finally fell into an exhausted sleep. In one hand, a drawing done by one of the kids; in the other, a sketch of Darius. Both so important. Both gone.

After that, she should be having a nightmare, but this was more of a dream, sailing through the heavens as majestically as an eagle soaring over a valley. The air was fresh and clear, cool for a change. The wind hummed steadily past her ears. Above that she heard . . .

Jingling?

Creaking leather?

She started to turn over and look, but a sandaled foot was planted firmly on her chambray shirttail, effectively pinning her in place. "What the . . ."

"Careful," Darius warned in a deep, rumbling voice. "Don't want you to go tumbling out the back."

Startled that he dared trespass on her dream, she opened her eyes.

She shouldn't have. "What the—" She *was* flying. "Where the hell am I?"

In a chariot, she knew that right off. On a blanket on the floor. No back end. No roof. No seat belt.

She sat up before giving the matter any intelligent thought, then when she realized how precarious her position was, she glued her back against the curved wall and wired both arms tightly around Darius's knee. She looked up, discovered he wore nothing beneath his tunic, and enticing as that could've been, it really didn't rank up there with saving her life.

"What's holding you in?" she asked.

"Practice."

"Not good enough." Keeping her arms around him, she glanced around the chariot, looking for something more permanent to grasp. What a joke! Who could be safe in a chariot flying through the sky?

She'd been wrong; she *was* having a nightmare.

"You might want to stand up and see this. We're almost there."

"Where?" She whispered a prayer; anywhere was better than here.

"Olympus."

Oh, of course.

He shifted the reins to one hand, reaching down for her with his other. She stared at his hand, wanting to hold it, remembering how good it felt to hold it, but frightened out of her wits at the thought of getting to her feet this high up. She didn't have an abnormal fear of heights. She could walk out on a balcony, all the way to the rail. She could race up a fire tower with the kids, all the way to the top. This she couldn't do.

"Alexandra."

Rationalizing that she could always sink back down to the floor, she gave in and placed her hand in his. Upon feeling his fingers close protectively over hers, enveloping her in a strong, warm cocoon that left only remnants of unease, she rose to her feet, whereupon she plastered herself to his side, not a breath of air able to pass between them.

"You may stand in front of me," he said, smoothly shifting her to the circle between the front of the chariot, his body, and his arms, his muscles bulging with the labor of holding the reins of two fiery stallions.

Almost as good as a seat belt, she thought sarcastically, as she white-knuckled the top edge and reluctantly admired the powerful black team pulling them through the sky. She peeked downward and saw they were as high as an airplane, and over the sea, to boot.

"Where's my inflatable cushion?"

"I have never crashed my chariot." A slight pause. "Well, not since I was very young and impulsive. But rest assured—" He nuzzled her neck, planting warm kisses behind her ear that made her knees weak, not something she needed right now. "I would do nothing to endanger my precious cargo."

She glanced at the floor of the chariot and saw nothing except the blanket . . . and her. Suddenly inferring his meaning, she warmed considerably. "Oh."

Even while guiding the team, he was able to squeeze her affectionately, though with a line like that precious cargo one, he didn't need to. She was pretty much his, she'd decided last night.

When she returned home, she was going to ask Griff if she could sleep on his couch for a while. That'd give her time to work her new job and earn a deposit on the cheapest apartment she could find, or maybe while clerking in the boutique, she'd meet someone who needed a temporary roommate. If Griff got tired of her, she'd ask Chef Ramon. Ever since she'd moved into the old carriage house, he'd been looking out for her. Feeding her. Checking on her. Moving club members' castoff furniture into her studio.

Darius could come visit her whenever he liked. He was a god, after all, and she understood he couldn't just leave his entire family and move to the Central West End. Besides which, she'd age normally and he, of course, wouldn't. She was thirty; he was about that. When she was fifty, he'd still be about thirty. When she was eighty, well, that was a ridiculous difference.

Would it be so bad to accept one puny little gem from him? One she could cash in, get a decent place to live with room to work, and purchase marble to sculpt another statue—one not so perfect next time. How was that different from accepting monthly maintenance payments? Just because this money wouldn't come from taxes, so what? It was the end result she had to look at here, and she wasn't in a position to be real picky.

As they gradually descended in elevation, islands grew larger, their hills, valleys, vineyards, and ports growing more distinct. But they passed over those and headed inland, toward the mountains.

"It's that one straight ahead," Darius said, his breath warm on her ear, promising more than his words. "Ah, wait'll you see it!"

Darius was quietly, thoroughly ecstatic, returning home with Alexandra in his arms, her body plastered along the whole length of his, heaven and Hades rolled into one. She listened attentively, nodding acknowledgment as he pointed out the different mountains where the Muses lived, the gates to Olympus, the Seasons who guarded them, the valley in which he'd crashed that one and only time, Apollo's herds,

Hephaestus's workshop, and all the rest. He circled above it all for her speechless wonder.

At least he hoped it was wonder. Few mortals had ever beheld Olympus. Those who made it as far as the gates saw only fog, and if they kept on, were repelled by the Seasons.

Dionysus's mortal mother lived here, yet a man who'd seen Zeus in all his glory had been blinded by the god's brilliance. At the first sign of any such trouble, Darius would whisk Alexandra away, though he did not anticipate a problem; she was a strong woman. Look at all she'd endured so far.

He hadn't understood her strength when he'd first met her. Hadn't really cared that she was warm and nurturing. He'd seen her solely as a talented perfectionist, so important to his goal. In dealing with the ups and downs of his statuehood, she'd revealed an unwavering strength of character. It would have been so easy for her to take all the gems he'd offered or accept the Pompeiian statue, yet she refused to act against her beliefs. So easy to run and hide, yet she'd returned to her studio, what was left of it. So easy to give up completely, yet she'd gone searching for a job to see her through.

Yes, she'd do just fine on Olympus. She had the strength to behold all the gods in their natural state.

When she'd seen everything from above, he steered the team to a safe landing, took her hand in his, and led her to Zeus's palace.

"Oh my God," she said, stopping in the very first hall.

"Alexandra, you mustn't keep honoring me so. You have permission to use my given name whenever you wish."

"Huh?" she said absentmindedly, staring at the new paintings, the very ones he'd noticed before in place of the tapestries he was used to. "Wow. *Vase with Five Sunflowers*, painted by—"

"Who was van Gogh? Art for one hundred, please."

"Right," she responded softly, automatically, the way a mother does when she's only half listening to a child. She examined the painting closer. "As I recall, this is listed as being destroyed by fire after World War II. And the other one—"

"What is *Venus and Psyche*? Art for five—"

"Stop that," she said, though with a smile. "Painted by—"

"Who was Gustave Courbet?"

"You're really going to annoy your family if you keep that up."

"You think?"

"Oh, I'm quite sure. Now that the wind's not roaring in my ears, tell me, why'd you bring me here?"

"I have to find out why I'm not, shall we say, *full-time* yet? And I couldn't leave you unprotected."

"I think the hooded sweatshirt guy tore the place apart. Maybe he was mad I was gone. Anyway, someone did."

"Don't forget Cytus."

She grinned. "Oh yeah, the big guy who wanted to drill your toe."

"No, he wanted to hurt me. *You* wanted him to drill my toe."

"Sorry about that." Her contrite smile pleased him.

"Does that mean you've given up the idea?"

"Yes."

"You're sure? Because last night, I seem to recall you throwing a goblet at my chest."

"Well, I still reserve the right to do that from time to time—you can be pretty insufferable."

"Me?"

"Not to mention egotistical." Her words were too soft to be taken as criticism. "But it won't be to turn you back into marble. So where do we start?"

"With my father, who, by the way, *told* me the curse was removed."

Hermes must have carried the news of their arrival to everyone. Apollo, Aphrodite, Athena, Hestia, Artemis, Hephaestus, Hebe—they all waylaid Darius and Alex with hugs and kisses and laughter. Alex, still overwhelmed by the chariot trip, Olympus itself, and the artwork, was nearly speechless as they introduced themselves, one after the other. Unlike meeting a lot of strangers for the first time, she wouldn't have trouble remembering their names; Greek art had been one of her favorite studies.

"My family," he said proudly, and she could tell they were important to him, as family should be.

Apollo played his lyre—the very first, very special one given him by Hermes, played only on special occasions. Aphrodite placed a honeysuckle wreath on Alex's hair and suggested Darius let her stay with them while he spoke with Zeus alone. Hebe seconded the idea, saying Zeus was in a snit over some unexpected, unresolved weather activity in St. Louis and likely to snap her head off. Athena fastened a necklace about Alex's throat.

"I designed it," she said. "Hephaestus made it. It's our way of thanking you for giving Darius back to us."

It was a pendant, a statue of a proud male in a short tunic and sandals, of exceptional workmanship, small and delicate enough for her to wear all the time; a miniature of Darius, and for that reason, she would treasure it when she returned home and couldn't count on his showing up anymore. It looked to be of solid gold, too, but she didn't dare ask. From the twinkle in Darius's eyes, he knew exactly what she was thinking.

A god walked up behind him, placing a hand on Darius's shoulder. Gray hair indicated he was elderly, though his face was unlined and he moved with ease. "Darius."

A startled expression crossed Darius's face, as if this were someone unexpected. He turned quickly. The smaller god engulfed him in a tight, back-slapping embrace, murmuring, "My boy . . . at last," over and over.

"That's Uranus," Aphrie whispered to Alex. "Our great grandfather. He's never met Darius, and he was so upset when he missed him the other day. You've done a truly miraculous thing, giving him back to us, but especially to him. Now the family's complete."

Family, Alex thought enviously, her gaze lingering on each member of the joyous group. So many of them. So happy to see Darius, to have him back in their midst, to touch him and hug him and clap him on the shoulder and talk to him.

A deep sense of shame suffused her heart. With one whack of a hammer, one tiny claw mark from a kitten, one gash from a heavy goblet, she would have deprived this family of Darius, and Darius of them. A family, which had always been so important to her because she had only one sister and a lot of questions, would have been exactly what she'd destroyed, no matter how inadvertently. How ironic.

She was envious that she could give him his, when she was helpless to find her own.

"Alexandra? Do you mind?"

"Hm?" She pulled her attention back to Darius, gripping her hand, anchoring her. "I'm sorry, what?"

"Do you mind if I leave you here and go talk to Zeus alone? You know, just in case."

"We'll take good care of her, Darius," Aphrodite said, with a small pout that he might not trust them.

"We won't let Cytus near her," Ares, god of war, and late-comer to the welcoming committee, promised.

"You might have more fun," Darius added as incentive. He leaned low, nuzzled her neck, and whispered in her ear. "And when I get back, we can go to my place."

She wanted to say, *That's fine, I don't mind, you go have a good talk.* But damn, nuzzling her neck like that turned her on so fast she couldn't speak. Could barely think.

"Maybe build a fire, have some wine, share our first of many sunsets to come. Sound good?"

Could barely nod.

Oh please, God, let him fix his little problem so I can quit thinking "hard as a rock" is a bad thing.

"I've come to ask why the curse which you said was gone isn't really gone at all!"

Hebe was right; Darius had no sooner entered the control room and opened his mouth than he could see Zeus was in a snit, running his fingers through his long, wavy gray hair, tugging at his beard in frustration, cursing the computer, demanding Iris get Hera in there to deal with her son.

Amused, Darius grinned. He'd been referred to as "your son" often enough as a youth, by either parent depending on the situation. Contrary to the Zeus he'd met the other day, this was more like being home again.

Zeus, his task chair jerking across the floor in tune to every move, an extension of his body, slapped the desktop with great force. "Why in Hades is it hailing in St. Louis? I didn't program that!" He glared up at Darius. "Seems to be centered in the Central West End."

Darius had more pressing problems, but he wasn't above

a little compromise. "Release me from this curse and I'll investigate." Not immediately, but no need to tell the old guy that he had far more urgent and more promising plans to make love with Alexandra ASAP.

"What do you want, you old fool?" Hera demanded upon entering the control room. She batted hanging plants out of her way, setting them swinging dangerously above the electronic equipment as she swept across the room toward father and son.

"He's your son," Zeus snapped.

"Darius, darling, hello."

"Take care of him."

"Something wrong?" she asked.

Again, with great effort, since he'd just blown it with his father, Darius remembered all Aphrie had told him about observing the social amenities. It was a great struggle, when he really wanted to get right to the point—again—but he tried valiantly, using Eddie Haskell as a role model. Now there was a kid who knew the social amenities.

"Mother, you're looking lovely today. Is that a new chiton?"

Tilting her head to the side but keeping her gaze on him, she studied him suspiciously. Maybe he'd overdone it. Come to think of it, June Cleaver never quite warmed up to Eddie like she did the other boys.

"What's this all about, Darius?"

"Well, I'm here to get Zeus to remove the curse. He said he did, but he didn't."

"Yes I did."

"Then how come I turned back into a statue last night! Do you have any idea how embarrassing it is to turn into a hunk of marble during foreplay?"

"I told you you'd get stuck," Hera said.

"Yes, Mother, I know. You were right." It didn't pain him to admit it; he had much to look forward to. "Now make him—can you please talk him into removing the curse? *Completely*."

"He did."

Darius glanced back and forth between his parents, though Zeus's focus was back on his computer. "But . . . last night . . ."

"Yes." She nodded, the way mothers do. "And I've decided you shall do so every night you spend away from Olympus, until you experience true love. And rest assured, you can do that only if you marry a goddess and give me grandchildren."

"What!" Rapidly putting the pieces together, he suspected Alexandra's nightly visitor might be a spy for Hera. Unconsciously, his hands balled into tight fists; consciously, he took a deep breath, filling his lungs, forcing himself to remain a picture of calm. Now was no time to let Hera know that threats against Alexandra awoke his protective instincts.

"And live here," Zeus said.

"Oh yes, thank you for reminding me. That's right, you must live here, because I want . . . *we* want to see our grandchildren grow up."

"I've found the woman I want. I've found true love."

"Now, Darius, that's just not possible. And I don't want grandchildren with mortal blood. We need new life here on Olympus. Full-ichored little gods and goddesses creating joy and mayhem wherever they go."

Her wistful smile made him ill. Here he'd thought only mortals made demands on him, wanting his gems. What a rude awakening. "This is blackmail."

"True."

"I won't stand for it."

Zeus snickered. "Then you'll be *stand*ing marble every night, son."

"You must release me!" He'd find a way to make it all work, no matter how long it took.

"Be reasonable," Zeus said. "Keep her as a mistress for however long you like."

Mistress! Just thinking about touching anyone other than Alexandra produced a bitter taste in his mouth.

"One more thing," Hera said. "Tell him."

Zeus sighed and turned away from his computer, focusing now on his son. "This rulership thing between you and Cytus—"

"It's mine."

"Yes, I know, but the thing is, it really needs a full time ruler. *One* full-time ruler. The two of you battling over it isn't good for the family or for Olympus. It certainly isn't good for my nerves. So your mother and I talked it over, and you've got one week to grow up and learn whatever it is she says you must."

They'd never, ever, conspired against him before. How far would they go?

"In the meantime," Hera said, "you'll continue to turn into a statue at sunset, just as a reminder. Incentive, if you will." As if she were relaying no more than the rules of a new game, she smiled.

It did nothing to ease his mind. Hera was known far and wide for her vindictive streak against women. He remembered the nymph Echo, doomed to speak only what she heard, and Io, plagued to madness by a gadfly. If Hera didn't get her way in this, Darius feared she'd surely go after Alexandra. With a spy, she'd know everything.

Or was it a mercenary, already in place?

"Tell him the rest," Hera said.

There's more?

"And if, at the end of the week," Zeus continued, "you haven't given in and married the goddess your mother has selected, then the rulership—including all your gems and all your powers—will go to Cytus. Permanently. You can have the gems or you can have a mortal wife, son, but you can't have both."

18

If anyone asked Alex how she'd spent her afternoon, only Darius would understand, as he was the one responsible for leaving her in a permanent state of carnal anticipation.

Aphrie had taken her under her wing, introducing her around, giving her a tour of Zeus's palace first, and then her own, the highlight of which was all the artwork that had been collected over the centuries. Even the structures themselves were artwork, with everything wonderfully preserved. Intricately carved pediments, metopes, and unending friezes that depicted far more emotion in the characters' features than anything outside Olympus. Probably not because man had lost the battle to the elements as much as man had never created such gifted work in the first place.

She'd been served the absolutely most divine food, consuming a zillion calories during their picnic on Aphrie's upper porch, during which they spiritedly discussed the evolution of art through the centuries. Quite an education.

Any other topic, and Alex never would have been able to string a coherent sentence together.

What was keeping Darius? Didn't he know it was rude to get a woman hot and then keep her waiting?

When she suddenly spotted him from her raised vantage point, she observed his quick, purposeful stride across the lush lawn toward the front door. Ooh, he was in an all-fired big hurry. Her mouth went dry. Forgetting the rest of whatever she'd been saying—or had Aphrie been speaking?—when the balustrade obstructed her view, she leaned across the tabletop, the better to see him.

Mm, mm, mm. Who would've thought a tunic and sandals could be so sexy on someone so . . . *male.*

Aphrie, noticing all this, reached over and gently tugged Alex's loose peplos until some leg was showing. Alex loved the feel of soft, shimmering silk on her skin; decadent, even erotic. She was alternately appalled that Aphrie insisted she wear it unbelted—it was open down the sides, the better, she said, to get Darius's attention—and delighted with a clear picture of just how easy it was going to be to get naked with him.

Well, heck, she was ready for some intimate attention. She'd already decided she wanted him, whenever and however she could get him. Why wait? Now that he was upstairs, striding magnificently across the stone floor toward her, she amended that to a *lot* of intimate attention.

"Leave it alone," she warned Aphrie, who was stealthily trying to undo one of the glitzy, barrettelike clasps on each side of the peplos. They gave her some modesty at hip level, holding the silk together in just the right place to hide her plain cotton underpants, which, no matter how much Aphrie protested they ruined the gown's sumptuous lines, she wasn't ready to part with. There were just some things a woman had to have.

Would Aphrie be offended if Alex told her to get lost? Or would Darius lead her away to some secluded spot? "Aphrie . . ."

"I think there's something I need to go do. Sorry, Alex," Aphrie said, rising. She winked, readjusting Alex's gown again to show even more leg. "Won't be back for, oh, a couple of hours, at least."

"There you are!" Darius bellowed.

"Ooh, if he weren't my brother, I swear my skin would tingle. Ta-ta."

Maybe it was the power of suggestion, but Alex swore her skin did start to tingle. Along with other organs.

Mindful of Aphrie's advice about letting her brother pursue her a little longer, Alex remained on the cushioned bench, though it wasn't easy when what she really wanted was to bounce up to greet him and throw her arms around his neck and suction her lips to his until he begged to come up for air. This bench was too short, but they could throw the cushions onto the floor and make a pallet.

God, he was a sight! Determination in his eyes, an arrogant tilt of his chin, very proud.

Mm, mm—

"Come with me," he barked, taking her by the hand.

Wow, this open gown thing really worked!

"Where're we going?" she asked, trailing after him breathlessly, thinking how to tell him in the fewest number of words that Aphrie understood completely and would be gone and wouldn't mind if they used her place.

"Home."

"You live far?"

"Your home."

"M-my home?" But that was hours away.

Alexandra, disappointed by the long trip in front of her, sat on the floor of the chariot, slumped against Darius's leg while he kept a watchful eye for anyone Hera might send after him.

"This thing come with a hidden bathroom somewhere?"

"No. Sorry."

Maybe Hera intended to give him the full week, just to cut him some slack, to give him an opportunity to see the error of his ways and return voluntarily.

Yeah, right.

"So, what, I'm supposed to hang over the edge and go?"

From the way she was fondling his thigh, he didn't think it was a bathroom she had on her mind. Ah, what creative hands! Always skimming, always circling, always patting, her fingernails raking higher and higher and then . . . *by Zeus!* she'd drop down and start all over again.

"Hang on." *A little higher next time,* he thought, smiling like a fool. "I'll have you down in a minute."

He landed on the tip of a rugged, uninhabited island off the coast of Portugal, knowing it was impossible to make the entire journey before sunset. If they continued on course, Alexandra would be left somewhere over the Atlantic Ocean with a statue, a pair of headstrong horses, and no way to navigate.

Even if they could have made it, he didn't want to continue. She'd been resisting his advances since the day he'd had hands to touch her, lips to kiss her, a need to assuage, and feet to carry him in pursuit. Now—*finally!*—she'd come around.

As she trotted away across the sand, the ocean breeze billowed beneath her gown, lifting and filling it like a sail. Amused to see she'd gone native except for the underpants, he didn't pursue her, not just yet, but led the horses to a cave, where he hid both of them and his chariot in case they were followed by Cytus, as it was doubtful he'd wait out the week to see if he won it all fair and square.

Then he carefully set the stage for her return. Food, drink, a small fire. Nice-sized erection, more to come.

She paused at the mouth of the cave, quickly taking in the scene he'd set. The breeze caught her gown again. He was quick to notice no underpants now, no hesitation as she stepped into their safe hideaway. They had at least an hour before sunset, and from the look in her eyes, she meant to make good use of it.

She smiled seductively as she removed the diamond clasps from her gown, one by one, clipping them in her hair.

The better not to lose something so valuable, he thought, though she could have a chariot full of them for the asking.

Disappointment edged in, unbidden, unwelcome. It grew slowly, persistently, in spite of his fight against it. Why *did* she want him now? Because she'd seen Olympus and all he had to offer? Because she'd finally realized what an honor it would be to lie with him now that he was whole, now that he'd beaten the curse—or so she thought. Because she hoped to gain by it?

Couldn't someone—just once—want him for himself?

He shoved his doubts aside. He wanted her. He owed her. And if he didn't get this taken care of by sunset, he'd be hard all night.

Unfortunately, Aphrie had befriended her, and Aphrie believed in social niceties. She'd have his head later if Alexandra told her he'd jumped her.

"Drink?" he asked, hoping she'd refuse and they could get down to business.

"Maybe later." She stood an arm's length away, studying him, waiting for . . . what?

"A bite to eat?"

"Well," she said, her gaze dropping slowly to his erection, "maybe something to nibble." Then with her head tilted becomingly, her eyelashes lowered, she smiled up at him. "Selena won't, uh, be back to clear this, will she?"

"I'll have her beheaded if she dares."

Who moved first? He hadn't a clue. In a blink, they were in each other's arms. No, they were all *over* each other. Arms surrounding, caressing, seeking to satisfy as their hands were content to touch nowhere longer than a few seconds, spurred on by moans of pleasure, groans of impatience.

His legs supported them only so long, and then, as she tossed the front of her peplos over one shoulder and climbed him—*by Zeus!*—saddling him with her center, he lowered them, his back against the floor of the cave, letting her sit astride him. Only she wouldn't sit so he could see her breasts bob and the pleasure on her face as he satisfied her. No, she sought to torture as she bent over him, brushing the tips of her breasts across his chest, his stomach, his thighs.

She snickered.

"What!"

She crawled up his length then, brushing soil and sand and cave debris off her knees. "Talk about down-and-dirty."

"How about we don't talk at all?"

"You mean I can't tell you how magnificent you are?"

"When I'm through. Get that gown off."

"Take it off yourself."

He untwisted it from around her neck, bunching it up beside him, rolling her over onto it, pressing hard into the saddle of her. From her moan of pleasure and the way her eyes drifted shut, he didn't think she'd be making any more wise-cracks about down-and-dirty. Or anything else.

As in everything else, her hands were never still. Even as he moved aside, cupping her intimately, pleasuring her with his hand, hers roamed constantly, plunging into his hair, tor-turing his nipples, grasping his erection.

"If you don't stop, I won't be able to go slow," he said.

"Who asked you to?"

"But you need—"

"I need you, Darius. Inside me. *Now.*"

By Zeus, he'd never—

Grasping him with one hand, pulling him toward her with her legs, she guided him in, moaning again as he filled her. Tight. So tight. So hard to hold on to his control, seeking a rhythm that kept her in that state of near ecstasy until he knew they were both about to burst. Then pulling away when she was too weak to resist, kissing his way down her breasts, her belly, her scar—he made points there, he could tell by the sigh that escaped her lips.

"My God, Darius," she said, gasping.

His heart skipped several beats to hear his name on her lips; she used it so seldom, yet said it so sweetly. He paused, thinking he could spend a lifetime hearing it over and over.

"Not used to twenty-first-century women?"

He gazed upon her face then, admiring how her smile was slightly higher on one side when she teased him. "No. How does one like it?"

"Bet you've never asked a woman that before."

He laughed. "You're right." Then sobered. "It never made a difference before. How would you like it, Alexandra?"

She had the usual reaction when he said her name. He

didn't understand why, but it always seemed to happen. A slight intake of breath. Eyes fluttering closed. A soft sigh.

"Alexandra?" Bracing himself above her, he pushed deep inside again, watching the emotions flit across her face. "You want it hard?" He gave her a three-stroke sample, then eased up. "Or soft?"

"No . . . way."

He smiled, but it was short-lived as she locked her legs around him and began her own torturous rhythm against him, slow and hard at first, then faster. "By Zeus, what are you doing?"

"Punishing you for talking too much."

He chuckled, said, "We'll see who wins this round," and slid his tongue into her ear and his hand between their bodies, ever mindful that, as much as he'd like to go on all night, he didn't have that luxury.

She sighed his name into his ear, right before arching her back, seeking and finding her climax, releasing him to follow her into ecstasy like none he had ever known. Not ever, in all the centuries he'd lived.

He rolled beside her, knowing what was soon to happen, dreading how it would affect her when she learned the truth.

Hoping to outguess Hera, he tried to vacate his body before sunset to forestall getting stuck, but she'd anticipated as much. It was not to be allowed. He fell asleep cradling Alexandra on his shoulder, careful that she be able to get free when he hardened, wishing she'd wanted him for himself, fearing she'd never consent to loving him again and he'd have to spend the rest of his immortal life punishing himself, remembering how wonderful it had been.

Alex lay on Darius's shoulder, watching the sunlight wane outside the cave, fairly certain he'd cease to breathe at sunset; they'd left Olympus so hastily, without any celebration, there could be no other explanation. Slowly, almost absently, caressing his chest with the tips of her fingers, she quietly took stock of what had just passed between them, knowing it was out of the ordinary.

She'd had lovers. She'd been married. She'd thought she'd made love before, but now realized with startling clarity that before today, it had only been sex. Making love was dropping your inhibitions and being yourself.

Well, she'd certainly done *that*.

Making love was being unselfish, ensuring your partner had a great time. She smiled to herself, knowing he had, knowing she'd surprised and delighted him. Making love was knowing he'd turn into marble at sunset and not counting it against him.

Or was that being in love? Knowing she was didn't scare her at all, for who could make love without first being *in* love? Not her.

It happened quickly, slow enough for her to see worry etched in a furrow between his brows—worry, she understood, that she might not forgive him for this—yet so fast that she didn't even have time to assure him it didn't matter. The furrow softened ever so slightly at the last moment, so maybe he knew, maybe he even felt her last kiss as his lips changed from warm softness to immobile marble.

She rose then, leaving him alone as she picked her way to the sea under a slim slice of moon, sad and regretful that he couldn't share this with her. Was this how the rest of her life was to be? Days with him, nights without? Or would his father take even that from her? She could live with whatever moments Darius could give her, she thought, telling herself she was that strong. She had to be. However, worrying that a more powerful god like Zeus could at any moment up the stakes, well, that was a little harder to bear. Was she *that* strong?

Why did she have this nagging feeling Darius didn't want her to leave the cave? He'd said the island was uninhabited. Taking him at his word, she bathed in the waves and paddled in the shallows. Being from the Midwest, she was ocean illiterate, thinking every unidentified brush against her leg was a shark or jellyfish or stingray, so after a few of those, she returned to the safety of shore, rinsed her gown, and spread it over a rock to dry.

She lingered to watch the moon sink beyond the horizon, then lay on her back and took it all in. Waves washed against the beach, rhythmic and hypnotizing, lulling her into a peaceful altered state. Stars, well, they were like she'd never seen at home and almost defied description; vast, unending, bright, so thick in number as to baffle the imagination.

Footsteps.

She bolted upright, grateful for darkness, needing more light to show her the way back to the cave, glad the moon had set and she'd be less visibly naked in the middle of nowhere.

But no, if she found the cave, if she were followed, something could happen to Darius, to the statue. She eased her way into the rocks this side of the cave, picking her way carefully, settling down into a crevice to listen and spend the night, hoping the intruder didn't hear her stomach rumble.

19

A quarter of the world away, Claudia was seriously considering setting her private detective on a different track: to find her sister. She'd stopped by to see if Alexandra was ready to come home with her yet and instead found a broken window, the inside of the studio thoroughly trashed. Then, inside the Ladies' Club, Eunice Nelson was bragging about the strings she'd pulled to get even with Alexandra for stealing members' jewelry, stealing the statue (*"If it ever even existed,"* she'd said snootily), destroying an antique bed (*What the hell was that about?*), sponging off the club's generosity for a year, bringing negative publicity to their doorstep, and a myriad of other transgressions. When it came to money, Eunice could be a real bitch.

While Alexandra would have been crushed to learn what Eunice, also an influential member of the Board of Directors of the Children's Home, had arranged for the children if she attempted to see them, Claudia knew she wouldn't go so

berserk as to destroy the studio. The children's artwork had
been ruined, too; Alex would never, ever do that.

So who had? Eunice wasn't bragging about destroying
any of Alexandra's work in order to teach her a lesson; apparently no one knew of the break-in. Maybe if she drove
around the neighborhood for a while, she'd find her sister
walking around, thinking.

She was mulling everything over at a red light when a
man with the oddest hat and funny-looking appendages on
his sandals opened the door and popped into the passenger
side of her Mercedes. At first she didn't know what to do,
what to say, but then screaming came naturally. He clamped
his hands over his ears, but didn't budge. She blew the horn
for attention—*Anybody with a cell phone, please, can't you
see this weirdo just got into my car? Call nine-one-one!*—
pushed the buttons to lower the windows so everyone could
hear her yelling, and fumbled through her purse for pepper
spray.

"Light's green," he said, snatching her purse away. "And
Alexandra's—"

"Alex—" She reached over and grabbed him by his . . .
dress? "You smarmy bastard, what've you done with her!"

"Hey, I'm on your side." Horns blared behind them. "You
mind? Better move before we get a little road rage going
here."

She held tight.

"She's in Portugal."

Of all the . . . Not in the mood for practical jokes, she
threw the passenger door open, and struggled and shoved
and pushed, trying to eject him onto the pavement. He was
stronger than he looked, though, and her seat belt hampered
her. She had to give up when he scooted next to her and
planted his left foot, wings and all, on the accelerator, giving

her no choice but to ignore the fluttering against her calf and steer through the city streets at double the limit.

"Too fast!" she cried, narrowly missing a fire hydrant.

He didn't seem to care.

"The light's yellow! Stop!"

He didn't. She swerved to avoid broadsiding a taxi, then had to concentrate on weaving through cars and trucks strung out in front of her, knowing she was closing in on the next traffic signal.

"All right!"

He lifted his foot from the pedal, *Thank you God!* She darted over to the curb in a loading zone, shifting the damned car into park before he could get his foot back on the accelerator. Then, taking a few seconds to gain the upper hand—she was really good at this—she flipped open her visor mirror and casually checked her hair.

"For someone who's worried about road rage," she said slowly, in the practiced manner she knew held a man's attention, "trust me when I say you shouldn't ever get behind a wheel."

"I'm more worried about what Darius'll do to me if I don't deliver his message."

"Darius again." She snapped the visor shut. "I wish I'd never heard his name."

"You may change your tune."

She flinched as he reached toward her, but he simply dumped a small but heavy black velvet pouch onto her lemon yellow lap. Cautiously keeping one eye on him in case he lunged for her, she peeked inside and saw what appeared to be gemstones, but no one carried a pouch of real ones around, so they must be fake.

"Alexandra's refused any gems to help the orphans because they'd likely be deemed stolen," he said. "You, though, seem to be able to turn your jewelry into cash without raising suspicion, so . . ."

Impossible. "You're saying these are real?"

"Absolutely."

"Uh-huh, sure." She reached for her purse, satisfied to note that he jumped like he thought she was going for sensitive areas. "I need my loupe."

He reached in and got it himself—a weirdo like him probably knew all about the hazards of pepper spray—then handed it to her so she could examine the gems for herself, which she did, very thoroughly because she couldn't believe what she saw.

"My God, they're real!" Awestruck, she ran her fingers through the magnificent stones, over and over, savoring the delicious feel of them. So heavy. So cool.

The tense mood in the car dissipated; a deranged killer wouldn't jump in her car and toss these babies in her lap. Come to think of it, she might have seen this guy at the preview. Maybe he wasn't so weird. Well, he was, but maybe he was on the up-and-up, too. Maybe even single; Alexandra could use a wealthy husband to support her while she sculpted magnificent pieces.

"These are for the kids?"

"No," he said, shaking his head adamantly. "Darius doesn't want to do anything that could get them or Alexandra in trouble. He knows you're a little short on money—uh-uh, don't deny it, he knows all about the diamond tennis bracelet, and he understands how important this search is to her, so those are to pay the detective whatever he needs to find your father."

Last meeting, the detective had promised they were so close . . . Why, with this increase in resources, with the extra manpower, the extra "grease" for slow-turning wheels, she and Alexandra might be meeting their dad within days! Maybe other siblings. Possibly some aunts and uncles. They could all celebrate Thanksgiving and Christmas together this winter. Ring in the New Year.

"And Alexandra's okay?"

"She's in Portugal. She'll probably tell you all about it when she gets back."

"Can you tell her not to go home?" She listed alternate suggestions, knowing Alexandra was too stubborn to take any of them.

"Will do. Now, you mind driving around the block so I can fly out of here without a bunch of gawkers? Zeus tends to get ticked off when mortals see me."

"Maybe if you wouldn't wear a dress—"

"It's a *tunic*."

"Uh-huh, and my sister's in *Portugal*. Right." Then again, she was sitting in her car talking to a man with wings on his sandals, who'd just given her a king's ransom in gems. "What the hell's she doing in Portugal?"

Darius, who'd sought *the* perfect statue for three thousand years with such single-minded desire as no mortal could ever comprehend, now was faced with an undeniable truth: Be careful what you wish for. The cliché, in fact, had been coined by the gods as warning to mortals who asked for too much. It wasn't supposed to apply to him. But at the moment, to his great frustration, his predicament indicated otherwise.

He cursed the marble holding him prisoner, cursed Hera's imaginative rein on his life, cursed whichever horse stomped its foot when he, Darius, was straining to hear every sound outside the cave, cursed Cytus for threatening Alexandra's life, and, in general, lay there flat on his back unable to follow and protect her and, frustrated, cursed every damned thing he could think of.

Where in Hades was she? Why didn't she return? He could yell for Hermes, who'd hear if he was nearby, though in truth he wasn't worth much in hand-to-hand combat, but if Alexandra was safe, he'd be giving their location away for no reason. Not good.

For hours on end, he considered bartering with Hera to release him from everything—the statue, the curse, and damn the rulership!—but as he would never agree to marry her choice of bride, she'd undoubtedly fix things so he could never come alive in any other statue either. Ever. Then he'd be back to nothing and could never touch Alexandra again. Never make love to her again. Though she might not be too keen on that right now anyway, since he still wasn't alive 24/7.

Finally she returned, a vision in shimmering white at the mouth of the cave one moment, a soft woman curled up beside him the next. He wanted to yell at her for scaring him— a god! How dare she! But then she pillowed her head on his shoulder, and he forgave her.

He wanted to pull her into his embrace and hold her forever. He wanted to marry her, have children with her, share life with her, but with Hera's short deadline, none of that was possible. He could appeal to Zeus, would have in the old days, but his parents had provided a solid, united front today.

Sunrise came, and he didn't dare move. Alexandra, who'd awakened a short while ago, was sitting cross-legged on her gown beside him. There was a basket of bread in her lap, and she was using his chest as a table, making her breakfast out of the food Selena had left the night before. How nice she made him fret half the night with worry, then used him as furniture before breaking the bad news that she wanted to go home and never see him again.

"About time," she said, without any discernible emotion.

"Where in Hades were you all night?"

Licking her fingers clean, she grinned. "Miss me?"

"I was scared to death Cytus would find you." If she kept licking her fingers in such an innocently erotic fashion, he was going to dump the food and ravage her. "Get this off me so I can get up."

"In a hurry to take me home?"

"More like in a hurry to thrash you for worrying me."

She laughed and casually waved off his concern. "Oh, I was being dumb. I went out to swim. Did you know this is the first time I've ever seen the ocean? Well it is, and I didn't want to waste it, and you said no one was around, so I figured, What the heck? Anyway, I thought I heard footsteps, so I hid until I figured out who it was."

He waited expectantly for more explanation, while she leisurely sucked a drop of honey off her thumb, taking far too long and using way too much tongue to be innocent, in his opinion.

"One of the horses," she said with a lopsided grin. "Stomping in the back of the cave. I guess the sound echoed out or something. Took me a while to figure it out."

"The food," he said, giving her one more chance to save her breakfast, needing to get up and control himself before he lay before her like a single-masted ship run aground.

She lifted one small silver tray, slowly sampled a cube of cheese, then set it aside. Not a hurry in the world. Totally oblivious to his discomfort. There were two silver bowls left, and he could have lifted them off his chest, but he was putting one hundred percent effort into not thinking about yesterday afternoon, about how hot and tight and eager she'd been. No blood was getting to his brain to figure out how to accomplish both tasks.

Finally she removed the first bowl. "Mm, this is really good. What is it?" She dangled a bite above his lips.

Maybe eating would distract him. He took her offering gently between his teeth, but her fingers brushed temptingly against his lips, sending more blood to nether regions.

"Darius?"

"What?" he growled.

"Ooh, testy this morning, aren't we?"

One of us certainly is.

She set that bowl aside and studied the last one, lingering over its contents, then glancing south of it. "And oh, there's another dish just showing up now. Not from Selena either, nope, this one's growing. Hm." She arched her eyebrows at him. "Impressive."

"Why in Hades are you so interested in food?"

Tossing the last bowl aside, she straddled him and said, "Because, stupid, I've been waiting all night for an encore."

Talk about cloud nine, Alex thought all the way across the ocean and eastern states. Floating across the sky in a chariot, visiting not-so-mythical-after-all Olympus, and sex with a god. She laughed, knowing she could never tell anyone. The first two she could share with Griff, of course. The last one, though, well, there was nobody she could confide to that she'd had down-and-dirty sex in a cave on a deserted island with a talented lover who, if he weren't really a god, would certainly win her vote.

She sighed contentedly.

"You okay?" Darius asked, standing beside her, steering the team westward.

Oh yeah. "Mm-hm. Think we'll be home before sunset?" They'd gotten a late start, for obvious reasons.

"Guaranteed."

Of course she knew sex wasn't everything. A large factor of love could make a less-than-talented lover seem quite satisfactory. She'd never know about that again. This was it for her. Darius was it for her. There'd never be anyone else ever again. He could visit whenever he liked; she'd be alone and waiting.

Did that make her some kind of sex slave? No, *whew*, she'd already decided on her course before they'd made love, before she'd discovered she was truly head over heels. She was mulling over whether that then made Darius into some kind of sex slave, when Hermes suddenly landed in the chariot, sandwiching Alex between the two of them. Good thing, too; she was getting cold.

"What's that up ahead?" Darius asked.

"Hail," Hermes said. "All over St. Louis, especially in the Central West End. A foot deep at least there."

"No way," Alex said. It was September.

"Zeus pissed off about something?" Darius asked.

"Oh I'm sure he is by now."

"He was complaining yesterday about hail," Darius recalled. "If it's not him . . ."

"It's Billy."

"No way," Alex said again.

"The computer," both gods said, Darius with dawning realization, Hermes with firm conviction.

"It still had some of the old weather programs on the hard drive," Hermes said. "He ran one, said he thought it was a game. Ha!"

Smart, computer-savvy Billy probably was having a ball. Maybe running the software intermittently, placing bets at school, making a little money on the side. Considering how a few ladies of the club were using the children as leverage against her, Alex hoped he'd borrowed as much as he could from everyone he knew and made a huge bet with one of them, especially that pushy Eunice Nelson.

"I deleted them," Hermes assured them.

"Too bad," she said.

"I told Claudia you were on your way back. Not that she believes me for a minute, Alexandra, but just in case, she said to tell you to go to her house, but"—Hermes grinned—"if I find you're too stubborn to do that, I'm supposed to talk you into going to Griff's or Ramon's."

"I'd rather go home."

"Griff's?" Darius said, as if he were being helpful.

"*My* home. The studio."

He tried again. "Ramon's?"

"Are you deaf?"

"I'll direct you," Hermes told him.

"You ever been kneed so hard you couldn't speak?"

Hermes jumped back, vacating the chariot in an all-fired hurry, scrambling over the side, cracking his shins on the edge. He flew alongside then, weaving a bit crookedly. "I can still direct him from over here."

"Fine. He'll turn back into a statue eventually, and then I'll walk home. In the *dark*."

Darius sighed. "Never mind, I'll take you home. I'll bribe Selena and the others to stay the night. Cytus may be afraid to do his worst in front of five women who can run to my parents with the truth. If you would promise not to hurt him," he said, bending toward Alex, "Hermes could ride the rest of the way with us."

"Sure." She grinned somewhat wickedly, just to remind Hermes she meant business.

"There you go, brother. Come aboard."

He did, but he kept Darius between them until they reached the studio, where white balls of ice clogged the gutters, blanketed the lawn, mounded against green trees and shrubs, and melted on the parking lot, allowing some of the black asphalt to show through. By far the prettiest winter wonderland she'd ever seen. And ooh my, a bonus—a lot of little dents in the half-dozen luxury cars parked at the club.

Hermes took flight during their approach. At Alex's quizzical look, he said, "I was with him once when he crashed."

"I believe it was you who got me drunk in the first place."

"Whatever. Watch that spot over there, Dare, looks awfully slippery to me."

With that kind of information, Alex white-knuckled the landing, but Darius handled it smoothly.

"I'll go tell Claudia you're here."

"Hey, Hermes," Alex said as he fluttered upward, "wait until sunset, all right?"

"You sure? She has some news from the detective."

"Has he found our dad?"

"Don't know for sure."

"Geez, aren't you the god of communication or something? How'd she *look*? How'd she *sound*?"

Sounding a bit miffed, he fluttered higher and said, "I don't carry rumors. You'll have to wait and see for yourself. What'll it be?"

Checking the sun's location, Alex figured a couple hours more or less after twenty-six years couldn't matter. Besides, Darius winked at her, jet propelling her hormones into overdrive again.

"Sunset," she told Hermes, trying not to sound giddy.

Darius urged her inside, out of sight, while he led the

team and chariot toward safe concealment in the garage. Unable to walk safely on top of the ice, she made her way across the yard by scooting her feet through the shallow lake of melting, marble-sized hail. Never knowing when she might want to paint just such a scene, she took her time to memorize the view, to study the ebb and flow and how small bits got caught between her toes.

The kitchen door hadn't been reboarded shut, but it wouldn't open, either. Peeking through the broken pane, she spotted overstuffed black trash bags lining the floor from wall to door. Someone had been cleaning.

Oh man, if they'd thrown out any of the kids' work . . .

She body-shoved the door open, lifted her long skirt out of the way—how did women used to live this way?—and ran into the studio, finding it pretty well swept clean. It was almost as if she'd never lived there, never worked there, never had the kids there, except for telltale marble dust ingrained into the hardwood floor, a lot of tack holes in the walls, and one stolen antiquity, probably still there because it was too heavy to toss.

"Well damn," she muttered, wondering if anything was left.

Overhead, a thump. Someone was still there, up in the loft, probably throwing her stored statues into more trash bags. Not that they were great works of art or anything, but they weren't broken and they were *hers*.

"Hey!" she yelled up the stairs, which were dark, rough, open, with no door at the top, and no answer coming back down. She charged up the treads, wishing she were in shorts so she could take them two at a time. "Hey!"

More thumping, from way back in the storage area that extended over the garage. She pulled the string to the overhead light; nothing happened. A little sunlight slid in through the dormer window. She headed toward it, nervously spinning this way and that as she heard different bumps and thumps.

Maybe she shouldn't be up here alone. Maybe it was an aggressive, pissed-off racoon. Talk about somebody who was going to be pissed off, maybe the jewelry store thieves were back, looking for the loot they'd left. They probably were responsible for trashing the studio in the first place.

In the shadows, a feminine voice said, "Claudia, no."

Her sister was up there? A woman afraid of dust bunnies and bats, in a stifling hot, dark storage loft, where the roof was so angled that she could only stand up straight in the very center or over by the window? This she had to see.

"Hey, Claudia," she called out. Thank goodness she was going toward the dormer, toward the light. It blinded her a little to what was around her, but nonetheless made her feel more secure. At the dormer, she paused, standing up straight, looking around. "Claudia?"

From the darkness behind her, cutting her off from the stairs, stepped a big man wearing a knee-length tunic and a belt studded with huge gems that glittered even in this meager light. No burglar, he.

Uh-oh. She'd been baited. "You're Cytus, aren't you?"

"Yes."

She exhaled with relief, knowing he had no quarrel with her. "Uh, you know that deal I was trying to work out with you? To drill between Darius's toes?"

"Very creative, I thought. But I have something better in mind now."

"But I, uh, changed my mind. In case, you know, you're thinking you might still want to do that. For me." Sounded lame, even to her, but she didn't want him to think it was *okay* to harm Darius. Didn't want him to think he had her help or approval. It was better if he thought he was alone in that; maybe he'd rethink it, change his mind, and go away.

"Call him," Cytus said. From his tone alone, the temperature in the loft dropped from sweltering to arctic.

No way, she thought.

"Call. Him."

"I don't think so."

He lifted his arm slowly then, so slowly that she couldn't help shifting her focus to it. Ah, geez, he was pointing a gun at her. Right toward her heart, if she wasn't mistaken. She didn't know what kind it was, didn't care, wouldn't know if it had a safety or if it was on or off. She only knew it was dangerous, would blow a hole through her or Darius, and she didn't want to call him. Cytus couldn't make her call him.

"Too bad," he said. Before she could react, he was upon her, grasping her wrist so hard that any second it would snap like a matchstick. "Nice hands."

What, she was supposed to say, *Thank you*?

Dragging her by the arm as easily as if she were a rag doll, Cytus grabbed her fingers roughly, splayed them on the windowsill, and anchored her there by her wrist. He also raised the window all the way and, without an ounce of detectable remorse, said, "Shame if this were to fall on your fingers."

No doubts in her mind now, she flew right past *But Darius is your brother, your own flesh and blood* and went directly to fighting for her life and his. She pulled hard, fought hard. She braced her foot on the sill, putting her whole body into it so that, if he let go, she'd fall on her butt. Frantically she reached around, desperately searching for a handhold on something—a wall, a rafter, a joist, anything she could use for leverage. Or as a weapon.

How could one brother threaten another this way? Didn't he know how much some people would give to even *have* a brother?

"I imagine a heavy window like this would crush your bones," Cytus said. "Yeah, good solid wood. Mash the joints pretty bad. I'm not sure if the surgeons could fix them well enough for you to move them. Or hold a tool." He smiled broadly. "Shame if you couldn't work again."

Out of options, she took her foot off the sill and aimed for his groin. He laughed at her futile efforts.

"Call him."

In the garage, Darius's coal black horses followed at his heels, whickering impatiently for their meal until he began to spread the bale of hay he'd brought along, strapped to the side of the chariot. His mind was elsewhere, fully immersed in anticipation of what was to come before sunset this day. Alexandra was a wonderful, responsive lover, full of surprises and passion and eagerness, who never once asked what he'd brought her. Truthfully, he was afraid to offer her anything at this point, as she was somewhat unpredictable at times and he was afraid she'd accuse him of trying to pay her. He'd work these things out as he went.

His reverie was interrupted by noises overhead; too big to be the mother cat, thankfully, as he didn't want to mess with any more sharp claws. He had only a week to figure out what to do and didn't need to get injured in the meantime and compound the problem.

There it was again. Stomping? A muffled squeal?

"Alexandra?" No reply. He opened the connecting door to the kitchen and called inside. Still no reply, yet there were more noises from overhead. Scuffling. Grunting. A slam.

If she was in trouble, if Cytus had arrived there before them, Darius didn't want to charge up the stairs as expected and race headfirst into trouble. No, he could better contain the situation with a little stealth. There was a back way up to the loft; he'd seen the stationary wooden ladder in the garage, no doubt left over from the days when hay was stored above. A little telekinetic warfare could go a long way if Cytus didn't see him first.

So he didn't call out again, but crept upward quietly, listening, analyzing all he heard. Halfway across the storage area, he heard Alexandra speaking, could tell she was purposely keeping her voice low.

"He's not here, you big ugly bastard."

As mad as she sounded, Darius couldn't imagine why she wasn't screaming.

"If he's not here," Cytus said, "then it won't hurt for you to call him, will it? But I promise you, it will hurt if you don't."

Bastard! If he harmed one hair . . .

"He's on his way back to Olympus. Why don't you go find him there?"

What a woman! Quite unlike Aara, who, long ago, had a chance to stand up for him but chose to protect herself instead. Funny, he couldn't even remember what the young queen looked like, what he'd ever seen in her.

When Cytus twisted Alexandra's arm, Darius knew time was up. She wouldn't be able to outwit him without getting hurt. No way he was letting this continue. He found a short two-by-four and sent it flying, whacking Cytus in the back of the head with it. Direct hit!

Cytus spun around. "You fight from the shadows like a woman. I would've thought better of you."

Darius stepped out into the light, grinning broadly, deceptively. "What's the matter, Cytus? Didn't get any telekinetic abilities when you took over the rulership? Guess that's because it was meant to be temporary, huh?"

"Afraid I can beat you hand-to-hand?"

"Not on my worst day. Alexandra, you'd better go downstairs while I teach my bratty brother a lesson." He widened his stance and delivered his favorite line. "Go ahead. Make my day."

Unexpectedly, Alexandra squared her shoulders and stepped between them, a most dangerous place to be. What in Hades—Dirty Harry never had to put up with this!

"Alexandra!"

"I'm not going downstairs to hide while you two bash in each other's heads or knock out each other's teeth or . . . or . . . or whatever gods do when they fight."

With a great degree of forbearance, Darius slowly exhaled. Of course she'd be against this, fighting with kin. Without a doubt, she was going to talk them both to death.

Cytus scooped up the two-by-four and stepped toward Alexandra. Darius had no choice but to sail a brick into his shoulder to stop him, landing it with a nice solid thud.

"I can't believe you two!" she said, as it crashed to the floor with an awful thump.

Too bad it missed Cytus's foot.

"How can you take your relationship so lightly? Darius, he's your *brother*. Don't you understand what that means? You two have *each other*," she lectured both of them. "You should rely on *each other*. Blood binds you together."

"I have lots of brothers," Darius said. "I don't need to coddle the one who wants everything I own."

"You have lots—" She groaned, frustrated. "You know,

some of us wish we had lots of brothers, even *one* brother, but we didn't get them. You don't know how lucky you are. You need to talk this out, get to know each other. Darius, you need to find out why he feels that way—"

"Oh I *know* why."

"And Cytus, you need to understand—"

"Shut her up or I will," Cytus roared.

"Alexandra, go downstairs."

"No!" She folded her arms across her chest and stood her ground. "Not until you two talk."

Cytus moved abruptly toward Alexandra.

Darius retaliated with a rusty old tool. "One more move like that, and I won't just stop you, I'll kill you."

"Kill—" she squeaked. "How could you!"

"Hold on, hold on," Hermes said, winging in, taking up a position next to Alexandra, his arms extended like a crossing guard.

"Get her out of here," Darius said to his older brother.

"Wait a minute."

"Wait a minute, nothing. You wanted me to deal with Cytus for you. That's why you made sure I came here and used her statue. Well, I'm here, he's here, let me deal with him. As of right now, I'm going to maim him."

"Uh, well, Apollo's convinced me there's something you should know first. You know how Apollo is, he has this thing about the truth."

Taking advantage of the distraction, Cytus rushed Alexandra. Darius bodyslammed him with the only thing he had—Hermes.

"All right, that does it!" Hermes said, unpiling himself from Cytus, scrambling to his feet. "I was going to be tactful about this, but you can just forget it."

"Don't worry, I hadn't planned to listen," Darius said.

"Cytus isn't your brother."

"Good!" He smiled at Alexandra and said, "Then you won't have anything to be mad about when I—"

"He's your son."

Ooh, bad. Darius shut his mouth, not finishing his sentence, not sure what to say next, not even sure if he could talk. If Alexandra wouldn't forgive him for bashing his brother, she sure as Hades wasn't going to like him killing his own son.

"How . . . ? Who . . . ?"

"Queen Aara," Hermes said, tugging Alexandra out of the middle, toward the window, leaving Darius face-to-face with a son he never knew he had, but who, on closer inspection, made him remember that same greedy look in Aara's eyes.

"But I thought she . . . I thought Zeus . . ."

"Nope."

Darius glared at Cytus. "What in Hades are you so mad at me for?"

"You should have come to see me, your *son*, when you drew your first breath."

"I didn't know about you!"

"And why not? You weren't dead. You were *around*. You talked to Hermes."

"Hey, leave me outta this."

"Didn't you even wonder what happened to my mother after she was caught with you?"

Darius roared, "I was having my own problems!"

"You, you, you, it's all about you, isn't it? The golden son. Zeus's favorite." He raised the gun toward Darius. "Well, we'll see how favorite you are when I'm through with you."

Darius had seen guns on television. He hadn't dissected them, never looked into how they worked. Wondered if he, like Superman, was faster than a speeding bullet.

"Give over the rulership of all gems to me."

Darius struggled to remain calm, remembering all the battles he'd had with Zeus over the centuries and how he'd sworn if he ever had children he'd never treat them that way. Knowing he'd need all his wits about him to defeat Cytus without pissing Alexandra off. "Now why would I do that?"

"For her." He turned the gun toward Alexandra, just a few steps away, too close to miss.

She glanced out the window, probably wondering if she should jump. "For heaven's sake, he's your father," she snapped instead. Darius heard the pain in her voice, knowing she'd never turn on her own. "The only one you'll ever have. Wise up."

"Shut up. Last chance, *Father*. What'll it be?"

Would she still love him if he gave Cytus everything? Not that she wanted the gems now, but given time, she might realize they could buy happiness for the children. He'd hate to give them all away and then find out she didn't love him without them. Perhaps he should barter to keep some in reserve.

"Half the rulership," he said.

"Wrong answer," Cytus said, squeezing his trigger finger.

Out of time, Darius flung himself in front of Alexandra, shielding her with his body. The gunshot was far louder than he ever imagined, the pain in his shoulder far more powerful than any cat's claws. It was far more than necessary to end life as he knew it.

"Darius!" Alexandra cried.

His wound was large. Ichor flowed from the chunk blown out of his deltoid, not so bad in and of itself, but in marble, it would be beyond repair. His limbs grew heavy. His heart slowed. There was only one way he could help Alexandra now. Only one way to give the woman he loved what she needed. Ignoring the pain, struggling against the heaviness as it suffused his entire body, with every last ounce of energy he had, he hauled himself upward into the position in which she'd originally sculpted him. Maybe she could touch up the marble somehow, disguise it with polymers or some new discovery. Maybe well enough that the statue could still fetch a decent price.

"Oh, Darius, no." Standing before him, she cupped his wound with her hand. The ichor had stopped, his heart too slow to push the flow. She touched his cheek gently, lovingly, and rested her forehead on his chest.

He wanted to circle her with his arms, feel her one last time. He knew he couldn't. He didn't have time for both, and the children would fare better if he assumed the exact position she'd given him, and the exact expression—though it was difficult and he didn't know if he could hide the sadness he felt at losing her. Had he told her he loved her? He couldn't remember.

He looked into her eyes, recognized love and unbelievable pain. He had to tell her.

"I . . . lo . . ." He could work up no more than a mere whisper. Could she hear him?

Why was the ceiling suddenly in his line of vision? Why was his head swimming? He'd experienced this before, when the movers had tipped him and once before that, when the king had thrown him out the window. Yet no one tipped him now.

He'd lost his balance. Afraid he'd fall on Alexandra and crush her beneath the heavy marble—whether he had a little muscle left or because he willed it so strongly, he didn't know—he twisted away from her.

"No!" she yelled. "The window!"

He teetered on the windowsill for a second, long enough

for her to grab him around the knees, throw her body on his feet and try to overbalance the load, but her weight wasn't enough to make the difference. Headfirst, he tumbled out the window.

He didn't fall end over end as he had down the cliff. The drop here wasn't far enough for that. Yet it was all too far. He saw the white hail below, melting, a darker surface beneath it, and instantly knew the statue would never survive the impact.

20

At dawn the following morning, Darius endured as a lone monument to a dream gone sadly awry, permanently and irretrievably stuck inside a deformed and dirty statue. Thirty centuries of hopes and dreams erased in one swift gunshot. Six days of nirvana, gone. Talking to Alexandra, impossible. Touching her, out of the question. Making love to her again, never. He lay on his back in the garden, canted to one side, his head lower than his feet. Mrs. Nelson had posted a guard to make sure the statue didn't "disappear" again.

Ha! Not friggin' likely.

The damage was irreparable; he knew that. Hera had let him out of a broken statue once, reluctantly, and said never again.

"Psst!"

"What in *Hades* are you whispering for?"

"I don't want to alarm the guard."

"You just landed in a tunic and winged sandals. If he hasn't shot you by now, I think you're safe. At least one of us is," he added morosely. He *reveled* in how morose he could sound.

"Boy, didn't take you long to get depressed."

"Excuuuuse me, I've only had three thousand years of practice."

"Still, let's look at the upside here."

"There is no upside, you fluttery twit."

"Well, you and Alexandra aren't competing anymore."

"We're not anything anymore, if you get my drift."

"The children will get the money they need."

"Can't hear you. I've got compost in my ear."

"You don't fool me, Dare. You posed yourself that way for Alexandra's benefit. And—even you'll have to admit this is a real plus—Cytus has lost interest."

So would Alexandra. Soon. He'd be auctioned off—for the statue hadn't cracked apart on impact—sent somewhere where he'd never see her again. She'd meet a man, fall in love, get married, and have babies, little golden-haired Alexandras, full of attention to detail, with talented hands that were always touching, feeling, learning, creating.

Why couldn't Hera see the possibilities? Why'd she have to be so prejudiced against his taking a mortal wife? Not all babies of unions with mortal women turned out like Cytus.

"Unfortunately, he didn't learn anything." Hermes rambled on about Cytus; Darius caught little of it. "We really needed you to handle him, Dare. He's out of control."

"Excuse me for not killing my son for you."

My son. The thought pulled at his heart, unwanted. Cytus had shot him; he should be incensed.

He knows I'm immortal.

He'd threatened Alexandra.

He was bluffing.

How ironic that Cytus had threatened the very person responsible for Darius learning anything about paternal feelings and family obligations. It was only because of her that he wasn't plotting some terrible revenge.

"We thought it was better if you were impartial."

"Oh yeah, I'm *solidly* impartial." He wanted to enjoy his misery. To look at Alexandra for the few days he had remaining. To study her so the memory of her didn't fade over the coming centuries, because memories were all he'd have. "You want me to deal with Cytus? Bring him by. Maybe he'll die laughing."

On Sunday, Alex tore through the trash bags in the kitchen, searching for her tools, finding them and a few clean clothes. Fortunately Darius hadn't landed on asphalt, but in the garden, the dirt softened by years of compost and hours of melting hail. She was racked with guilt over his falling out the window. If only she hadn't made any noise, Darius wouldn't have come upstairs. If only she'd kept her distance from Cytus. If only she'd left when Darius told her to.

The movers were very professional and careful, not to mention afraid of her, a puffy-eyed woman supervising every centimeter of the move back into the studio. She was rinsing mud off the statue when Hermes flew in, followed by Ramon carrying a casserole wrapped snugly in a gray sweatshirt to keep it warm.

"So that's what all the fuss is about," Ramon said, looking the statue up, down, and around as Alex cleaned it. "Griff said it was a mighty fine piece. Mm-hm, I'd call that 'lovestruck.'"

The guard had greeted him as Raymond. Was that really his name? Maybe he thought "Chef Ramon" sounded more foreign and experienced, chef-wise. Why else change it? She'd ask him after Sunday. Everything but the statue could wait until after Sunday.

"I'd recognize that look anywhere," he continued, undaunted by her sniffles or intense focus on polishing every tiny scratch. "Saw it in the mirror every day since I met my wife until the day she died, rest her soul. Pose looks good, too."

"At least he doesn't have his finger up his nose."

She didn't wonder if Darius had aimed for the original pose on purpose; she'd watched every second of his struggle. He was always trying to give her gifts. If he had to go—she started sniffling again, which made her eyes burn more, which made working difficult if not impossible, which just set the whole cycle in motion again—this was the best gift of all, a statue she could still auction for the children. And to think, when she'd met him, he'd been a self-absorbed prick.

When he . . . no, when *it* was finished this time, it wouldn't be perfect. She couldn't just "fix" gunshot marble.

She was tired of people always leaving her, damn it. When she was four, her parents had left. In a way, even Family Services left, ending their "relationship" when she'd turned twenty-one. As for her ex, well, he hadn't looked back.

Darius probably wouldn't be returning, either, but it wouldn't be for lack of her trying. It certainly wasn't his fault. She wouldn't even have the statue as a memento of their six days. Unlike a heroine in a romance, she wouldn't be pregnant with his baby as a reminder of their short time together. If she had time, she'd sketch him and keep the drawings. That way she could see him in motion, more as he truly was.

Oh hell, she could barely see the statue now through watery eyes, let alone work on it.

Ramon did his best to tempt her taste buds, removing a layer of foil and dishing out lasagna, practically under her nose. She nibbled at it, without looking. Hermes dug into his helping, purposely strolling back and forth in front of the guard and winking at Alex as if she were a partner in his plan to tease the poor man, who said absolutely nothing about Hermes' tunic or winged sandals. Hermes had been up to all sorts of tricks over the past two days, allying himself with Griff, hounding her to eat and sleep. Mostly she'd just ignored them.

Hermes tilted his head toward the statue now, as if listening, then he picked up the sweatshirt and said, "Ramon, he wants to know if this is yours?"

Ramon glanced around the room. "Who 'he'?"

"Darius."

"He can talk to you?" Alex said, feeling a warm, giddy glow flow through her, her attention ricocheting back and forth between the two brothers. "I thought he was too badly damaged."

"Nah, he can talk. He's very concerned about that guy who used to come around at night. He wore a shirt like this," he said. "What? I'm talking about an intruder and you're smiling like a puppy."

She didn't even try to stop. Why did it mean so much to her to have Darius this close, when she wasn't able to hear him? How much could he feel, if anything?

"What intruder?" Ramon demanded. "Jimmy know about this?"

Tuning them out, Alex squeezed a marble wrist tenderly, whispering, "Can you feel this, Darius?"

She jumped when Hermes murmured, "No," in her ear, startling her, "but he says you should eat."

He still cares. With grim determination, she worked harder, careful not to let false hopes set her up for another fall. "I'm not hungry."

"You'll make yourself sick. He's worried about you."

She gazed up at Darius's face. She'd seen sadness at first, then Ramon had pointed out the lovestruck look, and now, with startling revelation, she saw what was really there. In the midst of getting shot and regressing and falling out the window, he was worried not about himself, but about her, knowing how hard she'd work to see what she could do with the statue, that she wouldn't eat properly, wouldn't sleep regularly until she'd done every last thing possible, made it as nearly perfect as possible, in the hopes that maybe it would be good enough to bring him back.

While she doubted the statue could ever be perfect enough again, she couldn't help but hope that his parents, now that they'd had Darius back for a short while, would realize they'd been too tough and, maybe in the interest of family togetherness, they'd forgive a little gouge. Only time would tell, but there was one thing she could do for him right now. She turned on the television, tuning it so he could catch *Jeopardy!* then whispered in his ear that she loved him.

She loves me!

It made this harder to bear. The longest, most miserable time of day for Darius was whenever Alexandra slept, because then she wasn't touching him. Not that he could feel it, but nonetheless, her attention warmed a place inside him. At the pace she'd been keeping, her hours were unpredictable. Right now it was dark.

"What day is it?" he asked.

"Almost Monday," Hermes answered.

Hera had given him until Thursday to see things her way, to marry the goddess or lose everything.

"Look at Alexandra." She was curled up on the floor at his feet, where she'd fallen asleep working. Her concentration and misery were both so focused, it broke his heart, unable to help or comfort her in any way. It weighed heavy in his heart, too, to realize it was his fault the children couldn't come see her. "She's working too hard. She can't fix a gunshot wound."

"She knows that. She's just making you look good for the auction."

Alive, he'd had hopes of circumventing Hera's ultimatum. Stuck, he had none. "I need to talk to Hera."

Hermes knocked on the marble. "Gonna be kind of hard getting home, stuck in there like that."

"Ask her to come here."

Hermes laughed. "Don't waste my time."

"All right, then." Darius sighed, figuratively bracing himself. "Tell her I'll marry whichever goddess she picked out."

Hermes did a double take. "Whoa. Didn't see that coming." Glancing nervously toward Alexandra, he lowered his voice. "How can you do that to her?"

"It's what she needs."

Hermes squinted at the statue, at him. "You're going nuts in there, aren't you? I knew it, it was bound to happen."

"Listen, you're not here when she talks to me. She blames herself, all the time. 'If only I'd' this and 'if only I'd' that. It's tearing me apart seeing her like this, Hermes. I gave her the statue, willingly, and now she's blaming herself," he said. "I should've let her bash my head in days ago, but I didn't, and there's only one way I can help her now. If I draw breath again, I swear by the river Styx she'll have nothing to feel guilty about. She'll be able to move on with her life. So make the deal with Hera."

For the first time since marrying money, Claudia appeared to have dressed in a dark closet, one belonging to someone else, who was now missing a pair of purple plaid leggings and a green cropped shell, neither of which was very forgiving on a woman whose idea of exercise was firing a maid who didn't get all the dust bunnies out from under the bed.

"I don't like to see them misjudging you, Alexandra. I *thought* they were my friends, but since none of the bitches would listen to me . . ." Claudia glanced meaningfully at the stoic guard. After fifteen minutes of pacing the studio floor late Monday morning, she was still bemoaning the fact that, in light of all that had transpired, she'd been duly ousted from the one place she'd felt she belonged, the Ladies' Club.

Would the ripples from the statue fiasco never stop?

"Now, Claudia," was all Griff said. He tried to pat her shoulder and comfort her, but she didn't stand still long enough.

Kneeling back on her heels at the statue's feet, Alex sighed. When she worked long hours like this, she tended to get so caught up in every minute detail, holding her breath until all of a sudden she had to exhale. "I wish I never went to art school. I could be working at Wal-Mart or Taco Bell and living a normal life. One without a guard."

"Then you wouldn't have met the man who's put that smile on your face."

"I haven't smiled since Friday." Today was, what, Monday? When the hell was the auction, Sunday? She did catch herself smiling then, because she remembered Darius would've said Hades, not hell. "Anything that looks like a smile is purely your imagination."

Claudia snickered. "Yeah, I like watching you run your hands over a hunk of marble and pretend not to *glow*. Portugal must've been some trip."

She caught herself smiling again, and probably blushing, too. If she ever had enough money to travel, would she be able to find that cave? Spending an hour there would remind her how it felt to lie in Darius's arms. She'd feel closer to him.

Hermes, genuinely fond of Ramon's cooking, let himself in through the kitchen and waited by the table. While his relationship with Darius was different from hers, how horrible it must have been for him to lose his brother for three thousand years, then get him back for a few days only to lose him again.

"Maybe I need to find a better class of friends." Claudia shrugged and pasted on a cheery smile. "We've still got Ramon and Griff—oh my God!"

"What?" Alex asked, startled.

Claudia dashed over to the worktable and sprawled across it like a drunken hooker. "Oh . . . nothing." Hermes backed off, staring at her as if she'd lost her mind, while she, with nearly imperceptible little jerks of her head, indicated Alex should come closer, which she did, tentatively, in case Claudia was really cracking up over losing all her friends.

There, behind Claudia's reposed form, safely out of the guard's sight, was a sparkling heap of jewelry, the expensive stuff: diamonds, rubies, sapphires, emeralds, fiery opals, all set in gold and platinum. She didn't have to ask if Darius stole them. They'd been missing for days. There was even a police report to prove it.

"Wow," Griff said, then walked away to distract the guard.

"Darius thinks maybe it'll help your situation with the kids if you give these back," Hermes explained.

"*Darius?*" Too out of character, Alex thought.

Amusement sparkled in Hermes' eyes. "Yeah, quite an experience," he said, "him asking me to return something he's convinced is his."

"Whaddya mean *his*?" Claudia demanded, but was ignored.

"I thought they were Cytus's now."

Hermes shrugged. "Darius swears he's coming back, Cytus laughs at him. Stalemate." Lowering his voice, he said,

"If you return them, maybe they'll let you continue to live here. Maybe the children can come back."

She sorted through the pile, pulling out sets that went together, amazed and touched that Darius would voluntarily give up something about which he felt so strongly. From the time he'd first blinked, it had been his gems this and his gems that, never so much as a hairline crack in his egotistical, confirmed belief that he owned them all and had the right to repossess them.

"Claudia, you want to see these get back where they belong?"

"I wouldn't stoop so low."

Taken aback, Alex said, "Not even if it got you back into the club?"

"Not even if they *paid* me."

"Well, I don't have time to do it. Hermes?"

"Hey, I just carry messages."

"You brought these."

"That was for Dare."

Jimmy, not in uniform at the moment, popped in through the kitchen, said, "Wow," at the statue, "Holy cow," at the assorted piles of jewelry, and then, "Alex, you've got to give these back."

"You could at least look surprised."

"Hey, after yesterday, I'm sure these just showed up here." Amazingly, he didn't sound sarcastic. "Dave," he said to the guard, "you seen these? Oh relax, ladies, Dave's all right. He knows about the evidence—oh, that's right, you two don't know yet. I came by to tell you, the evidence from the jewelry store heist? It's gone. All of it. As of yesterday, vanished." He snapped his fingers. "There one minute, gone the next."

"So, what, it was cops trashing my studio looking for it?"

"Not a chance. That was probably the original burglars,

back to get their stuff. Charges have been dropped against you, by the way," he said, grinning broadly, "for lack of evidence. This your lasagna, Ramon? Don't mind if I do."

"You and me need to talk," Ramon said, pulling him aside.

The guard, who'd accepted Jimmy's invitation to see what the fuss was about, simply said, "Wow, and to think I didn't see anything," and then resumed his position by the door, only noting in the log when half a dozen club members filed through the door behind Mrs. Nelson.

In the face of her former friends, Claudia pulled herself together, held her chin high, acted as if nothing unusual had happened and she was going to sit down and have a plate of lasagna, thank you very much.

"We've been appointed to keep an eye on what's going on over here," Eunice said, her nose up in the air so far it must've been difficult to keep her eye on anything.

"My jewelry!" Barbara Denton cried, though Alex swore she couldn't possibly have seen it from where she was. Must've sniffed it out. She was on top of it now, though. "Look, Karen, isn't that your mother's brooch?"

The ladies of the club swarmed the worktable, all talking at once, grabbing jewelry, elbowing Alex and the others aside with dirty looks.

"*You*," Eunice Nelson said, staring at the lasagna as if it were stolen property too, then pointing a long bony finger at Ramon. "Obviously you're involved in all of this. You're fired. And if you're involved . . . Where's your no-account brother-in-law?"

"Brother-in-law?" Alex and Claudia asked together.

Eunice zeroed in on Griff. "You're fired, too."

Ramon, whose cooking skills were greatly admired, knew his value and stood his ground. "He has nothing to do with this. You have no right to fire him."

Alex glanced at Claudia in panic. Griff had just lost his job, too? Good Lord . . .

Dazed by this latest fallout, she stood there, speechless, while the ladies scooped up every last piece of jewelry down to the smallest one-carat diamond stud, searched the floor in case they'd missed any, then left in a parade of mixed expressions: joy at having their precious jewelry back, delight at being the ones to carry it back, smug *I told you so*s, and wicked *You're outta here come Sunday*s.

"I want a word with you," Griff said, following them out.

Alex turned to Ramon. "You and Griff're related?"

Ramon nodded. "He married my sister, rest her soul."

"And the both of you just forgot to mention that for years and years," Claudia said sarcastically.

Ramon, looking positively miserable, had trouble holding eye contact. "I have, uh, secrets. Don't look at me like that. An' nope, I'm not telling you, so don't ask."

Cytus barged in the back door, swaggering like he thought he was Zeus or something.

My son, Darius wondered, *or my enemy?*

"Well, well, well," Cytus said, circling him thoughtfully. "After that fall, who knew Alexandra could make you look so good again? I wonder, has she made you look too good for your own good?"

That answered Darius's question fast enough.

"Tell me, Dare, where do you think you'll be spending the rest of eternity, hm? Private collection? Art museum?" He chuckled, tracing the obvious flaw with his index finger. "Standing next to someone's swimming pool?"

"Go away."

"I wonder, is it too much to ask that they make you spit water out your mouth?"

By Zeus, what he'd give for the physical ability to make the brat swallow that laugh. It could even be telekinetic; he wasn't picky. "Go. Away."

"In a minute. Aphrie says I should talk to you. You know, give you a chance to change your mind now that you've had a couple of days stuck in there, thinking it over. Day and night. Night and day. Ooh, sorry, that must hurt. So that's why I'm here. Well, not really. I came for my horses, but I promised Aphrie, so what about it, *Father*? As far as I'm concerned, you've nothing to bargain with, but if you promise never to find a way to come back and fight me for the rulership, I could cut you some slack."

He couldn't believe his luck! Cytus didn't know of Hera's ultimatum? That by agreeing to a wedding of her choice, he'd be back on Thursday? Good thing; if Cytus knew, he'd steal the statue away and hide it from Hera. Alexandra might get hurt in the process; he had no doubt she'd fight him for it, even though it would be a losing battle.

It was better if the brat thought he'd given up. "As you can see," he growled, "there's no hope of repair here. No reason for you to threaten Alexandra again."

"No, no of course not. I have nothing against the woman, unless it looks like she can fix you, of course." He shrugged eloquently. "Looks like my problems are over."

"If you don't grow up, your problems are just beginning. Your aunts and uncles are very unhappy with your behavior." Good grief, he sounded like a parent.

"Well, now that you're gone for good, they'll come around and see things my way."

"*Your* way is letting too many of my valuables into the hands of mortals."

"*My* valuables."

"You fool! You've upset the balance of power. Have you

listened to no one? If mortals can simply go to a store and buy a bauble, what do they need you for? If they can make money selling them and then buy whatever they want, what do they need any of the gods for? By Zeus! No wonder Hermes came after me to deal with you."

"So what're you saying? I should take them all back?" He snapped his fingers. "Like that?"

"Obviously you lack the good judgment to fix anything," Darius growled, wishing he could throttle some sense into his son. "That'd throw world economy into chaos. You'll have to do it slowly, over time."

"That's the beauty of being in charge," Cytus said with a triumphant smirk that Darius wanted to wipe off his face. "I get to do things my way."

After Cytus's visit, Darius was even more determined to get unstuck. The brat was unpredictable, and there was no way to protect Alexandra while he was encased in marble.

"Mother," he said when Hera walked regally into the studio later that day, quelling the guard with an innocent smile that must've taken her centuries to affect so perfectly.

"I always know you want something when you call me Mother."

"I want out of this statue."

"Wait," Hermes said, interrupting. "Aphrie and I've been talking, Hera, and we think Darius has already experienced true love."

"You . . . and Aphrie . . . *dare* question me?"

Hermes shuddered from the chill, but persisted. "It's just that I was here. I saw it happen. If throwing himself in front of a bullet to protect Alexandra doesn't demonstrate true love, then what does?"

Yeah! Darius thought, wondering that he hadn't seen that

angle before. He'd been so absorbed in Alexandra's misery, more concerned with how to help her than himself.

"Purely reflex. He's immortal; it was no big sacrifice."

Darius objected. "I knew what an injury would do."

"Oh, so you thought about it? Then I have to think, why would you throw yourself in front of a bullet? To save Alexandra, of course! To demonstrate true love, which would win you your nights back. Which means it wasn't a selfless act after all, but a self-serving one."

"No!" How could he make her understand his only motive had been to protect the woman he loved? What gave her the right to judge the quality of his love, when he knew in his heart that it was pure and unselfish?

"I think there's a term for that," Hermes said.

"What's a Catch-22?" Darius said angrily.

Hera, looking in his general direction, gave him a quizzical look, then snapped, "I haven't the slightest idea. Now don't tell me I wasted my time coming here. Hermes says you agree to marry Galina."

If he could hang his head, it'd be on the floor. "That's right."

"Why?"

Only honesty would honor his feelings for Alexandra, his true love for her, even if Hera never would believe it. "Alexandra blames herself for what happened to me. If you let me out of here, she won't have anything to feel guilty about."

"Very good, Darius. Too bad you didn't come around and agree to marry Galina while you were still . . . mobile, shall we say? Now you won't have a body either."

"Oh. I'll need another statue?"

She grinned wickedly. "There's always the pendant Hephaestus made for Alexandra. It's quite exquisite."

Oh yeah, he really wanted to be no larger than Alexandra's little finger! There'd be a new item for *Jeopardy!*'s Double Letter category: *Once the ruler of gems, this god was reduced to living hand to mouth.*

Who was Darius Digit?

Better not to be snide to Hera, though, so he attempted a compromise. "Maybe something from a museum instead?"

"Very well, Hermes may try to find you a more suitable one." Hera headed for the door. "Deadline's still on Thursday, six P.M. After that, Darius, you'll forfeit the rulership and your powers, just as your father explained." She paused, turning for a last look at the statue. "I suppose I could still let you out of there after that time, hmm, maybe . . . if Galina's still interested, though you certainly won't have much to offer her. And Hermes, don't go robbing any museums. Zeus and I don't want to see your face on the evening news." She left without farewell.

"Three days!" Hermes objected, pacing agitatedly. "It took you three millenia to find a statue."

"Aphrie'll help," Darius said, formulating a plan. "So will the others."

"But three days!"

"I won't be so picky this time, I promise. Bring me anything."

21

On Wednesday, a succession of statues was paraded through Alex's studio. Among others, Apollo arrived with a good-sized male study, minus one arm and its nose. "Well?" he said to Darius, followed shortly by, "Yeah, I was afraid of that. Sorry." He took the statue and left before Alex could find out what was going on. Aphrie repeated nearly the same scenario, except the statue she brought was that of a well-endowed woman, bathing. Before she left, she installed a tall red pillar candle on the south wall of Alex's studio, with directions to keep it lit, creating good chi. "It'll help your reputation," she said.

God knew she could use the help.

At dawn on Thursday, Alex sat bolt upright on her mattress, knowing exactly what she had to do for Darius. Obviously, from what she'd seen so far, he no longer required something handsome. Barely pausing long enough to pull on a pair of shorts and T-shirt—only because a guard was parked inside her studio and Griff had spent the night on her couch again, saying he didn't like leaving her alone with a guard he didn't know from Adam—she charged out of the bedroom and whipped the sheet off the Pompeiian antiquity.

She studied the four-foot statue and, other than a lot of dirt, found nothing wrong with it—other than a tail, short horns, and two cloven hooves. "What do you think, Darius?" she asked, in yet another one-sided conversation designed to keep his spirits up, to prevent his going berserk in there. "Let's call him Mr. Pompeii, in honor of his human half." She began cleaning it with a madness formerly reserved for her own work.

In spite of being fired, Ramon still prepared lunch every day at the club, as many members didn't see eye-to-eye with Eunice's posse and neglected to cancel their reservations. He always delivered enough "leftovers" to Alex's to feed a small city. Hermes fluttered in right behind him today, sampling tidbits off of the stuffed-veggie platter. Cradled against his chest, he carried a tabletop statue of a king, carved in teak, for Darius's consideration. She didn't care what he looked like, as long as he got a second chance to get to know his great grandfather and his son, though she knew he would.

"Ask Darius what he thinks of this one," she said.

Hermes looked at Mr. Pompeii and choked.

"It's not that bad."

"It's downright *ugly*."

"What's he think of yours?"

"Never mind."

She studied his fair-quality offering thoughtfully, and remembered Apollo's damaged goods. "I thought he needed a perfect statue."

"No, he met his obligation to Zeus the first time around.

This is Hera's work, and 'suitable' was what she said, I believe. Trouble is, none of us is brave enough to ask her to define that."

"And three gods can't find one 'suitable' statue on this entire planet?"

Defensively, he said, "Anything with a security camera is off limits."

"I see. Well, I don't know whether Mr. Pompeii will suit Darius, but I was thinking, maybe once he's in it and has control, couldn't he statue-hop later?"

"That seemed like a good loophole to me, too, but he swears once he's back, he's never risking it again. Besides being claustrophobic, I think he's afraid of what Hera would do," he said. "What, Dare? Yes, unfortunately it's Thursday already." He winced as he listened. "Alexandra, he wants to know if you can have that ugly thing ready this afternoon."

She fondled its head. It was a beautiful antiquity, but Darius would be happier without horns. "Can I remove these?"

"No, they need them."

"They?" She laughed. "You make it sound as if it's a real creature."

"Of course it is."

"It is?"

"Sure. I haven't seen any for a long time, but they live in the forests and chase tree nymphs."

She studied it thoughtfully, evaluating how much work would be required below the waist, where skin segued into hide and the well-detailed grooves were packed with dirt, mud, and volcanic goo. "No way I can have it ready before Sunday," she said apologetically, regretting that she couldn't grant Darius's wish. "So I guess the tail and the hooves have to stay, too?"

"Absolutely." He waggled his eyebrows and said, "He won't be able to catch any nymphs without such a studly tail."

Having missed the deadline on Thursday, Darius bellowed, "If I'm not out of this statue soon, I'll go insane."

His only hope for Alexandra's eternal peace of mind now was that she'd have Mr. Pompeii finished by Sunday, that Galina would accept him without his gems, and that Hera would give in.

Claudia had badgered Alexandra into taking a break for a shower, then left, and the guards were outside chatting during their shift change.

"What makes you think you're not already?" Hermes asked, thumbing through the security log. "I mean, look what you've agreed to move into when it's ready." He shuddered.

"I'm bored. What're you reading."

"Guards' notes. Get this, they refer to me as *Mr.* Hermes, and not once do they mention my flying. They note the hail storms." They were centered mostly around this block and only when there were luxury cars in the driveway. Hermes dashed over to the home every time. "I'm still not sure I've erased all the weather programs off Billy's hard drive. Maybe he made copies."

"Is that a lawn mower I hear?"

"Griff wants the lawn nice for the auction. You know, anything to help Alexandra and the children."

"I think I hear a knock at the back door."

"Would you *relax*!"

"I can't. I'm going stir crazy. Is it Matthew? Or one of the kids?" he called after Hermes, who went into the kitchen and returned with a large envelope.

"It was Claudia's detective," Hermes said.

"What's that envelope? Open it and read it out loud."

"I will not."

Alexandra returned, her hair dark and straight because it was wet. Oh, how he longed to smell her spicy shampoo again! Since all her clothes had been tossed haphazardly into the trash bags, she resorted to wearing what she found first each day. Today it was khaki shorts and a red T-shirt that hugged her breasts, a great improvement over the baggy shirt she used to wear. She could walk around all day like that, and he wouldn't complain, but she didn't. In half a minute, she was bent over Mr. Pompeii, working. Nice view from the back, too.

Claudia charged in the front door. "Is it here?"

Alexandra didn't even glance up, but she did say, "What?"

"The envelope. He found our dad, Alex! He said he was dropping off an envelope with the information and a photo."

That got her attention. Darius wanted her to keep working on the statue; he also wanted that envelope opened, because he knew how much finding her father meant to her. Besides, a new topic would liven up the place.

"Really?" She used to look at him that way, with her eyes all bright. It was far better than the flat, exhausted look she'd had of late.

Claudia pounced on the large, white envelope and ripped one end open.

"Wait!"

Startled, Claudia clutched it to her chest.

"If you open that," Alexandra said, "we'll know who it is."

"Mm, yes, that's the general idea."

"Then we'll want to draft a letter. Or call him." Finally, she was taking a real break from her work, getting her mind on something else. Trouble was, she was so obviously torn between helping him and seeing what was in that envelope, she didn't quite know what to do with her hands, as they kept darting from the statue, to her wet hair, her tools, all over. "Or . . . or meet him."

"Yes!"

"No! I . . . I can't, Claudia. Not before Sunday. Darius needs to move from that statue to this one."

"So?"

"They're moving that one to the ballroom Sunday, and after that, who knows where? I have to finish the little one while they're still together."

"You mean . . . after twenty-six years . . . you expect me . . ."

"Yes! What's another couple of days?"

Without waiting for an answer, Alexandra knelt down to work on Mr. Pompeii's knees, but Darius caught the telltale glance over her shoulder. She was dying to know, but, as usual, her focus was too strong to break. Within seconds, she was back on track.

"Suit yourself," Claudia muttered, pulling out the report. A large photograph slipped free and fluttered to the floor. From his angle, Darius couldn't see it. Claudia picked it up, stared at it for a moment, said, "What the hell?" and then began laughing. After a few moments, she laid it all on the table, open, then left with a new bounce in her step.

What in Hades had made her laugh?

He wondered how long Alexandra could resist.

"You missed the deadline," Hermes said, for Darius's ears only.

"I know."

"I'll bet Cytus is celebrating his new wealth. Zeus said he gets your telekinetic powers, too, right?"

"Is there some reason you mention this, other than to torment me?"

"Nah, that's pretty much it. You can't help us anymore, might as well look on the bright side. Maybe he'll try a little telekinetic diamond mining, lose control, and bring the whole thing down on his head. None of us'd miss him. Well, Hera might, at Sunday dinner. Everyone was really looking forward to you being a regular."

"You do dinner regularly?"

"Oh sure, every Sunday. Have been for centuries."

Alexandra would've liked that, a family around the table.

"You know, Dare, *if* Mr. P. is done by Sunday, and *if* Hera finds it in her cold, black heart to take pity on you and let you out of there, Alexandra thinks you're coming back to be with her."

"I know."

"Want me to tell her about Galina?"

"Nah, you hate delivering bad news."

"It'll just be worse, the longer you wait. She doesn't deserve that."

"Grown on you, has she?" Darius asked, and Hermes shrugged, not putting his feelings into words. "Thanks anyway, but I have to do it in person."

Hermes looked at Mr. Pompeii and shook his head. "I don't think 'in person' quite describes *that*."

Oblivious to their conversation, all Alexandra could think was, *Our dad.* Stunned that he'd finally been found, she carved out more volcanic goo on auto pilot, so many thoughts running through her mind. After all these years, a dream come true. Their dad, alive. After finding their mother's gravesite years ago, she'd been afraid to get her hopes too high. Where did he live? What was he like? Did she look like him?

The envelope's right there.

Why had Claudia been laughing?

She took a step toward the worktable, then abruptly stopped. His life wouldn't change if she didn't contact him for a few days, but Darius still had a chance if she finished in time. She didn't want him to wait one second longer than necessary, and she didn't trust Cytus not to barge in and ruin everything, so she returned to work.

What would her father think when he found out she waited until Monday, all because of a statue? That he wasn't important? That she had her priorities skewed? Would he leave her again?

Watching Alexandra at work, obviously torn between two goals, Darius knew he'd been wrong; he wasn't going insane before, because he was now. Finally, something guaranteed to relieve his boredom, and Alexandra wasn't cooperating! "Hermes, you read it."

Standing by the table, Hermes looked it over slowly and said, "It's confidential."

"*You're* reading it."

"Yeah, but I'm not blabbing it."

"It's not like I can tell anyone."

Hermes continued reading. "Wow, who would've guessed? Hey, you know what?"

Darius growled, "I'm trying to find out."

"You can quit worrying about that guy, you know, the one in the sweatshirt. Looks like her father was checking on her every night, making sure the doors were locked."

"Who *is* he?"

Hermes grinned and resumed his slow torture. "So that's why he's been talking to Aphrie. You know, she's really good with relationship stuff. He told her he's stayed in the background all these years because he thought his past would ruin someone's life. I just didn't know whose, until now."

"Hermes!"

"The gardener. Griff."

Alexandra's head snapped up, ricocheting off Mr. Pompeii's left elbow. So, she'd been listening.

"Seems he was in prison for, hm, not sure, but it looks like he was out with some drinking buddies when they decided to steal some stuff. Anyway, his wife died of an aneurysm while he was locked up, and the two girls went to the home. End of story."

Griff! Alex thought, listening to Hermes' half of the conversation, checking out the nice new lump on her head. He knew she didn't care he'd been in prison. He'd made sure he was nearby since they were small children. He knew Claudia had been hocking her jewelry to pay for their search.

Was it guilt keeping him silent? Having firsthand knowledge of how guilt could be strong enough to run one's every thought, every motivation, she understood that it also could be powerful enough to force his silence, even on the day they'd all been weeding together, when it would have been so simple to just say, "It's me. I'm your dad."

Some people would say it was wrong to make excuses for him and the lies he'd told to keep her from suspecting, that she should confront him and tell him how hurt she was by both his actions and his inactions. But he already knew. Griff, the listener, knew so much already. Now that she and Claudia knew the truth, making a gradual transition to an acknowledged family was inevitable, because he'd stuck around all these years. He wasn't going anywhere. That knowledge alone lifted a terrible burden from her heart.

* * *

Just once Cytus wanted to visit when everyone was gone or asleep and no one would note his arrival. What was wrong with all these people? The gardener had practically moved in. The chef delivered food constantly, and it must have been good, because there were always takers. Alexandra's sister stormed in and out making demands. Club members paraded in and out whenever they pleased. Damn, might as well install a revolving door. The guard finally nodded off near midnight on Saturday.

"Whaddya want?" Darius asked.

"*'Whaddya want?'* Letting yourself go there, aren't you, Dare?" He strutted back and forth in front of the statue, snickering, showing off. Might as well get a little enjoyment out of this. "Oh, I get it. Twelve more hours and you won't be talking to anyone else ever again anyway, so why worry about your grammar, huh?" A layer of tools scattered about caught his eye. "Say, what's going on here? Oh my, my, another statue. And ready so quickly, too. She's a real wiz, isn't she?"

"It's not hers, so leave it alone."

"Don't underestimate my intelligence. You're hoping to use that, aren't you?" Only one solution to this new development—he poked around the worktable until he found a nice, heavy hammer. "Though I can't imagine Hera relenting, or you wanting to move into that ugly thing, maybe I should remove the temptation, hm?"

"You here to gloat—"

"Me? Gloat?"

"—or make a deal?"

"We tried that the other day, remember?"

"Then I'll make *you* an offer."

"Oh, I'm dying to hear what you think you have that I want." Since the statue was on a pedestal and taller than he, a power position over Darius was impossible. So he went one better, rubbing in Darius's plight by doing something he couldn't—pulling up a chair and straddling it backward—acting as though he sat in front of statues every day and talked to them. He juggled the hammer, too, from hand to hand, threatening and playful at the same time. Let Darius rack his brain trying to figure out which. "Begin."

"You may have all the gems."

"Uh, already do."

"And I'll never claim the rulership again."

"*Bor*ing. Excuse me while I practice my swing." He flipped the hammer and caught it deftly.

"And you have my deepest apology for not knowing I had a son, for not coming and finding you upon my first breath."

The hammer clattered to the floor. He'd waited three thousand years to hear those words. *If only it were possible!*

No, it must be a trick. He scooped up the hammer, acting cool. "You don't mean that. You're just saying it so—"

"So, what? So you quit trying to ruin my life? Sure, that'd be nice. But I still mean it, son, every word of it. You'll have it all, guaranteed, everything you wanted. And if you bust up that statue so I can't use it, I'm still sorry."

"I wanted a father."

"Oh," he said. "I see. No really, I do. I remember what it was like to fight with Zeus, but at least he was there. I know how badly the children want parents. Alexandra, too. Cytus, I've learned so much in the past two weeks, believe me. Maybe I'm ready to be a father, now. If you want. If you don't mind me practicing on you, making a few mistakes along the way."

"You think you can just waltz in here after three thousand years—"

Darius laughed wryly. "I'm hardly waltzing, kid."

"True." Cytus dared laugh, too, hoping this wasn't a trick. He'd need a witness, of course. Maybe get Darius to sign his promise in ichor. "And you want nothing from me?"

"Hey, a deal goes both ways."

"I knew it!" Maybe the hammer wasn't heavy enough.

"But it's nothing you'll mind."

Still, he could listen, maybe give him a chance. Give them a chance. He'd heard his grandparents and Darius and his aunts and uncles all talking and laughing around the table on Olympus before he'd entered the hall. He so wanted to be part of that. "Go on."

"Leave Alexandra alone. Let her finish the little statue. Don't interfere with me moving into it."

Cytus winced at the abhorrent creature. "You'll be too ugly to call Father, you know."

"Don't rub it in."

"I won't let a day go by without reminding you." He couldn't help chuckling then. "But I draw the line at chasing tree nymphs with you."

"Haven't you heard? I'm getting married."

"To . . . ? Oh, brave little Alexandra! You should've seen her when I threatened to smash her fingers. Wow, thought she was gonna take my balls off." He noticed Darius took a long time answering.

"Hera's picked out a goddess for me. Galina."

"But . . . you love Alexandra. Don't you?"

"I do."

"Then how can you just give her up?" Puzzled, Cytus paced around the tall statue. Too bad Darius didn't get to keep that body. They could go out wenching together.

Darius sighed. "It's better I let her go."

"This'll mean the end of life as you know it, you know. Ugly as sin."

"Don't rub it in."

"No wealth."

"I'm your father—"

"No power."

"See, the way it works is . . . you're supposed to make me feel better so I give you things."

"Doesn't apply." Cytus glanced at the antiquity pointedly. "Probably no sex again, ever." He tossed the useless hammer aside. "Okay—"

"Good!"

"—I'll let you know tomorrow." The guard began to stir, so Cytus headed for the back door. "I have to think about it."

"Whaddya mean, *think* about it? Where are you going? Come back here. Cytus! Right now. Come back here. Right. Now."

22

On Sunday, chariots lined up in the backyard of the Ladies' Club until it looked like the starting line for a horse race. Cytus came alone, as did Ares, but Apollo and Artemis, what, *chariotpooled*? Hephaestus escorted Galina, a beautiful, shy young goddess who sat where told and never said a word. Between Ramon and Selena's bunch, a variety of food and drink flowed abundantly. Claudia eventually commandeered Griff into directing the gods to park their teams and chariots on the lawn, scattered about in plain sight. Couldn't keep that woman down when she saw a theme going and, even though she was no longer in charge, she knew one-upping Eunice Nelson was a great way to get even.

Today had arrived too fast; Mr. Pompeii wasn't done yet. It also arrived too slow; Alex was impatient to find out whether Hera was going to allow Darius to return. To think, in a short while, she might have back the man she loved! He wouldn't look the same, true, but he'd still be everything she'd fallen in love with; funny, protective, generous, kind toward children. As for what kind of lover he'd be, well, she didn't know if that was even possible, but if it was, she'd just have to convince him that looks, as well as size, didn't matter.

"Do you still love him?" Claudia asked.

"Yes."

"Even looking like that?"

"What, you don't think he's cute?"

Alex had never fought for anyone before. Not really. Oh, she'd sulked and cried, but unlike this week, she hadn't *done* anything. When the children had been barred from seeing her, she should've banged on doors until the board rescinded that order, for the children's psychological well-being. She hadn't *fought back*. Her ex had left because she couldn't have children—she'd proposed adoption, but she hadn't *fought* for it. He'd also complained about her scar.

Well, okay, on that note, maybe it was a good thing he'd left. But she was so used to being abandoned, it hadn't even occurred to her to fight for the relationship. When she was a toddler getting dumped at the home, she'd had no say in the matter.

Well, she sure as hell was making a statement now. This little statue would be finished today, Darius was going to stand in front of her again, and she was going to tell him that if he left her, she'd hunt him down and put a leash on him until he was convinced she loved him and wanted him to stay around permanently. He'd probably get a big grin on that stupid face—Mr. Pompeii was *not* a handsome creature—and settle right in.

Apparently everyone else was eager to see today's outcome, too. Besides the family reunion that must have emptied Olympus, all three round-the-clock guards showed up, suspecting something big afoot.

The children, defying authority, arrived en masse. "You shouldn't be here," Alex said, unable to sound cross as she hugged them until they squirmed. They were going to be so excited when she told them she'd found her very own dad. "You'd better get back before you're missed. They'll worry about you."

Hermes put his arm around Billy's shoulders. "Sorry, Alexandra, this one's staying where I can keep an eye on him."

Billy groused, "That last wipe you did on the hard drive took care of the programs."

"Don't kid a kidder, son. One more freak storm and the computer goes back. Any after that, and it's curtains for you."

Billy gulped. "You mean . . ."

"Yeah."

As of yesterday, Mr. Pompeii was warm to the touch. This had to mean she was nearly finished—a good thing, since the big statue would be moved out soon. She kept hoping the lights would blink or the TV would come on, even though Hermes said Darius wasn't able to do that anymore.

Cytus wandered around the room, circling nearer Mr. Pompeii. If he tried to bash the little statue with a hammer, she didn't trust anything less than Jimmy's gun to stop him.

"Alexandra," Hermes said, sounding frantic. "The movers are here."

Upon hearing his brother's warning, Darius came as close to panic as he ever wanted to be. "Lock the damned door!" he shouted.

"Lock the damned door!" Alexandra echoed.

Dear, sweet Alexandra, your work is almost done. As he'd learned from the children, he crossed his fingers, though not literally, so he didn't know if it would help.

Time ticked by, punctuated by knocking, then banging, on the front door. Ladies, dressed to the nines, traipsed through the garden and rapped on windows, as if no one inside knew they were out there and wanted in. He didn't know how Alexandra could remain so focused. Polish, polish, polish.

Hera arrived through the back door, observed the prevenient crowd, and zeroed in on Mr. Pompeii. *"That's* the statue you want to use?" she said, horrified. She was probably picturing him across the dinner table, short and double-horned. She started laughing then, so hard she eventually doubled over with tears in her eyes. He'd never seen her so. "You'd be giving up your immortality," she said.

What was eternal life without Alexandra, other than eternal damnation? Though immortal, he might someday find another way. Hera might relent eventually. Trouble was, it could be five hundred years after Alexandra's lifetime. No, he wanted, *needed*, to be with her at any cost.

"I find it quite suitable, Mother," he said, trying to sound agreeable, knowing she could overrule his choice without batting an eye.

One minute Darius was frantically wondering if he'd come so close just to fail, the next he realized he was growing warmer and transferring to the smaller statue. *Yes!*

Elation was quickly replaced by a horrible pressure. "What in Hades . . ."

"Darius, what's wrong?" Hermes asked.

Abruptly, Alex sprang backward. "What? What'd I do? Should I stop?"

"Why's he screaming like that?" Aphrie demanded, cringing.

"It's too small," Hermes said, darting around nervously. "He's claustrophobic and it's too small."

Darius gasped, trying to tell Hermes to tell Alexandra . . . what?, he didn't know. Regardless, nothing came out of his mouth except groans. If he got stuck in this . . . tight . . . little . . . four-foot coffin . . .

Had Cytus made a deal behind his back? Was Hera just being a bitch?

Then all at once, he settled in, could breathe and move again. Most of the pressure was relieved, just in time, too, as the movers gained entry and carted the large statue away.

"Darius?" Alexandra whispered, gazing down at him in awe. "Is it really you?"

From behind, he felt the light pressure of her hand on his shoulder. It was bad enough being a diminutive, four-foot statue; now he had to step off the pedestal and face Alexandra.

The room was stunned into silence by an eardrum-shattering scream. "*That*'s Darius?" Galina screeched. "No way am I marrying *that*."

By Zeus, was he so hideous in the flesh? If so, he couldn't bear to frighten Alexandra, to make her scream.

"I'd rather be boiled in oil first!" The crowd parted as Hera's choice for daughter-in-law stormed out.

When Hera didn't instantly turn him into something worse and Alexandra didn't hit the floor in a dead faint, Darius's confidence was bolstered. Maybe she'd be okay with this. He turned, stretching up to his full height. If he stood up really, really tall—the marble creature had been crouched somewhat—he found he could maybe make four feet after all. At this level, he couldn't miss the dewy sheen of perspiration around the edge of Alexandra's scooped-neck tank top. And to think, his fiancée had just dumped him! He was unengaged. Unencumbered. *Free.*

Alexandra was neither screeching nor running. It was worse, much worse. She had her fists planted on her hips and fire in her eyes. "You were *engaged?*"

"Not at—"

"Just when the hell were you going to tell me? I never would've slept with you if I'd known you were *engaged.*" She spat it out like a dirty word.

He needed to clear this up. "It was arranged—"

"I don't care if it—"

Aphrie slapped her hand over Alexandra's mouth, muffling the rest of her tirade. "Sweetie," she said, "let the guy talk."

"It was part of the deal he made with Hera," Hermes said quickly, in Darius's defense, then flew out the door.

"I can handle this," Darius said.

"You think?" Cytus jabbed, then threw back his head and roared with laughter.

"Silence, you twit!" Hera ordered, to no avail. She drew herself up regally. "I've had enough of your behavior. If I can't have Galina as a daughter-in-law, she can be my granddaughter-in-law. *You* go after her and marry her. Maybe she can straighten you out so everyone quits pestering me about you."

"But, Hera." Cytus's belly laugh diminished abruptly, to a weak, beguiling smile. "Grandma—"

"Yeah," Darius said with a smirk, to which Hera snapped, "Don't even think I'm done with you."

Trumpets blared across the yard. Hermes flew in and said,

"Alex, quick, I just checked and lunch is over. You're supposed to say a few words before the auction begins."

Griff took one look at Darius and said, "He can't go like that! Stay here, I'll be back in a jif. Billy, you create a diversion."

"No hail storms," Hermes warned.

Alex tore through the remaining trash bags looking for safety pins to close the sides of the snowy white peplos Aphrie had given her. It was like searching for a needle in a haystack, not to mention how distracted she was by all the screaming outside. Apparently Billy found a way to empty the ballroom—without setting it on fire or activating the sprinkler system, she hoped. And she'd been worried about little things, like whether her gunshot-gouged statue would fetch enough money to see the home through another year. Well, the Ladies' Club's Forty-seventh Annual Auction would never be forgotten, that was for sure. Whatever Billy had done, he'd better be able to get them all back in there. Maybe with their adrenaline pumping, the bidding would be lively and competitive. A girl could hope.

She gave up on the pins, decided what the hell—might as well make a big splash—and attached Aphrie's two sparkly clips at the hips. Without underpants, no one would notice her lack of makeup, not even Claudia.

"Okay, he's ready," Griff said, chuckling at his handiwork as she joined Darius and him in the studio. Everyone else had left. "I give you," he added theatrically, "live and in person, the new and improved, if somewhat disguised, *Darius*."

She was taken aback by the two men in her life, standing side by side. With Griff's green rubber gardening boots taped tightly around the ankles to keep them on over his little hooves, Hermes' hat to hide his horns, and a pair of Alex's jeans rolled up at the waist and ankles to accommodate his short legs, Darius, a.k.a. Mr. Pompeii, was about as disguised as a two-year-old on Halloween. Beside him, looking proud of his efforts, stood her father.

"Here, put this on," Griff said, handing Darius a gray sweatshirt. "I'll need it back after the sun goes down, though—it keeps these old joints warm in the evening—but in the meantime, it'll hide the rolled-up waist."

As if any of the city's wealthiest wouldn't notice the four-foot homeless dwarf she'd fallen hopelessly in love with. Eager to get into the auction, she reached for his hand. She wanted, *needed*, him beside her. Only he really understood all they'd gone through together these two weeks.

"We best get going before—what in blue blazes are you wearing, girl?" Griff demanded.

"It's called a peplos," she replied, without taking her eyes from Darius, who shot her a lascivious wink.

"I call it a sheet, and a ripped one at that," Griff said. "Go find something that covers your behind when you walk."

"Aphrie gave it to me. It's very Greek."

"I don't care who gave it to you, you can't go into that ballroom lookin' like a two-dollar hooker."

"I like it," Darius said with a leer that made her heart skip a beat.

"So will every other male in there. She wants 'em looking at the statue, not at her."

She leaned forward and kissed Griff on the cheek. "You can start bellowing like my dad tomorrow, okay?" Then, leaving Griff speechless, she squeezed Darius's hand warmly and said, "Let's go."

* * *

"Good work, whatever you did," Darius told Billy, as they entered the ballroom last. Praise be, the attendees spent more time looking around nervously at the floor instead of noticing his odd getup or how exquisite Alexandra looked today. Her hair was tousled, her face flushed. On Olympus, he'd think nothing of it, but here, in this room of dressed-to-kill society women, she looked sexy enough to die for, and next to naked. And the men noticed. He squared his shoulders and stretched up to his full height, but no matter how tall he tried to be, they looked right past him.

Ah, well, who could blame them? She was stunning, even if they weren't looking at her face. And out of everyone there, it was his arm she'd chosen to hold as they entered the ballroom.

"Rats," Billy whispered next to Darius's ear.

Oh wonderful, he was the same height as a twelve-year-old boy. "What?"

"Em was great, you shoulda seen her, Dare. She started sobbing—she's really good at it—and all the women were trying to calm her down and asking her what was wrong, and she blubbered out that she lost her pet rat and she was afraid one of them would sit on it."

"And women are afraid of rats?" Darius guessed.

"Duh. Oh, I mean yeah, usually. And anyway, then we set the kittens loose under the tables." Billy saw the look of censure Alex shot at him and said defensively, "Hey, they're cute, we brought them along to find them good homes. Anyway, one of them romped across someone's foot, and that's when all heck broke lose."

"I think you should apologize for misleading the ladies," Alexandra said.

Billy laughed. "Shoot, when they see what you're *not* wearing, they're gonna forget all about this."

"It's called a thong," she lied. "And you're not old enough to notice."

Billy smirked and walked away.

As he led her toward a table, Darius said, "Sweetheart, any male out of his crib is old enough to notice."

"They're staring at you, not me."

"In your dreams."

"Well, if it isn't Beauty and the Beast," Hermes said. He pulled out a chair for Alexandra. Darius tried to scare him off with a scowl, but Hermes shoved him aside with his hip, setting off a brotherly scuffle that left Alexandra wrestling with an open-sided gown that didn't bend when she did. At least they were blocking everyone else's view.

Darius sat on one side of her, subjected to Hermes' playful attempts to pick her up on the other. At least she looked as if she knew they were playful. The rest of the family was scattered throughout the ballroom for the meal, Aphrie at a table here, Apollo there, and so on, all garnering a great deal of attention as the rat issue died down. It wasn't dinner together on Olympus, but it felt good to be in the same room again with all of them. Now that he knew what family felt like, he wished it could happen again; he knew Hera better.

During the introduction, when Alexandra was obliged to walk up to the stage and say a few words—not that he heard one of them—he felt the urge to rip the cloth off the table and wrap it around her waist. He kept his seat, though he was so agitated he nervously plucked red grapes off the centerpiece.

Alexandra returned to his side a few minutes later without anyone grabbing her, though many women swatted their escorts as she passed by. Patrick Pulsar scribbled in his notebook without taking his eyes off of her. The curtain went up, the statue was greeted with appropriate *ooh*s and *aah*s, and the bidding began.

Darius took her hand in his. As the bids escalated, so did her grip. By Zeus, but he'd forgotten she was so strong! Remembering that brought back clear visions of their tryst in the cave, and he thanked his lucky stars for long tablecloths and sturdy jeans. Would she lie with him as a beast? It was a rhetorical question, as Hera would no doubt finish what she'd started. If he could stay, though, he resolved that their love would be a pure love—though he wouldn't deny her if she came to him.

At the final crack of the gavel, he asked, "Is that a good price?" From the way Alexandra was hugged by Claudia and Griff and Ramon, all of the children, and many of the ladies of the club, he guessed it was. He felt great pride in that. After all, the statue was modeled after *his* body.

By Zeus, but he used to be good-looking.

He wished everyone would leave. He had so much to tell her, in private: not to feel guilty about what had happened to him, what was going to happen again when Hera finished what she'd started.

But everyone wasn't cooperating. The ladies of the club and their guests moved away, socializing near the front of the ballroom, in the hall, and out on the lawn, but his family did just the opposite, surrounding Alexandra and him at a table near the back.

"Don't backtalk me, Cytus," Hera snapped. "I told you what you had to do, now get going. Honestly!" she complained to Darius, "I don't know what I'm going to do with him."

"He just needs a father," Darius said, rising to stand next to Alexandra, a protective hand on her shoulder. "A strong hand to guide him. To love him."

"Don't be ridiculous!"

"I could do it."

"You? Galina refused you, remember? You've got about two minutes left—oh, you didn't think just because I let you watch the auction that I was letting you stay, did you? If you did, you were quite mistaken. You're going right back to a hunk of marble. And not a very good-looking one at that. I shouldn't wonder it ends up in a dark basement somewhere."

He felt Alexandra squeeze his hand, not in comfort so much as tight enough to hold on to him as long as she could.

"I'll keep you, Darius," she said. "I'll never let you go. I promise. And I'll be sure there's a TV for you."

"Aw, isn't that sweet?" Hera sneered.

Darius drew strength from Alexandra's touch. "You know, Mother, it occurs to me that in some ways, mortals have progressed further than we have."

Hera pulled out a chair, sitting as she said, "Do go on. I have to hear this," but not as if she meant it. "Tell me what you've deduced after so many centuries of absence."

Desperation made him go where few gods dared to tread, but his family's future was at stake, and if he'd learned one thing from Alexandra, it was the importance of family.

"Okay, strange as it sounds, I think we can take a lesson from them. I know it's unorthodox, but, Hermes, since I can't stay here and do the job, and you're my friend as well as my brother, how about you adopt Cytus? You know how to be a father. You can teach him how he's supposed to act."

"Maybe he doesn't want to learn," Hermes said.

"Yeah, maybe I don't want—" Cytus fell silent as Darius, who'd released Alexandra's hand, ambled over to him on boot-shod cloven hooves, then reached up and hugged him for a long moment before holding him at arm's length.

"Cytus, I heard you last night. Do you understand? I

heard you. You want a father. But a father's more than just making a baby. Sometimes it's knowing when you need someone else to raise your child, and sometimes it's being the one who gets the job. Listen to Hermes, he can teach you what you need to know. After all, he's my big brother. Where do you think I learned so much?"

Cytus was about to reply and, from the look in his eyes, Darius thought it would be profound, but they weren't to have this moment. Not yet. Maybe not ever.

"Cytus," Hera said, her voice cracking through the air like a whip. "Get going. Unless you *like* the idea of chasing tree nymphs the rest of your life, in which case I can always make you trade places with Darius."

A general "ooh" rippled through the back of the ballroom.

Darius turned to look at his mother, wondering if he'd just heard what he thought he'd heard. "You'd give me his body?"

With arched eyebrows, she said, "You want it?"

"I'd have the rulership back?"

"You'd be a sight better-looking, too. Just think, Darius . . . Cytus's beautiful body, immortality, wealth, and power . . . versus a Humane Society reject with the relatively useless lifespan of a mortal."

Alexandra could be his! All he had to do was give up a bratty son he'd met only a few days ago. He didn't even know him yet, not really.

But he knew better. "How dare you! You think I'd sacrifice my son for a few *baubles*?" he roared. As soon as he said it, he knew it was right.

"I'll bet Alexandra would marry you, too," Hera said, hitting him in his weakest spot. "What do you say?"

The fact that Alexandra would never have him, not that way, didn't matter; the decision was his alone. Alexandra couldn't have him as a statue and wouldn't have him if he sacrificed his son to get her. After the influence she'd had on him the past two weeks, it was a no-brainer. "No."

The collective gasp in the room was superseded only by the stampede toward the French doors opening onto the lawn, as no one wanted to be around to see how Hera was going to retaliate, what she would do to him or his beloved Alexandra. Only Cytus remained, moving to stand elbow-to-shoulder with Darius, symbolically showing his position.

"What did you say to me?" Hera demanded slowly, wickedly.

Louder, clearer, so there'd be no misunderstanding, he repeated, "No. I will not sacrifice my son to satisfy your emotional need for control and revenge. I won't be a party to it. Now, if you don't mind, I'd like to tell Alexandra how much I love her before you turn me back into marble."

Hera smiled and said, "Well done."

Was this a trick? He feared so.

"Finally," Hera said, "your son's impudent temperament has accomplished one good thing."

"What?" he asked tentatively, afraid by doing so, he'd fall into whatever warped trap she was setting.

"As if you don't know." Hera laughed. "Why, you don't, do you?" she said with amazement. "Only someone who has experienced true love—in your case, for your son—would give up what I just offered."

"I couldn't—"

"Yes, I know." Was that pride in her voice? "And I gave you every opportunity."

Why, the old gal wasn't so black-hearted after all! He'd thought he was caught in a hopeless Catch-22, and the solution had come so suddenly from a different direction, he felt blindsided. He couldn't believe it. Without Hera angry at him, what did this mean? What did it bode for him and Alexandra? What was that pure love crap he'd just been thinking? He wanted her in the worst way, *now*.

He suspected he was grinning like a fool, but without a mirror, who knew what this face looked like grinning. He wanted to kick Cytus and Hera out without preamble, but Aphrie's advice on social niceties had stood him in good stead lately.

"Congratulations, Darius," Hera said. "While I can't make you immortal again, or give you back the rulership, I can change you into someone I'd rather see across the dinner table." She actually *winked* at Alexandra.

At the same time, Darius felt himself changing, into what, he knew not. But he was steadily growing larger, taller than Alexandra—*yes!* The ripping sounds worried him at first, until he realized it was his costume, which hung on him in tatters. The neck of the sweatshirt almost strangled him, the jeans ripped at the seams, as did the boots. He winced—glad to know he could, but afraid, as he grew taller, to find she'd turned him into a Cyclops or the Incredible Hulk. Knowing he had to ask. Leaning down, he whispered in Alexandra's ear. "What's she turned me into?"

"Darius," she said, gazing up at him, and then said no more. Poor woman; speechless.

His hands flew to his face, touching it to determine what he could for himself. Regular nose, regular ears. Two eyes, thank Zeus; not a Cyclops. But this wasn't working, it only told him what he *wasn't*.

"Tell me," he insisted. Better to get it over with.

"Darius," she said, her head tipped back to look up at him. Then she seemed to understand, and a smile slowly blossomed across her face. "Oh. You're you again. Just like the first statue. Just like before."

He turned to question Hera, but a general uproar from the other end of the ballroom interrupted. There were cries of, "The statue—it's gone!" and "It was right here!"

"Oh . . . my . . . God," Alexandra said, glad it had disappeared in front of lots of witnesses this time. That damned reporter who'd been picking on her in print better get it straight this time. No one could make claims of theft now, except to the buyer's insurance company.

Darius squeezed her hand, pulling her out of the ballroom and into a quiet room down the hall. Alone together at last, able to move and breathe again, Darius suddenly didn't know where to start. There was so much to say! And if he didn't find a way to say it soon, he was going to have to find the nearest closet, pull her inside, and make mad, passionate love to her until everyone went away.

He'd told Hermes that love makes strong men weak. Turned out, it was just the opposite. His love for Alexandra had made him strong enough to do what was right.

"Marry me, Alexandra," he said, backing her against a wall, corralling her with his arms and body. He loved this woman so much! "I'm a powerless man now, I know, but I love you more than the sun and moon and every blasted star in the sky."

"It's not your powers I loved, Darius. Nor your gems. I want nothing from you, but you." Gold flecks sparked in her eyes, like a fire, and he knew her desire for him was as strong as his for her.

Between planting hot, sultry kisses all over her neck and teasing her ears with his tongue, he asked what had to be asked, "Can you live with Cytus being your stepson?"

"Are you kidding? Me, turn down being a *mom*? Not in this lifetime."

Her smile lit up the dark corners of his heart and warmed his soul. "Okay, then!"

Framing her face in his hands, he took possession of her lips, feeling no hesitation in her kiss. In fact it was so hot, it burned deep in his soul as he scooped her into the circle of his arms, hugging her against his chest, savoring the feel of her body against his, the memory, the passion. He had more to say, so much more. He had to get it all out, everything he'd thought was lost to him. To them.

"We'll have a dozen babies. Little girls that look like you, and—"

"Oh." Her expression was instantly crestfallen. Had he read her so wrong? "I thought you knew. The surgery— remember the scar? I can't have any."

Relieved that it wasn't something insurmountable, he glanced over his shoulder to be sure they were alone. "Sh, don't let Hera know," he said with a conspiratorial grin, and was rewarded with her soft smile. "I'm fine with it, but she expects—"

"Shouldn't you be quiet now so I can tell you how much I love you?"

He dipped his head, covering her sweet lips with his own. "Alexandra, my love, I *know* how much you love me, I *saw* how much you love me, every day, every time you touched the statue, trying to fix it, knowing I would take it if you could."

"I still want to tell you—"

"We'll have to come up with some creative explanations to satisfy my mother, but just moving to Olympus with me is enough for me."

"Oh." Suddenly she stiffened in his arms, wedging hers between them. "Darius, I can't. All my life I've been left behind, you see, and—"

He grasped her fiercely, not to hurt her or sway her, but only so she'd know the strength of his commitment. "I'll never leave you."

"Yes, I . . . I know. I don't doubt that."

"What, then?"

"The children, see, they're my little brothers and sisters. They look up to me. I can't leave them, not now. Not ever." Tenderly, she touched her hand to his cheek. "If you meant what you said earlier, then stay here. We'll adopt, or be foster parents."

"Wouldn't I need a job?"

"Hm, yeah," she said, smiling and snuggling back against his chest.

Could he stay here? It wasn't as if he'd be giving up his family; they could come visit any time, whereas, as a mortal, he'd no longer have the capability to go to Olympus. "I'm very good at *Jeopardy!*" he said. "Is that a job?"

"I imagine Alex Trebek thinks so."

"I know more than he does."

"Probably."

"Or if you teach me to read, I could be the best contestant they've ever had."

"You can't read?"

"Not modern English."

"We'll work on it. And we'll find something you can do." When she grinned up at him, he knew he was going to be the brunt of her wicked wit. "You'd need training, but I think you may have a knack for repo work."

"I know something I can do without training," he said,

dipping his head for another kiss guaranteed to leave her breathless. "Ow. What in Hades?"

"What?"

"I scraped my knuckles on the wall behind you."

Their playful, sexy banter died instantly.

"Are you bleeding?" She pulled his hand around and inspected it.

Yes, he'd have blood now, if he were mortal, not ichor. "Just a few drops."

She took his hands in his and held them near her heart. Waiting. "It would've happened by now, wouldn't it?"

"Yes."

"Do you mind so much? Being mortal, I mean."

"Not if it means having you. Do you mind being poor?"

Her smile returned. "Not if it means having you."

Epilogue

A month later . . .

The doorbell rang, a great bonging sound that was supposed to sound like Big Ben, or so the realtor had said
when Alex and Darius first looked at the house. It was a
rather grand sound in their small place, but she'd feel silly
with just the two of them living in a big home, even if they
could afford it on Darius's two incomes. Cytus had been
quite generous in signing the title to a diamond mine over to
Darius as a wedding present, and Hermes had manufactured
all the documents and references Darius needed to land a
position at the university, lecturing on Greek culture and
mythology.

Darius padded barefoot into the kitchen, wonderfully
sexy in a pair of jeans and nothing else. He popped the top
button. "She loves me." A sly look, and the second button
followed. "She loves me not."

"You'd better have five buttons on there or this isn't going to work out the way you want," Alex said, laughing at his antics.

Forget the door, she'd rather help him out of his jeans. She was only scorching breakfast anyway, trying to cook with Sabrina's playful kittens underfoot. If there was one person she missed right now, it was Selena.

Well, not *right* now.

She turned off both burners, met Darius in the middle of the kitchen floor—and she did mean *floor*—and helped him with the buttons.

"Honey, you forgot to wear briefs again."

He rolled her beneath him. "I didn't forget anything." Then he jumped, as if bitten. "Except to put the kittens out."

The doorbell bonged again.

"Good thing we didn't give the kids a key," he said between long, soulful kisses that melted every bone in her body.

"They'd come to the kitchen door. Must be someone else."

He rolled them over, running his hands up under her skirt, his thumbs skimming her inner thighs. "I love it when you're on top."

She gasped with pleasure even though, deep inside, something niggled at her. "Wait." She sat up, listening intently. "Do you hear something?"

"Better be retreating footsteps." He tugged her dress over her head and tossed it aside, knowing from experience that the kittens would be happy to romp in it for a while, giving them some peace.

Alex pressed her fingertips to his lips, letting him nibble on them as she tried to identify the sound. "Is that a cry?"

He groaned. "We have enough kittens."

"Omigod," she said, scrambling to her feet, "I don't think it's kittens. Quick, get the door while I get dressed."

Amid much groaning and muttering, Darius rose and adjusted his jeans with great care, while Alex wrestled her dress from dozens of tiny, sharp claws. She'd just gotten it back on when Darius returned, carrying a picnic basket. As soon as he set it on the table, the small cry resumed.

"Wow," he said, standing back and staring at it like a lost man, "we just filled out the paperwork last week."

"Uh uh, no way," she said, knowing a baby's cry when she heard one. She pushed the pink- and blue-checked blanket aside, then scooped up a tiny infant that couldn't have been more than hours old.

Darius said, "Wow," again.

"You don't understand, this isn't how adoption works here."

"I saw it in a movie once."

"Yeah, that's the only place it happens." She rocked the infant, patting it gently until there was quiet again. "Is there a note?" she whispered.

Darius snapped open a note. "Want me to read it?"

"Yes, but quietly."

"Dear Darius and Alexandra." His whisper wasn't very quiet, but the baby didn't seem to mind. "Hey, not bad for a month's practice."

"Keep going, Einstein."

" 'You know how much we want gran . . . ' "

"Grandchildren?" She shut her eyes, not needing to see the note to know where this was headed.

"Yeah, 'You know how much we want grandchildren. This'll get you started. Love, Hera and Zeus.' Well, at least it's more subtle than a thunderbolt," he said. "What's wrong? You look like you've just seen Cerberus."

She could explain away a three-headed dog easier than dealing with this. "Is it, uh . . . Is it . . . I mean . . ."

He held up several sheets of paperwork. "What's all this?"

She scanned them quickly, hoping to find her answer there. "Looks like official paperwork—boy, Hermes is *good*—listing us, hold it still, Dare, yep, listing both of us as birth parents. Oh yeah, like this'll be easy to explain." Not that she minded. Couples were adopting babies from all over the world these days. They could pull this off.

"Boy or girl?" he asked.

"Girl."

Darius's smile was as proud and strong as if he'd just delivered her himself. "We have a daughter. We'll call her Michaela, after the archaeologist who found and reassembled my statue. Without him, I might not be here."

"Sure, fine, whatever, but Darius, now tell me the truth, is she . . ." Whispering very softly now, lest voicing it made it so, she asked, "Is she, you know, a *goddess*? I mean, Hera said she wanted pure-ichored grandchildren . . ."

Darius tickled Michaela's chin and made her smile. "Yes, but Zeus loves orphans. So, I guess time'll tell."

"You mean you can't tell? How can you not know? You were a god—" He kissed her soundly, taking her breath away. "Okay, so you're still a god," she said with a grin. "But don't think that gets you off diaper patrol."

"I'm a fast learner."

The doorbell bonged again.

"Good. You'd better be a fast changer, too, because according to the paperwork, this little girl's only one of three."